The Best
AMERICAN
SCIENCE
FICTION &
FANTASY
2025

GUEST EDITORS OF THE BEST AMERICAN
SCIENCE FICTION AND FANTASY

2015 JOE HILL
2016 KAREN JOY FOWLER
2017 CHARLES YU
2018 N. K. JEMISIN
2019 CARMEN MARIA MACHADO
2020 DIANA GABALDON
2021 VERONICA ROTH
2022 REBECCA ROANHORSE
2023 R. F. KUANG
2024 HUGH HOWEY
2025 NNEDI OKORAFOR

The Best AMERICAN SCIENCE FICTION & FANTASY™ 2025

Edited and with an Introduction by Nnedi Okorafor

John Joseph Adams, *Series Editor*

MARINER BOOKS
New York   Boston

Without limiting the exclusive rights of any author, contributor or the publisher of this publication, any unauthorized use of this publication to train generative artificial intelligence (AI) technologies is expressly prohibited. HarperCollins also exercise their rights under Article 4(3) of the Digital Single Market Directive 2019/790 and expressly reserve this publication from the text and data mining exception.

THE BEST AMERICAN SCIENCE FICTION AND FANTASY 2025. Copyright © 2025 by HarperCollins Publishers LLC. Foreword copyright © 2025 by John Joseph Adams. Introduction copyright © 2025 by Nnedi Okorafor. The Best American Series® is a registered trademark of HarperCollins Publishers LLC. *The Best American Science Fiction and Fantasy*™ is a trademark of HarperCollins Publishers LLC. All rights reserved. No part of this book may be used or reproduced in any manner whatsoever without written permission except in the case of brief quotations embodied in critical articles and reviews. HarperCollins Publishers LLC is not authorized to grant permission for further uses of copyrighted selections reprinted in this book without the permission of their owners. Permission must be obtained from the individual copyright owners as identified herein. For information, address HarperCollins Publishers, 195 Broadway, New York, NY 10007. In Europe, HarperCollins Publishers, Macken House, 39/40 Mayor Street Upper, Dublin 1, D01 C9W8, Ireland.

HarperCollins books may be purchased for educational, business, or sales promotional use. For information, please email the Special Markets Department at SPsales@harpercollins.com.

The Mariner flag design is a registered trademark of HarperCollins Publishers LLC.

hc.com

FIRST EDITION

ISSN 2573-0797
ISBN 978-0-06-344147-7

Printed in the United States of America

25 26 27 28 29 LBC 5 4 3 2 1

"The Wonders of the World" by 'Pemi Aguda. First published in *Ghostroots: Stories* (W.W. Norton, May 7, 2024). Copyright © 2024 by 'Pemi Aguda. Reprinted by permission of the author.
"The Audit" by Olivie Blake. First published in *Januaries*, Tor Books, October 15, 2024. Copyright © 2024 by Alexene Farol Follmuth. Reprinted by permission of the author.
"The Three Thousand, Four Hundred Twenty-Third Law of Robotics" by Adam-Troy Castro. First published in *Lightspeed*, issue 166, March 2024. Copyright © 2024 by Adam-Troy Castro. Reprinted by permission of the author.
"Look at the Moon" by Dominique Dickey. First published in *Lightspeed Magazine*, issue 171, August 2024. Copyright © 2024 by Dominique Dickey. Reprinted by permission of the author.
"A Stranger Knocks" by Tananarive Due. First published in *Uncanny*, issue 60,

September/October 2024. Copyright © 2024 by Tananarive Due. Reprinted by permission of the author.

"An Ode to the Minor Arcana in a Triplet Flow" by Xavier Garcia. First published in *Death in the Mouth*, Vol. 2. Copyright © 2024 by Xavier Garcia. Reprinted by permission of the author.

"The Sort" by Thomas Ha. First published in *Clarkesworld*, issue 215, August 2024. Copyright © 2024 by Thomas Ha. Reprinted by permission of the author.

"Ushers" by Joe Hill. First published by Amazon Original Stories, November 1, 2024. Copyright © 2024 by Joe Hill. Reprinted by permission of the author.

"The River Judge" by S. L. Huang. First published in *Reactor*, March 6, 2024. Copyright © 2024 by S. L. Huang, LLC. Reprinted by permission of the author.

"The Witch Trap" by Jennifer Hudak. First published in *Lady Churchill's Rosebud Wristlet*, no. 48, September 2024. Copyright © 2024 by Jennifer Hudak. Reprinted by permission of the author.

"Country Birds" by Kij Johnson. First published in *The Sunday Morning Transport*, February 11, 2024. Copyright © 2024 by Kij Johnson. Reprinted by permission of the author.

"Why Don't We Just Kill the Kid in the Omelas Hole" by Isabel J. Kim. First published in *Clarkesworld*, issue 209, February 2024. Copyright © 2024 by Isabel J. Kim. Reprinted by permission of the author.

"Reduce! Reuse! Recycle!" by TJ Klune. First published in *In the Lives of Puppets*, Tor Books, March 2024. Copyright © 2024 by TJ Klune. Reprinted by permission of the author.

"What Happened to The Crooners" by Russell Nichols. First published in *Nightmare*, issue 144, September 2024. Copyright © 2024 by Russell Nichols. Reprinted by permission of the author.

"Fuck Them Kids" by Tatiana Obey. First published in *FIYAH*, #32, Fall 2024. Copyright © 2024 by Tatiana Obey. Reprinted by permission of the author.

"Yarns" by Susan Palwick. First published in *Asimov's*, July–August 2024. Copyright © 2024 by Susan Palwick. Reprinted by permission of the author.

"The Forgetting Room" by Kathryn H. Ross. First published in *FIYAH*, #30, Spring 2024. Copyright © 2024 by Kathryn H. Ross. Reprinted by permission of the author.

"The Weight of Your Own Ashes" by Carlie St. George. First published in *Clarkesworld*, issue 212, May 2024. Copyright © 2024 by Carlie St. George. Reprinted by permission of the author.

"Also, the Cat" by Rachel Swirsky. First published in *Reactor*, January 10, 2024. Copyright © 2024 by Rachel Swirsky. Reprinted by permission of the author.

"We Will Teach You How to Read | We Will Teach You How to Read" by Caroline M. Yoachim. First published in *Lightspeed*, issue 168, May 2024. Copyright © 2024 by Caroline M. Yoachim. Reprinted by permission of the author.

Contents

Foreword ix

Introduction xix

CAROLINE M. YOACHIM. *We Will Teach You How to Read | We Will Teach You How to Read* 1
   from *Lightspeed*

RACHEL SWIRSKY. *Also, the Cat* 18
   from *Reactor*

OLIVIE BLAKE. *The Audit* 59
   from *Januaries*

KIJ JOHNSON. *Country Birds* 78
   from *The Sunday Morning Transport*

TATIANA OBEY. *Fuck Them Kids* 85
   from *FIYAH*

S. L. HUANG. *The River Judge* 102
   from *Reactor*

CARLIE ST. GEORGE. *The Weight of Your Own Ashes* 132
   from *Clarkesworld*

XAVIER GARCIA. *An Ode to the Minor Arcana in a Triplet Flow* 148
   from *Death in the Mouth, Volume 2*

KATHRYN H. ROSS. *The Forgetting Room* 162
   from *FIYAH*

DOMINIQUE DICKEY. *Look at the Moon* 177
   from *Lightspeed*

ISABEL J. KIM. *Why Don't We Just Kill the Kid in the Omelas Hole* 202
   from *Clarkesworld*

JENNIFER HUDAK. *The Witch Trap* 211
   from *Lady Churchill's Rosebud Wristlet*

SUSAN PALWICK. *Yarns* 220
   from *Asimov's*

'PEMI AGUDA. *The Wonders of the World* 245
   from *Ghostroots*

TJ KLUNE. *Reduce! Reuse! Recycle!* 265
   from *In the Lives of Puppets*

TANANARIVE DUE. *A Stranger Knocks* 296
   from *Uncanny*

THOMAS HA. *The Sort* 317
   from *Clarkesworld*

RUSSELL NICHOLS. *What Happened to The Crooners* 336
   from *Nightmare*

ADAM-TROY CASTRO. *The Three Thousand, Four Hundred Twenty-Third Law of Robotics* 349
   from *Lightspeed*

JOE HILL. *Ushers* 356
   from Amazon Original Stories

Contributors' Notes 378

Other Notable Science Fiction and Fantasy of 2024 390

Foreword

WELCOME TO YEAR eleven of *The Best American Science Fiction and Fantasy*! This volume presents the best science fiction and fantasy (SF/F) short stories published during the 2024 calendar year as selected by myself and guest editor Nnedi Okorafor.

About This Year's Guest Editor

Born in the US to Nigerian immigrant parents, Nnedi Okorafor is a *New York Times* bestselling author and multi-award-winning author of science fiction and fantasy for both adults and younger readers. She also has a PhD in literature and two master's degrees, and is a professor of practice with the Interplanetary Initiative in The College of Liberal Arts and Sciences at Arizona State University.

In 2011, with her novel *Who Fears Death*, she became the first Black person to win the World Fantasy Award (which is an utterly baffling thing to type, given the award has been around since 1975). The original form of the award was a bust of H. P. Lovecraft, and Nnedi's acceptance speech was instrumental in getting the World Fantasy Award's governing body to change the award from its original form seeing as Lovecraft was a virulent racist.

Her novella *Binti* won both the Hugo and Nebula Awards. She won a second Hugo for her graphic novel *LaGuardia*, and that book also won the Eisner Award; her other comics work includes writing for Marvel's *Black Panther: Long Live the King*, *Wakanda Forever*, and *Shuri* series and for IDW's *Antar: the Black Knight*. Her book for young readers, *Long Juju Man*, won the Macmillan Writer's Prize for Africa. Her YA novels *Akata Warrior* and *Akata Women* both won the Lodestar Award (which is basically a Hugo for YA works), and *Akata Warrior* also won the Locus Award; and her first novel, *Zahrah the Windseeker*, won the Wole Soyinka Prize for Literature in Africa. In addition, Nnedi has a slew of nominations for these and other awards, and she has been inducted into the Science Fiction Hall of Fame.

Recent books include *She Who Knows*, *One Way Witch*, and *Death of the Author*—for which she notably received a seven-figure advance (and for which I suspect she will garner even more award nominations). Other works for adults include *Binti: Home* and *Binti: The Night Masquerade* (and all three Binti novellas were collected in the *Binti: The Complete Trilogy* omnibus), *Noor*, *The Book of Phoenix*, *Remote Control*, and *Lagoon* (an adaptation of which is in development at Amblin Entertainment). Other books for younger readers include *Like Thunder*, *Shadow Speaker*, and *Ikenga*. She's also the author of an autobiography/creativity book called *Broken Places and Outer Spaces*.

One downside of serving as guest editor is that your own work can't be included in the anthology. Which is unfortunate, because Nnedi had a great story called "Abracadabra" in *New Scientist* in 2024. (It's online, on the *New Scientist* website.[1]) She's a wonderful short fiction writer, so I definitely endorse checking that out, and I'd also heartily recommend her short fiction collection, *Kabu Kabu*.

Nnedi and I go way back together. We first met online when I was doing interviews for *SciFi Wire* (later known as *Syfy Wire* and *Blastr*), and I interviewed her about her novel *Shadow Speaker*. It was in that interview I learned that she and I had had the same rare spinal surgery (she for scoliosis, me for kyphosis, both of us ending up with rods attached to our spines). In her case, though, she was temporarily paralyzed for some time—which would directly influence *Death of the Author*, which features a disabled writer

---

[1] newscientist.com/article/mg26435213-900-abracadabra-an-exclusive-sci-fi-short-story-for-new-scientist

protagonist. Shortly after that interview, I convinced her to write a story for my first original anthology, *Seeds of Change*, which resulted in the amazing "Spider the Artist." (I later reprinted it in *Lightspeed*, so it's online there if you want to see what I mean.[2]) So in a lot of ways, her serving as guest editor is like our joint story coming full circle.

Visit nnedi.com to learn more.

Selection Criteria and Process

The stories chosen for this anthology were originally published between January 1, 2024, and December 31, 2024. The technical criteria for consideration are (1) original publication in a nationally distributed North American publication (i.e., periodicals, collections, or anthologies, in print, online, or ebook); (2) publication in English by writers who are North American, or who have made North America their home; (3) publication as text (audiobook, podcast, dramatized, interactive, and other forms of fiction are not considered); (4) original publication as short fiction (excerpts of novels are not knowingly considered); (5) story length of 17,499 words or less; (6) at least loosely categorized as science fiction or fantasy; (7) publication by someone other than the author (i.e., self-published works are not eligible); and (8) publication as an original work of the author (i.e., not part of a media tie-in/licensed fiction program).

As series editor, I attempted to read everything I could find that meets the above selection criteria. After doing all of my reading, I created a list of what I felt were the top eighty stories (forty science fiction and forty fantasy) published in the genre. Those eighty stories—hereinafter referred to as the "Top 80"—were sent to the guest editor, who read them and then chose the best twenty (ten science fiction, ten fantasy) for inclusion in the anthology. The guest editor reads all of the stories anonymously—with no bylines attached to them, nor any information about where the story originally appeared.

---

2 lightspeedmagazine.com/fiction/spider-the-artist/

The guest editor's top twenty selections appear in this volume; the remaining sixty stories that did not make it into the anthology are listed in the back of this book as "Other Notable Stories of 2024."

2024 Selections

Eight authors selected for this volume previously appeared in *BASFF*: Adam-Troy Castro (3), Thomas Ha (1), S. L. Huang (2), Kij Johnson (1), Isabel J. Kim (2), Susan Palwick (2), Rachel Swirsky (1), and Caroline M. Yoachim (4). With her fifth selection this year, Caroline M. Yoachim is now tied with Sofia Samatar for all-time most appearances in *BASFF*. 'Pemi Aguda, Olivie Blake, Dominique Dickey, Tananarive Due, Xavier Garcia, Joe Hill, Jennifer Hudak, TJ Klune, Russell Nichols, Tatiana Obey, Kathryn H. Ross, and Carlie St. George are all appearing in *BASFF* for the first time. This is Joe Hill's first appearance in *BASFF*, but of course he was *BASFF*'s first guest editor; nice to have him on this side of the ledger!

The selections were chosen from fourteen different publications: Amazon Original Stories (1), *Asimov's* (1), *Clarkesworld* (3), *Death in the Mouth, Vol. 2* edited by Sloane Leong and Cassie Hart (1), *FIYAH* (2), *Ghostroots: Stories* by 'Pemi Aguda (1), *In the Lives of Puppets* by TJ Klune (1), *Januaries* by Olivie Blake (1), *Lady Churchill's Rosebud Wristlet* (1), *Lightspeed* (3), *Nightmare* (1), *Reactor* (2), *The Sunday Morning Transport* (1), and *Uncanny* (1).

Several of our selections this year were winners of (or finalists for) some of the field's awards[3]: "A Stranger Knocks" by Tananarive Due (Locus and Ignyte finalist); "The River Judge" by S. L. Huang (Locus finalist); "The Witch Trap" by Jennifer Hudak (Nebula finalist); "Why Don't We Just Kill the Kid in the Omelas Hole" by Isabel J. Kim (Nebula and Locus winner; Hugo and Sturgeon final-

---

[3] At the time of this writing, several genre awards had not yet announced their lists of finalists, such as the World Fantasy, Sturgeon, and Locus awards, and the final results of some of the awards mentioned above won't be known until after this text is locked for production, but will be known by the time the book is published.

Foreword

ist); "Reduce! Reuse! Recycle!" by TJ Klune (Sturgeon and Locus finalist); and "We Will Teach You How to Read | We Will Teach You How to Read" by Caroline M. Yoachim (Hugo, Nebula, Sturgeon, Locus, Eugie, and Ignyte finalist).

2024 Top 80

In order to select the Top 80 stories published in the SF/F genres in 2024, I considered several thousand stories from a wide array of anthologies, collections, and magazines.

The Top 80 this year were drawn from thirty different publications: seventeen periodicals, seven anthologies, five single-author collections, and one single-story chapbook.

Thomas Ha had the most stories in the Top 80 this year, with three; several authors were tied for second most, with two each: Dominique Dickey, Zohar Jacobs, Alaya Dawn Johnson, Shingai Njeri Kagunda, Rich Larson, Aimee Ogden, and Caroline M. Yoachim. Overall, seventy-one different authors are represented in the Top 80.

In addition to the selections that were nominated for awards, several Notable Stories were finalists for various awards as well: "Judas Iscariot Didn't Kill Himself: A Story in Fragments" by James S.A. Corey (Sturgeon finalist); "I'm Not Disappointed Just Mad AKA The Heaviest Couch in the Known Universe" by Daryl Gregory (Locus finalist); "The Brotherhood of Montague St. Video" by Thomas Ha (Hugo and Nebula finalist); "Lake of Souls" by Ann Leckie (Hugo finalist); "The V*mpire" by P H Lee (Nebula, Locus, and World Fantasy finalist); "Another Girl Under the Iron Bell" by Angela Liu (Nebula and Locus finalist); "Evan: A Remainder" by Jordan Kurella (Nebula and Sturgeon finalist); "Three Faces of a Beheading" by Arkady Martine (Hugo, Locus, and Shirley Jackson finalist); "By Salt, By Sea, By Light of Stars" by Premee Mohammed (Locus winner; Hugo finalist); "What Any Dead Thing Wants" by Aimee Ogden (Nebula); and "Stitched to the Skin Like Family Is" by Nghi Vo (Hugo and Locus finalist).

Outside of my Top 80, I had about ninety more stories in contention this year, and the difference in quality between those that made it in and those that didn't was often razor thin—so in the end, many of the decisions came down to editorial instinct.

Anthologies

The following anthologies had stories in our Top 80 this year: *Death in the Mouth, Vol. 2** edited by Sloane Leong and Cassie Hart (2); *Far Futures* series edited by Jenny Johnston (2); *Northern Nights* edited by Michael Kelly (2); *The Black Girl Survives in This One* edited by Desiree S. Evans and Saraciea J. Fennell[4] (1); *The Last Dangerous Visions* edited by Harlan Ellison and J. Michael Straczynski (1); *Thyme Travelers* edited by Sonia Sulaiman (1); and *We Mostly Come Out at Night* edited by Rob Costello (1). Anthologies marked with an asterisk had stories selected for inclusion in this volume.

Other anthologies that published fine work in 2024 that didn't manage to crack the Top 80 include: *Deep Dream* edited by Indrapramit Das; and *The Crawling Moon: Queer Tales of Inescapable Dread* edited by dave ring. Overall, it seemed like a lot fewer anthologies were released in 2024; I hope that's not a trend that continues.

Collections

Six collections had a story in the Top 80 this year: *Buried Deep and Other Stories* by Naomi Novik; *Ghostroots: Stories** by 'Pemi Aguda; *In the Lives of Puppets** by TJ Klune; *Weird Black Girls* by Elwin Cotman; *Lake of Souls* by Ann Leckie[5]; and *Januaries** by Olivie Blake. Collections marked with an asterisk had stories selected for inclusion in this volume. Naturally, many other collections were published in 2024 that also contained fine work. All of the following were released in 2024 and meet the broad "American" focus of this book; some contained only reprints, but I'm

---

4 This was a Locus Award winner for Best Anthology.
5 *Lake of Souls* won the Locus Award for Best Collection.

Foreword

including them here anyway as part of my overview of the year: *Power to Yield and Other Stories* by Bogi Takács; *Jamaica Ginger and Other Concoctions* by Nalo Hopkinson; *You Like It Darker* by Stephen King; *Craft: Stories I Wrote for the Devil* by Ananda Lima; *The Proper Thing and Other Stories* by Seanan McGuire; *Death Aesthetic* by Josh Rountree; *Good Night, Sleep Tight* by Brian Evenson; and *The Skinless Man Counts to Five* by Paul Jessup.

Periodicals

Lightspeed* had the most stories in the Top 80 (11); followed by *Reactor** (10); *Clarkesworld**[6] (9); *The Sunday Morning Transport** (9); *Nightmare** (4); *Uncanny** (4); *FIYAH** (3); *Strange Horizons* (3); *The Magazine of Fantasy & Science Fiction* (2); *Psychopomp* (2); and the following all had one each: *Analog*; *Asimov's**; *Conjunctions*; *Fusion Fragment*; *Lady Churchill's Rosebud Wristlet**; and *New Edge Sword and Sorcery*. Periodicals marked with an asterisk had stories selected for inclusion in this volume. *Lady Churchill's Rosebud Wristlet* had a story selected for inclusion for the first time.

Appearing in the Top 80 for the first time are: *Baffling*; *Fusion Fragment*; *Lady Churchill's Rosebud Wristlet*; *New Edge Sword and Sorcery*, and *Psychopomp*.

Debuting in 2024 were *Psychopomp, Incensepunk Magazine,* and *Trollbreath Magazine.* Long-dormant classic SF magazines *Worlds of If* and *Galaxy Science Fiction* were revived in 2024 and released one issue each.

Permanently closing were: *Anathema: Spec from the Margins*; *Apparition Lit*; *Gamut Magazine*; *Mermaids Monthly*; *The Maul*; and *ZNB Presents.*

Aside from launches and closures, the big news about SF/F periodicals was that *Asimov's, Analog,* and *The Magazine of Fantasy & Science Fiction* were all purchased by a company called Must Read Books Publishing, a division of 1 Paragraph Inc. This is a seismic shift in the SF/F field—these three magazines are the longest-running

---

[6] Winner of the Locus Award for Best Magazine.

magazines in the field: *Analog* has been publishing since 1930 (originally as *Astounding*), *Asimov's* since 1977, and *The Magazine of Fantasy & Science Fiction* since 1949. Penny Press/Dell Magazines has published *Asimov's* and *Analog* since 1996, and Spilogale, Inc. has published *The Magazine of Fantasy & Science Fiction* since 2001. All current editorial staff were reported as remaining in place, and *Locus: The Magazine of the Science Fiction & Fantasy Field* provided this additional background on the acquisition:

> [Must Read Books Publishing] is financially backed by a small group of genre fiction fans. A major investor and board advisor is Michael Khandelwal, the founder of a writing nonprofit and Virginia's Mars Con toastmaster. Macmillan Learning Ebook consultant and developer Franco A. Alvarado has joined the group as director, design & operations. Leading the executive board is former Curtis Brown literary agent Steven Salpeter, who will manage the distribution, translation, and Film/TV rights for the company, as he does for other companies at his new firm 2 Arms Media.

For more, see bookpublishing.center; I felt compelled to share the URL, because it's annoyingly difficult to google "Must Read Books" given how many times that phrase has been used in listicles over the years. There's nothing on the website but placeholder text as I write this, but hopefully by the time you're reading this it will have more information. Time will tell if this is a good development for *Asimov's* and *Analog*—but it's certainly a good development for *The Magazine of Fantasy & Science Fiction*, which had been having such significant problems in 2024 (in which they only released two, rather than six, issues) that a lot of people in the field speculated that it might go out of business.

Acknowledgments

Many thanks to my assistant series editor, Christopher M. Cevasco, and to our in-house *BASFF* coordinator, Nicole Angeloro, for their tireless work behind the scenes. I'm also grateful to David Steffen, creator of The Submission Grinder, an excellent writer's market database that helps me keep tabs on what's opening, closing, and everything in between.

Likewise, I offer boundless thanks and appreciation to the writers who continue to breathe life into short fiction—especially those who carve out time for it even while juggling novel deadlines. And to the readers who seek it out, celebrate it, and share it with others: You're the lifeblood of this community. There are too few of us doing that work, and far too many readers out there who don't even know short stories are a thing. Special shoutout to Reddit user tarvolon, who organizes the Short Fiction Book Club over on r/Fantasy—doing excellent work to shine a spotlight on new and worthy short fiction.

Submissions for Next Year's Volume

Editors, writers, and publishers who would like their work considered for next year's edition (the best of 2025), please visit johnjosephadams.com/best-american for instructions on how to submit material for consideration. I also invite you to subscribe to my newsletter, *Robot Wizard Zombie Crit!*, if you'd like to keep up with me and my projects throughout the year. To subscribe (for free), just visit johnjosephadams.com/newsletter.

—JOHN JOSEPH ADAMS

Introduction

I HAVE A complicated relationship with the genres of science fiction and fantasy. It began long before I started writing stories (when I was twenty), back in my preteens, when I first developed my reading habits in the public library. My local library was always a place of adventure, safety, and freedom. I was at my most curious and entitled here. I could go wherever I wanted. I could pick up and look at any book if it was on a shelf. I didn't have to worry about what the book cost. I had my "Ring of Power," my library card. And so, in that place of knowledge, information, stories, and quiet, I didn't pay categories any mind. I meandered through the aisles, picking up whatever caught my interest.

This was how I ended up in the adult section and picked up Stephen King's *It* when I was only twelve years old. I lifted that heavy, ominous-looking tome, didn't even notice the label of "horror" on it, read the first page, and was hooked. Oh yes, throughout the weeks of reading it and for months after, I was terrified of storm drains, but I enjoyed that novel immensely. And so, my confidence in ignoring categories was solidified. Genre meant nothing to me. I would read Clive Barker's *Imajica* and then *Tiger Eyes* by Judy Blume. *Executioner's Song* by Norman Mailer and then *The Changeover* by Margaret Mahy. The library system in my neighborhood was not as diverse as it should have been, so books by people of color, particularly Black authors (globally), would come later, as I discovered them at the university level.

I wasn't a "gifted" kid, and I never saw any of this as unusual. My parents let me read whatever I wanted. I got used to dense, whimsical, informative, thought-provoking, bloody, uptight, unhinged, or childish literature. Expectations didn't hold me back or push me forward. I wasn't in the habit of resting in the comforting arms of the familiar, though when I did it was refreshing. I didn't need to control the narrative. I let the stories explain to me what they needed to explain. And I was open to whatever the library had to show me. Calling something "science fiction" or "fantasy" got no reaction out of me. Everything was everything. Boxes had no place in my reading experience.

That said, when I decided I wanted to get my stories published, stories that I never bothered to label or categorize, it was the community and genres of science fiction and fantasy that embraced me most. No matter what I cooked up, within science fiction and fantasy it was okay, it was normal, it was acceptable, and it was seen. But while working on my bachelor's, two master's, and then my PhD, I had professors telling me that what I was doing *wasn't* okay. Science fiction and fantasy were frowned upon, not viewed as "real" literature. I had professors who would even put that sentiment on the syllabus of writing workshop courses—"no science fiction, fantasy, or mystery." This never stopped me from writing whatever I wanted, but it certainly communicated to me that there was snobbery and a default Western point of view I had to navigate. (What is labeled "fantastical" often depends on your culture.)

Then I went to the Clarion Science Fiction and Fantasy Writers' Workshop (after Jamaican Canadian author Nalo Hopkinson recommended I check it out), and it was there that I felt my work was truly accepted for the first time since I'd begun writing years ago. I wasn't sure if what I was doing was science fiction or fantasy, but I also didn't really care. The enthusiastic embrace and fellowship in weirdness was what mattered to me. I was having too good a time, learning too much, and that was more significant than fitting into a box. After that, I started submitting to science fiction and fantasy magazines, and my work began getting chosen for anthologies. I found the openness there, too. I was writing about things like immigrant masquerades

Introduction xxi

who found work as brushes in carwashes, the ogbanje torturing a friend of mine with its coming and going, and people who could fly. That which was called "science fiction and fantasy" was freedom and open space I could occupy. Mostly.

This is what science fiction and fantasy means to me.

There are times when it feels like a box, but within it, technically, you can expect anything. There can be terror, fascination, the expected and unexpected, befuddlement, validation, transformation, alienation, worlds and universes, and it can also take you home. You can find stories about family, destiny, monsters, the future, the past, the never. And sometimes, you can find the nameless. And that's okay, too.

This is what science fiction and fantasy means to me.

Science fiction and fantasy is broad. Let it be broad. And it has many bloodlines. Not everything is a child of the science fiction and fantasy "Golden Age" of Asimov, Lovecraft, Lewis, Heinlein, Clarke, Tolkien, etc. My "Golden Age" names include Okri, Achebe, Soyinka, Ngũgĩ, but also the Nigerian town of Arondizuogu, the frivolous, proud, problematic spirit of the human-made country known as Nigeria. Understand that contexts, worldviews, points of view are not all the same, and all of those things play a role in the story that is told. I think it's difficult for many to understand this. My advice is that if something is new to you, then resist that urge to say/think, "I'm reminded of [familiar thing]." Just let that thing be what it is. Watch how you start seeing other literary bloodlines. Watch your world expand.

This is what science fiction and fantasy means to me.

This is my first time serving as an editor. It's a role that I never imagined myself taking. I knew that this would force me to stretch, and even when I was on the track-and-field team, I was known as the one who hated stretching. However, stretching makes you limber enough to weather being affected. Being affected leads to change. And as Octavia Butler wrote through her character of Lauren Olamina, "The only lasting truth is Change."

All this said, in order to do this, I returned to my basics. I threw all thought of genre aside and just read. Just as I did as a kid in the library. No expectation other than the search for a good and well-told story. I am not one who sees or pays attention to trends, and I think it would be a disservice to each story to seek out similarities. So no, no trends found here. Not by me. No similarities. Each story is its own beast, and I gathered quite the herd.

There's a story about self-love and acceptance and what one must sacrifice to arrive there; that one brought tears to my eyes. I was deeply touched by a story about complex sisterly love and death. There was a story that made me pause halfway through and get up and turn on all the lights . . . and the house alarm. And even then, it still had me looking over my shoulder. One story takes the concept of "passing" to a new level. There's a vicious little story that unflinchingly has the nerve to say all the things. (This was especially satisfying because of all that's going on in the world.) Oh, that robot who only wanted to fit in. There's a story that had me wondering what might be in the walls of my house. One story plays with and manipulates form, repetition, and the act of reading. In one story, I experienced the smooth mix of the mystical and the mundane and how some women audaciously navigate a patriarchal community. And more.

I went into this unsure, and I emerged so wonderfully affected. These stories did what the best science fiction and fantasy stories should do. I hope you enjoy this eclectic menagerie as much as I did.

NNEDI OKORAFOR

CAROLINE M. YOACHIM

We Will Teach You How to Read | We Will Teach You How to Read

FROM *Lightspeed*

SCIENCE FICTION

Iteration

THIS IS OUR story, simplified: Life. Loss. Transformation. Love. Death. Iteration.

The first time you get our message, you only find one thread. It mimics your language in its simplest form, a single strand of words laid end to end. You will have to work hard if you want to understand us properly. You must learn to hold more than one thread of language simultaneously in your mind.	This is our story, simplified: Life. Loss. Transformation. Love. Death. Iteration.

Don't worry, we will help you develop
the skills you need. We will keep one
simple thread unchanged. At first you
will glance back and forth
between these words and those. Your
attention is a strange, skittering thing,
but we believe you can learn
with repetition.

This is our story,
simplified:
Life.
Loss.
Transformation.
Love.
Death.
Iteration.

For you, we are relearning how to teach.
You can hear musical chords of multiple
notes, even two strands of differing lyrics
for short stretches of song. It helps to
memorize the words. Your mind has a
strange divide between learning and
knowing. Read both columns, please.
Every time.

This is our story,
simplified:
Life.
Loss.
Transformation.
Love.
Death.
Iteration.

Can you commit our simplified
story to memory? See just the shape of
the words and know what is there?
You have so little bandwidth,
there might not be any other way.
It is not ideal but we are
desperate.
We will repeat to help you understand.

This is our story,
simplified:
Life.
Loss.
Transformation.
Love.
Death.
Iteration.

This Is Our Story, Simplified

We read three times in the course of our lifespan: once with our parents to learn the story, once alone to add to the threads, and once with our children to teach them. History, science, philosophy, art. All we have ever known is here, in one thread or another, trapped in what—for you—would be a cacophony of overlapping words.

If both sides are simple,	This is our story,
can you do it?	simplified:
A series of moments.	Life.
The passing of parents.	Loss.
From reader to writer.	Transformation.
A new generation.	Love.
To persist when we're gone.	Death.
Our story continues.	Iteration.

We sense your struggle, it is still too much.	This is our story,
Have you memorized our story,	simplified:
simplified? Can you hear it in your head?	Life.
You are such strange creatures to have	Loss.
two eyes and yet to focus on only one	Transformation.
thing at a time. You can't read the words	Love.
on the other side of the page so you have	Death.
to simply know them.	Iteration.

Recognize them from the shape of the	This is our story,
lines. Sound would be easier, yes—	simplified:
you make far better use of your ears	Life.
as independent sensory organs	Loss.
than you do your eyes. But	Transformation.
we are determined to teach you to read.	Love.
Simpler still, simpler still. Can you at least	Death.
hold two identical lines in your head?	Iteration.

This is our story,   This is our story,
simplified: simplified:
Life.   Life.
Loss.   Loss.
Transformation.   Transformation.
Love.   Love.
Death.   Death.
Iteration.   Iteration.

Feel the doubling of it, hear it in two   This is our story,
different voices, somehow split your   simplified:
single focus of attention into two.   Life.
Do you see how they match, how they   Loss.
resonate with each other? Go back up   Transformation.
and look again. Try to capture the   Love.
sensation of reading both at once,   Death.
even for a moment.   Iteration.

Life

You are ancient, and we are fleeting. Such a luxury, to have so much time that you need not rush through everything at once. And yet you are so horribly inefficient, to not make more of the time you have. Think what you could do in a single lifetime if you could read more than one thread at once, think more thoughts at once, hold more experience in every moment.

You have a game with pictures, trying to
spot the differences, your eyes darting
back and forth between them. It is harder
with text. Don't focus on individual words
in each line, but look at the space between
them. Know what both sides say. Hold it
all in your head. Perhaps don't even quite
focus your vision.

This is our story,
with variations:
Life.
Loss.
Inspiration.
Love.
Death.
New translation.

Go back and try to read it all at
once—hold both versions in your head.
We are only asking you to read
two threads, though we
ourselves can do thousands.
Threads of love and hope,
threads of fear and death.
How many iterations will it take you?

This is our story,
simplified:
Life.
Loss.
Transformation.
Love.
Death.
Iteration.

This is our story,
simplified:
Life.
Loss.
Transformation.
Love.
Death.
Iteration.

This is our story,
simplified:
Life.
Loss.
Transformation.
Love.
Death.
Iteration.

This is our story,
terrified:
Loss.
Loss.
Endless attrition.
Death.
Death.
Desperation.

This is our story,
simplified:
Life.
Loss.
Transformation.
Love.
Death.
Iteration.

Loss

Our generations are synced in a way that yours are not. Iterations of our story are not staggered, not muddled like those songs that you call rounds. An entire generation reads together in a single voice, three times: as children with their parents, as adults alone, and as parents with their children.

But with each generation, the number of those who read our story is diminished. Many children refuse to learn their parents' words. There are too many threads, they say. There are so few of us remaining. Soon, our story will be lost forever. We must find another way.

We remember every word we read,
instantly, consistently, a perfect
rendition. There are those among
you with eidetic memory,
but even that is fleeting,
a lingering perception,
rather than a lasting record.
Insufficient.

How much story can you hold,
in a life as vast as yours?
Even if some threads
are lost
in the translation,
is it not better to have
a legacy, an afterlife
that echoes after we are gone?

This is our story,
simplified:
Life.
Loss.
Transformation.
Love.
Death.
Iteration.

This is our story,
simplified:
Life.
Loss.
Transformation.
Love.
Death.
Iteration.

This is our story,
simplified:
Life.
Loss.
Transformation.
Love.
Death.
Iteration.

We double threads for
emphasis,
contrast death
with life.
When you recreate
our story
do not lose this
information.

This is our story,
simplified:
Life.
Loss.
Transformation.
Love.
Death.
Iteration.

This is our story,
simplified:
Life.
Loss.
Transformation.
Love.
Death.
Iteration.

Transformation

Can you make the shift, from reader to writer, when you can only barely read? We fear that you do not grasp the urgency—you know our lives are short compared to yours but fail to comprehend the magnitude of the difference. We read three times in the course of our lifespan: once with our parents to learn the story, once alone as we write new threads, and once with our children to teach them. There is nothing else but this, we live our entire lives while reading, and the time it takes you to read three times . . .

> "This is our story,
> simplified:
> Life.
> Loss.
> Transformation.
> Love.
> Death.
> Iteration."

. . . is for us a lifetime.

We have been trying to teach you to read for several generations. We are running out of time.

This is our story,
simplified:
Life.
Loss.
Transformation.
Love.
Death.
Iteration.

This is our story,
simplified:
Life.
Loss.
Transformation.
Love.
Death.
Iteration.

This is our story,
simplified:
Life.
Loss.
Transformation.
Love.
Death.
Iteration.

We Will Teach You How to Read

Even in the simplest case, identical threads, we fear you cannot hold more than two. Please try. It is important for the translation. Understand us well enough to love us, to miss us when we're gone. Teach our story to your children.

This is our story, simplified:
Life.
Loss.
Transformation.
Love.
Death.
Iteration.

This is our story, simplified:
Life.
Loss.
Transformation.
Love.
Death.
Iteration.

This is our story, simplified:
Life.
Loss.
Transformation.
Love.
Death.
Iteration.

This is our story, simplified:
Life.
Loss.
Transformation.
Love.
Death.
Iteration.

This is our story, simplified:
Life.
Loss.
Transformation.
Love.
Death.
Iteration.

This is our story, simplified:
Life.
Loss.
Transformation.
Love.
Death.
Iteration

This is our story, simplified:
Life.
Loss.
Transformation.
Love.
Death.
Iteration.

Love

The gift of words we give to our children is our greatest expression of love. We want to give this gift to you, even knowing how hard you must work to receive it. Imagine our words, stretched into a thin vertical line...

T
H
I
S

I
S

O
U
R

S
T
O
R
Y,

S
I
M
P
L
I
F
I
E
D

... and set beside it all the variations, all our explanations, everything you usually read as a single stream of text chopped into smaller pieces and laid out side by side so we can fit it all within

We Will Teach You How to Read

our lifespan, each generation adding a new column to the story, stretching it ever wider.

There's a part of our story that describes finding you, our hopes and fears for you, and learning to communicate:

To even fit it on the page requires text a hairsbreadth wide, and it is still but a tiny fraction of our story.

Without our story,

life continues.
The loss makes space
for something new.
Our children
evolve, beyond
repetition.

This is our story,
simplified:
Life.
Loss.
Transformation.
Love.
Death.
Iteration.

Death

We are the last ones holding on to the old story. Our children are making something new. Please take these words we send you, read them, learn them, translate them into something your mind can understand. You might not add your threads and iterate as we do, but hopefully as you transform our words, you will keep some sense of the vastness of each moment, the illusion of holding more story in your mind than you are actually capable of holding.

This is our story,
one last time:
Life.
Loss.
Transformation.
Love.
Death.

This is our story,
simplified:
Life.
Loss.
Transformation.
Love.
Death.
Iteration.

> "Even if some threads are lost
> in the translation,
> is it not better to have
> a legacy, an afterlife
> that echoes after we are gone?"

It took many generations for them to teach us how to read.

Their lifespan was measured in mere inches of text.

It took far longer for us to learn to write on their behalf.

That timescale cannot be captured on these pages.

The blank space—the absence of their generations—would go for miles.

This is their story,	This was their story,
in translation:	simplified:
Life.	Life.
Loss.	Loss.
Transformation.	Transformation.
Love.	Love.
Death.	Death.
Commemoration.	Iteration.

Commemoration | Iteration

The entirety of their story has thousands upon thousands of threads. It is history told in moments that seem to happen all at once. It is science that progresses in increments almost infinitely small, and yet contains discoveries that even now we do not fully comprehend. It is their art, their language, their culture—everything they were determined to preserve. We have so much left to translate; this is only the beginning.

Give this story to your children, along with everything we have managed to translate, and perhaps one day the story will make its way back to the distant descendants of those who created it—ephemeral entities who, in the final generations of their decline, taught us a new way to read. When you teach this story to your children, do not start with all the threads at once. Instead, begin with a single line of text:

This is our story, simplified: Life. Loss. Transformation. Love. Death. Iteration.

RACHEL SWIRSKY

Also, the Cat

FROM *Reactor*

FANTASY

ROSALEE DIED, AGED seventy-six. Her oldest sister, Irene (seventy-eight), blamed their middle sister, Viola (seventy-seven), for sending Rosie out front to check the mail when she knew Rosie's inner ear condition was acting up. Viola, on the other hand, blamed Irene for not paying to get the garden path repaved last summer when they had the boys in to fix the porch.

The three sisters had never gotten along. They'd been born one, two, three—Irene then Viola then Rosalee—over the course of twenty-seven months, courtesy of prematurity and an abundance of parental amour. Their exhausted progenitors had expected them to share everything from possessions to personalities. As a result, they despised sharing anything apart from heartfelt and mutual hatred.

All three sisters had hightailed it away from home as soon as age and circumstance allowed—three teenage marriages, each more dubious than the last—but over the years, tragedy and/or mishap had struck thrice. One husband had died in a bar (where he spent the majority of his living hours, in any case); one had converted his mistress into a missus; and one had honest-to-goodness disappeared at sea. The financial strains of widowhood—combined with the indifference, incapacity, and simple ingratitude of the various children to which the sisters had given birth—had eventually driven them all back to the farmhouse to live like maiden aunts.

Also, the Cat

It was as if, in their elder age, their adult lives had unspooled, dragging them back to their childhoods—back to walls full of half-finished electrical wiring that Papa had abandoned because he didn't trust all that lightning in the house; back to the kitchen icebox with the drip pan that needed to be emptied twice a day; back to summers redly swollen with insect bites and winters nibbled blue by frost.

Irene and Viola had begun venting their ire on each other only seconds after finding Rosie's corpse. Once begun, the rants continued almost ceaselessly throughout the following days, subsiding only briefly for herbal tea. At night, when even tea couldn't soothe the savaged vocal cords, they rasped off to their separate bedrooms, where they continued to berate each other in their dreams, each pleased to be winning her points so eloquently until waking dashed her back to contentious reality.

Rosalee's ghost was understandably unhappy with the situation.

She had returned to spectral consciousness a few seconds after dying, the back of her head still pouring blood onto the garden path. Her body had not yet been discovered by anyone but herself, which had the virtue of giving her time to come to terms with the reality of her demise before being forced to cope with the concomitant reality of still being stuck in the world with her sisters, only now, as she would soon learn, without effective means to communicate her opinions.

"Does this seem fair?" Rosie had asked her corpse. "It does not."

If her sisters had heard her, doubtlessly one of them would have snapped at her in response that *life isn't fair*. She would have liked to reply: *Shouldn't death be, then?*

However, her sisters were elsewhere—and even if they'd been present, it wouldn't have made any difference: They, with their doggedly metronomic breath and circulating blood, couldn't hear her at all, no matter their proximity, not even when strolling right through her.

Rosie tried, nevertheless, to make conversation. For instance, when Viola announced that she was going upstairs to choose which dresses to send to the mortuary, Rosie followed.

"Not the polyester!" Rosie exclaimed, waving her arms in distress as she watched Viola sift through the hangers. "Oh, no, no—what are you doing? That was for a church play! I was a tree! Oh—no—I inherited that one from my mother-in-law—No! You can't be serious! *No one* should wear that color!"

The issue was simple: Viola had always envied Rosalee's wardrobe—but unfortunately, although all three sisters had gained weight after marriage and childbirth, Viola had gained more than the others, and so Irene would inherit the lot. Viola had made it her objective, therefore, to deny Irene whichever of Rosie's dresses she thought Irene would most enjoy.

This might have been tolerable, except that Irene's curmudgeonly tastes ran deep. Even at the age of ten, she'd dressed like the abstemious old woman it had taken her sixty more years to become. Given a choice between, for example, a cheerful bright red and a dumpy dried-puke green, Irene would always choose the latter. She regarded embellishments like lace with several degrees more disgust than an upright Puritan would regard a Roman orgy.

Alas, Viola knew Irene's taste very, very well.

Rosie followed Viola from dress to dress, striving desperately to be heard. "What about the pink one? Yes! Right there! No, no, don't put it down—Okay, the blue one, that's fine, too. It's right behind the one you're looking at—No, Viola, that's a dress I wore to *someone else's* funeral—*Oh, no.* You've got the key to my jewelry box. You're going to go straight for my husband's gold rings, aren't you? Viola! That's enough of this—Stop!"

Rosie planted herself directly in her sister's path as Viola went to lay her selections on the bed.

Viola walked right through her.

Glumly, Rosie went looking for Irene. She found her out front, endeavoring to scrub residual blood from the path where Rosie had fallen. This was characteristic of Irene, whose willingness to replace things barely extended to balding toothbrushes. She kept a box in the attic filled with torn wrapping paper, which she reused by taping it to packages in unsettling mosaics of reindeer, birthday candles, and the baby Jesus.

"This path was too old to start with," Rosie scolded her. "Viola's right. You should have had it replaced when we got the porch done. Look at all those cracks. One or the other of you is going to break your hip, if you don't die outright. How's it going to look to people in town if we all die the same way?"

Irene stopped scrubbing to examine her progress. She sneered in frustration at the persistent splatter. "Isn't this just like Rosalee?" Irene muttered. "Inconsiderate down to the blood."

"Oh, never mind," said Rosie. "Break your neck if you want to." A horrible thought occurred. "You won't become a ghost, will you?"

"Couldn't even be bothered to watch her feet, the stampcrab," Irene continued.

Rosie fixed a fastidious eye on her left foot as she drew it back to kick her eldest sister's rear end. Being insubstantial, however, Rosie's foot passed through Irene's worldly derriere, leaving Rosie's specter scrambling to regain her balance while Irene carried on her grumbling unaffected.

Although Rosie went to sit alone for the rest of the day, watching the sun slump behind the horizon, she could still hear her sisters shouting in the distance. Before her death, Rosie would never have guessed—and nor would anyone else—that she'd acted as something of a buffer between her older sisters. She'd argued just as bitterly and hated just as passionately. Yet now it was undeniable: In her absence, something important had changed.

The truth was that withdrawing any sister from the trio would have collapsed the balance between the others. With only two of them, there were no more shifting alliances to motivate negotiations and truces. There were only endless frontal assaults between opposing generals.

Through sheer vocal exhaustion, the hot war ended one morning in a ceasefire of a sort, though certainly not a cessation of hostility. Irene swore never to speak to Viola again; Viola swore the same back. The funeral, it was agreed, was to be arranged by notes deposited hourly on the neutral zone of the kitchen table.

For the first few early hours, Rosie felt relieved on behalf of her ears, but by afternoon it became clear that the only thing worse than the constant shouting was the unbroken silence. Not only had Rosie lost the ability to speak herself, but now she was without any words at all.

That night, when Rosie went up to the room that had been hers, and lay upon the bed that had been hers, atop the ugly clothing that had unfortunately also been hers, she was surprised to spy one of their childhood cats, Mrs. Fritter, loping into the room. The creature leapt onto her chest, seemingly untroubled by the fact that Rosie was recently dead.

Mrs. Fritter herself was many decades past the feline veil. Rosie held out her fingers for the dead cat to sniff. "Hey there, Missus," Rosie said. "We never did figure out what got you. Was there a wolf?"

Mrs. Fritter approached, and Rosie stroked her back. The animal circled several times before curling up.

"What did I expect?" Rosie asked. "They never listened to me when I was alive. No one did. Eddie—that was my husband, you never met him—Ed never listened to me either. To be fair, he was usually too drunk to listen to much. Certainly, too drunk to listen to the doctor about his liver."

Mrs. Fritter rattled a purr.

Rosie went on, "When I was a kid—nine, ten, probably, you were gone by then—I had this game pretending I was an actress starring in the movie of my life. You could've been my pedigree cat. I could've clipped one of my rhinestone pins right here." Rosie ruffled the tuft behind Mrs. Fritter's ear.

The cat bopped her head against Rosie's hand to start it petting again.

"I had a pair of those pins," Rosie said, a bit maudlin. "Viola lost the stones out of them. I bit her on the arm and broke her pencils."

Mrs. Fritter settled down as Rosie's hand resumed stroking.

Rosie continued, "I'd be at the bus stop, imagining the argument I'd have someday with the director of my autobiographical picture. How should we stage the scene where I was discovered? Should I be waiting for the bus? Weeding the garden? Should Viola and Irene be around so we could get some good shots of their faces turning green, or should we focus entirely on me?"

She shook her head.

"Now, I'm dead, and I'm still . . . here."

In the morning, Rosalee went out to the front porch. It was time, she thought, to fulfill her old aspirations, even if she had to do it on her own two ethereal feet. She gazed out at the flat horizon, wishing she had a hat and gloves and a suitcase so it would feel like a proper bon voyage. She took note of the brush of grasses against the sky, and the scent of open air, and the nearby copse of trees, and the little white car Viola had bought from her daughter-in-law at a discount—and she hoped never to see any of them again.

Mrs. Fritter came to see her off. The cat perched on the porch railing and washed her face.

Rosalee waved. "Goodbye, Mrs. Fritter!"

She set off on the road to somewhere.

A few minutes later, she was walking back toward the porch from the other direction, nothing in her head but blankness from the moment she'd crossed the property line. The shadows fell at exactly the same length and angle as they had before, cast by a sun that hadn't bothered to budge an inch.

Mrs. Fritter proceeded to wash her shoulder.

"Well," Rosalee started, but she wasn't sure what else to say. "*Well*," she repeated, sitting down on the porch steps until she gave up and started to cry. Mrs. Fritter jumped down from the railing, pushed her head under Rosie's hand, and tried to purr the tears away.

Irene's ghost woke after a heart attack landed her on the kitchen floor.

Two years ago, she and Viola had replaced the old fridge, and even called some boys to haul away the icebox. The new refrigerator's harvest gold door stood halfway open, leaking cold, expensive air. The carton of strawberries that Irene had been looking forward to all day had fallen to the ground with her, where it snapped open, spilling fruit across the linoleum.

Irene tried to pick up a berry, but her fingers closed on nothing. "By Saint Boogar and all the saints at the backdoor of purgatory! I *knew* these cost too much. I didn't even get to eat *one*."

Irene enjoyed antique swear words. They were not merely her favorite indulgence, but also her shield against slander. People with no sense of rhetorical wit said all sorts of nasty things about women—especially teachers—who let loose with mundane profanities, but you could shout, "Stop doing quisby, you fustilarian scobberlotchers!" in front of a whole classroom's worth of parents, and not-a-one would stop gawping long enough to complain to the principal.

Shakespeare was Irene's gold standard, but she delighted in anything sufficiently well-honed by centuries. Saint Boogar, for instance, found its origin in *Tristram Shandy*, whose eponymous narrator was a veritable fountainhead of insults.

As Irene aged, her elderly obscenities had lost some of their advantages, not because the average loiter-sack had gotten any more gumption, but because the wandoughts and fustilugs of the general public *expected* old women to use "outdated language." Even the rare parent who was not an irredeemable loiter-sack—a truly singular, nay possibly extinct breed—was far too parochial to distinguish between the tatters of childhood lingo and the sterling abuses of Shakespeare.

In the secret and desolate corners of what must grudgingly be called her heart, Irene had always hoped to meet someone with a tongue nimble enough to answer back. For the rightly educated person, retorts would have been easy. They could have called Irene a "klazomaniac" who'd keep on screeching even if you cut out her vocal cords, or a "muckspout" whose talent for constantly swearing was only outdone by her talent for constantly running her mouth. They could even have called her a "dorbel," a nagging teacher whose obsession with scolding and nitpicking made her a peer of the French scholar Nicolas d'Orbellis, whose name had been purloined to craft the insult. Irene took it as fact that the poor man, who had apparently once been forced to wrangle his own classrooms full of ungrateful lubberworts, had been unfairly defamed. It was just like students to sneak around slandering any competent teacher as "scolding" and "nitpicking."

The immutable ignorance of the dalcops that surrounded Irene depressed her, it really did. She consoled herself by flinging more insults until the feeling went away.

Also, the Cat

Irene was the nastiest of her sisters, a sentiment with which she would have happily agreed. As children, the three of them, being opposed to sharing anything, had carefully allocated their sins along with their dolls and dresses. Rosalee was selfish; Viola was resentful; Irene was mean. However, both Rosalee and Viola had found that, without their sisters' reinforcement, their worst traits were mitigated by the outside world. Irene remained equally nasty both in- and outside of sororal company.

When Irene's husband, Howard, had lost himself on an Arctic expedition, unkind people said he was searching for someplace warmer than Irene's heart. Unkinder people said he'd found it.

As soon as Viola heard Irene's body thud to the floor, she rushed stiff kneed from the back porch. At the sight of Irene's broken-down sprawl, she was sure her remaining sister was dead.

She lowered herself to check Irene's pulse anyway. Finding the expected absence, Viola released a whooshing sigh—not of grief or good riddance, but rather of gusty relief—as if she'd been holding her breath for all four years since swearing never to speak to Irene again.

"Really, Irene?" Viola asked, panting. "You don't say a word to me for four years, and now you're leaving me alone?"

"Giving up, eh?" Irene crowed. "I win!"

Unable to hear her sister's exclamation, Viola mused, "If you're dead, I suppose I've won now, haven't I?" She laughed. "I can't believe I won against *you*, Irene."

"Because you didn't win! I did!" Irene's eyes went wide with delighted realization. "Ha! I can talk all I want now. What a slovenly thing you are, Viola! *Buying* stuff and things. *Leaving* them everywhere. Not even *unwrapping* them half the time, you raggabrash. It's *intolerable* living with a driggle-draggle like you. You're as inconsiderate as Rosalee! And those plastic flamingo corn holders are the tackiest things I've ever seen! What do you want with them? What's wrong with our corn holders? When are you eating *corn?*"

Viola, staring down at her sister's body, asked listlessly, "What am I going to do? What if I *miss* you? What will I do *then?*" She shook her head. "Well, now it's all over, I suppose I may as well speak my mind."

"Over because *I* won," said Irene.

"How did you get so *mean?*" asked Viola. "You kept getting worse and worse. It's like you were *pickling* in your own spitefulness."

"Nothing wrong with pickles," complained Irene.

"How could you be so mean without saying a word? You could be mean with an eyebrow. You could be mean with your *elbow.*"

"I can be mean with my *toenail,* thank you very much."

Carefully, Viola picked herself up. Her joints creaked, the sound reverberating through her bones. She glanced toward the stairs leading to the second floor. "I guess the sunny bedroom is mine now," she said, referring to the room that had passed from Rosie to Irene. "Typical. The middle child gets everything last." She shuffled out, mumbling to herself about which funeral home to call.

"Watch you don't get fatter, too," Irene called after her. She sniffed. "Ridiculous tallowcatch."

"You're *both* ridiculous," said Rosalee.

The ghost of Irene looked up. She was not only surprised, but downright shocked to see the ghost of Rosie, who crossed her arms over her chest and looked back.

"You're dead," Irene informed Rosie.

"Pot, this is Kettle," Rosie replied, pointing to Irene's corpse on the floor.

Irene had known she was dead before this point, but the knowledge had occupied some passive, subconscious part of her deceased mind. Now, as it was forced to the surface, for the first time she really *understood* it. Her consciousness grabbed hold of the knowledge and ran around having a fit.

"Gadsbobs!"

"Awful, isn't it?" Rosie agreed drily. "You're dead. I'm dead. And *here* we are."

"Waesucks!"

"No one thinks about haunting from the *ghost's* perspective," said Rosie, who'd had a long time to maunder on the subject and no one to discuss it with. "*We're* not haunting the house.

Also, the Cat

It's haunting *us*. It's *always* haunted us. Think about it—we all escaped, and then it snatched us back."

"Drate-poke," Irene snapped back by rote, barely even hearing herself as she struggled for a grip on the situation. "Are Mother and Father here? What about Great-Aunt Nancy?"

"Just us. And Mrs. Fritter."

"The cat?"

Rosie snapped as her resentments shoved their way center stage. "Do you have *any* idea how horrible it's been in this house for *four years* when the two of you *wouldn't even talk?* Not one conversation! I *begged* you!"

"Don't try to tell me what to do," retorted Irene.

"You could have made up with her anytime. Now Viola's got however long to stew on things before she dies. You better hope she gets forgiving." Rosie narrowed her eyes at her eldest sister. She added, "Because ghosts giving each other the silent treatment would be *pathetic*," with the sinking feeling that was exactly what was going to happen.

Rosalee stayed out of Irene's way; Irene stayed out of Rosalee's way; Viola did as she wished, believing herself alone.

It was, in its way, a revelation for Viola. Not only was she apart from her hated sisters, but it was her first time living alone. From the day she'd left her childhood home until the day she returned there, she'd lived with her husband, Jack-the-Unzipper, who had no problem relying on her for housework and hot dinners even when he was relying on the new girl at work for horizontal refreshment.

Over the years, there had been many "new girls at work." Viola didn't know the precise number—certainly more than the eight or so with whom she'd become embarrassingly acquainted. High/lowlights included Bea, who at least had the manners to claim she didn't know Jack was married; Peggy, who'd optimistically bought a wedding dress; and Susan, who threw him over for his boss, triggering a monthlong sulk during which Jack had the gall to cry to Viola about female perfidy.

Jack's last "new girl" had successfully lured him into giving

Viola the ever-promised but never-before-delivered divorce papers. It was quite the acrobatic feat, given Jack's dread fear of alimony, perhaps assisted by the fact that Jack and Viola's youngest child had finally earned a high school diploma, thus relieving Jack of his even worse fear of child support. The new girl seemed to think he was a catch. Perhaps he was; judging by the increasingly evident ravages of smoking in his Christmas card photos, he seemed literally ready to cough up her inheritance any day.

He'd taken the waif off to New York City, which for some reason had always been "too expensive" whenever Viola asked to go. He called it "an extravagantly stupid way to waste money." Sometimes Viola tried to cajole him; sometimes she even begged. *It would be cheaper if we stayed outside the city,* she'd say. Or *Even if we don't go anywhere you have to pay for, there's still so much there!* Or *Damn it, if you can take your tramps to ski lodges, you can pay for me to see* Starry Night*!* But no. It was Jill who got to watch her face in the reflecting pool next to the Egyptian temple in the Met.

Viola considered that the worst part of this—worse than the difficulties of the divorce, worse than the revelations about bank balances and selfish children, worse even than seeing her husband strut off to New York City while she was forced into returning to the childhood home which had birthed all her miseries—the worst part of all was that the girl's name was Jill. It was intolerable beyond belief that her life had been wrecked by a nursery rhyme. Viola retained some hope that the universe would show enough sense of irony to throw Jack and Jill down a hill together, but thus far her ex-husband's crown remained lamentably intact.

After a few months alone (or so she thought), Viola settled into a pattern, going around the house unwrapping the plethora of packages that had so disturbed Irene. This would have made progress toward tidying if she hadn't kept ordering new items. Some of what she sent for was still gimcrackery (like the plastic flamingo corn holders which had made their way to charity and thence probably a landfill), but she also began ordering things that she found intriguing or even genuinely profound.

She read memoirs of movers and shakers; she pored over coffee-table books on the *Castles of Scotland* and the *Great Houses of Morocco*; she sighed at photo-essays of bright lights among smog-stained skyscrapers. Her vague, lifelong yearnings had solidified into wanderlust sometime after Jack moved east with Jill. Why should he be the only one who got to see whatever he wanted to see? Why should he get to move forward while she got yanked back?

Not that she intended to actually travel. A more confident or iconoclastic woman might have set off for parts unknown despite fatigue and stiff knees and an eighty-two-year-old heart. Viola never really considered it. She was used to regarding herself as middling in the way middle children sometimes do. Not as strong willed as Irene; not as cute as Rosalee; not particularly clever, not particularly talented, not particularly interesting. Certainly not someone who would do something extraordinary like explore the world for the first time while ninety crept closer on the horizon.

For a while, she became a devoted enthusiast of a television show about a food critic who traveled the world's backroads searching for oases of fine cuisine. Eventually, the metaphor began to depress her—that she could watch the world's wonders from a distance, but never really taste them. She found a show about a nun who visited art museums and watched that instead.

Rosie or Irene occasionally wandered through to harangue Viola about her viewing choices. ("We all have to listen to that, you know." "Is this suicide by boredom?" "Turn on the movie channel.") Viola never in the least registered their imprecations.

This is not to say that she never shuddered with the feeling she was living in a haunted house. She did. It was simply that the chills which shivered down her spine always came from leaky windows, and the horrible noises upstairs were never more than the settling of restive floorboards. Genuine uncanny activities— such as those times when Mrs. Fritter fell through Viola's lap while attempting to cuddle—never roused a single hair on the back of Viola's neck.

Rosie, for her part, saw no reason to change her routine just because Irene had died. She spent most days wandering the property with Mrs. Fritter until dawn and dusk swapped roles. The cat insisted on it; whenever Rosie tried to sleep past sunrise, Mrs. Fritter paced the length of her bed, caterwauling until the din forced Rosie out of bed. Rosie had no idea why. Maybe Mrs. Fritter was watching for ghost mice in the grass. Rosie had certainly never seen any.

Irene's ghost, on the other hand, was curdling with boredom. Insulting Viola was useless; nastiness lost its savor when your target couldn't hear you. Insulting Rosie was mildly amusing, but Irene could never get her to stick around for more than a few barbs. "Boil-brained, beslubbering giglet—" she'd shout, and by then Rosie would already be on her way out the door.

Bored out of her ghostly skull, Irene tasked herself with learning to control the television. It came to nothing but the occasional burst of static so rare that even she had to admit it was probably random.

Books, however, were different. It turned out that they could be pulled from the shelf—or at least something could, a sort of ghost-book available to be read until someone set it down for long enough that it faded away. The metaphysical implications were disturbing. Did books have souls, then? What did the soul of a book want? Could a book consent to be read? These questions occurred to Irene; she ignored them. In her opinion, all that was the books' problem.

Reading made the afterlife bearable. When Irene got fed up to the eyeballs with Viola's travelogues and the smattering of classics and popular novels in the parlor, she'd go up to the small bedroom to browse her father's heirloom volumes of Shakespeare. They were nearly one hundred and fifty years old by now; even their ghosts smelled like must and leather. Irene particularly liked Richard III for his sensible treatment of his cousins.

Although the cat, Mrs. Fritter, spent most of her waking hours with Rosie, she occasionally went to find Irene. It was unclear whether Mrs. Fritter's purpose was to annoy Irene, comfort her, or satisfy some other catly urge, but the most common result of her sociability was to be shouted at and chased away. Now and then, however, Irene would succumb to those parts of her which had failed to completely callus over, and she held Mrs. Fritter in her lap as she perused the soul of a book.

After a year or two, Irene realized the cat had gone. For some while, there had been no hissing, nor snuggling, nor ghost claws scrabbling on the hardwood. She was loath to admit feeling sad about some animal, but a misanthropic tear or two escaped her eyes.

Irene planned to ask Rosie about it, but the next time they crossed paths, she succumbed to the temptation to insult her sister's hair instead.

In the race to kill Viola, chemotherapy snatched the gold before pancreatic cancer could reach the finish line.

The moment Viola's sickbed became a deathbed, the atmosphere of the house changed in a way that would have been palpable to any ghost. It had gone from a place that held a living soul to somewhere only inhabited by the dead.

Irene barged into the sunny bedroom. "I saw what you buried me in!"

Viola's ghost squinted and tried to clear her eyes.

She was still lying inside herself, her corpse beset with a strange, transparent doubling. One set of blue eyes looked toward Irene while the other remained fixed unblinking on the ceiling.

"Get out of there." Irene jabbed her sister's arm. Her finger sank through flesh to hit spirit.

Viola flinched. Seeing her ethereal arm come loose, she set about pulling herself out of herself. Her joints moved fluidly in a way they hadn't for twenty years—which would have been more exciting if it weren't for the obvious cause.

"Scarlet!" shouted Irene, mind's eye filled with a vision of her corpse reclining gaudily in its coffin. "Scarlet and lace and rhinestone earrings!"

Viola snickered.

"I saw that puce nightmare you put me in for my funeral, too," added Rosalee.

Both Irene and Viola startled. Neither of them had noticed

Rosie's spirit leaning against the windowsill where she'd been waiting for the past several hours, anticipating the inevitable.

Rosalee waved. "Hi, Viola."

Viola glanced at Rosie, slightly sheepish. The puce had mostly been meant to annoy Irene. "Well, you *were* dead. How was I supposed to know you'd care?"

"Pfft," said Rosie.

A balloon of dread inflated in Viola's chest. ". . . Have you two been here the whole time?"

"Since the day I dropped," said Rosie.

With horrible inevitability, Viola's brain reeled through every embarrassing memory from the past nine years. She made a small noise. "I used to wonder if you two were talking to me."

"*Never,*" snapped Irene.

"All the time," said Rosie, "but you never heard." Sniffing, she took on a long-suffering tone. "*Not* that I *expected* you to. *None* of you *ever* listened to me when I was alive."

"Rosie," said Viola with a laugh. "No one could *avoid* listening to you."

Rosie's mouth went taut. "What are you talking about?"

"Ha." Irene snorted. "Isn't it obvious, you absurd skelpie-limmer?"

Skelpie-limmer meant *dreadful child*. Rosie would have been indignant if she'd understood what it meant, but Irene's blandishments were all the same to her. She'd never bothered to learn any of them except in as much to figure out that, like most curse words, they were mostly concerned with stupidity or sex.

Disappointed but not deterred, Irene continued, "Great horn spoon, Rosalee. You made a racket dawn to dusk."

"Singing, dancing, pretending to be in movies," Viola added. "Early in the morning, late at night, and any time in between."

"I never got *one* good night's sleep as a child except when you had pneumonia," said Irene. "Best month of my life."

Rosie glared between her sisters. Their accurate-yet-unsettling claims rose bravely against her long-held resentments but were no match for such well-armored forces of ego-defense.

Rosie turned on Viola. "Took your time dying, didn't you?"

"Sorry to disoblige," said Viola, affronted.

"Well," said Rosie, "now that you're dead, we can finally get out of here."

"Out of here?" Viola asked.

"Out of this house," said Rosie. "Away from this farm. *Out of here.*"

Irene clacked her tongue derisively. "Mumblecrust! What are you talking about, Rosalee? I've tried it hundreds of times, same as you. Walk off the property, and there you are, walking back again."

"Things will be different now," said Rosie, adopting her most tremulant and mysterious tone.

Viola looked with bafflement between her sisters as they tried to stare each other down. This seemed . . . unreasonable. She felt that she deserved more time to adjust to being dead before having to deal with anything else. She also felt like she had a headache. Did ghosts get headaches? She rubbed her temples. "I don't know what you're talking about."

"Ignore her," Irene told Viola. "This is just typical Rosie bespawl."

"It is *not*." Rosie tipped up her chin like an affronted socialite. "I know because of Mrs. Fritter."

". . . the cat?" Viola asked helplessly.

Irene felt a startled spike of anger as she remembered all those times when she'd thought about asking Rosie about the cat. She'd *missed* that cat, consarn it. "Why didn't you bring this up before? Where's Mrs. Fritter? Explain!"

Rosie sighed. She gave a little put-upon wave like a singer facing demands for an encore. "Fine. I'll explain about the cat."

Rosie did not explain about the cat.

Well, not immediately—not given that she suddenly had the opportunity to get more attention than she'd had in nine whole years. As much as Rosie had always liked Mrs. Fritter, a quirked cat ear made an insufficient audience for someone with as much pent-up joie de vivre as Rosie. Viola and Irene would also make an insufficient audience, of course, but at least they had human vocal cords with which to express admiration.

At Rosie's insistence, the three relocated to the kitchen. The remains of Viola's last downstairs meal lay on the table—a crumpled napkin, a glass with a splash of water, and a plate holding a few crumbs and a chicken's thigh bone.

As they settled, Viola's daughter-in-law, Kelly (who had somehow contracted the obligation to check in every few days on the woman she referred to as her monster-in-law), came in through the back door. She threw her coat on the counter and tossed her purse onto the nearest kitchen chair, where it fell through Viola's lap.

The sisters turned their heads to watch the luckless daughter-in-law head toward the stairs.

"That cumberworld is going to make a racket in a minute when she finds your body," Irene said to Viola.

Viola said, "Kelly will dress me in some ugly pastel skirt suit, see if she doesn't. Something a sanctimonious church lady would wear on Easter. That's what she did to her mother."

Rosie said, "If you think that makes up for what you did to us, it doesn't."

"*Scarlet!*" cried Irene. "*Rhinestones!*"

Viola snickered again.

Irene's turbulent anger sought the nearest target, which happened to be Rosie. She jabbed an incensed finger at her sister. "Enough of this prattling conversation about nothing! Rosalee, you pribbling beef-wit, can't you even bother to work your lazy mouth? Death's head upon a mop-stick, tell your story!"

Viola and Rosie regarded Irene unperturbed.

"You left out *fustilug*," complained Viola. "That's my favorite."

"I like *saddle-goose*," said Rosie.

Irene's mouth gaped open—no one was supposed to be *amused* by her outbursts, thank you very much!—but before she could deliver another torrent of abuse, the daughter-in-law's inevitable shriek filled the house.

Rosie said to Viola, "You've been found."

"Seems like it," Viola agreed.

Irene, furiously shaking, shouted at Rosie, "Explain! Now!"

So, Rosie explained about the cat.

It had been about six months ago as far as Rosalee could remember, timekeeping not being high on her list of posthumous priorities. The last crusts of snow had failed to crunch and melt under ghost-foot and ghost-paw as she and Mrs. Fritter roamed the property.

The family lands were fairly small. Although they were fallow now, every inch had been planted or explored by someone in the family line at one time or another. Nevertheless, it was difficult to survey the whole territory on foot without using a map. Woman and cat's daily wanderings drew them to some places frequently, and to others not at all.

Therefore, it was still entirely possible to find someplace their travels had not yet taken them. On the day in question, they found such a place: a nondescript hollow smelling of sage where a line of leggy bushes, undressed for winter, grew among patches of snow and dirt.

When Mrs. Fritter saw the naked shrubbery, her eyes lit with a wildness Rosie had never seen before. The cat bolted toward the westmost bush and began scrabbling at the dirt.

At first, Rosie merely watched, expecting Mrs. Fritter to lose interest. However, as the cat became increasingly frantic, Rosie, sighing, knelt to help.

The pair weren't digging up real dirt, not exactly, which was probably for the best, since they had only bare hands and paws to muster against the wintry ground. Yet in the same way that Irene had discovered that the souls of the books could be dislodged from their papery forms, Rosie now found that *something* was moving out of their way. She could see two realities at once: the intact patch of dirt that was part of the living world; and the growing, presumably spectral recess they were digging below it.

Mrs. Fritter stopped, so Rosie stopped, too.

The cat's ear cocked. Lonely, high-pitched noises came from the hole.

Rosie started to say something but caught her tongue.

Mrs. Fritter jumped in.

Leaping out again, the cat returned with a tiny ghost-thing in her mouth. It was a kitten, too young for its eyes and ears to open. It squeaked.

Rosie gasped. She hadn't meant to, but—a new ghost! She'd never seen another ghost besides Irene and Mrs. Fritter.

Mrs. Fritter glanced back at the hole as if she wanted to jump in again. She hesitated, tense on her paws. It seemed to Rosie that the cat was worried about putting down the kitten.

Rosie held out her cupped hands. Mrs. Fritter gave her a skeptical look, seeming to weigh how much she trusted her companion. The verdict came back in Rosie's favor; Mrs. Fritter dropped the ghost kitten into her palms.

It was such a tiny thing. Rosie laced her fingers around the shivering creature to keep it warm.

Mrs. Fritter carried up a second kitten, and then a third. By the time she brought up the fourth and final, Rosie had moved the tiny, squeaky ghosts into her lap to warm them in the folds of her skirt. She unfolded the fabric to make room for Mrs. Fritter, who obligingly climbed up to sit with her kittens.

Mrs. Fritter set to licking, sweeps of her tongue wetting the kittens' short, scraggly fur into cowlicks. They were too young to purr, but their complaints faded as they fell asleep against their mother's belly.

Rosie remembered the early days of her death—how it had been the cat who initiated their routine, leading Rosie to the back door every day and complaining until she followed Mrs. Fritter outside.

"You've been searching for them, haven't you?" Rosie murmured, quietly so the kittens wouldn't wake. "You had a litter before you died, didn't you? No one knew they were here. They must have starved. Poor little things. But now, everything's all right. They have you again."

Time passed. As Rosie began to worry about how long she could stay in her current position, Mrs. Fritter yawned and stretched. She took the first kitten by the nape and dismounted Rosie's lap.

"I can help carry them inside," Rosie ventured.

Mrs. Fritter ignored her. She turned to survey their surroundings. Her gaze fastened on a spot that Rosie would never have guessed a moment ago was different from anywhere else. Now, somehow, it was. Something about it seemed to glow—not the early grass, nor the dirt, nor the blue of the sky—something else, some nameless essence.

Mrs. Fritter approached the anomaly with the kitten in her mouth. She extended a paw. An ethereal glow shimmered over it like a beam of moonlight. The cat leapt forward and vanished, leaving only strange luminosity behind her.

Rosie exclaimed. The noise woke the other kittens, whose little voices cried back. She started to panic. How was she going to raise three ghost kittens? Did they need milk? Would they ever get bigger? What if they froze? Or starved as they had before? Could they die a second time?

Even as these worries clamored in Rosie's head, Mrs. Fritter bounded back through the portal, landing on the earth as if she'd never left.

Mrs. Fritter didn't have the kitten anymore. Perhaps she'd left it on the other side? Was the afterlife through there? Was Mrs. Fritter playing Charon, ferrying her kittens to the land of the dead?

Rosie watched with a sort of stunned feeling as Mrs. Fritter approached for a second kitten and then carried it into nothing. For the third, it was the same. When she returned for the fourth, however, Mrs. Fritter paused to lick her shoulder.

"You'll come back, right . . . ? After you drop the last one off?" Rosie asked.

Mrs. Fritter washed the area where her shoulder met her back.

"You aren't coming back, are you?" Rosie said quietly.

The mother cat bumped her head against Rosie's knee to elicit a pat on the head and a scritch on the chin. Purring, she took the last kitten by the nape and started to go.

Rosie reached out as if to pull them back. The mother cat growled softly and leapt away, tail lashing. Rosie dropped her hand.

"I'm sorry," said Rosie. "I'll miss you."

The cat gave her a slow blink of forgiveness.

Mrs. Fritter ran into the shimmering grass. The glow vanished with her.

Rosie took a little time to cry.

Afterward, she walked around the place where Mrs. Fritter had disappeared, but she found nothing other than mundane earth and cold air. Before going, she stopped to heap the ghost dirt they'd dug up into a memorial mound. It seemed right to leave something.

In all Rosalee's wanderings since, she'd never found the place again. The memorial, it seemed, was gone. She supposed that, like the ghost books, it had faded back into the material world.

At the table with her sisters, Rosie dabbed her eyes.

"So." Rosie tried to clear the lump in her throat. "I've been waiting for the two of you so we can do what Mrs. Fritter did."

"Have kittens?" asked Irene sourly.

Rosie flashed her a look of pure disdain. Her older sister didn't seem to have been affected by the story at all. Irene really was a nasty thing.

At least Viola was sniffling. "Rosie," she said, dabbing her eyes. "That's all very sad—and sweet, too, a bit, but . . . Maybe it's because I only just died, but I don't understand what it has to do with us."

"Ignore her, Viola." Irene rolled her eyes. "Rosalee's up to her usual mammering nonsense."

Rosie ignored her eldest sister. She spread her hands in a lecturing gesture as she embarked on her explanation. "What makes a ghost? Unfinished business. Our Mrs. Fritter died and so did her kittens, poor little things. None of them could move on until they were together again."

"Don't even *try* picking me up by the nape," Irene said.

"You think we have to leave together," Viola said.

Rosie shrugged. "Mom and Dad and—heck, basically everyone—expected us to do everything together. Seems like the universe agrees."

Viola glanced at Irene. "What do you think?"

"Mammering nonsense," repeated Irene, but her expression was thoughtful.

Later, Rosalee realized she should have told her sisters she *didn't* want to go.

First, Viola wanted a night to sleep on it. Then Irene declared it was a waste of time that would never work. Then Rosie tried to appeal to their sisterly feelings, but for some reason they were unmoved by her many anecdotes of victimization. Then Viola, having slept on it for two nights and an afternoon, insisted on staying until after her funeral.

"You both got to see the preparations for *your* funerals," Viola said.

"Yeah, it was so exciting to watch you two exchange notes," muttered Rosie.

"*Scarlet*," said Irene. "And *rhinestones*."

Rosie challenged Viola. "You just want to memorize every time someone slights you."

Viola waved her arms as if to suggest that this was such an obvious and natural thing to do that she had no choice in the matter. "Why shouldn't I want to be informed? I might see them again in the . . . whatever you call it—the after-afterlife."

"It doesn't matter," Irene broke in, "since Rosalee's delusional."

Rosie turned on Irene. "If I made it all up, then where's Mrs. Fritter?"

Irene hesitated then made a *pshaw* noise before stomping away.

Rosie was not deterred.

She had only one goal now: leave. If that didn't count as unfinished business, nothing did.

Rosalee knew of exactly one place where the world could fissure. True, up to now she hadn't been able to find the rift through which Mrs. Fritter had escaped, but this time she'd have Irene and Viola with her. Obviously, once all three of them were there, the world would open up again.

(*Will it?* asked a tiny part of Rosie. She ignored it.)

Once Viola and Irene saw an actual exit right there in front of them, they couldn't possibly keep being so unreasonable.

(*Couldn't they?* asked the tiny part of Rosie. She told it to shut its stupid mouth.)

She formed a plan, tucked a ghost-volume of poetry into her pocket, and went off to lie.

"You're sure you saw the cat around here?" Viola asked Rosalee as the three sisters trudged through the musty-smelling humidity, searching the property. Rosie and Viola felt phantom itching on their calves as they passed through the overgrown grass. Irene's calves, however, did not, being protected by the most boring spectral pants the sour-minded sister had been able to imagine.

Rosie put on an expression of wounded indignation. "Absolutely, completely, one hundred percent," she said with fraudulent passion.

"Calm down," said Viola. "I'm just asking."

"Hmff," puffed Irene, walking behind.

Rosie had begun this trip quite pleased with herself. Irene and Viola had agreed to come surprisingly quickly after Rosie told them that she'd seen the ghost of Mrs. Fritter from a distance on one of her afternoon rambles, perhaps because Rosie had learned from her previous mistake and told them she thought they should stay away.

The only problem was they'd been out for at least a couple of hours now and, so far, there were trees and weeds and buzzing insects that made Rosie's intangible skin twitch, but there was no sign of anything shiny.

"Why are you so sure it was the cat?" asked Viola. "If it was that far away?"

"Because I'm sure," retorted Rosie. "You think I can't recognize my own cat?"

"It can't have been more than a blur," said Viola. "Maybe it was a skunk."

"It was *Mrs. Fritter*," Rosie snapped.

"Give it up, Rosalee," said Irene.

Rosie and Viola stopped to look back at their older sister. Irene stood planted about ten feet behind them, arms crossed over her chest.

Irene smirked, which was never a good sign. "You didn't see the cat. You never saw anything at all."

Rosie feigned indignation. "That's not—Of course I—"

Irene cut her off. "Don't try it, Rosalee. *We're* not stupid just because *you* are."

Rosie shrank a step back. She was usually inured to her sister's insults, but the naked simplicity of this one had an unexpected sting.

Viola's forehead creased. "You were trying to trick us into leaving?" she asked Rosie.

"No!" Rosie protested.

Irene pointed an accusing finger at her youngest sister. "Then what's in your pocket?"

"Nothing!"

Irene turned to Viola. "It's a poetry book. She was planning to recite a few elegies before we dearly departed. Don't take my word for it. Look for yourself."

Viola made a grab for Rosie's pocket which, deflected, became a grab for Rosie's rear. Viola adjusted her grip while Rosie struggled to fend her off. They grappled until Viola managed to jab a finger into Rosie's left armpit, which Viola knew from childhood fights was particularly tender. Rosie yelped and twitched involuntarily, giving Viola time to snatch the poetry book with a triumphant yawp.

Viola read the title with disgust. "Collected elegies!" She waved indignant arms. "I told you I wanted to stay until after the funeral!"

"And how long are you going to want to stay after that?" Rosie shouted back. "How long am I supposed to wait to get out of here?"

Irene laughed. "I heard her practicing. '*Shall we take the act to the grave? The ravenous grave?*' Her poetry reading is almost as ridiculous as her plan." She clacked her tongue. "You don't even really know where the cat disappeared, do you, Rosalee?"

Tears burgeoned in Rosie's eyes. "It has to be close—I think I see the line of bushes—If we just go back—"

"Rosalee, you're a flap-mouthed leasing-monger," said Irene. "That cat went through where she found her kittens. That's where she finished her business. It's got nothing to do with us."

"But we're together now—" Rosie started.

Irene scoffed. "Come on. Even you can't be this daft. If all we had to do was go together, we'd have gone at Viola's deathbed." She sliced her hand decisively through the air. "We're stuck here. It's obvious. I only came along to see your face when you realized it."

"No—" Rosie's voice broke. "That can't be true. I've been here so long. I can't bear it anymore."

"Truth doesn't care what you want," said Irene. "And neither does anyone else."

Rosie's whole face was wet. "You don't have to be so mean."

"*You* don't have to be so selfish," said Irene.

Rosie's hands clenched. "I'm not being selfish!"

Viola broke in before Irene could respond. "You act like what anyone else wants doesn't matter! I told you, Rosie! I want to *stay* for my *funeral*."

"But—" started Rosie.

Viola glared back with contempt. "I'm going back to the house. Kelly and Archie have probably been there for hours. Now I've missed everything they have to say because of *you*."

Viola stormed off.

The oldest and youngest sisters stood in silent reproach for a few long minutes until Viola was out of hearing range.

Rosie pleaded, "Irene, I—"

Irene gave Rosie the sweetest smile that she could dredge from its quivering hiding place in her soul. "Thanks for the outing."

Rosalee watched through watery eyes as her eldest sister left. She considered waiting to follow them both, but she couldn't bear the thought of being stuck with them in the same, dim rooms where she'd been stuck all along. She turned toward the outskirts of the property instead and went wandering, searching for somewhere that shimmered.

Viola's funeral passed. The relatives remained, fixing up the house for sale.

Viola felt sullen as she sat on the dresser in the sunny bedroom where she'd died, watching her son and daughter-in-law arrange the house for sale. It was fun hearing what people had to say, "very Mark Twain" according to Rosie, although she hadn't read the book for decades. Viola mentally stored every slight as ammunition to use in postmortem altercations once the living had given up their ghosts—assuming the various relatives turned up in the same afterlife, of course.

So far, this conversation was light on snubs, but then again, it was also light on words. Mostly, Archie was sniffling by the window frame he was supposed to be fixing while Kelly silently unpacked the dresser.

How like Archie. Her son had always been a brooding child. He was like Rosalee if Rosalee had been inclined toward self-scourging rather than foisting recriminations onto perfectly innocent sisters.

And how like Kelly. That most execrable of daughters-in-law was leaving the poor boy to cry without a single "there, there." What a termagant. (One couldn't live with Irene without picking up a *few* words.)

Into the stillness, Archie said, "I know Mom wasn't nice."

Not nice? A slight. Viola cataloged it.

Kelly snorted. "To put it mildly."

Viola cataloged that, too.

"But it breaks my heart sometimes," Archie continued. "I'm not sure she was ever happy. If only . . . I mean . . . I wish I could have . . ."

The sliding of dresser drawers was the only sound in the gathering pause.

Archie looked up at Kelly. His wife remained focused on her work, face averted, but Viola saw her son's upraised expression. Tears blurred the blueness of his pupils, and exhaustion bruised the skin under his eyes. His face, usually near white—he was an indoor sort of boy—was patched and red from rubbing. He made a noise in the back of his throat, part clearing and part sob.

Viola, softening, decided to de-catalog his last few affronts.

Archie sighed into the quiet. "I don't know."

Kelly still didn't look up. "It's not your fault."

Her daughter-in-law's voice was soft but stiff, almost annoyed. Archie barely seemed to hear.

"I know," he said.

"Do you?"

"*Yes*," Archie protested, followed by, "Dad didn't help."

Kelly snorted again. "Thank goodness you didn't inherit whatever gene it is that causes his dick to spontaneously dive into the nearest canal."

Archie frowned slightly. "He's been faithful to Jill." He paused before mumbling, "I think."

"He probably can't find anyone else who'll take his old ass," said Kelly.

"I think he regrets things with Mom. He cried, you know. When I told him she'd died."

"Really?" asked Kelly.

"Really?" asked Viola.

"He said, 'She was my first love.'"

"Huh," said Kelly.

"*Huh*," said Viola.

That was nice to hear, somehow. She added a little positive tick to her mental catalog. She didn't have many of those.

"None of them were happy," Archie went on.

"You mean Rosie and Irene?" asked Kelly.

Archie nodded. "I didn't see much of them growing up. I mean, you know how Mom felt. But I didn't *have* to see them much—you could just tell."

Kelly shrugged. "Irene seemed plenty happy whenever she screamed at me."

"I guess . . ." Archie admitted, "but addicts are happy when they get their next dose, too. They can still be miserable."

"Sometimes I wonder whether they'd all have been happier if they'd started drinking. I guess Rosie's husband did enough of that for the whole family," Kelly said. "I don't see why you're wasting time worrying about Irene. She spent plenty of time yelling at you, too. Honestly, I don't see why you're worrying about Rosie either. Or your mother. How many happy memories do you have of her? I bet you could count them on one hand."

"More than *that*," Archie said with a frown, but Viola noticed he didn't say how many.

Come on, Viola thought, there had to be at least a few dozen. Right? There was that national park trip when all four of the kids were in grade school—well, up until she and Jack had that argument over the tents and they had to go home . . . and there were those milkshakes she used to make with Archie on weekends until she realized it was making both of them fat . . . Oh, just after she brought home Archie's first baby sister, that had been a good time. Archie was such a sweetheart, helping out in that cute-but-unhelpful way toddlers did. Viola had to redo everything on the sly so she wouldn't hurt his feelings. But even then, there were those hours-long shouting matches at night after Jack came home five hours late, rumpled and smelling like someone else's brand of cigarettes . . .

Viola's fingers fretted at the hem of her sleeve. How many happy memories did she have at all, really, in her whole life?

Archie continued, "They all got . . . stuck. Sometimes I wonder what Mom would have done if she'd been born twenty years later."

"People have always been pressured into things," said Kelly. "You're making excuses. It wouldn't have changed anything. She could have done things differently if she wanted. She chose to be what she was."

Viola's eyes narrowed. She knew the girl couldn't hear her, but she responded anyway. "Meaning?"

At the same time, Archie said, "Don't be mean about her."

Viola smiled. Sweet boy.

Kelly continued, "It's easy for you to be maudlin. *I* was the one who had to deal with her. At least, by the end, I was free from those other two horrors."

"*Kelly*," Archie said, chastising.

His wife finally looked up. She took out a last shirt, threw it in the donation bag beside her, and banged the drawer closed with her hip. "You can't make me do everything and blame me for how I feel about it. She was a monster-in-law. It wasn't cute because she was old, or because she was sad, or because she had dreams that never came true. If she wanted to be something else, that was her responsibility. Not mine—and not yours."

Kelly stopped, breathing heavily after the gust of words. She looked over at her husband; he was fully crying now, though silently, tears streaming openly down his cheeks as he didn't even try to cover his face.

Viola, who had been stunned by the vehemence of Kelly's speech—no, not speech, self-important *sermon*—suddenly sparked with anger. She leveled an accusing finger. "You witch," she growled, not caring that Kelly couldn't hear. "Leave my son alone. How dare you."

Kelly's face had softened. She spoke gently. "She was the parent, Archie. It wasn't *your* job to take care of *her*. It's not your fault."

"But Dad—" Archie started.

"—doesn't matter," Kelly finished. "At some point, we're in charge of ourselves."

Viola stared at them. Her anger had fizzled out. The pit of her stomach—even though there was nothing in it, could be nothing in it; even though it was ethereal and not really a stomach at all—felt horribly heavy and swollen as if she'd eaten something terrible that had lodged in her so deeply she'd forgotten it wasn't part of herself.

None of the three of them, the two living humans or the ghost, moved for several minutes. There was no clock in the room to tick, but insects droned outside in the humidity.

Archie looked down at his feet. He wiped at his eyes, and then looked up again, staring glassily out of the window. "I just wonder."

Kelly said, "I know."

After a while, Archie picked up his hammer and returned to the broken window frame. Kelly opened the next dresser drawer. Viola went up to the attic to sit by the dormer windows overlooking the farm and think.

Viola had never brought it up with her sisters because she'd been afraid they'd laugh—but sometimes, when they were little, she'd had fantasies they could be friends.

The fantasies were always strange and hazy because it was so hard to picture. When hatred is your bedrock from the time you understand other people exist, it's not a thing you can just get away from. Viola's hatred for her sisters had metastasized before she knew what the word *sister* meant. It was in her fingertips and her tongue and her toes even now when they were all transparent. She could get as far as imagining the three of them as dolls with stitched-on smiles, but the daydream fell apart as soon as she tried to imagine what those sewn-shut mouths would say.

After moving out to get married, Viola had realized that, while they all knew that their parents had planted the pernicious seed of hostility by forcing the three sisters to be alike, the truth was that their parents had also watered, fertilized, and nurtured that seed into bloom by pitting the sisters against each other. When one sister achieved something the others had not, whether easy or extravagant, she became the favorite, showered with praises and treats. The esteem never lasted. Soon enough, Rosalee would get a compliment on her choir singing from the mayor's wife, or Irene would win an attendance award, and favor would pass.

Viola hadn't been the favorite very often. Perhaps that had made it easier to see what their parents were doing. While Rosalee and Irene brawled for approval, Viola watched carefully to snatch up the scraps.

A person could learn to like scraps. A pat on the head—savor the comfort, remember it. A secondhand dress with checkered trim—hang it up and treasure it. The next pat would be for another head, but they couldn't take back the first one. The heirloom Bible and earrings would be doled out to Irene and Rosalee who "deserved the family legacy," but the secondhand dress hanging in the closet never passed judgment.

Except when she gained weight. Then it felt like the dress *was* judging her, the same way it felt when Mom laughed any time Irene called Viola a heifer (during the days before Irene became a cussing expert). Then the dress became a reminder of all the things she *didn't* have, the same way Jack had been every time he came home moping over some "new girl at work." At least she could put the dress in the back of the closet where she didn't have to look at it.

After Rosalee's failed attempt to find Mrs. Fritter, Viola had been gnawed by a parasitic worm of a thought: Perhaps the universe *wanted* them to act like the dolls with sewn-on smiles. Maybe it wasn't satisfied by their simply being together; maybe it wouldn't let them go until they all gave in and got along. Could that be their unfinished business?

No, how horrible. To make them responsible for each other's fates? That was how everything had begun in the first place. Their whole lives, they'd been twined in a horrible dance, a quartet with the house taking the fourth position, continuing long after their parental choreographers were gone. How could they reconcile even if they wanted to? When you keep stirring volatile chemicals, you can't be surprised when they explode.
Sometimes things don't have to mix. Sometimes things are separate.

When Viola was done thinking, she went to find Rosalee because Rosalee was easier to persuade than Irene.
"You *really* think you've got a plan that will work?" Rosie asked with a skeptical squint.
"Positive." Viola paused to consider. "Well, maybe about sixty percent."
One corner of Rosie's mouth dipped downward, but she allowed it was, "Still worth trying, I guess."
Viola told Rosie that the next step was finding Irene. Rosie complained and tried to convince Viola they didn't really *need* Irene, did they? When that line of persuasion didn't work, Rosie tried to wheedle Viola into at least *telling* her what the plan was before they went off searching for their sister, but Viola found it exhausting to think about trying to explain things twice. More accurately, Viola found it exhausting to think about having to *debate* things twice. She had no desire for a double helping of nitpicking.
In order to make her reasoning more palatable for Rosie, Viola called this "wanting to get everything done at once" rather than "wanting to spare myself a headache (and by the way, I still think it's unfair I have to deal with headaches when I don't even have a real head)." Eventually and grudgingly, with a bit of stomping and a bunch of sighing, Rosie gave in.
The problem was that Irene had been hard to track down ever since the elegy incident. Even though Rosalee was the only one who'd actually *expected* to leave that day, the failure had disappointed all three of them in a way they did not understand. It

had the feeling of a final condemnation, the turning of the key in the lock of the prison door that would cage them here forever.

However, it still felt odd for Rosie and Viola to see how badly the incident had affected Irene. She had, after all, gloated almost unbearably at the time about how she'd "defeated Rosalee's mammering." Yet since then, she had become sullen and shadow-eyed, avoiding both becurst farmhouse and belated sisters in favor of haunting remote crannies of the property. Her invective had fallen silent; her glowering was squandered on rodents and spiders.

In contrast, the other two sisters were perfectly able to rely on their usual comforts. Rosalee, for instance, had a lifetime's experience of feeling hard done by when reality refused to reshape itself for her convenience. Whether her peevishness was unreasonable (as in most circumstances) or reasonable (as in this case), she used the same technique to channel her angst—namely, swanning around with great sighs and lamentations.

Thus far, Viola had been able to entertain herself by spying on Archie and her other relatives, but when the need arose, she'd soon be able to resort to her own default behavior of passive-aggressively doing chores while snapping at anyone who asked: *everything's fine, don't bother about me, here's your damn laundry*. Granted, her ghostly state made most chores impossible, including laundry, but Viola's self-martyring instincts were no doubt up to the task of finding substitutions.

As for Irene, well . . . Even Irene, the erstwhile vulgarian herself, didn't know why salutary activities like flurries of abuse now failed to raise her spirits.

In an inchoate and unarticulated way, Rosalee and Viola had begun to suspect that the cause might lie with Irene's stagnant disposition. During those all-too-short years when Rosalee and Viola had moved away from the farmhouse and their parents and everything else that had made their childhood what it was, they'd found their worst vices alleviated by their new surroundings. In their outside lives, they had been sometimes affable, even occasionally friendly. This meant that now, from time to time, the two ghosts were able to marshal their admittedly minimal social skills and tolerate each other's company.

For Irene, there existed no such possible relief. She had never done anything—never *wanted* to do anything—but ferment like a herring buried beneath an icy patch of Scandinavian ground. She faced an eternity of nothing but sisterhood—which by her lights was far worse than an eternity of almost anything else.

In any case, Rosie and Viola had to expend significant time and effort before locating Irene near the border of their farm, sitting in the mildew-scented dark under the fallen roof of a shed that had been built for some unknown purpose and then likewise abandoned.

"Leave me alone," Irene said, not even bothering to call anyone a canker-blossom.

With a *pshaw*, Rosie waved her hands in defeat and turned to go. Viola took her arm to stop her from leaving.

"This is important," Viola said.

Irene shrugged.

"You'll want to hear it," Viola added.

Irene repeated herself.

Rosie rolled her eyes. Viola decided it was time to bring out the big guns.

"Rosie was wrong," Viola said.

That got Irene's attention. She liked other people being wrong.

Irene turned around. Viola found her sneer oddly reassuring; apparently, Irene's hateful self remained somewhere beneath that mopey facade. Rosie, however, did *not* find the sneer reassuring, given that it was at her expense.

"Of course Rosalee was wrong," Irene said. "She's always wrong."

"I'm *done* with this," Rosie said, turning dramatically on her heel. Viola grabbed her arm again.

"Well?" Irene snapped as if Viola was the one delaying things. "Are you going to say what this is about or not?"

Viola ignored the provocation. "Rosie thought our business was finished now that the three of us are dead. Our business *isn't* finished. It's just beginning."

"Tsch," said Irene, waving her off. She looked dangerously ready to turn her back again.

Also, the Cat

"Will you just give me a *chance?*" Viola complained. "Look, we've been stuck here with each other our entire lives. We were still stuck here even when we were living in other places."

"Rosalee's been running her mouth about that for years," Irene said. "So what?"

Viola spread her hands as if revealing a truth in the empty space between her palms. "Everything has always shoved us together. Our *destiny* is being *apart.*"

Neither of Viola's sisters seemed impressed by this revelation.

Viola tried phrasing it a different way. "Our unfinished business is to *leave.*"

"I knew this was a waste of time," Irene muttered.

"Don't be stupid," Rosie said to Viola. "We can't leave the farm. That was the *first thing* I tried."

"No—See, Rosie, you weren't *entirely* wrong," Viola replied, earning a *tsch* of indignation from Rosie and a *tsch* of dismissal from Irene. Viola continued, "You said we all had to be together, and we did. Just like Mrs. Fritter couldn't leave without her kittens, we couldn't leave until we were all here. But now we *are* all here." She looked between Rosie and Irene. "Have you tried leaving since I died?"

"Well . . ." Rosie said, sounding defensive. "I mean, I'd tried so often . . ."

Irene pitched in, "I don't do things that are obviously a waste of time."

"That's what I thought," said Viola. "Do you see what I mean? Now that we're *all* here together, we can *all* leave to go our *separate* ways."

"Like leaves dispersing in the wind," Rosie said in her best poetic voice.

"More or less," Viola agreed.

"It can't be that simple, can it?" asked Rosie.

"Some things are simple," Viola said. "When you were alive, how many times did you lose your glasses and then find them on your head?"

Rosie looked indignant. "Never. Why would *I* need glasses?"

Viola strove not to roll her eyes. "Okay then, thought your TV was broken, but the cord had just been pulled out of the socket."

"Never," Rosie repeated before admitting, "but I *have* thought my curling iron was broken when Eddie tripped the circuit breaker."

"See?"

Rosie bit her lip. Sometimes she did that to look cute, but this was an unstudied gesture, awkward and thoughtful. "You know? I think you're right. After all this time, it just seems . . . right."

Fretting nervous fingers, Viola turned to their eldest sister. "So, uh . . . What do you think, Irene?"

Despite Irene's pinched expression—which had been growing more and more contemptuous throughout her sisters' exchange—Viola entertained a thread of hope that Irene's disdain might be a mask to conceal her vulnerability. Alas, that hope unraveled as Irene coughed a laugh and pulled to her feet.

"Do whatever you want. Just leave me out of it."

"Irene—" Viola began, but before she could voice her protest, Irene had already begun to stalk away.

Viola closed her mouth on her unspoken objection. She and Rosie both watched Irene disappear into the ever-growing grasses, heading in the opposite direction from the farmhouse at a surprisingly rapid pace.

"Don't tell me we're going to have to run around and find her a second time," Rosie complained.

Viola shook her head slowly. "I think we're just going to have to try without her."

"Will that work?"

"*I* don't know." Viola shook her head again then suddenly stopped to laugh. "You know, life never made any sense. I guess there's no reason for the afterlife to."

"Maybe life and death should both get their act together," Rosalee said.

"Well." Shaking away her anxieties, Viola rubbed her hands together as if cleaning off dust. She turned a determined gaze on Rosie. "Tomorrow, I'm going to wake up at dawn and follow the sun East. With any luck, I'll get to keep on going. You should go wherever you want, Rosie, just as long as you don't follow me."

Rosie didn't even pause to think. "I'll go West. I've always wanted to go West."

Viola chuckled. "Gonna take Hollywood by storm?"

Rosie's expression went stormy. Viola realized the comment had come across as a slight. She raised a conciliatory hand.

"Sorry, Rosie. I was joking. If there's a ghost Hollywood, I'm sure you'll be a star."

Rosie, who did not quite believe the apology, arched a skeptical eyebrow. Nevertheless, she chose to forgo pursuing the subject. She asked, "Do you think it's all right if we leave at different times?"

"If we're all doing our separate things, why not?" Viola scratched her elbow. "Why? When do you want to leave?"

"Sunset," Rosie said with the kind of flat intonation used to signal something should have been obvious. "When else are you supposed to ride off at the end of the movie?"

Viola chuckled.

Rosie smoothed the hair behind her ear. "So, this is goodbye, then."

"I guess so!" Viola agreed.

Rosalee took Viola's hand. With a flourish worthy of a close-up, she bowed to give it a kiss. "Dearest sister, I sincerely hope never to see you again."

Viola felt some sort of sentimental obligation to wander the farm, taking one last look. She kept waiting for a wave of nostalgia, but none came. It was more like riptides of awkwardness, sudden swells dragging her into memory. Not even anything traumatic, really, just stupid things that made her flinch. Here: that dirt patch surrounded by stones where Rosalee's friends left Viola out of their games. There: behind the shed where Irene tricked her into sticking her hand into a bucket of live bait.

Oh, and over there: the old carriage house where guests stayed sometimes. That was where she'd said the stupid thing to Great Aunt Nancy about how it was easy to stay skinny if you weren't lazy. Aunt Nancy had cried, and then later Viola heard her mother reassuring Aunt Nancy that "Viola can be a little brat sometimes. I don't know where she gets these ideas," as if Viola hadn't just been repeating something she'd heard from her mother in the first place. Viola often remembered the incident at night. Sometimes it hurt more that she'd upset Aunt Nancy; sometimes it hurt more that Mother could just betray her like that without even pausing.

Where were they now? Aunt Nancy? Mother? Had they died with all their business finished? What had their mother's business been? *Traumatize your daughters then sit back and watch the show?*

Viola felt guilty about her indifference. You're supposed to care about your home, aren't you? Even if you hate it?

Well, supposed to or not, she didn't.

She did end up spending time with her books of photographs. Their slick smell, which still rose from their ghost pages, made her stomach feel shiny with anticipation.

To go East! Those were the museums she'd always dreamed of in her deepest heart. Not the Louvre or the Uffizi Gallery— however beautiful they looked behind the nun on TV—but the Metropolitan Museum of Art. And the Smithsonian! Where she could see the Star-Spangled Banner, the *Spirit of St. Louis*, the microphone from the Fireside Chats. Viola was going to walk past brownstones; stare up at goddesses carved into marble facades; explore tall ships in Boston Harbor. She was going to stand in the spray of Niagara Falls and, thanks to ethereal resilience, she could even dive down it if she wanted to. She flipped through her books until dark, but every beautiful Mediterranean villa and French vineyard only made her itch to head for Central Park.

After a night's fitful sleep, it was dawn. Viola wasn't surprised to find the porch was empty, its steps layered with sawdust that the sisters' ghost footsteps couldn't disturb. The goodbye she'd exchanged with Rosalee yesterday had felt final. Even if Irene had known Viola was leaving, she'd never have come. She'd probably be cackling with joy up in the attic.

Viola took a deep breath. She straightened her ghost hair and her ghost dress. Not that anyone would see her—or would

Also, the Cat

they? If there could be a ghost cat, why not ghost elevator operators and ghost cigarette girls? Maybe Rosalee would get her ghost Hollywood after all, full of departed swains and starlets.

Maybe.

Hopefully.

She set her feet to the path and went.

Rosie slipped into the front room to watch as Viola set off. She didn't call out; they'd said their goodbyes. As Viola passed out of sight, Rosie felt a little choked up. She'd always been sentimental.

Now that she had made the decision to go West, Rosalee couldn't imagine how she hadn't decided to do it when she was alive. She'd wanted to all her life, hadn't she? At least, all of her life before she did her best to stop wanting things.

She'd only been fifteen when she took up with Eddie. Neither of them came from families that believed in taking time between taking vows and making babies. She already had one squalling in her arms by the time Eddie decided that alcohol was the best cure for an ex-bachelor's boredom. If there was more boredom after you'd drunk your first five shots, he believed, then the answer was to keep drinking until you were either cheered up or passed out. Eventually, instead of not caring much about family life, Eddie stopped caring much about life at all.

Rosalee had rocked the baby and thrown her ambitions out with the bathwater. Well, what else was she going to do? Ambitions are halfway thrown out by the time you grow up, anyway, especially ambitions of stardom—which, let's be honest, are about as likely as a manifestation of your long-dead childhood cat appearing to pester you about going outside.

Could she even remember—*really* remember, down to her bones—a time when going to the cinema *wasn't* about counting pennies and wrangling kids? When she was a child, going to the theater had been different; it had stirred a promise of wonder and beauty in her chest. She remembered the promise. The feeling was gone.

Had been gone. She could feel it flickering again like a single bulb coming back to life on the long-dark frame of a backstage mirror.

Through the window, Rosie kept watching the empty road that led away from the farmhouse, honestly expecting to see her middle sister pop back onto the porch any second. She watched long past the time it should have taken for Viola to walk off the property and then kept watching longer. She watched and watched until it was ten in the morning, and then eleven, and then noon, and the porch was still empty.

The porch was still empty.

Viola was headed East! Or maybe she'd disappeared in a puff, or ended up in the afterlife, or who knew what—but whatever had happened, she wasn't *here* anymore.

Rosie still had hours before her planned departure. She wished Mrs. Fritter were still around so she could say goodbye with a pat on the head, but the cat had napped long ago. Rosie went to find Irene instead—well, again, she'd always been sentimental. She couldn't find her, though, and eventually gave up.

As dusk settled, Rosalee stood at the base of the porch steps, looking back up at the railing where Mrs. Fritter had been perching the first time she'd tried to walk away. Viola's daughter-in-law had stripped the paint off so they could redo everything for the sale. Too bad, since the porch had just been redone. Wait, no, it had been almost ten years! She laughed.

Sunset flushed the western horizon pink, and Rosalee headed toward the lights and the cameras.

Irene was having none of it.

Unfinished business? By the double-barreled jumping jiminetty, she wasn't going to let some bobolyne like destiny push her around. Maybe some people really did die with "unfinished business," whatever that meant. Certainly, the common froward barely possessed the wherewithal to tie their own shoes. But it wasn't as though *she'd* ever asked the universe for its opinion, thank you very much.

Besides, Viola and Rosalee had told her to do it, and there was no way she was going to obey *them.*

Irene stayed in the farmhouse, and why not? When it contained an appropriate number of sisters, which was to say absolutely none, there was nothing wrong with the old place. If Viola and Rosalee were correct that the three of them had been fated to go their own directions—note the *if*; it was a pretty long shot that either one of them would be right about anything—then she'd chosen the direction "staying put."

During the day, various factions of nieces, nephews, and hangers-on tramped all over the house. Irene had never bothered to keep track of Viola's and Rosalee's broods; she registered them as an anonymous blob. That was, until she had the nasty surprise of finding her *own* children mooching around the kitchen. The gall! So, she wasn't good enough when she was alive, but now that the smell of inheritance was in the air, the estranged sorners ran in like dogs after the dinner bell.

Irene spent several creative hours swearing at her perfidious progeny, but their living ears heard nothing. For the first time, Irene missed her sisters a bit.

A bit.

Eventually, the parade of useless relatives became a parade of useless home buyers who squinted at things and yawped about widening windows and knocking out walls. The family that settled in had both a daughter and a son. This offended Irene's anti-sibling sensibilities, but their parents never forced them to interact with each other so that was all right.

The daughter got a bad-tempered pet rat for her birthday that bit her a lot. When it got sick, the family let it die. Although it was particularly absurd to imagine why a pet rat would become a ghost, the next day when Irene went to look, there the thing was, nosing around its cage. Irene reached in to take it out; it chomped down in hello; thereafter, they were best friends.

Most days, the rat rode around on Irene's shoulder, chit-chit-chittering as Irene paced the house making her own acrimonious observations. The rat proved to be a surprisingly good listener who enjoyed Irene's secondary occupation of settling in the armchair to read aloud from the family's regrettable collection of tasteless paperbacks. (The armchair had once been designated for the father; eventually, with an appropriate but subconscious apprehension, he bought a second sofa.) While

Irene sometimes threw the soul of a particularly stupid technothriller across the room, the rat itself was an undiscerning literary connoisseur. It was perfectly content to listen to anything, including the occasional time travel romance that Irene felt vaguely guilty about pulling off the shelf.

From time to time, Irene wondered what had happened to her sisters. By now, had they passed through some rupture like Mrs. Fritter?

Ridiculous. How incredibly stupid to walk into who-knows-where just because the entry is shiny. Even if she *did* see a portal like that, Irene was planning to cling to the Earth like an angry barnacle.

Here, she had a rat, a bountiful quantity of dubious-quality books, and a pair of teenagers to learn new insults from. Fulfilling? Perhaps not. But who said life should be fulfilling? She could be unfulfilled if she wanted to.

She told the rat as much. It seemed to agree.

OLIVIE BLAKE

The Audit

FROM *Januaries*

SCIENCE FICTION

Day One

7:15 A.M.: I'M TRYING something where I wake up early. It's not going well.

9:45 a.m.: Okay, this time I'm definitely up. I have an interview at eleven, and according to my roommate—let's call her Frances—I am, quote, unbearable when my blood sugar is low. She says I need time to digest and a person can't live on black coffee. I point out I'm currently fully alive, and she says fully is a stretch. Frances is the kind of person who makes me want to go back to bed. I love her and assume she will leave me someday.

10:15 a.m.: I've drunk all the coffee and picked irritably at a bagel. Frances looks over my shoulder and asks who I'm talking to. I say the internet. She makes a face and says am I journaling, and I say kind of, not really, it's just something I have to do for the audit. She says I had better explain what the audit is. I tell her the only people reading this will already know what the audit is. She glares at me, so I guess I'll explain.

10:35 a.m.: The Life Audit pilot program uses the latest AI technology to determine a person's capacity for accumulated lifetime wealth. The idea is that youth is wasted on the young, who have no money. Frances looks over and says I am being too facetious and to really explain myself. Fine. By the time a person enters their fifties or whatever age involves sufficient discretionary funds to go places and do things, they're mostly too tired, which is the root of most middle-age crises, or seems to be, as far as I have understood the impetus for any of this. It's frankly astonishing that this pilot program even passed. I think the older generations dying off left some room for social experimentation. Frances says don't say that, but it's too late, I said it. Anyway, I'm not sure how this works exactly, but I wanted to travel and I didn't want to work, so I signed up as soon as I graduated. Basically, they're going to determine how much money I'm likely to make, and then they'll give it to me up front as a loan, and I'll have ten to fifteen years to get my kicks before I have to start working. The small print says that if you die before the loans are repaid the plan is to take it out on your family, but my parents are already dead and they had no living relatives either. So mostly this is robbing the bank. Frances agrees, although she has chosen not to participate in the pilot program. She says it feels too much like astrology, which she is far too practical for, being profoundly a Virgo.

10:39 a.m.: The agoraphobe downstairs shoves a broom into the ceiling because apparently we're being uproarious. For the millionth time, I tell Frances that we're moving as soon as the audit check clears. She says not to count my chickens because I might still be considered worthless. She means it too. The agoraphobe slams the broom again, beseechingly. I begin to two-step from a place of vengeance.

10:55 a.m.: Well, I'm going to be late.

11:17 a.m.: I'm late, but so are the auditors—when I check in, the receptionist tells me they're running thirty minutes behind schedule. I settle into a sterile-looking office chair with my forms and a granola bar that Frances shoved into my hand after I stomped around the kitchen, and someone immediately calls my name.

11:34 a.m.: An auditor dressed more like an HR rep than a lab technician shows me into a room with a surprisingly banal touch screen tablet. When I make a joke about playing a game or getting my biometric data sold he grimaces and says the technology is more important than the hardware, which feels a bit like a comment on penis size. I can tell I've gotten off on the wrong foot so I ask how his day is going, and he says well, we're

The Audit

behind schedule, so, you know. Then we stare at each other for a second before he points to the tablet. Just press start, he says.

12:37 p.m.: I stumble out of the auditing room with the sense that I just came from a really intense therapy session. I've only been once or twice because I couldn't afford real therapy, just whatever was offered at the student counseling center, which was honestly not very illuminating. Most of the audit involved me answering questions that got more and more ephemeral as I went. At first it was simple demographics and then it was questions about what I thought would happen to my soul after death or had I ever really known a love without obligation. I have at least three headaches. I ask the receptionist when I'll find out the results, and she says they'll be emailed to me as soon as they've been reviewed by an auditor, likely twenty minutes or so. I say I've seen pizza delivery take longer, and she says haha in a polite way. So I leave.

12:55 p.m.: I'm on the train when my results arrive in my inbox. The results are so destabilizing I immediately send a screenshot to Frances. She says she's leaving the office and will meet me at the apartment, please don't have a meltdown. I say no promises.

1:23 p.m.: I throw my keys on the dish we keep on the bookcase and pick up one of Frances's daily affirmation cards. I forgot to pick one up on my way out. It says, "Embrace the unknown." Fuck you! I shout. Then the agoraphobe picks the wrong day to slam a broom.

4:56 p.m.: Well, here is what happened when I went downstairs to pick a bone with the agoraphobe. First, I noticed he was not an eighty-year-old Italian woman like I had assumed. Second, I realized he was a hoarder. His apartment was a strange labyrinth of bookcases that led to a tiny bistro table with those blue rattan chairs you see in Paris in the one spot of light in the entire place, next to which was the broom, propped against the window. The shelves were packed with books facing every which way. I forgot to be angry, sort of. I explained about the audit, and the agoraphobe said he'd done the audit as well. How much did he get? I asked. He opened his mouth to tell me but then I heard an incredibly unbelievable din, such that

I was completely distracted. What the fuck is that, I said. Well, it can't be you, so it's probably your roommate, he replied. So then I remembered about Frances and came up to tell her I was fine and she could go back to work because I wasn't going to have a meltdown, it could wait until dinner. She pursed her lips and said fine. Then I went back downstairs to the agoraphobe, who explained to me that he had a special exception to do the audit from home, it wasn't necessary to go down to the office. I said, glumly, did you get forty million dollars too? He looked hard at me for a second, and I realized he was young, maybe even younger than me. No, he said, I got a very reasonable seven hundred thousand, which is about as much as the average American woman makes over her lifetime. I said but you're not a woman, in a questioning tone, in case I was wrong. He said no, that was exactly why it seemed fair. Then he poured me some tea and asked me what I planned to do with forty million dollars. I said I had no idea, that was part of the problem. He said part of the problem? And I said yeah, the other part of the problem is that when I turn thirty, I have to start working, and I have to do the kind of horrifyingly dull, capitalist work that produces forty million dollars, and I have to do it until I die, because that's the deal with the audit. Oh, bummer, said the agoraphobe.

5:15 p.m.: Frances is reading over my shoulder again. That's it, you went over and drank tea? Yeah, that's it. Then she's quiet for a second and asks if I want to order pizza. For some reason I can't stand the thought of it so I suggest Thai instead.

9:18 p.m.: We eat companionably and watch some baking competition shows and Frances doesn't ask me what I'm going to do with forty million dollars. She does ask me when I get it, and I say, actually, it's in my account right now. She says do you have to pay taxes on it? And I say no, the pilot program has an exemption, because the taxes come into play later, when I'm actually earning the money. She says hm interesting and asks me if the audit told me what career I'm going to have. I confirm yes, part of the reason my deadline is thirty instead of thirty-five or later is because I have to go to grad school, first for chemistry

The Audit 63

and then for law. I'm going to be a very particular kind of executive officer that I currently lack the technical background for. Woof, says Frances. And she's a paralegal.

10:38 p.m.: Frances goes to bed. The agoraphobe texts me (I gave him my number because I am really tired of the broom, to which he said in a slightly not-joking tone that I can pay him cold hard cash to stop). In the text he says: Did your audit ask you if robots dream? No, I reply, and then ask him if his audit asked him what heaven looks like. No, he says. We keep going like that back and forth for a while wondering why my answers were worth forty million and his were worth a literal fraction of that until I feel myself drifting off. So I tap lightly on the floor. No need to shout, he texts me.

11:58 p.m.: I expect to fall soundly asleep, but instead I lie there thinking about grad school, which I was trying to avoid, because I really thought that only aimless people who didn't know what to do with their lives went to grad school. And ironically, I was so sure about my life for a second there.

Day Two

9:43 a.m.: Frances asks me how long I have to do this journaling thing for and I tell her just a week. She gives me a look, like, hm. I say what. She says nothing. I say seriously what and she says you're already behind, I heard you moving around at six this morning and you're only now starting to type. I ask: Are you implying something? She says: No, I am stating it directly. The agoraphobe texts me to keep our voices down. I text back no offense but something is seriously wrong with your apartment. Come down and listen, he suggests. I roll my eyes and tell Frances not to move at all for twenty minutes, to prove a point.

10:16 a.m.: The agoraphobe and I ended up having a consultation over coffee. He asked me does this taste sour or bitter to you? And it took me a while to decide. He explained sour means the beans were ground too fine, bitter means they're too coarse. I said I think it might, possibly, be sour. He said okay I'll brew some more. By the time I remembered I'd meant to go back upstairs, there was an incredibly ominous din from overhead.

"You see? You're animals," said the agoraphobe. Then he asked me if I wanted more coffee and I said yes. It wasn't really that sour.

11:25 a.m.: I realized he was having to journal as well and asked him how that was going. He said oh it's fine, it's no different from what I normally do, and then he asked me what I normally do, which is when I realized I was two and a half hours late for work.

12:15 p.m.: My boss isn't happy with me. More later.

8:46 p.m.: I ended up having to close and do inventory with Quintina, who is mostly fine but lately has been talking a lot about a mole she needs to have looked at. She keeps forgetting I am not a doctor.

9:27 p.m.: Frances tells me I'm supposed to explain where I work and why I didn't quit my job today despite having forty million dollars in my checking account. I work at a used bookstore that is also a café. I am sometimes a bookseller, sometimes a barista depending on whether people are feeling a more pressing need for literature or caffeine. It's a very covetable job in that the owner is very rich and makes most of his profits selling rare books to private collectors, so it doesn't really matter whether I am any good at my specific job (I'm not). Frances points out that I, too, am rich. So rich that it doesn't really make sense for me to keep the retail job that I specifically said I was going to quit the moment the audit money came through. But that was last week, I point out. She asks me what's different about this week. The answer was obviously everything, even though it was nothing. You're handling this very immaturely, said Frances. She was wearing a face mask to improve her healthy glow. The agoraphobe took issue and texted me to say he was trying to sleep.

10:11 p.m.: The agoraphobe opened the door even before I knocked. He wasn't wearing pajamas and had a book in his hand and was clearly not going to sleep. I realized I didn't even know where he slept. Is there a bed in this mess? I asked. No, he said, every night he shrinks down and sleeps in a little shoe that he keeps on the window ledge. It took me a few seconds to realize he was fucking with me because something about his

The Audit

apartment feels absent the usual rules of time and space. Sit down, he said, I'll put the kettle on.

12:57 a.m.: He does have a bed. There isn't much to say about it. It's a bed with a blanket and a pillow and next to the bed is a tower of books, on top of which sits a rotary phone he says could be used as a weapon if necessary. I said are your parents dead too? And he said interesting question, no, they're alive, they're just profoundly divorced. I thought this was an interesting choice of words. We seemed to bring out the interestingness in each other in a way that seemed mutually impressive. He explained that this apartment belonged to his maternal grandmother and most of the stuff in it was hers—he wasn't personally a hoarder, he just didn't have the energy to move it all to storage, and anyway he was making his way through the books (some of which were very bad, others just deeply anti-Semitic). I asked about the agoraphobia and he said well, I don't care for disease. The way he said it made it sound reasonable, like any wellness choice he had made and stuck to. He said not to be insensitive but what are you doing with your journaling week? And I said why would that be insensitive? And he said you just seem, you know, emotionally constipated. I thought about being insulted and chose not to be. Then, below an unbelievably chaotic noise that must have been Frances getting ready for bed, the agoraphobe asked if I could place an order for a book for him tomorrow, one of those coffee-table art books he already has hundreds of. I said wait a minute, I never asked, what did the audit say about your life that it was only worth the average American woman's lifetime earnings? Then I realized how horrific that sounded and felt embarrassed. Don't be embarrassed, said the agoraphobe, it's not your doing. Then he added that he was going to continue doing what he already does, which is essentially freelance journalism. Think pieces for very niche audiences. I said why did you do the audit? And he said well I mentioned the disease thing, right?

1:15 a.m.: Eventually I went home and tried to sleep, although it was difficult because I was thinking about how to spend the forty million dollars. I might as well spend it, because I owed it no matter what—it was contractual. Before the audit,

I signed a really long agreement (Frances read it for me) that said no matter what the audit said, I would have the money and owe it back. So now I have it, and I owe it back. But I don't like this thought exercise so instead I think about the agoraphobe. What is he journaling about? The bitterness of his coffee? In retrospect, I think the end result was fairly well ground.

Day Three
8:35 a.m.: Frances comes into my bedroom and suggests I really do something today, something expensive. She says she's been thinking about it and she thinks we should sign some sort of financial agreement. I ask what she means and she says well, she didn't really think I'd end up getting so much money, so she hadn't considered it before but what if I wanted to live somewhere really fancy and she wasn't contributing as much? And I say what if I wanted to live alone? And she says well, do you? And I say no and she says I really prefer you don't waste my time with stupid questions, and then she says don't write that down. But Frances isn't the boss of me even if in many ways she absolutely is.

9:00 a.m.: I make it to work on time. Many hearty congratulations to me.

12:15 p.m.: Break for lunch. Quintina asks me if the mole seems darker today. I ask if she means like a mood ring. Then she asks me about the audit and I tell her my results. She asks me if I'm worried that someone might kill me for the money, and I say they don't get it if that happens, it's not like normal money, it doesn't really belong to me in a way where it can be transferred to another person. It's not inheritable, because I owe it back. I can't transfer the loan to anyone else either, it has to be me. She looks at me hard for a minute and says wow that's lucky. Then she asks for a bite of my peanut butter sandwich and I say Quintina, please. But I give it to her because I don't even really like peanut butter. It's, you know, fine.

5:14 p.m.: I'm closing up at the front when my boss comes over to tell me he heard about the audit. If I'm going to quit I have to give him two weeks' notice. I say I don't know yet if I'm going to quit, I mean, I wanted to travel, so I was probably always

The Audit

going to quit, but I'm not sure yet of my exact timeline. Don't you have a limited amount of time to spend it? says my boss and I have a weird little panic inside of my chest. Oh god, I have to see the whole world before I turn thirty. I mean sure, maybe I could have traveled later in life like a normal person, but until I turn thirty I have *complete freedom* and then it ends. Wasn't this supposed to let me be young? I should be making mistakes right now. I was ready to be reckless—that was my whole plan. So why am I suddenly so terrified of making a mistake?

6:47 p.m.: The agoraphobe pats my free hand while I breathe into a paper bag. It's not so bad, he says. Maybe I should just spend some of the money, dive in cold. I ask him what he's doing with his money. Mostly grocery deliveries, he says. But what about your recklessness? I ask, and I'm grateful he doesn't ask me to explain. I did rent a movie last night that I might otherwise have tried to stream, he says, and asks me if I ordered him the book he wanted. I forgot. What's the deal with rococo? I ask. It feels reckless! he says enthusiastically—like, with so much enthusiasm I realize I've never seen him get excited before.

8:19 p.m.: I ask him about the profound divorce of his parents and what made it so profound. Oh, they hate each other so much and so specifically that it's obvious they used to have a thriving sex life, says the agoraphobe. I ask does it bother you, observing sexual tension between your parents? He asks me does it bother you, having dead parents? I have to think about it for a second. My mother died when I was really young of a disease she'd been struggling with for a while, and even though he always knew the end was near, her loss made my father very quiet. Or maybe he was always quiet? We didn't talk very much although he was extremely diligent about our nightly dinners. The food was usually simple, and lunch was always a neatly packed bento. He was much older than my mother and died after some struggle with heart failure. I used to take the train back every weekend to sit with him for an hour on Saturdays and then return to school. He told me not to visit at all and focus on my studies, so the weekly visit was, like most things between us, a very quiet compromise. He never wanted me to be anything in particular except for focused on my studies. He did get to see the telecast of my graduation, so there's that. And then he died on a weekday, between visits. Didn't you just graduate a few weeks ago? asks the agoraphobe. Yes, I say. He doesn't say anything else, just pats my hand again. Upstairs Frances has brought in a mariachi band, or she's just getting things together in the kitchen for her nightly salad. From down here it's not very clear.

Day Four

    7:04 a.m.: Frances points out that I've been spending a lot of time at the agoraphobe's and asks if I, too, am becoming agoraphobic. I say no but I don't really like heat. Or bugs. Or crowds. She lifts a brow and says nothing in a way that's very offensive. I say I'll go outside today, just to prove it. She asks what expensive thing I have planned, if I'm going to charter a jet to Paris or something and if so, could she come with me. It occurs to me that's totally plausible given that it's Friday and we can just go for the weekend, it wouldn't be a big deal, literally nothing is stopping me except that I have work tomorrow, which I could very easily quit. Two weeks' notice is honorable but, like, does it matter? I sit here thinking about it for so long that Frances leaves for work.

    9:17 a.m.: "I know I don't leave my apartment but I do technically have a schedule," says the agoraphobe when I knock on the door. I say okay, can I check your coffee for you? And he sighs loudly but says fine.

    10:23 a.m.: The coffee today is slightly acidic so he makes a fresh pot. I notice he has a small vegetable garden on the ledge outside his kitchen window, which I didn't pay attention to before. I ask him if he misses the outside world. He says no, he's kind of always been like this, it's just that now he's allowed to stay inside instead of being forced to go places or do things. I ask him what he's used his money for today and he says he bought himself good butter and pink salt. Why is it so easy for him? I was paralyzed in the bodega by two kinds of chips. I'm out of ibuprofen and can't decide whether to buy name brand or generic. I should see a therapist or something. The agoraphobe says I can talk to his therapist if I want. I say I didn't re-

The Audit

alize he had a therapist. He says of course, everyone does, plus he can be agoraphobic and mentally healthy at the same time. I ask if that's actually true and he thinks about it for a second. Yes, he says.

11:37 a.m.: I would miss the first weeks of spring. I would miss the fall, the leaves crunching underfoot. I would miss walking by to see the first Christmas lights twinkling on in shop windows. I would miss those hot summer days when the city feels alive again. I would miss, most of all, the feeling of walking around and knowing that nobody knows where I am, or what I'm doing. And anyway, sometimes bugs get inside the house. Even the agoraphobe has a flyswatter.

12:31 p.m.: I go to the park for a bit because the agoraphobe has to write. I decide I'm going to honor my first instinct and do whatever I want to do, whatever it is, whenever it occurs to me.

1:15 p.m.: "Why are you here?" says my boss.

3:45 p.m.: Quintina's mole does seem a little oddly shaped today. I knew it, she says in a melancholy voice. Then she tells me the book I ordered will be in on Sunday, which is another day I have off. I tell her I'll come in anyway, and then I do some inventory.

5:47 p.m.: I think about getting flowers for Frances, to put on the kitchen table. I think about buying a loaf of fresh bread. I think, Frances would want some chocolate, and then I stare at the chocolates in a fancy shop for almost forty minutes. In the end I buy nothing and go home. And then I stop and go back to the florist.

6:32 p.m.: The agoraphobe answers the door and looks confused. I don't understand, he says, you brought me flowers? I said yes, I don't know, I guess. He says those are definitely flowers, and they're definitely for me, so . . . He trails off. I realize he's making a point and say you can say no if you want. He rolls his eyes. Come inside, you're making a racket upstairs, I have a migraine.

7:01 p.m.: He fingers the petals so gently I have the strangest feeling, like I want to sweep up his fingers and press them to my lips. Recklessness. He asks me what I'm smiling at and I say oh, I didn't realize I was smiling. He asks if his book has come in. He asks if I remember what perfume my mother wore. I close my eyes and think only of sun coming through the open window, a soft pink shade of cotton they only seemed to make in the late eighties, the way the house used to smell. The agoraphobe says his mother wears a vintage peach-scented perfume, something almost saccharine, he's been trying to figure it out but he can't—he points to a package of three different perfumes that aren't it. He closes his eyes and smiles. I want to ask where his mother is now, and I think maybe it's too invasive, and then I think no, it's fine, if he never wants to speak to me again I'll just move. Where's your mother now? I ask. He laughs. Indoors, he says, and I laugh too.

8:34 p.m.: I hear Frances clomping around and come upstairs. The flowers are beautiful, she says. Then she says, there's some kind of party this weekend at one of those fancy rooftop bars. I say do you want to go? And she thinks about it for a second and says no, I want to stay home and read, this antitrust case is so labor-intensive and I spend all day trying to avoid this one senior associate who thinks I'm prettier when I smile. I'm too tired to grind on some guy, she adds, the weight of my youth is just too burdensome. She yawns widely and asks if I'd be okay rewatching a show we've both seen four times all the way through (it was canceled halfway through its second season). I say sure, why not?

11:44 p.m.: Frances falls asleep on the couch. I pull the couch blanket over her. The agoraphobe answers the door and says I just remembered that my audit asked me a math problem, did yours require any math? I say no, did he know the answer? He says maybe, it involved the Pythagorean theorem, which I know because there's a song that goes with it, so maybe I solved it correctly, I don't know. I wonder what makes me so valuable when I am unquestionably the most boring person in my life. Hey, thought, announces the agoraphobe, what if you put some of the money in a savings account, wouldn't the interest generate enough money for you to pay back some of your loan? An interesting loophole, I say. I didn't read my contract so I don't know, and Frances is asleep so I can't ask her. Let's find out, says the agoraphobe.

The Audit 71

1:23 a.m.: Looks like nothing specifically prohibits it, says the agoraphobe. I've stopped reading because my eyes hurt. The ceiling twinkles with plastic glow-in-the-dark stars. Has my book come in? asks the agoraphobe. Are you dying? I ask. The agoraphobe turns to look at me. How did you know? he says.

1:35 a.m.: Oh man, I say, oh man. I can't do this again.

2:01 a.m.: The agoraphobe texts me. We're all technically dying, he says.

Day Five

7:15 a.m.: Frances is on the couch reading a book I got her last month when I had no money and also no second thoughts about my lack of money. She laughs to herself and I think, I knew it was a funny book. I met Frances when we lived in the same hall in our freshmen dorms. She slept with my roommate, then they dated for a while, just a couple of weeks, long enough that Frances and I ended up walking in and out of the building together sometimes. Then she sat next to me in the dining hall and when we both ended up in the same French literature class I sat next to her and it kept going like that until I stopped knowing how to define myself without Frances as a benchmark. For example, I am funny at parties, but less funny than Frances. Let me pay your law school tuition, I say. She looks up from her book with a frown. No, she says. But I want to make things easier for you, I say. She sighs heavily and says things being easy isn't the point, but let me know when you charter that jet to Paris.

9:00 a.m.: "If you're going to quit, I need two weeks' notice," my boss tells me again. Quintina mocks him from where she's stacking the orders that have just arrived. When my boss leaves to take a phone call, I ask Quintina if she needs money to see a doctor about her mole. Oh, I'll get around to it someday, she says with a shrug.

12:00 p.m.: I ponder my lunch choices. Sushi? Pizza? Expensive patisserie? In the end I have a peanut butter sandwich and am reminded of everything that is wrong with me. I wind up so furious that I storm into the travel section and pull three books off the shelf at random. Sofia. Lagos. Seoul. There, job done. I pull up a browser page on my phone to book flights. Then

Quintina tells me the book I ordered got here early, and that by the way, I could use it to incapacitate intruders. She mimes lifting a boulder as she drops it on the table in the back room where we all eat lunch and leave rings from our coffee mugs. The coffee back here is bitter. My brain is pressing in and I flip through the pages. Rococo. Characterized by elaborate, ornamental stylings. Maximalism. Wealth.

5:25 p.m.: The agoraphobe doesn't seem all that surprised to see me. It's not an imminent death, he says. I hand him the book and he says thank you. He closes the door and I go upstairs.

5:32 p.m.: Frances hasn't moved, although there are chocolate wrappers all around her and crumbs on her sweatshirt. She pats the spot next to her on the couch and I sit. There is a really good joke, one that makes me laugh-cry every time, and I do. The agoraphobe texts me to keep it down up there.

8:12 p.m.: What do I want? I have all the money in the world. What do I want? What do I want? Time feels like it's slipping away from me. It's already been five days. I can't breathe.

10:16 p.m.: You know, I know we don't know each other very well, but it seems to me you're handling this uncharacteristically poorly, says the agoraphobe, pouring me some herbal tea. He says he tried four different blends before he arrived at this one. I ask him what he writes about, and he thinks about it for a second. I have a tendency to intellectualize my emotions, he says, and also lately I've been writing about you. Can I see? I ask him. He shows me his recent entry, which is much longer than mine. He has basically recorded everything I said verbatim. I have a very good memory, he tells me. I say wow, this reads like a play or something, did I really say all of this? Sometimes I embellish, he says. Me too, I say.

11:01 p.m.: I owe you an apology, I say. Then we both sip our tea for several minutes in complete but companionable silence. It's pretty good, and I'm not really a tea person. I'm thinking I'll try bone broths next, the agoraphobe says. I lean over and kiss him on the lips. He seems surprised for a second, then slowly melts into it. His lips are soft. He smells a little too sweet, like

The Audit

an overripe peach. Was that the apology? he says. No, it was a different thing, I say. I kiss him again, then a third time. I trace the back of his neck with my fingers. I think about holding his hand in the snow. I think about the way the moonlight falls on his sheets. I think about bright white linen. I think about what matters to me and come up empty, except for Frances. I have so much time, I realize. So much time to fall in love. So much time to choose my future. So much time to call a therapist, any therapist, I can afford to have several therapists at once, which I really need to do. Why am I so weak for a ticking clock? The agoraphobe kisses me back and pulls away. That was nice, he says. Thank you.

12:46 a.m.: Later, when we're lying in his bed and looking up at the glow-in-the-dark stars, I think about high-interest yields and whether the contract gets forfeited if I go to prison. What if I literally rob a bank? Take my youth away from me, I don't deserve it, I don't know how to use it. The agoraphobe looks over at me and says there must be a hell of a mess going on in that head. I can't remember who I used to be. I can't remember who I want to be. Maybe money is the root of all evil. Maybe they made a mistake! I sit up in bed, forgetting I'm naked. I'm going to tell the auditor he made a mistake, I say. The agoraphobe leans up to kiss my spine. I bet he'll love that, he says.

Day Six

4:43 a.m.: I wake up with a jolt and the agoraphobe is writing, one leg propped up on his chair, wearing only his boxers. He looks over at me and says nothing. I ask him if he ever sleeps— I'm realizing now that I've never seen him do it. He says he's on a dozing schedule. Part of me wonders if this is a complex psychological thriller, if he's meant to represent some part of my inner psyche, he's too weird to be real. Seems a highly congratulatory thing to think about yourself, he says, and goes back to writing.

6:15 a.m.: At some point I must catch his dozing schedule, because when I wake up he's nudging me with a fresh cup of coffee. He reminds me I was going to confront an auditor today.

I say yes!! Thank you for reminding me!! I sip the coffee almost without noticing and then I say wow, this one is good. The agoraphobe looks smug. Yes, I really think I cracked it, he says.

7:02 a.m.: Frances doesn't think this is a good idea, but she says that at least I seem like my usual self. She says what are you hoping for, you know, from the new audit? I open my mouth as if I have a perfectly reasonable answer and then I realize the thing I'm about to say is nothing. I hope they say I'm worth absolutely nothing, the whole deal is off, I'll just have to figure it out on my own, the way real people do. But that is absolutely insane, and not even true, because I want to travel. I really like to travel. In theory, that is all I want to do. I quickly google what seems like an appropriate lifetime earning for mid-level management, which sounds boring but might not require too much additional education or extensive work hours. Something that would allow me to come home at five and take a few weeks off during the summers. I do the math and come up with about five million. Okay, thinking five-million-dollar thoughts for you, says Frances, toasting me with an iced latte that I really should have bought for her before I decided to give my fortune back.

9:17 a.m.: The auditor isn't happy to see me. You're already in the system, he says. Your audit has already been run through the program. This is it. I ask him if he, by chance, wants thirty-five million dollars. Please leave, he says.

10:21 a.m.: The agoraphobe doesn't answer the door when I knock. For a moment I have a panicked thought: Could he have gone out? Is he dead? I knock again and he answers. I'm on with my therapist, he says, and asks if I want to join in.

11:05 a.m.: The agoraphobe's therapist says it's not appropriate for her to treat me but she does think it's worth asking myself why I'm so paralyzed by my unexpected windfall. She suggests that I try to turn it into art. I ask, turn what into art? She looks very tired.

12:34 p.m.: My theory is she's assigning you homework so that your overthinking becomes someone else's problem, the agoraphobe tells me after we make out a little on the bistro

The Audit 75

chairs. The sun is streaming in and I can only think of pastries. Come with me, I say. No, he says. But I just want to sit in a café with you. No. Come on, it's not that bad. No. The sun will feel so nice, the pastries will seem fresher, the air is—No. What if we went for a walk? No. Is being trapped in this apartment even good for your health? Irrelevant. I don't understand, you're young and free and the whole world is your oyster, what is so fucking wrong with you that you want to stay trapped in here? Wow, he says, and closes the door in my face. Goodbye.

4:12 p.m.: I take myself for a walk. I buy the pastries. I don't charter a jet but I book two tickets for Frances and me to Paris, first class. I google "capsule wardrobe" and buy everything the article recommends. I buy a new pair of shoes and an outrageous hat. I buy expensive champagne to celebrate the trip that Frances and I are taking to France. I buy Frances a new capsule wardrobe in multiple sizes, in case I get some of it wrong. I email the funeral home and request a more lavish headstone for my father. I put a quarter of the money in the highest-yielding account I can find. I hire two accountants, without telling them I've done so, to check each other. I book appointments with fifteen different therapists. I buy the fancy weed.

9:56 p.m.: I mean, I'm excited about Paris, says Frances, but I don't know if I can get the time off. Just quit your job! I say in exasperation. She looks at me with a grimace. I'll figure it out, she says, but don't do it again. Next time you spontaneously book a vacation, consult my calendar. I realize I need to quit my own job.

10:11 p.m.: I begin drafting my two weeks' notice to my boss. I get distracted by my phone, which has no messages. Then I change my mind and ask for a week off. Personally I find Paris overrated and you'll need to ask Quintina to cover your shifts, my boss replies. I look over at my phone. No messages. I stand up and start to stomp around in a figure-eight pattern. Nothing. After several minutes of this I email my boss back. Thanks, I say. I think about asking him what he does with his money, but I guess I pretty much already know. He buys peanut butter for the break room, for the store he owns that doesn't really make money in its day-to-day business, that he opens himself every morning and chooses not to leave, just because he can.

Day Seven

7:01 a.m.: I check my phone. Nothing. Frances knocks on my door and reminds me to eat breakfast. I call back yeah okay. She leaves for work early, so she can get some stuff done before we leave for Paris, even though I tell her again that she can just quit her job. She says you are really testing my patience. I feel a moment of crushing fondness.

7:16 a.m.: The agoraphobe doesn't answer the door when I knock.

7:32 a.m.: I'm sorry, I text him from outside his door.

7:45 a.m.: I text him: I shouldn't have said or done any of that. I just want you to feel how I feel, that's all.

7:56 a.m.: I almost go back up the stairs when I see that he's typing a response. I see the shadows of his feet on the other side of the door. I like it in here, he says. I rush to type back. I know (Delete.) I was just (Delete.) I shouldn't have (Delete.) I like being with you I just (Delete.) Can you forgive (Delete.) I know we don't really know each oth (Delete.) I just have all this money and (Delete.) I guess I'm kind of freaking out because I (Delete.) I just want (Delete.) Do you think you can (Delete.) What if I stayed h (Delete.) Do we have a fut (Delete.)

8:07 a.m.: The message I send says: If I make sure there's no disease, can I bring you something?

8:09 a.m.: I see his feet pace slightly on the other side of the door. Okay, he says.

12:43 p.m.: Frances texts me: Eat lunch.

2:32 p.m.: Frances texts me again: Make sure you have comfortable shoes for Paris.

2:56 p.m.: Frances texts me again: I should really just quit my job.

3:41 p.m.: Frances texts me again: Do you think you could pay for an accident to befall that senior associate. Burn after reading. Lol

3:44 p.m.: Frances texts me again: Don't literally burn but yeah delete just in case we do go through with it.

The Audit

4:41 p.m.: Frances texts me again: What are you doing, anyway?

9:54 p.m.: It took me most of the day to finish my errand, but eventually I send Frances a picture. It's an arrangement of paintings on loan for twenty-four hours from a bunch of private collectors. Most are rococo but I did choose a few others, like Van Gogh's sunflowers and *Wind from the Sea* by Andrew Wyeth. It's of an open window with translucent lace curtains, blowing in a way where you can almost taste the salt.

9:56 p.m.: Frances texts back: Holy shit, that's what his apartment looks like?

10:04 p.m.: The agoraphobe stands in front of each painting for a long time. He looks at all of the textures and colors and pieces. He explains to me things I didn't know about composition, about the values of the paint, about where the subject matter came from and what it means, the profoundness of the ordinary. My fingers flutter beside his and I feel like I'm floating. I feel like money finally has a point. I feel like the clock is ticking. I feel my future weighing down on me. I feel the grains of my youth being wasted. I reach for another pastry, my hand still holding his. It flakes tenderly apart.

11:11 p.m.: We move the mattress to the floor and fuck with an extravagant view of all the paintings. Briefly, the agoraphobe dozes. Thusly, my week of journaling ends. I don't know what I'm doing, only that if I'm lucky it will hurt. Recklessness is mine at last.

KIJ JOHNSON

Country Birds

FROM *The Sunday Morning Transport*
FANTASY

> You would like to hear how it is in old age?
> Certainly, not much is known about that country
>   —Czesław Miłosz

FOUR YEARS AGO, Jan is awakened by a brilliant flash of gray-white light in her right eye. She is lying on her left side, face half-buried in her pillow, so she thinks nothing of the fact it is only in one eye, instead wondering first about the color, which is more like static on an old television than a flashlight—and then, how someone with a flashlight (for that is what it has to be, a flashlight) was able to shine it into her second-story bedroom, past the heavy curtains, and straight onto her face. She is not afraid. On some level, she knows already that this flash is no outside threat.

But at her age, waking up in the night is followed inevitably by heaving out of bed to pad to the bathroom, and so she sits up. The light is gone (it was only a flash, after all), but as she lifts her head, she feels a sensation as delicate as plucking a petal from a violet. It is inside her eye—at the back of her eye, where the only nerve she knows of is the optic nerve. After that tiny flicker there is no more sensation. But she knows it's bad.

She does all the appropriate things: right eye covered and her head leaned carefully forward, left eye fixed on the ground at her feet as Dave, her husband, helps her into the empty offices of the eye specialist who meets her early the next morning (a Saturday). And as it happens, it is not the detached retina they all fear. It is only a few blood vessels torn loose from the back of her eye. A retinal tear. It's a fairly common occurrence, he says, adding some information she misses but Dave gets. This has been scary; thank god for Dave.

"But there's a blur," she says. "When I look at the wall."

The specialist says, "The occlusion is in front of the optic nerve, yes."

The blur dims one of his eyes as she turns to him. "Is it always going to be there?"

He tips his head to one side, like a sparrow. "Well, it might be. When you're young, any loose matter in the eye settles to the bottom." She has a sudden vision of her eyeball's floor littered with threads and scraps, like a sewing room after a big quilting project. "But in older eyes, the vitreous humor—the fluid in your eye—dehydrates with age. It gets thicker, more like a gel, and things don't settle as quickly. It might take a while before the occlusion is out of your line of sight."

"How long?" Jan says. Her pleasures are all pleasures of the eye: bird-watching, cloud-spotting, reading, embroidery.

He says, "Maybe a year or two, but your brain will learn to ignore it before that."

But it doesn't settle, and her brain doesn't learn to ignore it. The occlusion remains obstinately in her focal point. If she flicks her eyes to one side, she can evade it for an instant before it slides back into its place. She cannot observe it directly, as it's inside her eye, where the strange magics of focus and inversion happen, but after she looks at a bright object, it seems clearer. She senses more than sees that it is vertical and branched, bipedal.

A year later, when she is getting her glasses replaced (this thing in her eye has affected her prescription), her optometrist, who is a bit odd and likes science fiction as much as she does, says, "Oh, it's like you have a tiny alien in there! Nice. Like, it's got little legs and a head." And since he is beaming a giant light directly into her dilated pupil, she also sees it sharply for the first time.

"It's not an alien," she says. "It's a bird."

*

She only sees it clearly at the optometrist's, but it is always present, a bird-shaped blur at the center of her world. But she knows from her more conventional bird-watching: That's how birds *are*. You catch a fat shape in a distant oak that isn't a branch, or you see a group of triangular darknesses bobbing against the vivid green of a soccer field, or you see specks scattering across the sky, and you say: *bird*.

Her eyes have never been good; she has never, even with glasses, seen a bird clearly that was not an illustration in a book or a specimen in a museum—and once, there was a Carolina wren that strayed into her garage when she and Dave were changing her oil. It stood on the hood a scarce foot away, fearless and curious, long enough that she still can remember the brassy color, the dustiness of its feathers. Except for that, this bird in her eye is how she has always seen birds.

She imagines it as a grackle, a crow, a finch, but it is none of these. It is Jan-specific, a new and very endangered species.

Endangered, yes. Learning that it still obstructs her vision after two years, the optometrist (and then the ophthalmologist he sends Jan to) explains that there is a simple laser surgery that would break up the occlusion. The smaller pieces would still be there, but they'd be easier for her brain to ignore. Some might even dissolve. When she inquires further, the specialist clarifies, "Well, it's simple, but it's not risk free, no. The occlusion is right in front of your optic nerve, so there's a slight risk of burning that nerve, which could cause blindness in that eye." Medical specialists love their conditionals, but Jan already knows she won't do it. Her eyes, imperfect as they are, are the only ones she has, and she cannot afford to lose them. Dave understands.

And . . . well, the bird. She's gotten used to it. It's become part of how she sees, the thing that stands in the center of things, the thing that makes her pay attention to the things that are off to the side.

Dave has floaters in his eye too. This comes up during the initial diagnosis and again when she is deciding about the laser

Country Birds

surgery. She interrogates him: Where, how many, what do they look like? But his answers aren't very helpful. There are some; they just look like grayed-out places where his peripheral vision is fuzzy.

"So, you can't see what they look like?" she asks. For some reason she hasn't told him hers is a bird.

He says, with the laugh that means this isn't going to be the absolute truth, "Like the inside of my eyeballs." But two days later, when they are driving home from the Costco and the car is warm and dark and they are both facing forward, he adds, "They're a little like fish. I guess. Like they're swimming in a muddy river."

This isn't the first bird in Jan's body.

There has been a sparrow in her heart since she was twenty, since the night she woke up in terror feeling wings thrumming in her rib cage. She didn't see a doctor for it, and she has never told Dave; it went away so quickly each time that she wondered if she was dreaming, and by the time she realized she wasn't, it had stopped frightening her. It mostly sleeps, but every year or so, after too much coffee or a lot of stress, she feels the flurry of wings again. *Calm yourself,* she whispers, and presses her hands against the flutter: *It's okay.*

And another, later, in her thirties: When she tore the ligaments in her right knee, the sick pale gray of the pain was accompanied by a flushing heat like the breast feathers of a brooding hen, and that's how she saw the entire slow process of healing: a ruffled, slightly angry chicken watching over the damaged ligaments.

And then, her depressions: They were always birds, greasy and bedraggled and struggling in an oil spill, frightened of and then grateful for the hands that pulled them free, the Dawn dishwashing soap, the warm, calm corner to recover in.

As she ages, the birds collect in her body, nestle into her hollowing bones.

Last year, she read a very old Sufi story, *The Conference of the Birds* by Farid ud-Din Attar. All the birds of the world gather on a quest to find the Simorgh together, the Simorgh being a sacred bird that none of them know except by rumor. All the birds have personal reasons for going; everyone gives a speech or two. Birds drop out at every stage of the quest, like the ever-shrinking brackets in a college sport. In the end, the last, determined few find the Simorgh, which is themselves. Or that's how she remembers it. Perhaps her birds are collecting to become a new Jan.

Jan meets a very old woman in a Scottish church. That sounds like a fairy tale, and it even feels a bit like one to Jan, but it is not: She has been traveling without Dave and stops in a pretty chapel built of stone the color of honey, because it is Sunday and she thinks that listening to thirty voices (it turns out to be thirty) singing together will be pleasant, as it is. Afterward, she drinks coffee from an urn set up to one side of the nave, and meets the very old woman she noticed in the front row, whose hair is the color of winter lakes, who is curled like a shepherd's crook, who has a red-and-pink crocheted afghan hung over the front bar of her cardinal-red walker. She is hard of hearing, so Jan stands close. In the warm light of the chapel, the blurred bird in Jan's eye is apparently standing on the very old woman's shoulder.

"What are you seeing?" the very old woman says. They have been talking about the weather, the rides they are waiting for, the chapel itself. At first Jan thinks she is asking about the altar cloth or the stained glass windows, but then she tips her head like a sparrow to peek up at Jan and says, "I have them too," in a voice soft as pigeons. "The birds, all the birds. More every year."

"Birds?" Jan repeats, taken aback.

"You'll see," says the very old woman. "We all get them, though maybe we don't all see them as birds. But you and I . . ." She grins and Jan sees the very young woman that once was this very old woman. "Oh, we're lucky, we are."

Jan cannot help but smile back. "Lucky?" She seems to be incapable of doing more than repeating whatever the very old woman says, like an echo or a parrot.

"It's not really an ending," says the very old woman conversationally. "Do you think I am a witch?"

They are in a honey-colored chapel filled with light and people who are, at the moment, kind. "*Are* you a witch?"

The very old woman unexpectedly reaches up a hand as fine-boned as a sparrow's foot and touches Jan's forehead with her finger. She sounds slightly surprised: "Well, perhaps I am! But you'll see. It's birds. It's all birds."

There will be other birds.

Jan falls on a patch of ice in Wisconsin and breaks her wrist with a sound she feels as much as hears, the flexible snap of the breaking wishbone after a holiday meal. After this, she takes supplements as directed and learns to walk more carefully.

The whirring, thrumming bird in her chest is at last taken to the doctor and then the hospital for tests. Changes are advised.

For a long time now, a bird has been making a nest in her left hip, a painful obstruction that *kraks* like a raven when she climbs the stairs. Eventually she has surgery and it is gone until, two years later, it moves into her right hip. Ousted again, it nevertheless visits from time to time, more as the years go by.

Sometimes gulls stab at her face, her throat, pulling free the little crabs that hide there.

Her vision eventually fades until she can no longer read easily, and even the bird in her eye is lost into the gathering shadows. After the cataract surgery, she sees it is where it has always been, but now there are more, a flock of tiny, undifferentiated dark birds off to the sides of her eyes. She is never alone.

Dave dies. A second bird moves into her chest, as miserably lumpish, as outsized and immovable as a cowbird chick, a hatchling that refuses to leave.

The birds accumulate: dry feathers under her skin, her hollowing bones filled with restless rustlings. Jan forgets people she has loved, even the reasons for the various pains and discomforts. But the birds stay. She sleeps in a flock without knowing why they are there.

Jan doesn't see what the very old woman meant about any of it, until she does.

Many years from now, there will be a night when, after quite a lot of pain and confusion, the birds shake themselves free of her, one by one. They are as tall as she is, clustered close, gabbling as though meeting at a family reunion, preening disordered feathers into place and stretching their wings into complex curves that intersect like Gothic arches. They stand on moss as thick as a carpet; overhead, it is smoke gray but growing lighter.

"Well, that's that, then," says the bird that was in her eye. It is dark gray and its breast is white, like a junco, but its head and throat shimmer with colors new to Jan. It is speaking to the other birds, and they reply: coos, caws, croaks, liquid silver and brass gongs and felt mallets on rosewood.

This is not a place Jan knows, but then, it's been a long time since she has really understood where she is. "Where *are* we?" she asks.

"Does it matter? We're leaving," says the bird.

"Can I find Dave?" she says. "He only had fish."

"Why not?" says the bird. "We're all going up."

And she is surrounded by flapping wings and songs, the laughter of birds, and she realizes suddenly that she has wings as well, and she is flying as well, and singing.

TATIANA OBEY

Fuck Them Kids

FROM *FIYAH*

SCIENCE FICTION

"WHEN ARE YOU finally going to stop gallivanting among the stars and give me some grandkids? You're not getting any younger."

At the decrepit age of thirty-five, Jaz had developed titanium skin to her mother's favorite question. A couple of years ago, the question had used to wound her. Now, the sharp edge of her mother's words had dulled, and they bounced off her armor of indifference. One would think that her mother would give up after all these years, but it was an old joke between Jaz and her sister that since their mother was one of the first colonists to settle Jupiter's moon Europa, stubbornness had been genetically modified into her bones.

With the fork of greens halfway to her mouth, Jaz raised her eyebrow and asked, "What do you need more grandkids for, anyways? Don't you have enough?"

"Whatever happened to that nice boy you brought over a couple of years ago?" her mother asked. Too bad her question was drowned out by her sister's youngest child wailing in the highchair.

The toddler had been happily chomping on carrots, but for some reason, they were now screaming and launching their food across the table. Jaz's sister, Faye, burst from the kitchen, carrying two plates she had been making for the twins. She placed the plates on the table, then swooped in and pulled the toddler from the highchair.

Jaz remembered when, back in the day, Faye would never go anywhere without having everything done up, looking so astral she could attract any suitor into her orbit. Now, the roots of her sew-in were showing, baby vomit adorned her sweatpants, and her complexion seemed drained of vibrancy ever since giving birth to her oldest ten years ago. Jaz honestly didn't understand why anyone decided to have one kid, much less four.

She seriously couldn't believe her mother expected her to do the same. There were technologies now where you could pop a baby out of a tube in nine months, but should she allow some genetic parasites to demand the best of her energy, time, and attention? Absolutely not. No, thank you.

"Kids, get to the table!" Faye yelled.

Bare feet pounded down the hallway, and the five-year-old twins burst into the room, bringing with them a storm of noise and chaos. The baby continued to wail. The oldest plopped into the chair right next to Jaz while wearing a pair of those translucent gaming glasses.

"No games at the table," Faye reprimanded.

Her ten-year-old niece, Aden, set the glasses down on top of the table, almost knocking over Jaz's "grown-up" drink if she hadn't reached to stabilize it in time.

"Is Daddy going to make it home?" one of the twins asked.

"Sorry, starlight, he's still working on the dome. They found a fault in one of the panels and if he doesn't replace it soon, we could become so cold we'll never wake up. He's out there protecting us."

"Technically, before we freeze, we'd asphyxiate from the lack of oxygen first. If we somehow survived all of that, then we'd have Jupiter's radiation to contend with," their mother added, ever the scientist. At the horrified look on the twins' faces, she clarified, "But the dome has multiple layers so one broken panel isn't going to hurt anyone. It's just bad optics on Resettlement Day. No worries, my little seedlings, we learned to employ contingencies in our first year."

"*No games at the table!*" Faye snapped, her patience wearing thin.

Aden was a second away from rolling her eyes but thought

better of it before her mother's glare. Was Jaz that much of a little shit when she was younger? They said that kids were cute and precious and all, but no one prepared you for the attitude.

Aden tossed her handheld communicator next to her glasses. Then, with barely a glance at her dinner, she blinked up at Jaz and beamed. "Can I ride in your spaceship?"

"No," Jaz said automatically. She shoveled the rest of the greens into her mouth, a delicious reminder as to why she was willing to put up with her mother's obstinate questions and the flurry of her sister's kids. Jaz could endure anything for good food, and her mother was the best damned cook in the universe.

For that reason alone, there was no galaxy big enough to keep her from missing a family holiday.

Later that night, Jaz helped her sister clean up the kitchen. The toddler had been put to sleep in a crib that rocked when it sensed sound and projected 3D images of Europa's wildlife dome off the walls, but even the latest technology didn't keep Faye from anxiously looking toward the bedroom. The toddler, as Jaz understood it, could be quite the escape artist. In the other room, the older children were watching the holiday broadcast with their grandmother.

"How you been?" Jaz asked, now that they had time to themselves. She scraped food off the plates into the recycler and then placed them into the automatic washing machine that cleaned, dried, swallowed them up, and spat them out in the appropriate cabinet of the kitchen.

Faye sighed in response, which was all the answer Jaz needed. "It would have been nice if their father had been here, but of course they had to call him in to work. There are others on his team, but somehow, he's the one they always call in for an emergency. On a holiday, no less!" she vented. "But I guess I shouldn't be complaining. At least his job is important enough that he isn't likely to lose it, but I wanted better than the life we grew up with, you know? Our mother did nothing but work all of the time."

"We turned out fine." Jaz shrugged. Faye looked at her as if she wasn't so sure about that, and she rolled her eyes under her sister's scrutiny. Not helping to improve her sister's opinion any, she leaned against the kitchen counter and asked, "Hey, do you think I could borrow some money?"

Her sister threw up her arms, as if she was yet another problem piled on top of all the others. Jaz quickly continued, "I'm just a bit short, but I'll pay you back the next time I visit. You know I'm good for it."

"When are you going to get a *real* job?" Faye asked. Ahh. There was another one of those questions Jaz had welded her armor against. But unlike their mother, Faye had no real expectations as she shook her head, pulled her communicator from her pocket, and sent over the money. "You know Mom thinks it's drugs, right?"

Jaz didn't care what their mother thought, or at least, not anymore. Good thing her big sister was a bit more supportive.

"You're the best, big sis," she said. "And I'll pay you back, I promise."

"Just . . . come by more often. I miss talking to you, and the kids barely get to spend time with you."

Jaz scrunched her face in disgust, and honestly couldn't imagine what they would even do together. "Maybe when they get to the age when they're not leaking fluids."

"They are always leaking fluids!" Faye wailed. Jaz laughed at her sister's misfortune. She grabbed the multiple to-go plates that she had made for herself and gave her sister a quick hug before sweeping out of the kitchen. "See you later!"

She found the twins and her mother asleep on the couch, cuddled together under the insulated blankets. The television was still broadcasting the celebrations from multiple domes, showcasing grand light displays of drones that twirled through the air.

Sometimes, at rest, her mother once again resembled that young botanist who dedicated her life to terraforming Europa, who nurtured plants from the moon's manufactured soil. Her mother was one to show her love through work, through laboring to transform a harsh frozen moon into a place where her children could thrive. Jaz didn't get comforting hugs and nightly kisses growing up, but clean air and fresh food. Years later, in her retirement, her mother doted on her grandchildren in a way she never did with her own children.

Unlike Faye, Jaz found it hard to be bitter about their upbringing, for it was their mother's absence that allowed her to pursue her own interests. It taught her how to entertain herself and how to be content with being on her own, a skill she found useful while traversing long stretches of space.

And despite the claims made by all the settlement ads thrust into her face while growing up, she didn't feel empty or unfulfilled with her child-free life. Society might consider her a black hole, but in truth, she was a galaxy.

"Happy Resettlement Day, Mom," she whispered, and kissed her mother on her cheek.

She made sure to check that she wasn't forgetting anything, especially the food, before walking out of her sister's house.

The artificial lights of the dome mimicked nighttime. Rail lines zipped overhead like titanium clouds unraveling across the sky, creating a constant overcast that streaked shadows across the hempcrete homes constructed amid forests of bamboo and public gardens. Farther beyond the dome's clear sphere, mountainous drills cracked through the blue-veined ice of Europa's surface to deliver water to various dome habitats. From the streets of her sister's house, she could see the jungle dome situated farther out, always on the horizon like a sun that never sets.

She approached her spaceship, which occupied an entire cul-de-sac compared to the smaller railcars that the neighbors used to traverse the dome. The exterior of her ship was painted a nebula purple and the words *Furious Astral* were sprayed across the hull in electric yellow. The ship had three prongs—the cockpit at the center and two turret lasers on either side. It was an absolute beauty, if she did say so herself. It had curves all sexy and sleek, with a design that sliced through the speed of light like an assassin's throwing knife.

She put her finger on the DNA lock, and the wing-door swiveled on its hinge and rose into the air. The lights automatically came on as she dipped inside, except for the bulb above her cot that flickered in and out. Unfortunately, that nuisance was always on the bottom of her repair list. When she delivered her to-go plates safely into the refrigerator, she noted that the bathroom door was ajar. She didn't remember leaving it open, but she slid it shut as she passed and headed toward the front of the ship.

She sat down in the pilot's chair, and it immediately conformed to her shape from years of use. She fit her fingers into the worn divots of the steering wheel, and the ship's dashboard lit up in greeting.

With a press of a button, the engine gave a great purr, and the neighbors across the street peeked out their windows when the thrusters blasted air and heat across their yards. The neighbors were always reporting her for noise violations, and Jaz sent them a middle finger as her ship ascended, higher than the roofs of their homes, higher than the rail lines, and then higher than the pointed buildings in the dome's downtown sector.

There were certain procedures one needed to follow to get off-planet, so she sent a message to air control, and then leaned back and crossed her feet onto the dashboard while she waited for her turn in the queue.

She was engrossed in her alien smut and chewing on pecan pie when they finally called her name. She tossed the book onto the dashboard and dumped the crumb-infested biodegradable napkin with the other fast-food wrappers on the floor. After licking her fingers, she snapped a helmet over the short natural coils of her hair.

The hole at the top of the dome slid open as she approached. She steered through four layers, each layer adjusting from the artificial gravity of the dome to the low gravity of Europa's atmosphere.

She ascended into the stratosphere, and as she looked down, she saw hundreds of domes that pockmarked Europa's cold surface. Some domes glittered with the city lights of human activity, and others held an aquarium of sea life or bloomed with the luscious foliage of green terrariums. As she traveled higher, they all looked like bright white pimples ready to burst on the moon's porcelain surface.

There had only been one dome when her mother first arrived on the colony ship, and now, there were hundreds. Despite the population growth, Europa's colonies paled in comparison to the might of Mars. Right before the Earth's environmental collapse, colony ships were sent to different celestial objects that could potentially support human life. By the time her mother's colony ship landed on Europa, humanity had already developed Mars into the new center of the universe.

"Breaking atmosphere," Jaz reported to air control as she pointed the nose of her ship toward the sky. She never grew tired of this part as the ship rattled and a red film burned around the windows. The ship's acceleration pressed her against her chair, and she was reminded of her first time at a Mars amusement park. Exiting atmosphere felt like that moment when the roller coaster rumbled to its greatest height. Beneath her, she could see the widening curvature of Europa. The ice blue of the planet gradated into a darker hue, as wondrous as the colors of a sinking iceberg.

One day, Jaz wished that her mother would understand that a rejection of the ground wasn't necessarily a rejection of her. Her mother had spent her entire life building a thriving world for her children to inherit, and Jaz . . . didn't want it. She wasn't built for dome life and artificial gravity. She was too much of a planet in elliptical orbit—coming close for a few days for the holidays and then whipping out as far as she could toward freedom.

She broke through the thermosphere and all resistance fell away as the planet's gravity released her. The sight of Jupiter filled her vision, and the bands of burnt orange and pale beige overwhelmed her with a sense of awe. The beautiful gas giant always felt as if it was reaching out, examining her with that great red eye, and kissing her off with stormy encouragement.

Loose wrappers from various way stations' algae burgers floated past the window until she flipped a switch overhead and activated the ship's internal gravity. Something loose rattled around in the back of the ship, and she hoped that nothing had broken. Either way, she had an appointment to make, and she didn't have the time to check on the problem.

After she navigated around the dust and debris of Jupiter's rings, the endlessness of space welcomed her.

Sometimes, she couldn't comprehend how space was simply

a means to get from one point to another for some people, and not a destination all of its own. Her mother had traveled on a colony ship, eager to land and settle and to leave the stars behind, but they called to her daughter like a lighthouse guiding wandering ships to port.

Nowhere could you find such beautiful, perfect, and peaceful *silence.*

"HEY, AUNTIE!"

Jaz whipped around to the sight of her ten-year-old niece clutching the ship frame, barefoot and in her flower pajamas. At first, she couldn't believe her eyes, and then she screamed, "WHAT THE FUCK?!"

"Aden Mae Juniper! You are in so much trouble! Wait until I get my hands on you!" Faye yelled at her daughter through the communicator screen. "I cannot believe you would do this! You are grounded for life; do you hear me? Grounded. For. Life!"

Aden slumped in the copilot's chair, looking all contrite ever since Jaz had explained the situation to her sister and she had started yelling. When Faye finally paused to take a breath, Aden mumbled, "I'm sorry, Mommy."

On the screen, Faye rubbed at her forehead and turned to Jaz. "How did this happen?"

She glanced over at Aden, who anxiously fiddled with the frayed ends of one of her twirling pink braids. "I think it was the bio-lock. I have your biometrics saved for, you know, insurance purposes, but I've been having trouble with the sensors lately. It must have figured Aden was close enough and let her in."

"I've been waiting for her father to come home from work, so I guess waiting up a little longer can't hurt. How long will it take for you to get back?"

"Yeah, about that," she said slowly. "I've got an appointment to make, and I don't have time to turn around. I'm going to have to deliver her tomorrow."

"Excuse me?!" her sister said. "Absolutely not! You are not going to get my daughter caught up in your escapades!"

"Oh no, did I also mention that I've been having problems

with the communications? Sounds like you're cutting off," Jaz said as she reached for the button to end the call.

"YOU BRING MY DAUGHTER BACK RIGHT—"

Her sister's voice sputtered out. She glanced over at Aden, who stared at the faded black of the screen in shock. Her niece looked up at her, with eyes as bright as her chipped glitter nail polish. She asked, hopefully, "You're not taking me back?"

"Looks like you get to ride in the spaceship, after all," Jaz huffed. "Everything will be fine. Just sit there and be quiet."

Her niece mimed bolting her lips closed, but that didn't last long, when she glanced at the book Jaz had tossed on the dashboard. The cover was flipped up to display a blue-muscled alien with a double-pronged schlong. "What's that?"

"Nothing," Jaz said as she snatched it and stored it away.

She took the ship off cruise control, which she had activated before calling her sister. The call had made her later than she had already been, and she was going to have to gun it to make her engagement on time.

Without hesitation, she floored the pedal.

Aden released a scream that ripped through her eardrums. She turned to find that her niece had fumbled out of the chair and the acceleration had pinned her to the closed door of the cockpit. With an annoyed grunt, she lifted off the pedal and reached back to grasp at the smiling daisies of Aden's pajamas. She dropped her niece back into the chair.

"You didn't tell me to put my seatbelt on!" her niece shouted, shocked, as she scrambled to lock the seatbelt around her chest. It clicked into the mechanism.

"I ain't your momma," Jaz scoffed, and then raced toward the stars as if they were a finishing line.

Shango was the largest space station in the entire galaxy, positioned right at the shit-end of the asteroid belt. It was named after a Yoruba god because astrologists ran out of the Roman ones to name things. The station acted as a gateway between the inner and outer planets and was an epicenter of commerce and trade.

And like all ports of trade, it was a hive of criminal activity. Not somewhere one should bring a kid, but she needed to recharge on energy.

"What do you mean you're not going to make it?" Jaz growled into her wrist communicator. In the corner of her eye, she monitored the mechanics as they recharged her ship.

"I'm sorry. The babysitter is sick and I'm not having any luck finding anyone else. I'm not going to make it," Jaz's copilot, Katya, apologized. "You might be able to hire a last-minute copilot. I've sent over references of some people I know."

"*Come on, Katya.* Can't you leave the brat at home alone?"

"She's two!"

"Aren't they, like, walking at that age?"

"Oh my stars, Jaz, check out my references. Or see if you-know-who would be willing to team up."

She hissed at that suggestion. Absolutely not.

"Or maybe you should just sit this one out, then?"

"And what? Let someone else claim my title?"

"Sharing is caring." Katya laughed. "I'll see you next week for girls' night."

"Wait—" Jaz groaned when Katya hung up on her. The references popped up on her screen afterward, and she dragged them immediately to the recycle bin.

When she looked up, the mechanics had finished their work. She transferred all the money that her sister had given her to the mechanics for the recharge. If she wasn't in need of money, maybe she would do the responsible thing and sit this race out. Eh. Who was she kidding? She would still race even if she had all of the money in the world.

She returned to her ship, sat down in the cockpit, had her seatbelt buckled, and had finished all of the preparations to depart when a bright pink hairband in the copilot's chair caught her eye. Wait a minute. She turned in her seat, looking for her niece.

"Aden! Where you at!?" she yelled. When she heard no answer, she released an annoyed sigh and got up to find the brat. Panic set in when she couldn't find her anywhere on the ship. She checked the toilet, under the thin blanket of her cot, and under the weaponry shelf. Then she spotted her, through the window, *outside* of the ship.

"What did I tell you about leaving my sight!" Jaz demanded, storming toward her. "I told you to stay on the damned ship!"

She found her niece ogling a ship parked two spaces down. She pointed and asked, "Isn't that a T-48 model?"

"I . . ." Jaz paused and properly looked at the spaceship. It was indeed a T-48 model. Although with some garish modifications. It had an extra plate of armor that sacrificed speed for protection, and the blast cannons were far too powerful, so much so, that the kickback could affect steering. But some people liked big guns. "Yeah, it is. What do *you* know about spaceships?"

"I love ships!" she exclaimed. "I want to drive a spaceship just like yours when I grow up. It's my favorite model to drive in my virtual reality game."

How cute. But her niece's words gave Jaz a terrible, *terrible* idea. Her niece was tall enough that with Katya's space suit and helmet on, no one would be able to tell that she was underage. Besides, who bothered carding roid racers, anyways?

"Who is the brat? I know she ain't yours."

Jaz growled as she turned, and as she feared, the owner of the monstrous spaceship hadn't been lurking all that far away. She crossed her arms, and hilariously enough, her niece did the same beside her. They both glared at Damien, who only smirked, amused.

She and Damien had been rivals ever since she joined the racing circuits, but not only that, he was also her ex. When they had first gotten together, she had been clear that she didn't want any children and he had claimed he didn't want them, either, but after four years he had changed his damned mind. He dumped her for a woman ten years younger and now had a newborn at home. And yet, he spent more time on the circuits with her than with the family he claimed to have wanted. But whatever. That was in the past. She and Damien had a strictly rival-appropriate relationship now.

"She's my sister's kid," Jaz muttered.

"Faye's kid? I haven't seen her in forever. How is she doing?"

he said as he swept back his locs. "Oh wait, today is Resettlement Day, ain't it? You got any of your momma's food?"

"Faye is fine, and no," Jaz snapped, despite the fact she had four plates currently on the ship. She grabbed her niece by the hand. It was warm and clammy, and thankfully, not as sticky as she feared. She pulled the girl back toward the ship.

"Ah, come on, Jazzy. I haven't had any of your momma's greens in years," Damien said, following behind them, with an uneven, sharp gait. He had an artificial leg to replace the one he had lost in a bad crash, the one he had suffered right before he had broken up with her. It made him reevaluate life and what he wanted or whatever. For her, it was still a betrayal.

Her eye twitched. "Don't call me that."

Once she pushed her niece back inside of the spaceship, she snapped the door closed behind her and collapsed against the metal of it.

"Who is he, Auntie Jaz?" her niece asked, too young to remember when she had brought him over for the holidays.

"He is our number one enemy," Jaz responded, and Aden repeated that word in awe, as if an enemy was only a thing that existed in her video games.

Then, there was a knock on the door. She groaned, stomped over to the fridge, opened the ship door, and stuffed one of the plates into Damien's chest. He grinned that goofy-ass smile that still made her stomach do barrel rolls all of these years later. She reminded herself that he had a wife and a kid and that she was no one's sidepiece. "Maybe that'll fatten you up enough to slow you down."

"Need help keeping up?" he teased.

"You wish. Eat my space dust."

She slammed the door in his face and then turned with both hands on her hips. There was no way she was going to let Damien have any more wins. She grinned at her niece, who was plenty tall enough to see over the dashboard. That was enough for her.

"Let's get you in a suit."

The race began on the edge of the main asteroid belt, on the underside of an asteroid as large as the Shango space station.

With Katya's helmet obscuring her face, Aden gazed out of the window from the copilot's chair and watched all the other ships line up next to them. The one immediately on their right was painted to look like a stylized comet, all blazing reds and nova oranges, with a driver wearing a helmet spray painted the same colors. On Jaz's left, Damien's big beast of a ship idled next to her. The manufactured horns on his and his copilot's helmets mimicked the thick arms of his hulking ship.

Instead of being intimidated by the colorful characters not commonly found in her little Europa dome, Aden swiveled toward her and asked, excited, "Can I help? I've won lots of races. I've earned so many points that I've unlocked the super ultra-rare gold skin."

"This isn't some game," Jaz scoffed. "Having a copilot helps with response times, but I'm redirecting all system operations to my control panel. You don't need to do nothing but sit there and not distract me."

"But the others have copilots. Are you sure you don't need help?" she asked, genuinely concerned as pairs of pilots continued to join them at the starting line.

"Relax, kid. I've been driving *actual* spaceships since I was sixteen," she said. She had been recruited as a copilot after getting caught racing one of the dome's smaller railcars. Eventually, she saved up enough money to afford her own ship and crew. After a pause, Jaz winked and said, "Don't tell your grandmother."

She and her niece shared a conspiratorial smile.

A red light burst awake in the distance, twinkling like a dwarf star against the backdrop of space. Jaz felt mesmerized by the light, as the afterglow of it often faded into her dreams. The ship's engine purred underneath her like a wild cat that she had carefully tamed with years of attention and experience. Eventually, all sound vaulted into the void of space, and it was just her and the red antenna light installed into the asteroid.

It turned green.

Jaz slammed her foot atop the pedal, and the nose of her ship raced against the others. But an asteroid race was never about pure speed. In her opinion, the best pilots were the ones who understood how mass and force acted against one another to become a force all their own.

Damien blasted an asteroid directly in front of her, shattering the rock into pieces that flew in all directions, setting off a chain reaction and sending all the nearby asteroids into movement.

"Watch out!" her niece yelled.

Jaz blasted the incoming asteroid at just the right angle that the resulting shards bounced off of one another, pinging against each other like a casino billiards table, until a shard struck the window of Damien's ship. He flipped her off as she sped past him with a wild laugh.

The asteroids moved and shifted like a living maze, but she prided herself on seeing the pathways. Ahead, the fastest route was quickly closing as two asteroids threatened to collide. She activated the additional boosters, which drained the ship's energy faster than normal but gave her just a little more speed.

"We're not going to make it!" her niece yelled as she clutched the armrests of her chair. The asteroid scraped the roof of the ship with a screech, and Jaz whooped when they squeezed past.

The ship shook when someone blasted them to their right, hitting their starboard plating. Aden screamed and pointed. "They're shooting us!"

Jaz spun the ship to escape the line of fire, and their opponent's gunshots whirled around them like a spiral of light. She abruptly slowed and flipped back. For a brief moment, the rival ship hovered beneath them with a top painted like a flaming comet, before she positioned at their rear. She aimed the turret lasers, and bright lights flashed with each shot.

The opposing ship attempted to evade out of the way of her gunfire, and it exploded in all those garish colors when it crashed right into an asteroid. She straightened the ship and, with an eye on the ship's battery, directed more energy to the thrusters to return back to course.

Warning lights flashed and blared within the ship, set off when the starboard plating had been shot. She snapped off her seatbelt and stabilized the wheel with her feet, to reach up to the ceiling to turn off that annoying light.

"You're driving with your feet!"

Jaz settled back into her chair. Asteroids revolved around her like partners in a swing dance, and the music played in her head as she danced right along with them—twirling, spinning, and swinging to the beat. So many people mistook space to be a silent void, but if you listened closely, it could play music for you.

A light flashed in the corner of her eye. She ducked underneath the attack. An asteroid moved out of the way to reveal Damien racing beside her, neck and neck. They briefly glanced at each other, and a smile tugged at the corner of her lips. Both at once, they activated their thrusters to full blast, damn the consequences.

"Go, Auntie, go!"

The end of the asteroid belt was straight ahead, pulling her forward with the grip and strength of Jupiter's gravitational field.

She glanced at Damien inching a little past her, aided by the gigantic thrusters of his ship. Without hesitation, she careened to the side. He veered left to avoid the collision, straight into one of the asteroids. He blasted it apart, but the kickback slowed him down and Jaz sped ahead.

She spiraled toward that hole, as if she was once again a child, aiming toward the opening in Europa's dome that would offer her everything that she ever wanted—if only she was brave enough to reach for it.

She burst through the asteroid belt into sparkling infinite outer space.

Jaz settled back and grinned at her victory. She hadn't won a race solo in a long time—wait, no, that wasn't true. She smirked down at her little niece, but her smugness fell away at her niece's ashen face. There was a reason why Faye refused to ride passenger if Jaz was the one driving. She grew concerned that she had scarred the girl for life. After all, a virtual reality game was far different from the real thing.

But then, Aden exploded with the force of a small supernova.

"THAT WAS SO AWESOME!" she cheered.

Jaz laughed, and they clipped off their seatbelts and hugged each other in their excitement. It was an unfamiliar feeling to have someone else in her family who understood her love and passion for the stars. Aden asked brightly, "Can we go again?"

Jaz laughed and smiled. "When you get your pilot's license." Then, she realized that they were drifting through space, completely out of power. She activated the radio and contacted Damien, who had slid to a stop beside her. "Hey, can I borrow a charge?"

He laughed at her. Despite their complicated relationship, she knew she could always rely on him. At the end of the race, he was still her best friend.

"No problem. I'm coming, Jazzy."

The next night, Jaz descended back onto the quiet streets of Europa's quaint little neighborhoods. Aden spilled out of the ship once the door opened and raced to meet her mother waiting in the front yard. Faye tucked the girl into her arms, and looked up at Jaz and glared at her. "You didn't do anything too crazy?"

"Just a meeting I had with someone that owed me money. That's all," she said. "Nothing too crazy."

Jaz could tell that Faye did not believe her, but she returned to fussing over her daughter, and when Aden snuck a look at her, Jaz winked. It would be their little secret.

Faye told Aden to get back into the house.

Without hesitation, Aden turned to wrap Jaz into a hug, and then she yelled, before running into the house, "Thank you, Auntie Jaz! I can't wait for next time!"

"If you do good in school!" Jaz called out. That was what she was supposed to say, right?

Faye looked between the two of them as she tightened her robe. "Perhaps it's good that you two got the chance to spend some time together. She's been obsessed about spaceships ever since her dad got her that game. Thank you for bringing her back in one piece."

"Of course. I wouldn't let anything happen to my little niece," she said, and was surprised when she meant it. "Here."

Jaz activated her communicator and transferred the money

she owed. With her winnings, she was able to fix the damage incurred during the race. The repairs were so costly that she was practically broke again, but at the end of the night, all she needed was enough for a recharge.

With a pause, Faye asked, "Are you going to tell me what really happened?"

"You really don't want to know." Jaz waved goodbye as she turned toward her ship. She paused and looked back at her sister, who looked as if anxiousness had been haunting her face ever since her daughter had snuck away. She asked, "Why do you do it?"

Of course, her big sister knew exactly what she meant. Faye crossed her arms with a sigh. "It's a lot of lows, but the highs are worth it. All of the rough days just seem to disappear before those small moments of joy. I might not be as amazing as Mom, but like her . . . love is my legacy."

Jaz looked back at her ship, all bandaged and patched up, and smiled. "Yeah, I get that. I love you, Faye."

"Love you too, Jaz."

She returned to her ship. As she ascended from the street, she noticed a light in the window and the sight of her niece waving at her from the glass. Maybe kids weren't all that bad. Maybe she should spend more time with her nieces and nephews. Maybe she should stop by more. But you know what was the best part about kids?

Giving them back.

Jaz blasted off into the stars.

S. L. HUANG

The River Judge

FROM *Reactor*

FANTASY

THE FIRST TIME Li Li buried a corpse, she was nine years old. Her father had been shut up inside one of the inn's private dining rooms all day. At such times it was understood that he was never to be disturbed. The rule had been drilled deep in Li Li since she was a small child—whether she had fallen on the riverbank and matted her hair with blood, or a patron of the inn became belligerent with drink and flung wine in her mother's face—knocking to interrupt her father was strictly forbidden.

Such times were for *business*, he always said. Meetings with business associates, planning for the inn's future. How could Li Li's mother expect the place to prosper if she did not respect the undisturbed peace needed for such work?

This time, only one other man had joined him. Li Li hadn't seen the man arrive, but her mother had waited on them with the finest meals and wine, the door always shutting firmly again when she had barely crossed the threshold to leave. Li Li had been ordered to get on with her usual long list of daily chores, gathering the washing and scrubbing dishes and packing out the night soil from the latrine buckets. But some rebellious river current always seemed to draw her into baiting dragons, including tempting her father's fury.

When she snuck close to listen through the wall this time, however, she couldn't hear much of interest. Only her father's voice rising and falling in conversation with the other man's.

Then the two of them laughing together, her father much louder and longer.

She was still listening when everything went silent.

Li Li scurried from the door in apprehension of being caught. Her father's temper might be the chief concern, but both her parents disliked her tendency to lurk around corners and in shadows. They disliked a great many things about her—she had once eavesdropped on them telling people she was "strange and cold, like a stone" and "not a proper child at all." After that, she'd sat up on a hill once for half a day, challenging herself to stay perfectly still. It took so much strength that she decided being a stone was a compliment and had begun testing her muscles with stillness as often as she could. She had always been stocky but small, and the other children in the town tended to be surprised at her strength, when they deigned to notice her.

She had stayed motionless as granite by the door for a long time today, lest a sound give her away. When that sudden silence reverberated so deep and strange, she threw herself back into her chores with an overdone vigor, as if to prove she'd never left them. She had relocated to the kitchen to sweep out the hearth's charcoal and ash when her father's silence bloomed into several loud crashes and thumps audible through the entire inn—which after a short time evolved into shouting at her mother.

That, at least, was very normal.

Li Li's mother kept her voice low, though the front room was empty of patrons this time of the afternoon, especially as travelers through the town had been dribbling off since the new magistrate had arrived. In contrast, Li Li's father never seemed to worry about potential patrons at all, even when the inn wasn't empty. None of the guests ever seemed bothered by his taking his house in hand, anyway.

His voice snapped off in furious declarations, vibrating through the walls about how *this isn't your concern, the inn would have been ruined, it was the only way* . . .

Li Li did what she usually did when her parents argued: She made herself scarce and still. As unnoticed as a shadow on the wall. If this argument followed the customary routine, her father would shout at her mother and then her mother would storm through the inn to find Li Li, raining down cruel digs and extra chores as if passing on a bucket of vitriol that was too hot to hold on to for long.

Li Li knew how to navigate such attacks as little as she knew how to handle her mother's interleaved spikes of affection or proclamations of her child's preciousness. In a bid to stay out of sight, she slipped into the back storeroom of the inn, intending to hide out among the earthenware pickling jars and stacked dense heads of winter cabbage.

Until she saw the dead man.

He sat slumped against the great cisterns of wine in the back of the storeroom, his head fallen forward from its own weight. His clothes were finer than any Li Li had seen, his robes spreading in layers of wide, embroidered skirts, and fur-trimmed leather armoring his legs where they stuck out in a stiff sprawl. Crimson stained the luxurious clothes, a shining wetness slowly creeping wider from below the man's collar and across his chest. More blood dripped from his manicured beard and mustache, leaving a spotted pattern upon his lap.

Li Li was so fascinated she momentarily forgot her parents' fighting. She had seen a dead body before, of course, but not like this, in rich clothes dumped in the back of a storeroom. She stared for several long moments, watching for the tells she always tried to squash when staying motionless herself. The rise and fall of breath, the twitch of eyelids, the shift of a cramped muscle . . .

No breath moved the man's lips or chest. His eyes were half-lidded and filmy, and one wrist had folded against the ground at an odd angle. His skin had gone white with a hint of purple, like the inside of a taro root, and the blood was beginning to dry into the color of rust.

Dead. Li Li felt very proud of herself for such a definitive conclusion.

Curious, she crouched down and scooted closer to the body, staying on her knees as if standing too tall might wake the man from wherever he dwelled on the other side. Then she reached out a daring finger and poked it against his cheek.

It was shockingly cold. And soft. And still felt like human skin. Li Li jerked her hand back.

Only then did she notice something behind the dead man: a fine black hat with long, swooping wings that lay crushed against the floor. She was not old enough to recognize it as a mark of high office, but she would recall it later.

From the front room drifted in the bitter hiss of her mother. "... *that kind of business here at the inn* ..."

Li Li's father snorted back something much louder—a lot of words about "*just think it through*," and was her head empty, and no good wife would peck at such trivial objections. Then a sudden series of bangs and slams, as of someone moving about in anger. Li Li froze, a nebulous idea cobwebbing through her that she must be violating some rule by finding the corpse, much less touching it, and would be shouted at until her ears rang, and then have mountains of extra chores piled atop her. Like scouring out all the latrine buckets on top of the usual collection of night soil to sell to farmers, until the smell got in her nails and hair and clung for days ...

After a moment's thought, she crept out of the storeroom as if she'd never been, and in a roundabout fashion snuck back into the front room. Her mother slumped at one of the empty tables, a cold cup of tea untouched before her. Li Li's father was wrapping himself in heavy layers to go outside.

"I have to go downriver and speak to Elder Mu," he said, without looking at his wife. "The investigators might arrive before I return. Make sure they have no cause for questions."

Li Li's mother raised stricken eyes. "But what about—"

"Just take care of it! Must I do everything for this family?" Her father shut the door hard behind him. A gust of cold settled in his wake.

Li Li's mother noticed her daughter then, and Li Li tensed. But to her surprise, her mother only reached out for her.

She came obediently.

Her mother crushed her in with both arms, face pressed

against Li Li's hair. As usual when this happened, Li Li stood very still until she was released.

"Go play," her mother told her, sounding sad. "Outside, eh?" Li Li went.

Outside was frigid. Li Li wrapped her arms tightly around herself and counted out the three thousand steps over to the shipping house on the river where her cousin Li Jun lived, stamping her boots every few paces to keep the numbness at bay. Her father and mother didn't like her playing with Li Jun, but they couldn't stop it on account of being family.

But Li Jun wasn't at home. Only her mother, Auntie Ru, a large and muscular woman who was tearing the hide off a couple of boatmen so loud the paper vibrated in the windows.

"River licenses? Do you think I give three farts for the capital's nonsense about river licenses? You're paid what the ledgers say you're paid!" Her gaze fell heavy on Li Li.

"My elder cousin . . . ?" Li Li asked.

"On the river, most like. *Ai! How dare you turn your back on me!*" Auntie Ru grabbed the case from her counting rods and began to beat the two boatmen around the head with it.

Li Li retreated. She'd heard her parents muttering about her cousin's family—how Li Jun ran wild, and how Auntie Ru didn't act proper in the least. As a widow with no sons, Auntie Ru had been permitted to inherit her late husband's shipping brokerage, and Li Li's father made frequent bitter remarks toward the way she ran it. And toward his dead brother for marrying her in the first place. And toward Li Li whenever he paid enough attention to notice her associating with the family more than he liked.

He needn't have worried so much. Li Li didn't like her aunt much, either.

Now she walked back to her family's inn and paced about the yard with gloved hands over her tingling ears. The chickens fluttered about and squawked at her, and she scattered their evening meal early, her fingers becoming stiff sausages. The temperature plummeted until it knifed into her bones and teeth, but she stayed outside until the gray sky became grayer and she stopped feeling the tips of every extremity.

When she went back in, two patrons sat at a table, their rumpled clothes those of merchants off the water, their faces red and bunched with impatience. "Girl! We've been waiting an age. Hot wine and rice, and kill a chicken for us if you have it."

"Yes, Uncles." Li Li went back outside through the kitchen, grabbing the sharpest butchering knife on the way. A single swipe to catch a chicken; she held its warmth tight against her body and sliced with one swift move. The blood drained fast and practiced and red upon the frozen ground.

She took the bird back into the kitchen to prepare and went into the storeroom to get the wine—where she found her mother heaving at the arm of the dead man, tears dribbling down her jaw.

The corpse had collapsed on its side now but had shifted only a few paces closer to the back door.

Li Li looked at her mother, looked at the corpse, and then back at her mother, who was not scolding or sniping but instead giving the distinct impression that their roles had reversed, and her small daughter of less than ten years had become the authority who had walked in on *her* doing something untoward.

Li Li pointed at the front room. "Guests," she said.

She walked past to ladle out bowls of cloudy yellow wine, then returned to the kitchen to prepare the food. The men ate and she sent them on their way, but by that time another patron had arrived demanding a meal and lodging. Li Li cooked and served, made up a room, and scrubbed out all the plates and bowls and pots once the man had retired.

By then it was full dark, an oppressive pitch aided by the overcast layer smothering any moon and stars. Li Li took a candle to the storeroom.

The room was empty, save for the dead man, who had now been wrapped—badly—in a length of rough cloth. Li Li moved past to where the back door was ajar.

Her mother stood in the patchy grasses behind the inn, shoving a spade against the ground, each motion barely chipping away another sliver of frozen dirt. Her breath huffed out in a gasping sob with every hit.

Li Li went back inside and brought the sole lodger a full

hot pitcher of wine, no extra charge, and peeked out to make sure his room only saw the road. Then she listened until she heard his drunken snores and bundled back up in her warmest clothes.

She walked the three thousand steps to her cousin's place. All was dark, the living quarters behind the shipping house shuttered up tight. Li Li carefully lifted the latch of the toolshed where her aunt kept supplies for the vegetable patch. She borrowed a pickaxe and a digging knife and hiked back, stopping every so often to heave the heavy pickaxe from one shoulder to the other.

When she returned, her mother's body formed a curled crescent motionless around the haft of the spade.

Li Li thumped the pickaxe off her shoulder and sent the sharp end into the ground. Then again. And again.

Her mother roused at that. The two of them worked into the deep night, wood hafts blistering their hands. Then Li Li helped her mother drag the man out of the storeroom and into his shallow grave, where they packed the frozen clay tight atop him.

The next day, Li Li's shoulders ached and her hands cracked and bled. She wrapped her fingers in cloth and went to return the pickaxe and knife.

"What did you take those for?" asked Li Jun.

"I had to bury the dead," Li Li said.

Li Jun laughed. She was three years older than Li Li, tall and lithe like the eels that slithered down the river, and her hair stuck out as wild as if she'd not only been out on the frigid water but swimming its depths. Maybe she had. "Make sure you bury them deep," she said. "Otherwise they'll come back as ghosts."

Li Li did not laugh back. She had seen ghosts before, but only of her ancestors, and only in dreams. The idea of the dead man haunting the inn did not scare her, but it did annoy her. He had no right to invade her home.

She resolved to keep a close watch for ghosts.

She was still watching when, two days later, the Empire's investigators arrived.

They stayed at the inn.

They stayed at the inn, and demanded lodging and food

The River Judge   109

without offering coin, and were rude to Li Li's mother, complaining that the food was too dry and the wine too weak. Then they interviewed every man in town and many of the women.

Li Li's father returned at midday but kept himself scarce, leaving his wife to wait on the interlopers. She stayed meek to them and then snapped at Li Li in the kitchen for peeling too much meat off the winter melon.

When the investigators went out to chase down anyone they decided to suspect, a handful of the townspeople congregated in the inn's front room in their place, and Li Li's father emerged to gather with them. Together they hunched over drinks, voices bouncing tense off the wooden walls.

"What will we do? How could they know so fast?"

"Some damned mouth must've talked."

"Even the swiftest boat would take more than a day from Bianliang. I heard it was sorcery; an omen came of the magistrate's death . . ."

"Why would the Imperial augurs be casting their eyes all the way down here?"

As Li Li retreated back to the kitchen, she heard her father grunt. "Same reason they pay just enough attention to send these grasping judges in the first place," he said. "Mark me, our worth to the capital is merely what they can scrape out of our pockets and stomachs . . ."

A weight seemed to hang over the inn all day, a heavy darkness that made the candles gutter and the rafters creak. Until that evening, when the townsfolk returned to the front room but the investigators did not—and all with a sudden roar of good cheer as if an overstretched noodle had finally snapped. The men laughed and shouted and toasted each other in every variety of the inn's wine, and the center of the party seemed to be Li Li's father.

"To Brother Li!" they cried. "A true man of the Empire!"

Wine sloshed and another sloppy cheer went up—until they saw Li Li watching and quieted.

"Eh, it's all right, Brother Li's daughter knows not to yap, don't you, girl?" said a younger one of the Tong brothers. Li Li knew him vaguely—the Tong family did a good deal of business with her aunt, and the eldest Tong brother had two daughters a bit older than her that Li Jun was fast friends with. Sometimes the three deigned to allow the littler cousin to join their group—which Li Li always did, even if they made her take enough bruises to prove her worth. They were bigger and could always wrestle her down, but she never gave in.

Like a stone.

Elder Tong was staring at her, and Li Li realized he expected an answer. Her parents often scolded her for letting grown-ups' questions linger in the air for a moment too long. "Yes, Uncle," she said.

The men's hands unclenched, their faces relaxing back into easy smiles.

"I'd best be off, anyway," Elder Tong said, rising and reaching for his fur-lined cap and outer wraps. "My elder brother thinks setting off for a delivery up in Ying Province might be in order, just in case anyone gets around to asking questions . . ."

"About today, or about your 'deliveries'?" said another of the men, with a tone in his voice that Li Li had come to recognize as a joke. The others guffawed.

"You want to stop benefitting, that's fine with us! Go on!" Elder Tong roared, laughing harder than any of them, while the joker raised his hands and hastily declared his lack of any desire for a change.

"To Brother Tong and Brother Li! Heroes of the Empire!" the men cried raucously. Elder Tong brushed them off and slapped Li Li's father on the shoulder.

"After today, Brother Li's talents far outstrip those of us lowly boatmen. Shall we do some cleanup for you on the river, Brother? We can take the boats, find a convenient swamp . . ."

"Oh, no, no, I couldn't ask such a thing," Li Li's father said in his booming voice. "The cleaning part is easy, just a trifle. I wish you good hauls and a swift return."

Once the men had all left, Li Li's father staggered to bed sauced with his own drink and fell into a motionless slumber. He might have been mistaken for a dead man himself, but for the snuffling snores reminiscent of a rooting hog.

Li Li went to pick up the scattered wine bowls and to wipe

up the drink that sopped tables and benches. She wrung out the wet rags and went into the storeroom for a bucket and mop.

Her mother sat on a stool in the back, staring at two more corpses. Li Li couldn't see their faces, but the hems of their skirts had the silken trim of the two Imperial investigators.

Li Li's mother raised her eyes with something like hopelessness, sweaty hair falling across her face. The spade leaned against her knee, her hands drooped across it like the branches of a shrub that had given up against too harsh a clime, with no willingness left to lift its leaves toward the sun.

Li Li curled her own hands. Her scabbing blisters crackled against themselves.

No men from the government came for some time after that. None of the people in the town had any sort of ear into the capital, or knew any reason the magistrate was not replaced or more investigators sent. Li Li continued working at the inn alongside her parents, although, slowly, her father disappeared more often and returned sodden with wine, and her mother snapped less and retreated into a hollow shell, her skin beginning to shrink tight against her bones.

Over the years, as if now by custom, here and there another body would appear in the storeroom for the women to tidy. A tax collector who had come to raid the residents' pockets. A regular merchant from off the river who'd been suspected of slipping overweighted stones onto the payment scales. A boatman who became sloppy with drink every time he came through and made aggressive attentions on married women. Then another man from the capital who'd proclaimed officiously that he had come to enforce the river's ferry licenses, as he'd had information that many in the area were in violation—and a few weeks later, his cousin from a nearby village whom the gossip reported as having leaked such business about his neighbors. Once, a poor but handsome local man who'd caused trouble for a friend of Li Li's father by competing over a marriage contract.

Sometimes, after a disappearance rid the region of some acknowledged pestilence, Li Li's father would get a few grins or nods from select guests, and he would always smile back and put on a genial act of ignorance. Occasionally more investigators arrived, but they either came and left again or ended up in the storeroom like so many others.

Traveling the river was dangerous, everyone knew. Storms and cutthroats and serpents of the river's wide depths . . . The people of the villages in this bend of the river were well used to donning a wide-eyed innocence. See nothing, hear nothing, speak nothing of their own, not to some uncaring government official from far away.

And every time, once night fell, Li Li and her mother would drag the bodies out into the dark, heaving a growing collection of digging tools along with their burden. They'd discovered, eventually, that a nearby bog provided the most forgiving ground for grave digging, soft muck that would suck down a buried corpse with no outward sign, and that only froze across the very top layer in winter. It still took half the night to drag a body such a distance, and then to excavate enough mud for even a shallow covering. In cold months it might take the whole night, as they broke through the ice to where the swampiness somehow still churned warm beneath.

The river itself might have provided a more secretive maw, but the inn had been built far back from potential spring floodwaters, and an easy walk for a sailor or merchant was not such for dragging a corpse.

Li Li imagined the men's flesh decaying in the bog until their bones settled into the depths and crisscrossed atop each other. Like chopsticks thrown into the bottom of a basin to wash. Stacks of latticed chaos.

It was not until she was fifteen that the Empire sent another magistrate.

The position had remained vacant for so long that the local magisterial compound had become overgrown with knotweed, its ornate scrollwork broken in places and the tiles of its sweeping roof crumbling or chipped away. The retinue that preceded the new magistrate ordered the men of the town to scrape the weeds free and make every meticulous repair, with no mind paid to the labor that would ordinarily occupy their days—the fish that failed to come fat and fresh to market, the crops struggling untended, the dike walls and building stilts in need of this season's maintenance.

A muttering resentment blackened the town. Li Li was old enough now to comprehend it. The people did not need or want a new magistrate—for any rulings, the military governor in the nearest prefectural city could be appealed to, and conveniently, he was so far away and his attention on so many more important matters that here in this bend of the river they could live their lives without interference. The governor's lack of attention might mean he was also no reliable source of justice, but that was all right, too, because this tiny bustling town and its surrounding tiny sprawl of villages and farms could largely oversee itself. Small squabbles were solved by a clean verdict of fists, larger ones sometimes by a gang of one man's friends banging on the other's door in the dark with the silver flash of a knife, or sometimes more civilly by their neighbors dragging them before a wealthy estate like the Mus' for a judgment. The Mu family were not true nobility of the type who had such heaven-granted judicial authority, and their eccentricities and occasional viciousness were well-known, but a decision with their teeth behind it was one all would respect. Most considered it a fair enough court for these parts, out here on the rural reaches of the Four Great River Deltas.

And sometimes, a person who upset the balance of this bend in the river would simply disappear.

Bones in a chopstick pile.

Li Li did not, at this point, remember the previous magistrate very clearly, although somehow the image of his noble hat smashed against the floor had stuck in her mind with the sharpness of recent detail. She could not recall whether they had buried it with him.

The new magistrate arrived off the river amid a great fanfare of silken banners and golden bells, far beyond anything Li Li remembered seeing in the town. But this part of the river had been burgeoning bit by bit, its vibrancy and traffic flourishing, and perhaps someone thought it merited notice. Certainly the sole local inn had lately been humming through every watch of every day.

Most of that work had been falling on Li Li. Her father had grown increasingly absent, more often than not returning only to raid fistfuls of silver from the inn and depart again . . . Even when home, he intruded so much, while completing so little, that it sometimes seemed questionable whether their workload truly lightened with his presence. Her mother still rose at the same time and moved among the same chores, but over the years had faded to a weary remoteness, and Li Li would frequently find her gripping a door frame or a table and staring at nothing.

The last few months the inn had gained the assistance of Li Li's cousin as well—after Li Jun's mother had succumbed to a hemorrhagic fever in late summer. The shipping business had gone to Li Li's father, who promptly sold it to the Mus for a tidy sum. Li Jun had approached her uncle with a humble but passionate argument not to sell, promising she could do the work of the ledgers and even go out as a helmsman herself and report everything back to him. But Li Li's father would not entertain the notion.

"I shall do my responsibility by my brother," he said to her, "and find you a decent marriage contract. A difficult order, I dare to guess. Of course, you're not to blame for how you were raised—if a plant is allowed to grow to weed it will naturally become hardened to proper pruning."

Li Li, eavesdropping as usual, knew her cousin well enough to see Li Jun's posture knot into the tightness of angry defiance, even if she was wise enough not to challenge the uncle who now held control of her life.

Instead, she unloaded in long monologues to Li Li later about how she was going to go off and join the Tongs on their boats for good, just as soon as they would have her. Li Li did not think it likely. Tong women might be just as brawny as the men, saying all hands were needed when scrubbing down a salt barge, but what was accepted on the river was not the same as the ways of the town, and the Tong elders wouldn't pick a fight with Li Li's father.

Practicality would win out. Li Jun might be older, but she had never been practical enough.

Today Li Li let her cousin's usual complaints fade into the background, drowned behind the day's never-ending duties. Her feet ached and her hands had split in stinging cracks from the washing. Her father had chosen to forgo supervising the inn today, as he often did, leaving it to Li Li and her mother and cousin. When Li Li's mother entreated him to please stay and help, this one time—he told her he trusted her, and wasn't that flattering? That he could delegate the family income to her entirely, that it made him proud . . . and she wouldn't prove him wrong, would she?

Li Li's mother flinched and hunched, a hand going to the side of her abdomen. She'd been making that same motion commonly of late.

"Lie down, Auntie," Li Jun said, her face crinkling in concern. "You don't look well. We'll take care of the guests and then bring you some tea and tonic broth."

Li Li had the distinct feeling she ought to have said that first, but she hadn't thought to. A dark scorn spiked as she watched her mother hobble to her room—one that had been biting at Li Li more and more often. Guilt lapped vaguely on its heels: Children were to protect and provide service and support to their forebears; it was what children existed for.

But if her own father wouldn't care for her mother's weaknesses, why should she?

She followed Li Jun to fetch wine for the packed front room of guests. Too many guests. The new magistrate's presence certainly hadn't damped the number of travelers, at least not yet. Some of those travelers would have brought their own provisions for her to cook, but the inn wouldn't have enough meat to feed the rest—not until the Tongs returned with more stores for the town.

Li Li was already bracing for the endless complaints sure to pelt down upon them. The inn had better have enough wine.

She didn't want to know how the men might react if the inn didn't have enough wine.

At the entrance to the storeroom, however, Li Li almost ran

into her cousin's back, where Li Jun stopped stock-still in the doorway.

Piled behind the barrels were the familiar stacked limbs of ever more bodies. Rich clothes, limp hands, slack faces. And this time a very large lot of blood, seeping across the floor as if a barrel of dark fruit wine had spilled across it.

The dangling limbs were too many to easily count. More than her father had ever left them to take care of at once before . . . Li Li's scorn at her mother's weakness sharpened into a white-hot anger at her father. *Does he not realize how long this chore takes?* And now her mother leaving her to it alone . . . !

"Aiya," whispered Li Jun. "Look, it's the new magistrate."

The same swooping black headdress lay a bit apart from the corpse pile. The visceral stamp of the first man, six or seven years ago, had never left Li Li's memory.

"What do we do?" Li Jun asked.

"We clean it up," Li Li said. "That's *our* job. Father does his business, and he says it's his women's job to clean up."

"The other disappearances . . ." Li Jun was clever, which was good, because it saved Li Li time explaining. She had no concern that Li Jun would cause any trouble. Li Jun was of the local populace, and family besides, and everyone knew how the government officials stripped prosperity from the villages and played games with the residents' livelihoods. How pretty women were advised to appear less so when near the eyes of government men, and how their husbands were advised never to step in, lest they lose more than a wife.

"We'll have to deal with it after the guests go to bed," Li Li said, assuming the authority of experience.

As if in response, rowdy shouts erupted from the front room, demanding what was taking so long with the meat and wine. Li Li's eyes crawled over the corpses. A hopelessness wanted to throttle her. How many bodies to drag? How many trenches to dig?

Li Jun seemed to be thinking the same. "Could we get them to the river? I could swim, weight them down in one of the caves . . ."

Li Jun might be older, but she was ignorant of the way dead bodies sagged like sacks of rice in the shape of a man. "We'd need a mule and a cart for that," Li Li said.

They'd need to rid the inn of the bodies the same way they always did. Li Li's fury at her father welled up and up, flooding her. Drowning her.

"Where are those useless wenches?" came a yell from the front room. "Meat, girls, or I'll butcher the lot of you instead!"

Li Li recklessly wondered what would happen if she walked out of the inn and left it all undone. Would her father have to bury his own corpses for a change?

But no, her cousin and her mother would do it, her mother falling and fainting, and though Li Li didn't strictly love her mother, she did feel a familial duty, and the image reeked of an injustice so vast it made her teeth hurt. But the prospect of dragging so many out to bury—and with so many guests who would already keep them up late into the night with demands and complaints, that the wine was too thin or the beds too cold, or that the inn did not have enough meat—

Li Li's eyes flashed wide.

"Cousin?" Li Jun said. "What is it?"

Li Li had begun moving, retrieving the cleavers. Knives in hand, she appraised the body on the top of the pile. It stood to reason a man would not taste different from a goat or a hog.

And she knew how to butcher those.

"You get the wine," she said to Li Jun. "I'll bring the meat."

The guests went to bed full and happy, and the inn even had a surplus of shanks that Li Li placed on hooks as she had been taught. Only this time she took some care to disguise any humanlike foot or hand or expanse of bared and hairy skin.

Once the guests had been calmed and put up, and any repeated whines or calls for yet another cup had been dealt with, Li Jun helped Li Li mop up the blood from the butchering and burn the men's clothes. Tomorrow the guests would not only tell tales of a well-stocked inn, but rhapsodize about how warm the place had been kept on a blustery night. What luxury!

"Your father is a hero," Li Jun said in a hush, as they finished. "I never knew!"

Li Li snorted. "He's not a hero. He only does the easy part."

"Maybe he'd let me help," Li Jun said. She spun the mop to *crack* it against one of the pillars of the back room. "I've done summers with the Tongs keeping ruffians off their boats, and I'm just as good with a knife as them. My mother said she'd marry me to the first boy who could swim longer than me or beat me in a fistfight, and I'm not married, am I? And the Weng boy drowned trying!"

Li Jun loved telling that story.

"You oughtn't be so proud of not being married," Li Li said. "Your parents are dead. Now you're dependent on charity until you do find a husband."

Li Jun's eyes narrowed. "Why, though? The Tong sisters are going to take over the salt barges eventually, their father said so, and the Mus don't have a son, either, and they taught their daughters to hunt tigers. We aren't any weaker than them. Besides, you're right, you and your mother run the whole inn, your father doesn't do anything. I bet I could do his other 'business' just fine, too." She made a stabbing gesture in the air. "I've heard of groups of female bandits in the hills. Maybe I'll go join them."

Li Li had heard such tales, too. She wasn't sure she'd like that. Women annoyed her just as much as men, most days. She wasn't even sure she *was* a real woman; she seemed to be cursed in some way—her women's monthly water still had never come, at this point surely backing up its toxins into her blood. Meanwhile, the eyes of the boys in the town skimmed past and through her, which was just as well since she was repulsed by them in turn. She was old enough now that Li Jun and the Tongs bragged openly in front of her of their ever-escalating obscene exploits—Li Li was pretty sure they'd even "done things" with *each other* while out on the boats, which they said didn't count. Li Li was unclear on whether this was because they were all girls, or if because they were all involved then none of them could score anything above the others, but all of it sounded so distinctly unenjoyable that she secretly dreamed of worming her way out of ever sharing a marriage bed.

Sometimes men didn't get married. Rarely, but sometimes. Maybe she could become a man. Gossip said one of the Mu daughters had done that the other way around, but rules were different for rich eccentrics who taught their daughters to fight tigers.

The River Judge

"I could be a bandit," Li Jun was saying. "A hero of the hills. Like your father, but not leaving all the work to the womenfolk. I bet I'd be great at it."

She produced a knife and threw it in one move. The blade buried itself in a doorjamb across the room, the handle vibrating with the force of it.

Li Li walked over and wrenched it out. "You'd better not say such things when the Imperial investigators arrive."

Her cousin's expression went shocked and tense. Maybe from nervousness. Maybe eagerness.

Li Li sighed and handed the blade back. "Just don't say anything, right? They'll come eat all our food and go away again."

Unless my father kills them first, she added silently.

Li Li had spent no serious worry over her cousin knowing the truth. But she ought to have remembered a far deeper concern than Li Jun telling tales about what she knew: Her cousin was uncontrollable.

Without consulting Li Li at all, she conspired with the Tong sisters, who had just come back downriver with their family. The Tong girls spread wild rumors of a wakening water demon among the surrounding towns, and Li Jun plunged into the deep, gray fathoms of the river and swam below every one of the investigators' boats during the last days of their approach, holding her breath so long they neither saw a ripple of her arrival nor when she surfaced afterward.

When the investigators disembarked at the inn they jumped at every small sound, dark moons pressed out beneath their eyes and their fine beards and caps awry.

"*Something knocking at our boats—*"

"*A river demon, everyone is saying so!*"

"*It must have been that which devoured the magistrate and his men, we mustn't stay long . . .*"

"*It's this place, this place is surely cursed!*"

Li Jun came back to the inn rather insufferable. "I fixed it all, didn't I?" she bragged. "See, I *told* you I'd make a good hero."

"It's not done yet," Li Li said. "And you should have asked first. This isn't some game."

"Stop being such a mud-stuck clam," Li Jun said. "They swallowed it like fish bait. They're going to leave and no one is ever going to come back to bother us, you watch!"

Such a plan might have worked. Even Li Li had to admit it, though she refused to say so aloud.

If only it hadn't been for the ghost.

After so many years of corpses, Li Li had ceased to worry about ghosts. She knew ghosts could enter the world at times, everyone knew such a thing, but they were so rare, and so often mysterious in their methods of manifestation, and as likely to bestow beneficence as to make trouble. More importantly, Li Li's father had been killing people for enough years that Li Li had become jaded to the possibility that one might return.

Until this magistrate did.

He didn't visit in dreams, the way Li Li's ancestors had on brief flickering occasions. He didn't make his presence known through strange events, either cursed or blessed, nor did he return as animal or insect, nor through cold or wind.

He came as a shadow.

The inn was abuzz with it the next day, the day the investigators had been hastening to depart, with their report of the magistrate's demise via river demon. But four of the six investigators had seen the magistrate in the night, along with another three guests.

They talked in hushed voices of his shadow sliding silently out from cracks in the darkness.

Reluctantly, the delegation's leader determined that they must remain longer and seek communication with the apparition. He assigned himself and one of his men to depart to a neighboring town to find a spirit medium, giving his other four unhappy subordinates strict instructions to keep watch for the ghost.

Traveling for a medium would take at least a full day and night. The four remaining investigators lurked sour and white-faced around the inn, and Li Li tried to go about her duties as if she did not feel the weight of a dozen panthers scrambling up her back. Her cousin was even jumpier.

"What if he tells them somehow?" Li Jun whispered while

they cleaned out the lodging rooms, no matter how Li Li tried to shush her. "What if he can tell them who killed him?"

"My father's gone again anyway," Li Li said. As had become his habit, he had disappeared up- or downriver before any investigation descended.

But the thought snuck up from her heart, in the greatest of familial betrayals: No great loss, if they do come for him. After all, hadn't Li Jun said herself how Li Li and her mother were the ones who truly ran the inn?

If the investigators took her father away . . .

No more long absences while only returning to yell at Li Li and her mother or plunder the inn's savings. No more finding fault with their work while barely moving to help with the inn's chores, only drinking and heckling and reminding them that it all came from him.

No more bodies left in the storeroom for them to clean up at the most inconvenient times, while he alone raked in the whispered adulation of any in the town who knew.

Her prior disrespectful words had been nothing but truth: Her father only did the easy part. Any of them could kill a man just as well, couldn't they? It didn't take some great skill to stab into rich soft skin that was sopped with beef and potent rice wine, did it?

She made a retreat into the kitchen and ground tea and cardamom and pepper, too much and too fast until she struck too hard and the pestle cracked.

She stopped. Forced herself to stillness. The spices had scattered across the counter.

Maybe, with her father gone, her mother might cease being so sick and weak all the time. At least her mother worked hard. At least she did what needed doing. A small, fleeting part of Li Li wondered if, with her father gone, her mother might become a figure she would gladly pay daughterly duties toward.

Besides, Li Li was discovering that she despised injustice even more than weakness. Not because of any soul-deep sympathy for her family and neighbors, but because of the way it added up so wrong and out of joint, like a ledger that wouldn't match itself. The world ought to balance.

It ought to, and it never did. The rich government officials took whatever they wanted, and Li Li's father killed whomever he wanted, with Li Li and her mother crunched in the fissures of it all and working their hands to bleeding.

She returned to her chores and allowed herself to imagine a future where her father met some timely end. With his nuisance removed, her mother could gain widow's rights to the inn, the same as Li Jun's mother had. They'd finally be able to run it in peace, doing a hard day's work and then retiring to bed without worry . . .

Thus it was that when Li Li came into the back storeroom to lock everything up for the night, and she saw the great swooping headdress shadowed on the wall by a light that came from nowhere, she stopped cold and still as a rock but did not turn away.

Li Li stared at the shadow. She did not feel afraid.

The inn was quiet. The remaining guests would be in bed, trying to sleep—or failing to sleep, what with word of a ghost about. Most had fled with nervousness at such an interaction, leaving the rooms near-empty for once.

The shadow elongated slightly, the body growing taller and thinner. Somehow, the magisterial headdress simultaneously stretched wider, until its authority yawned to near comical levels.

"Do you speak?" Li Li inquired finally.

The shadow was silent.

"Are you here for vengeance against my father?"

Again, no reply. No movement.

Li Li wondered if the magistrate even knew her father had been the one to assassinate him. When she'd chopped through the gristle of the body, she'd noted the knife wound that gaped between the back ribs.

If the ghost didn't know who had been responsible for such an end, she supposed she had now told. But the shadow had not extinguished itself.

What else might it be seeking?

With a start, she wondered if her own actions had caused this manifestation. Cooking human flesh . . . could such a thing release a restless ghost? After all, even among the ardent admirers of her father's activities, most would frown on what she had done.

The thought made her angry. *Those* men had not been working their hands raw to help ill mothers defray exhaustion when dumped with such inconvenient corpses, and she was sure how they would judge her nonetheless. But her solution wasn't of some inferior moral character. It was *clever*.

"They won't find your remains," she declared to the ghost. "If it's my father you want to point at, though—is that it? Is that what you're looking for? Well, if he didn't want anything found, he should have done it himself. The old magistrate, the one before you—he's buried in the yard out by the larch tree, and anyone who—"

The shadow winked out.

Li Li stood in the empty night, stood long enough for her feet to grow stiff against the unmoving ground, stood stiller than any rock face on a carven mountain. The strange righteousness that had filled her had burst as suddenly as it appeared, leaving a vague void behind.

She'd told on her father. Her family, her elder. Her *father*. An act against Benevolence, against nature, even more than eating human flesh.

She should be flooded with guilt and shame.

Instead, something had begun to sizzle and bubble within the emptiness like when the river churned with typhoon-fed floods.

Something very like excitement. Or power.

The inn was awoken by screams.

Li Li struggled out of sleep in disorientation, deep dreams still snatching at her. The light had begun to turn, almost at dawn—almost when she would have been rising anyway—

Someone screamed again. Li Li was struck by the sudden instant certainty that the scream belonged to her mother.

She was on her feet without being fully awake, racing outside without proper outerwear or boots, her breath fogging with the late-autumn cold and her ears ringing with the aftermath of those screams. The first edges of dawn cracked weak and watery over the yard.

Others from the inn were stumbling out into these last dregs of night. The few guests who had remained—and Li Jun, too, wrapped hastily in a blanket, the Tong sisters with her, strapping young women who stood with the confidence that they were no longer children. Li Li hadn't known they'd stayed over with Li Jun; they usually lived out of their boats.

Li Li's eyes raked across the yard—and found her mother.

Her mother, who knelt a few paces before the larch tree, her worn thinness suddenly in such sharp relief that her fragility seemed shocking. Someone had chipped up the clay beside her.

The four remaining Imperial investigators surrounded the shallow grave beneath. One leaned a pickaxe haft against his hip, another had discarded a spade upon the ground. In the pitted earth, a half-unburied human skull stared from naked and collapsed sockets. His fine clothes had turned to dust, roots twining through where his flesh had been. But somehow the swooping magistrate's hat was still as broad and black and fine as the day his corpse had appeared in their storeroom.

Within Li Li, the surprise of it warred with smug satisfaction. She'd told the ghost, and the ghost had communicated to them, even with no spirit medium to interpret.

Now the scales will balance. Everyone will get what they deserve.

"Explain this, innkeeper," said one of the investigators to Li Li's mother. He bit the words so sharply that spit flew forth with them.

Li Li's mother hunched over against the ground, shaking her head over and over, not in defiance but desperation. Her breath keened high and hard, so fast she couldn't seem to speak.

Li Li did not feel sympathy. Her mother had always reacted with overly high humors. Once the investigators had taken Li Li's father away, and the inn slipped back to normal, all this frenzy would recede and everything would turn calm.

One of the other men turned to his partners. "The snake cannot move without the head—the husband must also be involved. Bind her and take her to the magistrate's compound. The chief will decide if they face justice here or if it's to be prisoner transport to Bianliang."

The words took many heartbeats to coalesce into meaning, so contrary were they to Li Li's expectations. Why would they—but her mother hadn't—

They *assumed*—

Li Li began to call out—what, she hadn't determined; she only knew that this was not the way she had meant anything to go. Before she could, her mother launched herself at the feet of one of the investigators.

The motion was one of supplication. As if to clutch at their hems and press her face upon their boots in weeping entreaty.

The man's lip lifted in a sneer. In that moment, with a movement that was almost casually slow, he moved the pickaxe from against the side of his leg.

The head of the tool thumped against the ground in front of him. Directly in the path of Li Li's mother as she fell at his feet.

The dirt-clodded spike of the pickaxe plunged through the soft skin just below her jaw.

Her cries cut off with a wet crunch. Her limbs flopped boneless against the ground in the sudden silence.

"Stupid woman," said the investigator. "At least now we won't have to—"

A choked gurgle cut him off as the edge of the spade *thunked* straight into his throat.

The investigator struggled against suddenly folding limbs, his eyes casting about in confusion. He hadn't seen Li Li grab the spade off the ground. Hadn't seen her heave it upward with all her strength.

People always underestimated her strength.

She yanked the spade back from his neck, and blood fountained forth, more than she'd ever seen when butchering animal or human. The other three investigators had begun to move by then, hands fumbling for the blades at their sides. Li Jun's knife took one of them in the chest. The Tongs tackled another with a shout, pounding him into the earth. The last man stumbled in his shock, and Li Li heaved the spade again.

Its dull metal rang hard against his skull.

He clattered onto the ground. Li Jun dove in to grab the man's own short sword, and she plunged it through his body as if driving a fence post.

The Tongs stood up. The elder of them pressed a nonchalant hand against a bloody slash that gaped her forearm open. The younger gripped a jagged rock in one hand. Bits of white bone shone through the face of the man unmoving below them.

The elder Tong sister jerked a chin at the inn's few patrons who had braved the haunted night. Three of them, all men, watching with slack jaws and wide eyes—two merchants from off the river and one man from a neighboring village who'd stayed to sleep off his drink.

"We'll have to kill them, too," the elder Tong said. "They saw."

"No—please, we won't—" started one of the merchants, at the same time the other began to shout, "How dare—!"

Li Jun's newly retrieved knife found the shouting man in the liver.

The man who had begged broke into a panicked run, but the younger Tong dropped her rock to grab one of the short swords and caught up with him easily. She loped back over to join her sister and Li Jun in surrounding the final man.

"Wait," Li Li said.

The others stopped, their expressions aggressive questions. The only sound came from the still-dying merchant whose gut Li Jun had buried her knife in; he curled on the ground with moans ever more thready and pitiful. One of the cocks crowed suddenly, calling out the start of the day in an unsettling contrast.

Li Li approached the local man. "You're not from off the river," she said. "Do you know what my father did here?"

His chin trembled in a nod, his ragged mustache shaking. "I heard—rumors, miss. Only rumor."

"Would you ever have told men like these?" She pointed back at the dead investigators.

Shock suffused his face. "Of course not! Never."

"Good. Speak nothing of this, either. Remember what protection this place has given you."

"Yes, miss. Of course, miss. We are all loyal to your father, miss."

Li Li tasted bitterness at that, and her hand twitched to complete the violence here, but she held the judgment at bay. Instead, she said, "Go home to your family."

He wasted no time in scrambling away, backing up with jerky bows. By that time the man on the ground had stopped moving. Everything had stopped moving.

Li Li let the edge of the spade fall to the dirt, let her hand grip tightly against its haft. She didn't want to turn around. Didn't want to look at her mother's body.

She didn't want to look at the rest of the bodies, either. *So much to clean up . . .*

She hadn't meant for anything to go this way.

But she hadn't started any of it, either. That had been the investigator, and the vile officials before him, and most of all—

Li Jun stepped over and rested a hand against her shoulder. "You did right. None of this was your fault."

"I know," Li Li said. "It's my father's."

Rumor said that when the investigators' leader learned his four subordinates had been devoured by the river demon, he and his right-hand man scurried straight back to the capital, convinced they had enough for their report after all.

Rumor said the capital seemed prone to forget the magisterial post existed, after that. Or perhaps they tried to assign men to it and failed, until a harried minister looked at the judiciary lists and decided leaving one remote bend of the river to the military governor was good enough.

Rumor also, however, now knew the name of Li Li's father, and knew embroidered stories of a skeleton found beneath his inn, stories whispered as often in admiration as in judgment. They were carefully never whispered where they might reach the ears of Bianliang—not that they likely would have been deemed important, by those far away whose wish was to ignore such a troublesome rural town. Even so, Li Li sometimes wondered if she'd been wise in sparing the local villager's life. Her generosity was returned to her, however, when still other rumors reported how her father heard the tales being told of his name and how he shook with fear as he ran. He fled toward the western mountains with no glance back at the inn or the living daughter he left behind.

The daughter was just fine with that.

Li Li and Li Jun smartened up the inn with some help from the Tongs, and Li Li made certain to declare to the right ears that her father's other "business" was finished and had disappeared along with him. Most took this to mean that no more skeletons would be buried in the inn's yard, and indeed, none ever were again.

The law technically provided no way for Li Li to come into ownership of the inn, as her father was still alive, and even if he had not been, as an unmarried daughter she would not inherit. In this bend of the river that lacked a magistrate, however, no one was too fussed about each and every stroke of law. Li Li declared that of course she must keep up the inn for her father in his absence, and that was enough for most people not to question.

If any questions did arise, they were not heard for long before mysteriously going silent.

Thus, for the next four years the inn at the bend in the river gradually became even busier and more prosperous, growing into a well-known stop for hungry traders. And if gossip whispered anything else about the inn and its young proprietor, it was wise enough not to whisper too loud.

Four years was how long it took for Li Li's father to decide the law would no longer remember his name, and then to return to claim his wealth.

Li Li was wiping down tables when his shadow loomed up in the door. He stepped inside with his chest puffed out in assumed ownership, then stood in the center of the clean and polished front room, fists on his hips. His eyes crawled over the walls and tables, the customers comfortably tucking in food and wine, the expanded wings that had been added on with their newly carved wooden screens and the delicate brushwork scrolls Li Li had hung upon the walls for both aesthetics and luck.

His shape sucked away the smooth balance of the space more than any shadow from beyond the grave. Cold gripped Li Li's heart, as if another ghost had entered her home.

That's all this man was. A ghost.

She straightened her clothes and approached him. From the way his eyes slid uncertainly she could tell he did not recognize her until she said, "Hello, Father."

His smile slipped, just a touch, before it shuddered back into place. "I see my inn is not as well-kept as it could be, but not ruined. Good girl. I knew you'd handle things until I returned."

Li Li had come to consider her natural lack of expression to be an asset for just such moments as these. No stirrings showed on her face.

"You must be so tired," she said to her father. "Come into a private room. I'll bring you a meal."

He grunted and took what he considered his due. Li Li served him stew and steamed buns and noodles simmered in sauce, along with the inn's most fragrant wine. He rambled on about how he'd returned to sell the property, as innkeeping life no longer fit him.

When did it fit you? thought Li Li. *When have you ever kept the inn?*

"I have a few buyers nibbling about. And I don't want you to worry; I'm only considering the ones who are also willing to bring a bride price. We'll get this business done."

Li Li barely blinked at the casual assumption she would be sold off as a rich man's concubine. This must be what it felt like, to have power.

"I've been doing your business," she said instead.

Her father's wine-glazed eyes wobbled over to her, uncomprehending.

"*Both* your businesses," Li Li added silkily.

She pulled up a chair and sat beside him, leaning in against the table as if they shared secrets in a conspiracy. "Let's be truthful, Father. You never did those businesses yourself, anyway. I've been doing both since the beginning. For ten years now."

Her father licked his lips, a quicksilver nervousness darting through his eyes for the first time.

"You're feeling heavy," Li Li said. "That's a mineral sleeping powder in the wine. It's very potent."

And made everything much more tidy and convenient, she'd come to find.

It took a moment for her father's eyes to grow wet and wide, and then he jerked as if to lurch up or swipe at her before falling heavily back in the chair. "Can't. You . . ." His lips flapped against the words until they were unintelligible.

"None of this was ever yours." Li Li's voice became a slither. "I saw so clearly, by the end. You claimed ownership but left every meaningful task to us. Because this bit now, it's no work at all, is it? To kill a man who's soft with meat and wine, and only full of air and words."

Her father tried to answer. Fear suffused every line of his face.

Li Li's knife moved with the whispering speed borne of four years of practice.

That night, Li Li straightened her inn with great care. She had plenty of meat stored up for the inn's travelers—the ones who would leave to travel onward, rather than those who would best serve by staying on her hooks to fill the bellies of the next . . . those she judged to be too much like magistrates or fathers, or the rude oglers or complainers who demeaned and demanded.

The inn never wanted for traffic, here on this busy bend of the river. If not everyone made it up- or downstream, well, everyone knew the river was dangerous. Full of cutthroats and smugglers and undertows and ghosts and demons.

And Li Li. Who met and judged, just like a magistrate.

Tonight, however, she made a very special soup only for herself.

She waited for Li Jun to come back from the river—to come back from making the river more dangerous, as one of those smugglers and cutthroats who caused so many to hoard their silver in fear. Today she came from accompanying the Tongs upriver, returning with hulls that bulged with silver and salt and spices, dried fish and pickled vegetables . . . all "donations" from choice estates, as Li Jun laughingly liked to say. She and Li Li added her share of the silver to a lockbox below the inn floor, alongside the establishment's own quickly expanding riches.

The inn was becoming impressively flush. Nobody had ever asked how the two cousins had come to run it, or how they had achieved such success. At least, nobody had asked for long.

The River Judge

Li Jun had spoken with great prescience, those years ago: They did a very good job without any husbands at all. Or fathers.

Tonight, Li Li left her cousin in charge, and she carried her freshly made soup up to her mother's grave on a hilltop overlooking the town. The streets and buildings spread out below, multiplying outward in a slow creep every season as the town expanded. Beyond them the river stretched wide and fathomless, a muddy gray-gold snake draped across the landscape, the farms on the other side tiny at this distance.

Li Li sat with her mother, and she leaned against an ash tree and drank her special soup while she watched the sun set.

Her home had never felt so peaceful.

CARLIE ST. GEORGE

The Weight of Your Own Ashes
FROM *Clarkesworld*
SCIENCE FICTION

ALICE WANTS TO hold a funeral for me, which is disconcerting because I'm not dead. But humans, like all aliens—and certainly all single-forms—have their own idiosyncrasies.

I'm used to the idiosyncrasies, of course: I've lived on Earth—in my tertiary body, at least—since my hatching in San Francisco, grew up in a cramped apartment in North Beach and am very much a Californian, an American, and an Earthling, if not a human. (I refuse the terms Earther and Terran, which may be in fashion but have no charm.) I can't pretend it was always easy growing up here, and humans do have specific biological quirks that will forever baffle me: sweat, for one, and also the garbled hallucinations more commonly referred to as dreams. But despite its many abhorrent flaws, Earth—like any other world—also has its small joys, its thousand little wonders that you simply can't find anywhere else. Garlic bread, for instance, and dim sum. Butterflies. Magnolia trees. Trick-or-treating. Kandinsky paintings. It's my culture, just not my only culture. My home, my life—but only one of four.

Well. One of three, now.

Three weeks ago, I died in a catastrophic bus accident on my way to UC Berkeley; simultaneously, I was hibernating on Myr in my primary body, hibernating on Banquo in my quinary body, and meal prepping on the *Valorous Raccoon* in my secondary body. (The literal name of *Valorous Raccoon* is closer to *Scav-*

enger Animal That is Righteously Courageous, but more often than not, I prefer my own translations.) Dying has a way of grabbing your full attention; for several minutes, I lost all awareness of my secondary body before forcefully slamming back into it. Fortunately, shock allowed me the emotional distance needed to compose two Earthbound messages: one to my doctoral advisor, apologizing for not making our meeting, and one to Alice, reminding her not to worry—yes, my tertiary body had died, but I was fine and already working on travel arrangements back to Earth, and if she could just make sure my remains—whatever was left of them—were delivered to a reputable alien-friendly mortuary, I would handle everything else. Then, instead of making those arrangements, I had a small breakdown on the galley floor when my captain walked in and, concerned, asked if I was okay.

But that was weeks ago. I'm feeling much better now. It's Alice who's struggling, really.

I knew there would be *some* awkwardness, of course, especially as my bodies vary in form. I'd wanted to leave Banquo behind, considering the only thing I'd miss about that icy hell-rock was Jwa—but my quinary body is a fraternal body, for lack of a better English term: male, with a brightly feathered crown, and noticeably shorter than my female forms—which *are* identical, save the odd injury, cosmetic choice, and level of sun exposure. It'd be . . . easier for everyone, I told myself, if I left the *Valorous Raccoon* instead. Alice, especially, might have trouble recognizing me as *me* if I suddenly showed up as a man—and I would be a man because I use male pronouns in that body. (Some well-meaning human friends have described me as trans, but I'm not entirely convinced the label fits and often find difficulty translating my gender in English, despite having spoken the language all my life. Simultaneously living in several different bodies and cultures means simultaneously experiencing several different gender norms and expressions, and it can be difficult to translate those multi-bodied experiences to fit a single-form's conceptions and expectations of gender.)

The primary differences between my secondary and tertiary bodies are these: tattoos (my secondary body has none), skin color (milk white rather than a near-human alabaster), crown and cape colors (red and white feathers rather than black and white), and a significant limp (my left hip is slightly fucked from a fall that my tertiary body never experienced). Otherwise, my features are identical, my weight very similar, my eyes still round and dark. I stopped wearing my dark eye makeup in favor of neutrals, my tank tops and coveralls in favor of vests and plaids. I don't look like some long-lost sister. I look like *Yonder*. I look like *me*.

But Alice doesn't see me anymore.

We met years ago in grad school. Same field of study, cultural xenology, but with different focuses: Alice's primary interest is culinary traditions, whereas my dissertation—if I ever finish it—is on comparative ghost stories. There are a surprising number of nonhumans in the program, given Earth's rather dismal nonhuman population, but I'm the only Myriad student at UC Berkeley, and it can be . . . disheartening to see how even other species react when they realize I'm not single-bodied like them. It's not like junior high, at least—we're all too horrifically busy for that sort of active bullying; instead, it's the casual slur, the occasional shudder, the inappropriate question, or wildly incorrect assumption that would be insulting from anybody, but is *especially* egregious from other xenology students—and often faculty, too.

Alice, though, has always been different. Her immediate questions were not about masturbation, nor did she play devil's advocate to "prove" that I was a liar, deluded, or inorganic; mostly, her questions were about food. Alice made me comfortable. Alice made me laugh, and when I eventually did share pictures of my other bodies, Alice looked at them with wonder, rather than horror, and I thought—I really thought—

Dying is no small thing. I never expected it to be easy. But when I stepped off the shuttle, when I finally got through customs and saw her again with my own two eyes . . . I thought Alice would hold me. I thought she would say my name and cling.

Instead, Alice flinched and looked away.

*

Now I'm here, standing in my living room, holding my own urn. "It's not right," Alice says from behind me. "She—I mean, *you*—you *died*. It's not fair that you won't let me mourn."

Is that what I'm doing? It doesn't feel like it. I've never thought of myself as controlling before. It's not the kind of person I want to be—who am I, to dictate someone else's heart? Still, what is there to mourn? I'm *here*.

This isn't the first time I've died. It's the second—or fourth, depending how you count. My biological mother laid seven eggs, but one never hatched, and another was obliterated when a fire destroyed an entire incubation center. Thankfully, the other eggs were scattered throughout the stars: There's a reason Myriads say *scatter the nests or shatter the shells*—a proverb usually translated as *don't put all your eggs in one basket*, but again, this lacks poetry.

I can't remember my egg deaths, but I *do* remember dying as a child: A devastating illness swept through my lunar colony, causing terrible skin sores and mouth lesions. All my feathers fell out, and I remember hibernating as much as possible: The doctors had hoped it would heal my quaternary body, though at the time, I was mostly concerned with avoiding the pain. Unfortunately, dying often triggers a kind of hypnagogic jerk, a last-ditch survival reflex, so rather than sleeping through my death, well. One moment I was awake in my tertiary body, playing tag with my siblings in Washington Square—and in the next, I was *also* awake on that far-off moon, bleeding from my gums and writhing from a terrible, crushing agony as my two tiny hearts gave out. *I'm scared*, I remember thinking, as blurry hands and faces frantically rushed around me. *It hurts; I'm SCARED—*

And then my quaternary body died, and I was back in San Francisco again, on hands and knees in the dirt, gasping, with my littlest sibling, Gray, screaming their head off for our parents.

Was I cremated back then? I don't know. It doesn't matter so much, only—it's a strange thing, to see your own remains, to know the weight of your own ashes.

"It doesn't have to be a human funeral," Alice says, more gently. "You know that, right?"

I do. Alice has proved more than willing to participate in customs both outside her own specific upbringing (white, Protestant, Upper West Side) and outside the greater human culture in general (largely isolationist, and . . . rural, for lack of a better word). We've tried so many new things together: Martian séance festivals, galactic liquor tastings, the perplexingly named orbital bungee jump (*never* do this). Alice has always been curious, respectful, game for anything. If I wanted to hold a specifically Myriad funeral, I'm sure she would willingly participate.

But that's not the problem. The problem is—outside of a few frankly strange religious denominations—Myriads don't *have* funerals for their tertiary bodies, or *any* body save the final one. The whole idea of it is . . . odd. Unsettling. Like having a funeral for an amputated limb.

"Actually," Alice says, when I tell her this. "There *are* humans who bury lost limbs."

Disconcerting. Not the practice, itself, but the fact that I've lived here my whole life and never knew that: never been to a leg funeral, never read a single story where a character's limb was laid to rest—or, better yet, became a haunted limb because it *wasn't* laid to rest. I could live until I'm a hundred and sixty and still miss so much of the world. It fills me with dread, some days; I don't know how single-bodied species handle it. At least, I have four bodies to walk with, see with, taste with.

Had. I had four bodies.

Yes, there's something to mourn. There's something for *me* to mourn, but Alice—

"Anyway," Alice says, "this isn't just an arm, Y—you know. It's your *body*. It *died*."

I remember, I almost snap, because I *do* remember—pinned, bleeding, and extremely conscious when the bus went up in flames. *I'm scared, it hurts, I'm SCARED*, and then—

Boom.

But that's not the problem, either. It's not that I died, because I'm still alive. It's not the annoying dash of existentialism, the useless smidgeon of trauma. Those things, I can manage. Badly, perhaps, but I can handle them.

But Alice won't say my name anymore, and I don't know how to handle that at all.

I start to argue, but Alice begins crying again, and it's just . . . easier, ultimately, to compromise. That's what relationships are, right? I need to be reasonable about this. No, I won't do a large ceremony. Yes, we can do a sea service. Yes, Alice can say a few words while I scatter the gray clumps of my tertiary body to the water below.

What Alice says, weeping:

"Yonder, I love you. I miss you."

Like she's alone by the water. Like I'm a ghost, after all.

The next few weeks are . . . difficult.

Alice is avoiding me, which is challenging, considering that we live together. She stares at me, but won't *look* at me. She'll speak to me, but never touch me. Sex isn't an issue, fortunately, as we rarely bother fucking anyway: Alice is a "sex is fine, but what about tiramisu" ace, and my sex drive only kicks in twice a year. But I already miss holding her. I miss how softly she pets my feathers. I miss snuggling close while watching some whodunit, exchanging increasingly outlandish theories and laughing into her shoulder whenever we're both wrong.

Everyone reacts differently to traumatic events. I'm trying to imagine this from Alice's point of view, which is difficult because Alice will only ever die once. That scares me, if I think about it too much. It's not just her, either: Gray, my *VR* crew. My human parents, who I already lost. Our relationship was . . . complicated . . . but when they died, that was it: no second chances.

When I think about losing Alice like that, I ache to grasp her tightly with both hands and feet. But Alice doesn't need that. She needs time, space. I can give her that. I can stop being selfish and give her that.

"I swear to Christ, if you call yourself selfish one more time," Gray says.

Gray is my only sibling who still lives in the Bay Area. There are five of us, all adopted: Gray is the youngest, human and Chinese American, and dresses in whatever historical fashion they're interested in at the time: Lately, it's all dyed mullets and bright colors, very queer glam rock. We had little in common as children, but as adults, we've bonded over a bitter and grief-struck love for parents who raised us, loved us, but wouldn't accept our names. (It's not quite the same, of course: I don't consider Felicity a deadname. I did once have five given names, after all, and unlike Gray, it doesn't hurt me to hear them—but choosing one or more for yourself *is* an important Myriad rite of passage, and the fact that my human parents found that disrespectful, inconsequential—that *did* hurt.)

Gray is here providing moral support via empanadas while I focus on my other post-death problems: paperwork. There is an unholy amount of it. This would be true even if I was simply and irrevocably dead, America being a melting pot of bureaucratic nightmares, but is wildly complicated by my status as both living and nonliving. Three bodies, one consciousness! How is that so difficult? It's not like state, federal, and planetary governments haven't had time to prepare! First Contact (between our species, at least) was over ninety years ago, and yet here we are—with forms for new ID cards and new health insurance and even national *and* global visa applications because, suddenly, it's become unclear if I count as either a US or Earth citizen, as my secondary body—this body—was born on a planet in the distant Red Fox galaxy.

"So, you're trying to keep from getting deported *off-planet*," Gray says, "and your girlfriend can't even bother hugging you 'cause you've got red feathers and a limp now?"

"No ink, either," I say, too bitterly. All week, Alice had kept fetching me cardigans, even though Earth still feels very warm in this body. I'd assumed it was residual anxiety, overprotectiveness—Alice has always had something of a sweetly chivalrous streak. Turns out, she's simply discomfited by the sight of my bare arms.

Be fair, I remind myself. "It's complicated."

"It's weak," Gray says. "*She's* weak."

I smile. Gray has always been stubborn, bull-hearted, righteously indignant. As a child, I'd found those qualities very tedious; now, I love them for it. "It must be strange," I force myself to say, reluctantly. "Seeing me this way, for her *and* for you—"

Gray leans back. The flat line of their red mouth speaks annoyance. The high lift of their red eyebrow says, *bitch, remember to whom you speak.*

I laugh. Still. "It's not the same, and you know it. When you used to have nightmares—"

"Ugh, you *promised* to stop bringing that up—"

"I didn't hold you with these arms," I remind them. "When we played tag, I wasn't in this body. You've never held these hands before. Can you honestly say—"

"Yes," Gray says, and immediately takes my hand.

I stop.

"Sure," Gray says. "It's strange. So? Who gives a shit? Lots of things are strange for a while, and then we get used to them—or else we stay limited and narrow and fucking sad."

Gray's grip is firm and reassuring, and I swallow, unexpectedly emotional. I've missed this; I've really missed someone else touching this skin. Desperately, I will my body not to do anything weird, like grip Gray's hand even tighter, or—God help me—cry. "I'm trying. I'm really trying to give Alice time to—"

"No," Gray says. "This isn't new behavior. Alice has always been limited."

I frown. That's not true. Alice is open, adventurous. Alice and I are partners; we *grow* together—I thought we did, at least. "That's not what you said when she moved in with me. *And then they were roommates*, you said."

"Yeah, 'cause you're my sister, and I'll support you even when you make lousy decisions with your heart—but I haven't *liked* Alice since she refused to go meet your *Raccoon* fam."

I wince. "It's complicated," I say, which is annoying because I'm repeating excuses. "She *did* want to meet them," I say, which has the benefit of being true. "I don't know how you got the idea that Alice is some sort of bigot, but—"

Gray waves their free hand. "Yeah, whatever, she's probably not a *horrible* person. But come on. You always worry about her feelings. When does she worry about yours?"

That's not true, either. Is it? Doesn't Alice worry about me?

Gray lets go of my hand, and—entirely without meaning to—I grab them again, clinging. Then *I* try to pull back, embarrassed—but Gray refuses to let go.

"She loves me," I say, and hate how uncertain my voice sounds. She *does* love me, a version of me, but maybe—
"Okay," Gray says, the unspoken words clear: *if you say so.* "But Yonder . . . does she *know* you?"
And I can't answer the question.

I do eventually make a solid dent in the paperwork and set up an appointment with an immigration lawyer. Gray helps (the empanadas do, too), but by the time they leave, my hip has gone stiff, and the stress and frustration has built into a deep ache between my shoulder blades. I take a mild painkiller, turn on some Vivaldi (*Nisi Dominus*, to be specific), and collapse onto my bed, whilst simultaneously waking up my primary and quinary bodies. I stare up at three different ceilings: taupe (here), brick red (Banquo), and something close to fuchsia (Myr). A few weeks ago, I would have seen gunmetal gray, too, and I miss it, the *Valorous Raccoon*. I even miss things I used to hate, like the gravity going haywire and rebooting in the middle of meal prep, all my diced vegetables floating—and then all my diced vegetables fucked.

I might never see my canteen again if I stay in this body in this life.

But I made my choice, didn't I? Music keeps me from wallowing: I turn on some chime-pop on Banquo and grunge-hymns on Myr and listen to the wondrous mesh of discordant melodies, a habit that Alice has always found strange. *Isn't it jarring,* she asks, and it can be—loud, unpleasant, overwhelming. But you can also create such *symphonies,* and there can be such lovely surprises, too, when a chant, a clacking, and a lullaby synchronize into something unlikely and transcendent. I love art that is created this way, collages and remixes of . . . anything, really: music, monologues, poetry, prayer, color. There's a beauty in capturing multiple sensations over space and time—and, it should go without saying, drugs are best experienced like this, too.

I hate listening to multiple conversations, Alice says, and it's true: Myriads are more biologically suited to that sort of thing: I can hold multiple conversations at once, provided they're simple enough, and complete multiple small tasks, so long as they don't require any serious focus. Most things do require focus, of course, and so mostly I alternate bodies—but there is a *glory* in these small moments of being fully awake as no single-bodied can be.

Hey, Alice sometimes says—no, she's saying it right now. "Hey."

I sit up. Alice is leaning in the bedroom doorway, watching me fondly. No, wistfully—with love, yes, but also with loss.

Alice sits beside me. On Banquo and Myr, I turn down the music. I could go back into hibernation, but I don't want to; I don't *feel* like it. I feel—

Hip-sore (here). Hungry (Myr). Thirsty (Banquo). Cold (Banquo). Frustrated (everywhere). Anxious (everywhere). Tired (everywhere).

Alice, very tentatively, takes my hand. My breath catches.

"I know it's been . . . difficult lately," she says. "That I've been distant. I'm sorry."

I exhale, squeezing her hand gently. She smiles a little, squeezing back.

"It's just—"

No. No, don't ruin it—

"I feel like I'm cheating on her," Alice says. "On you."

Immediately, I want to pull my hand back. I don't, but on Banquo, I get up and stare out the window. Another snowstorm, white and wild. I resist the melodramatic urge to walk into it.

"You aren't," I tell Alice. "I'm not a different person. I'm just—"

"I *know*," Alice says, sharp. "I'm just telling you how I *feel.*"

I know how you *feel*, I think, unfair and bitter—but then, maybe it isn't so unfair. Maybe Gray was right, at least a little; why *are* Alice's feelings always prioritized over mine?

On Myr, I walk to the window, too. Clear, pink skies, and three visible moons.

"*I* feel like you're leaving me," I tell Alice.

"I'm not—"

"You're never around," I say, and inside, some resentful dam bursts. "Even when you're here, you're not. You keep treating me like I'm fucking *gone*—"

"I don't—"

"They could deport me, Alice! Do you understand that? Do you care how *I* feel because *I'm* terrified all the time, of losing my home, losing you, even taking the goddamn bus now—"

Abruptly, Alice turns away. "I don't want to talk about that."

"Well, what if *I* need to?" I yell, forcing her to face me. "Do I have to handle everything on my own? The paperwork, the loneliness, the memories. You know I remember it, right? This body didn't bleed, but *I* bled; *I* saw the flames; I *felt* it when—"

But Alice only says, "I *can't*," and leaves, slamming the front door behind her.

I collapse back on the mattress, closing my eyes. There's a window here, too, but I don't bother looking out. I'm too exhausted to get up, and anyway, it's not the window or view I want it to be. Too many city lights, and I ache to see stars.

So, I go see the stars.

I wait until the blizzard on Banquo passes; then I leave my secondary body behind and gear up, venturing out to find a nice, isolated snow hill—excellent for stargazing, quiet conversations, and very cold picnicking, assuming you don't need oxygen to breathe, which, of course, I do. Jwa, however, does not.

Jwa is less a friend than a fate-bound, a term he finds superstitious and sentimental because he is, and always has been, a cantankerous little shit. We first met as children on that lunar colony; we both died on that lunar colony, too. I lost contact with him and everyone else I'd loved there—my parents, my teachers, my friends—because children rarely get to make their own choices, and all my *other* parents decided I needed a clean break to move on. But that break had been devastating; it had been anything but clean, and I remember longing for adulthood because it meant that nobody could ever make those choices for me again.

(I wouldn't go back to being a child, not for anything, but lately I wonder if maybe I'm just shit at making the right choices for myself.)

Running into Jwa last year—in this frozen truck stop of a planet, no less—well, those were astronomical odds, miracle odds, and to hell with what he says about it. We've never had very much in common, anyway, save our shared bleak history, and also this: Jwa is Untold, the only other multiple-body species that I know of. (The actual English exonym is Untoldan, but that's so ungainly; I prefer the root word.) Unlike me, Jwa has ninety-seven identical bodies, all of which look rather like a hickory-horned devil caterpillar, if those caterpillars were faceless, translucent, the size of a human arm, and beaded with one hundred and twenty dark eyes. Ninety-seven bodies *is* rather high for his species, but extremely typical of Jwa, who's always had to win absolutely everything.

Case in point: "You wouldn't see *me* wasting around on a planet where I can't even breathe the air."

And: "I've only lost *one* body, unlike *some* people I could mention."

And: "I *told* you to stop fucking that puffed-up amputation."

Amputation is likely the handheld's best approximation at some derogatory word for *single-bodied*. We often rely on translator apps; I prefer not to, but the Untold communicate entirely by colored flushes and secretions, which I'm as biologically incapable of producing as Jwa is unable to process vocal speech. We make it work for us: Jwa can usually decipher the rough meaning of my hand gestures, and I can work out his general mood by whatever color he's oozing. Currently, his bodies—there are four of them—are coated in dots of rose-pink goo, which means he's a little sad/sorry/pitying, but mostly smug as hell.

With effort, I bite back on a lecture about allonormative assumptions. "No," I tell him. "You said not to date *any* single-bodied person because you're conventional and boring."

"Because I'm not a reckless idiot," Jwa insists, flushing an indignant buttercup.

This is an old argument: Jwa thinks most Myriads are reckless idiots for spreading themselves out across the universe; in turn, I think *he's* an idiot for wasting so much precious life in a solitary collective. If he'd lived this way as a child, he wouldn't be around now to brag about having only died once. *Scatter the nests*, I told him, to which he'd asked, *is it still a nest with only one twig*, and I'd said something very cutting and mature like *fuck off* because, really, we just bring out the worst in each other.

Today I'm prepared with several choice insults—but then Jwa flushes a bitter forest green and says, "They see us as bugs."

Well. Yes. Despite his obvious sentience, some humans probably *would* see Jwa as a bug, just like some caw and jeer at me, asking if my father fucked a Northern cardinal. "Humans—"

"Not just humans," Jwa interrupts. "*All* amputations. And not just me. Not just bugs."

"I don't—"

"Bots," Jwa says. "Clones. Monsters. Parasites. Non-people. Non-sentients. *Less* than."

Demons, I think, despite myself, not because I often actually get called a demon, but because the true English exonym for my species is Legion, not Myriad—and that absolutely was *not* chosen as an allusion to the ancient Romans. It infuriates me when I think about it, so I try not to think about it. I try to enjoy my silent rebellions, my superior translations; I try not to be consumed by my anger, but—

"We frighten them," Jwa continues, greener than I've ever seen him. "We're *more* than them, so they make us less. They can feel justified that way: We're less, so we don't matter."

I think of middle school, then, and the casual slurs I still hear, and all the single-bodied people who've shuddered when they realized just how different I am. Every species in every world across the whole universe is the same: fearful and hateful and *small.*

But I don't let it consume me; I won't, because—

Individual *people*—not bodies, but *people*—aren't all so limited or sad. Individual people—like Gray, like Jwa—are small, sentient wonders of their own. You can meet them and learn them and hate them and touch them and watch the bright, beautiful stars on a tiny, white world with them. You can change them and be changed by them, too. Sometimes for the better, sometimes for the worse.

Alice is her own sentient wonder. But are we really changing each other for the better? How can we be, if she doesn't see me? *Did* she ever really see me?

I still don't know. I want to think so. But I look at Jwa and his four green-glowing bodies; I look at the stars and think of my *VR* crew—

And I think, yes, I already made my choice. But it's never too late to make a better one.

When Alice gets home, I tell her, "I think you should meet my other bodies."

Alice actually stops midstep. "I'm sure I will," she says, with an unconvincing smile.

"No, I mean soon. After everything . . . I think it's important."

Because I'd told myself it was complicated, that I shouldn't read too much into it—Alice had already seen the pictures, and she hadn't been upset then—but the truth is Alice *had* been excited about meeting my *Raccoon* fam. She didn't back out because she was uncomfortable with *them*. It was only when she remembered the crew also included *me*, that—for the very first time—she'd be in the same space with *two* of me: cooking, talking, holding her hands . . .

That's when Alice backed out of the trip.

"Okay," Alice says now. "But let me hit this deadline first."

"Sure," I tell her—but once that deadline passes and Alice comes up with another excuse, I secretly begin the dual journeys back to Earth. Banquo is a quick portal hop, but Myr takes six, and two of those portals are notorious for traffic backups and passport fuckups. I hibernate through much of the journey, and in the meantime, catch up on my dissertation reading; in the meantime, update my immigration lawyer; in the meantime, live in the stilted quiet with Alice.

And then finally, it's time.

"Alice," I say, stepping into the kitchen. "My other bodies are here now. They're coming up the elevator."

The coffee mug slips out of Alice's hand, rattling against the countertop. "What? But we said—and I'm not dressed—"

"I can already see you," I remind her.

"Well . . . I *know* that, but look, we said we'd wait."

"Yes. And then you kept postponing."

Alice crosses her arms. "You *know* how hard it's been lately. If you just—"

"Alice," I interrupt, as patiently as I can. "I don't actually need your permission to come into my own home in my own bodies."

Alice visibly wrestles with that.

"I just don't think it's a good idea," she says after a moment, not looking at me.

"Okay. Why not?"

"Well, I just . . . I don't know if I'm *comfortable* with that. I mean . . ." She flounders. "I know they're all you, but it's just . . ." *Weird*, she wants to say. Or *creepy*. Or *fucked up*. Or *you seem so neat in theory, but only if I don't think about it too much*.

"I don't care," I tell her. I punch in the door code with my primary body and follow my primary body inside with my quinary body.

Alice freezes.

I walk over, stand beside myselves: three Yonders, all in a row. Maybe I could be mistaken for identical twin sisters and their brightly feathered kid brother, but that's not who I am. That'll never be who I am.

"I know you didn't want this," I tell her. "But I need you to see me, Alice."

"I do!" Alice says, eyes watery. "But this is just so—"

"Do you?" I interrupt, this time with my primary body, "or have you—"

"Been pretending that I'm some human with feathers." I run my hand through my secondary crown. "Because—"

"I'm not human," I say with my quinary body. "I was never human. I was never single-bodied. This is me. This is all me. The scattered ash—"

"And this—"

"And this. Each is *me*, Alice. I'm Yonder, your Yonder, and I'll—"

"Never be human," I say, simultaneously with all of my bodies—

And Alice shudders.

And I know.

At first, Alice waits for me to pack my bags.

And then she keeps waiting.

And then she waits some more until finally, she realizes I have no intention of packing anything. This is *my* apartment. She moved in with *me*.

The Weight of Your Own Ashes

"But . . . you aren't *staying*," Alice says, and it takes me a moment to understand what she means. She isn't just talking about this building; she means UC Berkeley, the doctorate program, Earth. With three bodies and four lives, surely this is the one I'm leaving behind. She's waiting for me, I realize, to take my bodies and go home.

But I *am* home. I was born here, and even if I hadn't been—this is where I chose to build my future, and no one, certainly not my new ex-girlfriend, will take that choice from me. I long to tell Alice that; I want to be cold, confident, devastating. But I'm still too heartsick, and eventually, I just point at the front door, watching Alice close it behind her with a quiet click.

And that's it. It's over.

I do cry, then, in all my bodies, even, because it's always difficult saying goodbye, even if the person you're saying goodbye to isn't the person you thought—and especially when you've had to say goodbye a lot, recently. (I'd told Jwa my decision before I left Banquo. He'd gone silent, glowing mournful blue approval. Then, quickly turning pastel pink and condescending: *Finally. I thought you'd NEVER figure your shit out.*)

(I'd dumped snow on him and promised we'd meet again. We will. I'm sure of it.)

Eventually, though, I get tired of crying, and annoyed at myself, and pretty hungry, too, so I start chopping vegetables with my secondary body, while I clap my quinary hands to gospel-EDM, and lean out the open window in my primary form, listening to breaking glass and laughing people and a neighbor singing a Spanish love song. Tomorrow, I'll have appointments to keep (my immigration lawyer is *not* thrilled with how I keep causing her more paperwork), and also messages to send, travel arrangements to make, dissertations to work on, siblings to hold hands with—

But tonight, I just want to sit back and unwind, comfortable in all my skins. Tonight, I'll listen to the joyous small symphonies of my apartment, my neighborhood, my world.

XAVIER GARCIA

An Ode to the Minor Arcana in a Triplet Flow

FROM *Death in the Mouth, Volume 2*

FANTASY

BLOOD ON GOLD teeth looks dope as fuck.
    Tre feels bad thinking that. Feels bad that that's where his mind goes as his fist comes down again on the man's face. The brittle crunch of broken nose bones barely audible beneath a boom box blaring some Memphis rap group's new album; sound cranked to drown out any screams. The man's labored breathing somehow keeping time with the music's barren snares and coked-up hi-hats.
    Tre collects himself, panting and ignoring the ache in his fist as he watches blood bubble and gush from the man's nose to run over his mouth and teeth.
    Hell, blood on gold teeth does look dope as fuck, though.
    He'll have to keep that in mind for when he finally films his first music video. I mean, like goddamn, it's '92. People expect violence in videos, demand it even. But again, Tre feels bad thinking this, feels bad indulging in these selfish thoughts as he deals out so much pain to an absolute stranger. But he has to, has to or else he'll vomit from the guilt. Because seeing violence in videos is one thing and choosing to actively hurt a man until he's broken and bleeding is another. And Tre doesn't want to think about what making that choice means about the kind of person it makes him.

An Ode to the Minor Arcana in a Triplet Flow

I want it, I need it, I'll take it. It's mine. I want it, I need it, I'll take it. It's mine.

Another punch to the kidney and the room suddenly smells like piss.

Tre isn't a violent person. He's an artist. But come on now, this right here? As much as he hates it, as much as it makes him sick, it's necessary. Tre can perform at all the local shows he wants to and rap his ass off better than any other local fuck with a mic, but without funding, without money to pay for studio time and producers and radio spots and who knows what the hell else—everything the hell else, really—hype and talent mean nothing.

Tre throws another punch to the side and this time something breaks.

The man coughs up blood all over his piss-stained legs.

Tre knows what hard work pays off to in this country. Cuban on his father's side, Haitian on his mother's, so growing up, his dad used to say things like hard work was in his blood. But that never felt like a compliment. Like when folks say, "People from Latin America and the Caribbean are just so hardworking." Oh really, that's so nice, you really think so, actually please go suck a dick. Those are such obvious lines to get Black and Brown immigrants doing the work that white people don't want to—sorta like telling your little brother he's the best at making PB&Js, just so that he'll make one for you while you keep on playing video games.

So, when his mother's brother came to him with an idea on how to get some funding for his music, how could he not pay attention?

"Go see Papa Wilky," his uncle says, "the man's got eyes and fingers everywhere." And Tre knows what that means, has heard his name around. A local Haitian businessman everyone seems to do business with, no matter what it is. And yeah, sure, business. Business like dope, guns, girls; business like anything like, even weird shit like Santeria, Vodou, and brujeria, and whatever, whatever, anything's clever as long as the man is willing to fund his music.

So, Tre goes. Goes to this dusty-ass strip club around the way. Papa Wilky, by reputation, has offices all over the city, some that were even nice. So, who the hell can say why he'd chosen The Ladies of Babylon as a meeting spot. Strip clubs and titties on a Friday night are one thing; it's just straight up off-putting when you're there to talk about that one thing that's the only thing you do want to talk about.

But what choice does he have? So, Tre goes, goes and opens the door to a blast of pink and purple neon, to the steady pounding of overmodulated 808s screaming distortion over a soundscape so raw it's just as much noise as it is music. Bass so aggressive it physically hurts, with them hi-hats tick tick ticking away alongside a voice from one of them triple six boys, discordantly low and melodic and singsonging murder raps in a Memphis triplet flow.

I want it, I need it, I'll take it. It's mine. I want it, I need it, I'll take it. It's mine.

Tre reminds himself why he's there and walks straight past a light-skinned girl already topless on stage, thong as blue as her hair, and makes his way up to the bartender. No line, no wait. Nobody else at the club this time of day except some sad old man.

"Hey, I'm here to see Papa Wilky."

The bartender hardly looks his way, never stops cleaning the glass in his hand.

"I know you are. Take a seat. He'll come get you when he's ready."

So, Tre sits down, not even ordering a drink. Too nervous for drinks. Too nervous to do anything but wait. Not that he has to wait that long, either, barely a song passes before two enormous bouncers walk up to him. Tre stands up.

Scarcely even a word, they pat Tre down then and there. Nothing to hide. He isn't stupid. And then, again, no words needed, they lead him away. And Tre figures that the old man by the front of the stage must be tipping oh so nice because that blue thong is off and to the side by the time Tre passes them both. The light-skinned girl catches him looking and gives him a little wink. Good luck charms come in weird places.

Tre fixes himself up and puts on a mean-looking face as they lead him into a back room and close the door. No more pink and purple neon, no more triple six boys rapping murder; just the steady thrum of the bass beating against the wall.

The room in the back is a weird-looking office slash lounge slash church. Near the far end is a heavy table where sits a man in an all-red pantsuit talking on the phone, goons lounging around him itching for a fight. But Tre isn't looking at them. Tre is looking at the man in the red pantsuit. Papa Wilky. Tre meets his gaze and Papa Wilky holds up his finger like one moment please, Tre. Your dreams can wait.

So, Tre waits and looks. The room has such a different vibe from the strip club on the other side of the door. Not at all what he was expecting. Atmospherically dark, the ceiling is decked in hundreds of tiny, dangling Christmas lights washing the room out in warm primary colors. More worship than business, the place looks like an active shrine, a mix of Indigenous faiths and Catholicism, Cuban Santeria and Haitian Vodou, all chimerically mixed together in a way that is all of it and none. Shrines against the wall that display everything from orisha stones inside soperas, to rotting fruit, cloyingly sweet, to pictures of people in little plastic bags, baby shoes, shells, icons, and statues of saints and animals in various shapes and sizes—like Santa Muerte in her seven-colored robe—right beside bones and rum and images and artifacts that are neither Santeria nor Vodou, but more like tourist Voodoo, haphazardly placed alongside incongruous likenesses of famous actresses and singers, mysticism distilled through an MTV lens muddying the African diaspora religions into pop art worship and culminating into a kind of spiritual Disney World.

But as silly as it all looks, all jumbled up together, there's also something comforting about it too. There's something about the shared history of it all, there's something about the familiarity of its gaudiness, there's something about the way it reminds Tre of his grandparents that makes him also think of his father and his mother and his uncles and his aunts and his brothers and his sisters. There's something about it that, for just a second, Tre almost believes in it too.

Finally, Papa Wilky hangs up the phone. Tre meets his gaze.

"Papa Wilky, thank you for meeting—"

"—You listen to this shit?" Papa Wilky says. A big smile on his face, ear-to-ear, toothy, cheap salesman white, as he points to the air.

"Um, hip-hop? Yeah, I listen to this shit. I actually do this shit."

"We all do shit, boy. Even my dogs do shit."

His goons burst into laughter. Joke wasn't even funny.

"Come on, sit," he says, motioning to an empty chair. "Hip. Hop." Feeling out the words. Toothy smile still on his face. "Bunch of noise to me. Gives me a headache. Whatever happened to them old soul records? Now *that* was music."

A pause. Tre doesn't know what to say. Why the hell is he here, then? "You know your uncle, Michel, he gave me your tape, you know?"

"I know he did. Sorry for the headache."

Papa Wilky looks at him a long moment, no more toothy salesman smile, just two yellow, rheumy sick-man eyes. Them infirm eyes staring into Tre's own.

Then he bursts into laughter and Tre can breathe again.

"No headache. I'm not one of those old men who shakes his fist at the world wondering where the time went. I'm a futurist, Tre. First thing you need to know about me."

"Glad to hear, sir."

"And none of this 'sir' shit. If we're going to do business together, then we've got to be family. You got family, Tre? Besides your fool uncle. Any brothers and sisters?"

"Yeah, nine, actually. Nine brothers and sisters. Big Haitian/Cuban family. You know how it is."

And then something seems to brighten in his eyes. Something mean and playful over the yellow sclera of his unhealthy eyeballs. Some look that makes Tre sick.

"Yes, I know how it is," the return of the toothy smile. "And by the way, I already knew that. About your nine brothers and sisters, I mean."

Whatever the fuck that means. Tre composes himself. "So, we are? We are doing business together?"

"I had already decided before you took one step into my

club. You see, Tre, I want to be immortal. Don't laugh, now. But I want my name to be remembered for more than just girls and blow and all of that garbage. So, I ask myself. How? And then your uncle comes to me and says to me, listen to my nephew, what a good rapper he is. Rap rap rapping all over these cassettes. All he needs is a little money and he could be big. Live forever on the radio. And that's when I tell myself. That's how. I help you become immortal, and so I become immortal."

Tre's turn to smile big.

"Papa Wilky. Honestly, man. You won't regret this."

"I know I won't. But like I said, Tre, I know things. I know you've done things. I know you've put in work."

And there it is: the fine print.

Tre spends the next ten minutes in a daze, half listening to what Papa Wilky has to say. About some man who lives in a big house on a big hill, isolated and alone. About how he owes Papa Wilky money, about how Papa Wilky is patient but not that patient, about how Tre and Papa Wilky are family now and family do things for one another, about how all Tre has to do is go up there and take care of this man, does Tre understand what he means by take care of, of course he does, Tre is a smart kid, he knew that about him the moment he walked into his office.

Tre only nods. When you're willing to say yes to anything there's no room for negotiation.

I want it, I need it, I'll take it. It's mine. I want it, I need it, I'll take it. It's mine.

"Okay good. It's all settled. Pat will go with you. Pat, go with him."

"Wait. Now?" Tre asks as a man he assumes to be Pat hands him a pistol.

"Glock 19," growls Pat, immediately moving to the side to pick up a boom box after handing him the gun.

"What's that for?"

"For the screams." And then that smile again. "Oh, and one more thing. This man. He has this chair he loves, always talking about this chair. Before you . . . finish . . . I want you to humiliate him a little bit. Make him strip, tie him to that chair, and just beat on him for a little bit."

"Why?"

"Because it's funny." And at that Papa Wilky explodes into laughter. A laughter that turns into a phlegmy coughing fit before being swallowed up by a blast of southern hip-hop as soon as the door is opened.

Pat drives Tre a long way out of the neighborhood. The drive feels long and awkward but thankfully silent. Tre isn't a killer. True, he has hurt people before, but never murdered. And in the silence of the car ride, he can't help but ask himself if this is worth it. But no matter what angle he comes at it from, no matter how much he tries to play devil's advocate, muster up his soul, the answer always comes up yes. In the end, yes, it's all worth it.

Because what's the alternative? Like, seriously, what? Is he to be like his dad and his uncle and their dads and their uncles and everyone the hell else in his family? Trabajando como buey, growing old and poor and sad and frustrated with nothing but frown lines and callused fingers to show for it all?

No. In the end, one man's life would have to be worth it. It would all have to be worth it. To choose to actively hurt a man until he bleeds, to make a choice about the kind of person he is, what it means to be the kind of person he is, it would all have to be worth it. Because for Tre, there is no alternative.

Tre makes up his mind just as Pat starts parking. They pull up into some secluded area where they can't be seen from the road, that isolated house only a five-minute drive from where they are. Pat insists they wait another three hours for when it gets dark. Three hours of more silence, three more hours of contemplating death and prison and the future. Three more hours until he gets everything he's ever wanted.

Around the three-hour mark, another car pulls up beside them. The driver, not even getting out of the car, passes a black bag to Pat.

"What's that for?" Tre asks.

"For later," is all Pat says.

Then more silence. Then it gets dark.

Then Pat finally turns to Tre.

And now Tre wishes it were three hours ago. Three hours ago, when he had more time to contemplate. Three hours ago, when Tre didn't have to make the choice to become the kind of person that makes these kinds of choices. Three hours ago, when Tre was still Tre from three hours ago.

Pat makes eye contact with Tre.

"Showtime. May the Minor Arcana take flesh tonight."

And what the hell does that mean?

No time to think, no time to ask, Pat jumps out of the car, gun and bag in hand, and runs out into the bush toward the house. And Tre follows, gun in tow, panic creeping into his gut, wondering what deal he's really made with Papa Wilky, and not the one regarding music, what Santeria, Vodou, Voodoo, pop art, horror movie bullshit has Tre agreed to. And what did it really matter? The time for regret and questions has clearly passed as Tre follows Pat through the bush, making their way through and then emerging into a clearing, and then he sees it: an enormous house on a distant hill, dark and isolated beneath the waxing crescent of a new moon. Pat squeezes Tre's shoulder. And the excitement in his eyes makes Tre's stomach lurch in disgust, but he still follows him up the yard to the back door.

And blood on gold teeth does looks dope as fuck. But only if you got no soul at all left up.

Tre throws another punch and hits the man square in the mouth, gold teeth spilling out and across the piss-covered floor.

He stands up, his hand sore as hell and bleeding. He can't do it anymore, can't beat on the man for a second longer. He looks so pathetic, it hurts to look at him; all naked and bloody and broken and tied to this massive weird-ass chair in the middle of the room. This whole thing has been so goddamn weird, Papa Wilky was right, there was a room with nothing in it but a massive chair. But it isn't just one chair, it's three. Three massive chairs descending in size; three massive chairs without armrests, more like thrones, arranged one next to the other in the middle of an enormous room within an enormous house. The man tied to the leftmost chair, the largest. No one to hear his screams, no one to help, no sound at all but the continuous ever-present lament of them triple six boys rapping death in a Memphis triplet flow.

Tre takes out his Glock 19. Pat walks up beside him.

"You should beat on him some more," he says.

"Why?"

"Because it's funny." Pat flashes him a smile that makes Tre's stomach lurch. Though it doesn't have the same stopping power as Papa Wilky's sick-man grin.

"No. I'm done."

"Done? Are we done?" asks the naked man on the chair, slowly. Painfully. Blood bubbling from his nose and dripping down into his mouth. A look on his face that for just a second looks very much like another fucking smile.

Tre points the gun at the man's forehead. The man in turn raises his broken, battered face to meet Tre's eyes.

"I want you to know it is an honor, Tre."

What the fuck?

How does he know my name?

Tre looks at Pat then back at the man. Meeting his eyes this time. "What?" Tre asks, confusion and panic roiling in his gut.

"Shoot him," says Pat.

"How do you know my name?"

"I want you to know it is an honor. I mean that, Tre. I will live forever in your music."

And this time, Tre knows he sees it right, the man is most definitely smiling, ear-to-ear, jubilant and peaceful, and then Tre notices that it isn't just that, not just the awful grin, the naked man on the chair is fully hard, his cock erect and stiff and pressing against his belly as he leans his whole upper body forward, toward the muzzle of the gun.

"Shoot him," Pat says again. "Do it."

Blood dripping from his toothless mouth, the smell of urine in the air.

"Here sits the King of Teeth."

Bang.

The man's face explodes in a wash of blood and bone.

Tre holds the smoking pistol, his hand shaking only just a little.

"Good," says Pat. But Tre can't hear him. He can't hear anything.

He'd never taken a life before and what the fuck was that all about?

His hand begins to shake even more than it already is when he finally feels the wet warmth of bodily fluids, red splashed across his face and dripping thick down his lips. And now he feels like throwing up again, but now is not the time for that. He forces his attention, all of his concentration and focus back onto the music. Back onto those minor-tone synth leads, so dark and heavy over a lo-fi soundscape, grizzled and dirty and distorted and punctuated by a chorus more like a group chant with its violent repetition before giving way to a new voice, not melodic this time, but gruff and wild, deep and angry, spewing paranoia over the unending beat of those eternal 808s.

I want it, I need it, I'll take it. It's mine. I want it, I need it, I'll take it. It's mine.

I have to, I can't lose. That future, it's time.

Tre finally lowers the gun and faces Pat.

"Let's get out of here." He pauses. "I need to get out of here." Something crashes and breaks in the hallway just outside the room. "What the fuck was that?" Tre says, his heart pumping. Papa Wilky had said there wouldn't be anyone else at home, had promised nobody else would be there, and now Tre is pointing the gun at the empty doorway and why the hell did he agree to this?

A woman steps into view.

"Oopsie, I dropped my drink." She giggles. Standing fully nude in front of them, blue hair flowing down her side. Tre's eyes wander over her breasts and body, not out of arousal, but out of sheer confusion. She meets his eyes and smiles as if she only just then realizes she is naked. She lets out another little laugh, not a scream, a laugh. She doesn't run or yell or hide, she looks at him all shy and high and drunk and walks right into the room.

"The fuck is this?" Tre says, and looks to Pat. And Pat glares back.

"No survivors, Tre. Shoot her. You know what you agreed to do."

"Papa Wilky said there'd be nobody else here," Tre says, trying to sound all tough and in control, but his voice is oh so shaky.

"Doesn't matter. Shoot her. No survivors."

Tre looks back to the naked girl walking toward him, wobbling and tripping as she does so, so deeply intoxicated she can barely even stand, and only then does Tre realize that in her hand is a little carving knife.

Tre points the gun right to her chest. "Put that fucking knife down!"

And in response she rubs her heavy breasts in a *see if I care* taunting playfulness. Waltzing right into the room, Tre can do nothing but take a big step back, pushing the gun forward like he really means it.

"Shoot her, Tre."

She flashes him another smile before she sits down in the middle chair. A dead man sitting to the right of her; to the left an empty seat.

"I wanted to thank you for including me, Tre," she says, lifting up the little knife. Letting out another girlish laugh. "I wish I still had my drink, though."

"Put that down, I said."

"Shoot her, Tre."

"It means so much to me, you have no idea."

And then she raises the little knife up to her ear and with one hand on her lobe stretching the ear out tight, the other holding the handle of the knife, she begins to cut. Begins to saw and slice away at the fleshy bit between ear and face; blood spilling down her cheek.

"Ouch, ouch, ouch," she says as she rips the ear clean off, tossing the bloody thing to the floor before starting on the next one.

"Please, stop," Tre says meekly, his eyes stinging and filling up with tears. No thought but wanting to run, and knowing Pat will shoot him if he does.

"Shoot her," says Pat, like it's his fucking catchphrase. "No survivors."

She drops the second ear beside the first one, blood gushing down her neck and chest. And this time Tre raises the gun and aims it at her head, he just wants this all to stop. Because what's

happening? It wasn't supposed to be this way. It wasn't supposed to be like this at all.
"I will live forever in your music."
"I'm sorry."
"Here sits the Queen of Ears."
Bang.
Only the music.
"I just want this all to stop," says Tre, mostly to himself.
"I know. I'm sorry," says Pat, gently taking the gun from him. "Look, it's almost over. Take a seat."
And Tre sits down in the third and final seat, smallest of the three. Pat walks up to him and looks down at Tre, as would a kindly friend. "We all have so much faith in you, Tre. We know you will do great things. Become immortal in the airwaves. It's an honor seeing you become this. Papa Wilky wishes it could have been him, but his eyes aren't what they used to be. So, it's me you're with. Sorry about that. But I'm just here to witness. A Page of Eyes and nothing else."
"Witness what?" Tre says, and this time the tears do come. He's scared and shaking and the guilt is building in his chest and making him want to puke. All he wanted to do was be better than his parents, make something of himself, and now he's stuck in this room of chairs and bodies. Why won't that music fucking stop?
Pat kneels and starts going through the black bag that he brought with him. Slowly rummaging, so gentle in his movements. Tre looks and only a part of him wonders what's inside, the other half is broken. And then Pat pulls out something wet and dangling, dripping only just a little bit of blood onto the floor. It takes Tre a moment to realize what it is he's looking at. Some kind of cord, some kind of necklace, some kind of necklace with pink and fleshy bits hanging down from it.
Pat meets his eyes.
"Nine tongues," Pat says.
And then that part of Tre that was human, the part of him that was left alive, it breaks.
Nine tongues. Nine siblings. Nine brothers and sisters.

All of them gone, all of them murdered, all of them mutilated and hurt and cut and defiled, all for a dream that was Tre's alone. All of their memories, all of their childhoods, all of their teenage years spent so closely together, all of their laughter and smiles, all of their futures, all traded in for a promise that Papa Wilky gave inside of a strip club.

Pat holds it out. His eyes wide and pleading.

"I cannot force you to take it. I cannot make you. You have to take it for yourself, Tre. You can't understand this now, I know. But if you take it. If you'll take it, it'll be done. And you won't die, forgotten, nobody, like your parents and their parents before them. You'll be immortal. You'll have it all."

Tre meets his eyes. And he hates himself for finding any of that appealing. Hates himself for still wanting it. Images of his father's callused hands flashing in broken pieces across his inner eye. The same callused hands his brothers and sisters would have eventually had. Tears freely streaming down his face.

I want it, I need it, I'll take it. It's mine. I want it, I need it, I'll take it. It's mine. Forget it, it's over. It's nothing, stop crying.

Stop crying because it all has to be worth it. Papa Wilky's promise has to be worth it. Tre thinks back to Papa Wilky's shrine inside of that strip club. Tries to imagine it. Because there's something comforting about thinking of it. Something about the shared history of it all, something about the familiarity of its gaudiness, something about the way it reminds Tre of his grandparents that makes him also think of his brothers and his sisters. Tre thinks back to that shrine inside of a strip club because there's something about it that makes Tre believe in it too.

And choosing not to believe in it means Tre's become someone he can't possibly be.

So, Tre reaches for the necklace. Taking hold of it, careful not to touch his family.

"Nine tongues hanging beneath the silver tenth inside your head," declares Pat as he slowly stands.

Tre puts his head through the garland of tongues and lets it dangle from his neck.

"There sits the Knight of Tongues."

And Tre settles in his seat, third and smallest but it seems to fit him right.

"Forever live the Knight of Tongues."

And as he relaxes into it, pushing back into the chair, he can feel the future creeping up on him and it feels so very warm. That future that was once only a dream, he can feel it coming now, can feel it nearing. The world around him vibrating like the thrumming of overmodulated bass. Quivering and shifting, making way for a new dawn. A dawn that is being heralded by the gravelly voice of a rapper singing murder in a Memphis triplet flow.

KATHRYN H. ROSS

The Forgetting Room

FROM *FIYAH*

SCIENCE FICTION

THE LITTLE FAMILY was sitting around the dining table enjoying the pancakes, scrambled eggs, and hashbrowns that Henry, the father, had made for breakfast. The kitchen was warm and rich with the starchy smell of oil and fried potatoes. Adom, the son, was squeezing syrup onto his cakes and snickered each time the bottle spluttered. Anika, the mother, kept glancing at the boy out of the corner of her eye.

"That's enough, now," she said at last, her voice stern. The syrup bottle had just let out the biggest splutter yet, and Adom dissolved into a fit of laughter. The sticky maple goo had sprayed the table some, making the scrubbed wood look like it had broken out in a sweat. Anika stood and headed straight to the sink to wet a towel. Adom placed his large eyes on his father, looking apprehensive.

Henry raised his eyebrows at him. His son smiled but did not make a sound as Anika came back and began wiping the syrup drops before they dried.

"C'mon," Anika said as she worked. "Go get your shoes on. School starts soon, baby." Adom jumped lightly from his chair and ran down the hall. Henry looked at Anika. He could tell she was tense, edgy. "I can take him," he said as he scooped up their dishes. The wood was scrubbed clean, shining and raw as if it'd just been sawed.

"No," Anika said with a glance at the kitchen clock behind

her. "You won't have time. Looks like you should get going, too." She straightened up and looked at him, and her eyes softened. Henry smiled. "You okay?" he asked.

"Always," she answered with a quick wink. Half an hour later, Anika had dropped Adom off at school and Henry was sitting in his car in a patch of traffic.

People on the street walked by quickly with their heads down, shoulders laden with bags, hands filled with coffee cups or phones. Henry had the window cracked and let his gaze slip from one face to the next as he rolled slowly along. The sun was high, and the air was pleasant on his face. He closed his eyes for a moment and exhaled, thinking briefly of Adom and wondering what he might be doing in school just then. The radio was turned down low, but Henry could just hear the remnants of "Summer of '69" as the song faded into dead air. He smirked as a memory of himself and Anika singing along loudly and badly with Bryan Adams washed over him. They'd been cruising downtown, the moon bright above them and the air warm, and Anika said the song was so stupid, but she knew every word. That had been a long time ago, well before Adom was born, maybe even before they were married.

A horn honked. Henry started and glanced in his rearview to see the person in the car behind him gesturing animatedly. He pulled forward and raised his own hand in apology. Outside, the street was getting louder. A motorcycle zipped past, and two dogs began yipping as their owners chatted idly on the corner. The radio was now playing tinny static, so Henry twiddled the dial until a voice broke through the fuzz: ". . . anything in your head you just *don't want to be there*? If you said yes to any of these questions, then we have an offer for *you*."

Henry paused with his fingers still on the dial.

"A child at my son's school showed him and some of the other children a graphic video," a woman's voice said suddenly. "My son is only in the fourth grade, and he came home upset and confused, and . . . asking too many uncomfortable questions . . ." Henry frowned. He increased the volume and put up his window to mute the street. The woman's voice, confident and clear, went on: "The other parents and I got together and decided a group session in THE FORGETTING ROOM is just what our children needed. Now, their innocence is back intact, and they don't have to worry about anything until *we're* ready. It's truly a lifesaver."

The voice changed again, this time to the smooth enthusiastic tone of a salesman: "The technology is simple," it said with gusto. "Once THE FORGETTING ROOM is in your home, it's ready for immediate use. Thirty minutes inside and any memory you choose is totally erased thanks to supercharged electromagnetic radio wavelengths that permeate the mind on a molecular level. Developed by retired aerospace engineers . . ."

The light turned red, and Henry slowed to a stop. He stared ahead, no longer seeing the cars gliding across his view as they zipped left and right on the black road. He gripped the steering wheel, listening.

Weeks ago, little Adom walked in on them making love. In the warm dark his soft voice rang out clear as a bell: "Momma?"

They stopped quickly and looked; his little shadow filled their doorway, backlit dimly by the light from the hall. Anika quickly sat up, covered herself, and went to him.

"What's the matter?" Henry asked from the bed. A stomachache, but Adom's focus had shifted.

"What are you doing?" he asked them. Anika glanced back at Henry as the question hung in the air. Soon the three of them were in Adom's room tucking the boy back into bed as they gently explained. He had questions (*But* what *were you doing with Momma, Baba?* he asked earnestly, his small face filled with concern), and they fielded them all as tactfully as they could. The night ended with a story. Henry read while Anika rubbed Adom's belly until he fell asleep. When they turned out the light and tiptoed from the room, Adom was breathing as deeply and peacefully as a house cat.

"That couldn't have gone better," Henry joked once they were back in their room. He slid beneath their covers lightly, and Anika settled beside him. He looked at her and saw her face was filled with worry. "What is it?" he asked.

The Forgetting Room

She shook her head. "I just wish he hadn't seen that," she answered.

"It doesn't seem like he saw much of anything," Henry responded as he settled into his pillow. "It's okay. It happens."

Anika shook her head again. "I know, but I just . . . I wish it hadn't."

"What do you mean?"

"He's just so young," she said, and looked at him with wide eyes. "It's probably confusing no matter what we say, and you know how he chews on things, his mind working them over until they're spent. He's so thoughtful." She looked up at Henry with a small, apprehensive smile. "Like you."

Henry pulled her to him and held her hand in his. "Trust me," he said gently. "It's okay. I saw my folks once or twice when I was a kid and forgot all about it in no time. Didn't you ever walk in on your parents?"

"Never. And you still remember—you just said."

Henry frowned thoughtfully. "I guess you've got me there, but it wasn't a big deal. They sat me down just like we did Adom, and it was all right. I was okay." He looked down at his wife appraisingly, aware that she was just like how she saw Adom— chewing things over until they were spent. He could practically see the wheels turning in her mind.

"What if—" she began, but Henry stopped her.

"Hey," he said, and gave her a squeeze. "Everything's fine. We handled it. There's nothing to worry about. Adom's fine, okay? And if he has more questions, we'll handle those, too." Henry squeezed her hand. She squeezed back and nodded but said nothing; her eyes were fixed on their bedroom door. She leaned her head against Henry's chest, and he held her. In time he fell asleep, but she stayed awake for a long while.

"The room must not be in use for more than thirty minutes," Henry read aloud. "Use may cause mild brain fog and migraines at first, but that should subside after a few days depending on frequency of use." He and Anika were sitting at the breakfast table with the laptop in front of them. "It says here that installation can be done in an afternoon. Maybe we could do it next Saturday?"

Anika was frowning at the screen with her eyebrows furrowed. She removed her reading glasses and looked at Henry. "That should be okay . . ." she said, still frowning. "God, this all sounds so incredible."

Henry nodded. It had sounded that way to him, too. He'd barely given it time to sink in that morning in the car. Aerospace engineering, electromagnetic radio wavelengths, a total wipe of only what you wanted to forget. It sounded like a science fiction movie, but once the advert had finished, he'd called Anika right away and told her to look it up.

"Do you really think we should?" Anika asked. It was the third time she'd asked since they'd been sitting there.

"Only if you think it's right," Henry answered. "The testimonies sound good to me and, I don't know, this could be helpful for us and for Adom. What if it happens again?"

"We could just be more careful . . ."

"Yes, but we're careful now, and things still happen. This would be like insurance."

"But you said you were fine when it happened to you," Anika pushed.

"I am fine," Henry agreed, "but I was thinking about what you said about things just . . . not happening. What if he sees something frightening on TV or at school or has a horrible nightmare? Maybe if I'd had the choice back then, I would have forgotten some things. I know I could've used it . . . like when I passed out during dissection day, or when I deleted that entire file at work and we had to stay late salvaging it, or that time—"

"But aren't those small things? Little embarrassments?" Anika interrupted.

"Absolutely, but that's my point. What good do they do us? Why keep them with me? Because they're there even if I don't want them to be . . . and it could be for bigger things, too."

"Like what?"

"Well, like the other night. Adom *is* young and he doesn't need all that in his head. I mean he can hardly even understand it. Or . . ." Henry paused. "Or like when Adom was born. Having to stay in the NICU all that time not knowing whether . . . why remember it? He's here now and he's happy and healthy and all that memory does is haunt me. The room's safe, it's easy, it's affordable . . . why not?"

Henry was right. The rooms had been on the market for a little over a year and there wasn't even a whisper of anything negative about them. The testimonies he'd heard on the radio were just the tip of the iceberg. So many had so much to say, so much to praise. Just the idea of a mind wipe when one needed it most was doing people so much good.

Anika nodded, and her eyes changed, clouded over with the memory of their little boy born silent and so small. "You're right," she said at last. "You're right."

"Yeah?" Henry said excitedly. Anika nodded.

"But we'll need some ground rules."

"Okay," he agreed.

"Let's not use the room more than once per day," Anika said, writing the rule down on a piece of notebook paper.

"Is it unsafe?" Henry asked.

"Well, it says no more than thirty minutes of use . . ." Anika answered, checking the website again.

Henry looked where she was reading and frowned. "I think that just means thirty minutes at a time, not cumulatively."

"Is it advisable, though?"

"I don't see anything here saying we can't use it more than once a day so long as each session is within the time limit . . . but if you're just not comfortable with that we can make it a rule."

Anika closed her eyes and exhaled. "No, you're right," she said. "We might need to use it a couple of times in a day. Who knows what can happen . . ."

Henry felt a flutter of anxiety. "I didn't mean it like that; we don't need to worry about everything. I just think it can be on an as-needed basis, rather than restricting it to one time for one thing per day, you know?" Anika looked at him, and he saw her face relax.

"No, that does make sense," she said. "Okay. But let's try not to use it too, too much, right? Especially for Adom. As needed. Only when necessary."

"Deal," Henry said. They high-fived. "Okay, what else?"

"We only use the room when both of us are home. That way

there's always an eye on Adom if one of us is using it alone, and one can keep an eye on the other if we're using it with him. He can't be in the room or the house totally alone."

"Good idea," Henry agreed, nodding. "One of us should always be on standby."

"Right. But what if we want to use it all together?" Anika wondered.

"I think that should be okay," said Henry. "The room has a timer, so family sessions should be fine. But again, only as needed."

Anika nodded and scribbled the rule down. "Anything else?"

"Check-ins?"

"Check-ins," Anika repeated and wrote it down. "Just so we know how everyone's feeling."

They looked at each other, and to Henry's delight, Anika smiled a genuine smile. "Saturday, then?" she said. Henry opened the website's "Booking" window.

"Saturday."

The reviews seemed to ring true. Shortly after it was installed, Anika went to Adom and asked him if he could remember what he saw that night. At first, he was confused. He was lounging on the couch beside Henry, sipping on a juice box while a cartoon played on the television before him, half listening. Anika put a hand to his face and asked again. "Can you remember what you saw? When you came into Mommy and Daddy's room the other night?" Henry glanced at them, watching his son's face. Adom looked at Anika for a moment and then nodded determinedly. "Good," she said. She clicked off the TV and reached for him. He stood up and fell into her arms. "Can you keep that and all your questions in your mind? Think about them as much as you can. We're going to sit for a while and listen to some music."

Henry began to rise, but Anika held up her hand. "I've got it," she said, and smiled. "You just keep watch." She lifted Adom onto her hip and carried him down the hall, stopping before a heavy metallic door with a glass window one foot high and across at its center. On the wall beside it was a keypad and glass-plated screen. Anika carefully punched in a series of numbers and a smiley face appeared, winking at her. With a click the

The Forgetting Room

door opened and a message appeared: *The Room is Ready for Use. Please Enter.*

Anika walked inside, closed the door behind her with a snap, and settled on the little bench at the room's center. She situated Adom on her lap and then pulled his soft head toward her chest. He placed his cheek against her heart, and she covered his face with her hand gently, kissed him atop his woolly head. "Just sit and listen, okay?" she said to him, and he only sighed in response. Anika hesitated and looked around her. The room was a soft eggshell white and totally bare except for its seat. With a quick clearing of her throat, Anika said, "Begin," and the lights dimmed.

Henry made his way down the hall and stopped at the door. He looked through the little window and could see his wife and child sitting there as serenely as if they were on a park bench. Anika was holding Adom to her like she did when he was an infant, and the boy had his small arms wrapped around her shoulders. Henry could hear the "music," which was actually the hum when the room was in use. It sounded like a great wind blowing through an empty desert, and he could almost feel the breeze.

They soon were using THE FORGETTING ROOM nearly every day. Jokingly, Anika began calling it her therapy. Whenever something distressing or upsetting happened, Anika would hurry Adom into the room and sit with her arms around him until the alarm dinged and both their minds were clean. If a cartoon Adom was watching got too scary, Anika would shut it off and rush him to the room. If he came home from school tearful and claiming he'd had a bad day, Anika would whisk him back into that room. She stopped asking him what had happened, only whether he could remember it. Henry waited outside and watched them, saw the way Anika's shoulders would relax as the room hummed along. Every unpleasant thing had a shelf life of just a few hours, which made them both worry a lot less.

It didn't matter how old a memory or experience was, either. She might remember something mildly unpleasant—a bad flu she'd had when she was eighteen, a discouraging phone call with her mother, a fight with Henry—and retreat to THE

FORGETTING ROOM. She would emerge half an hour later glowing and serene. She smiled more. There was less everyday stress. Things that used to make her lie awake at night when she thought Henry was asleep no longer visited her, and she slept soundly. They hardly argued about anything. The days began to blend. Henry would ask Anika about something only to realize she must have erased the conversation from her mind. It took him a few times to realize he couldn't even ask her why. More and more, he found he was the only one who could hang on to anything.

Though he had advocated for it, Henry hadn't yet used THE FORGETTING ROOM. Mostly he was on standby for Anika or keeping an eye on Adom, but even when the room was free, he talked himself out of using it. The possibility of erasure elated him, but the opportunity to actually do so, to alter his own mind, scared him. He would pass that heavy door as he walked down the hall on his way to the bathroom at night or coming back from checking on Adom, and it felt cold and sterile. The feeling reminded him of a field trip he'd been on when he was young—they'd gone to the zoo and there had been an ice palace to house the polar bears. The walls were covered in real ice, and walking past them seemed to sap the warmth from his very body. He could still see the hallways of that habitat, ice blue and echoing, but there was a pleasantness in the memory that the room didn't hold. It merely made him feel cold.

As winter approached, THE FORGETTING ROOM saved the day left and right. When Adom had stumbled upon the closet with his unwrapped Christmas gifts, a quick pop into the room fixed him right up. Someone had been rude to the family while they were out shopping, and Anika returned so upset that she insisted on a session to calm her down and restore her faith in humanity to boot. On Christmas Day, there was a nasty fight between Adom and his cousins. The parents each agreed to use the room so that the children, and they themselves, could put it behind them. Henry, on standby, watched outside as the group sat together on the bench and the floor since there were so many. The children were still tearful. Anika was clearly distressed. The next day they celebrated Christmas anew, and Henry was the only one who remembered.

"You need to empty that big head of yours," Anika would say to Henry every now and again when she caught him deep in thought. Her words playful but true, she would wrap her arms around him and hum like the room.

"Why?" Henry would ask, hoping she had a reason that would release him.

But each time her answer was the same: "Why not? Why carry what you don't have to?"

One rainy evening toward the end of spring, Henry came home to the hum of THE FORGETTING ROOM. He frowned as he closed the front door behind him and looked around the empty kitchen.

"Anika?" he called as he dropped his keys on the island. "Adom?" All was quiet save for the humming. "Anika?" he called again. He moved toward the hallway and stopped. There was Adom in the living room, fast asleep on the couch. Henry headed for him but stopped. He could see the boy was breathing deeply, his face washed in soft gold lamplight. Henry headed into the hall instead.

The window in the door of THE FORGETTING ROOM was glowing bright like a spotlight, splashing the wall with white. Henry checked the time quickly—he wasn't late coming home, and Anika hadn't said anything about needing a session. Faintly, he began to feel the beginnings of annoyance. He walked up to the window and peered through it. Anika was sitting on the bench with her back to the door. Henry checked the timer. Five minutes. She had five minutes left. He exhaled slowly. At that moment he wanted to rap on the door and pull her out, but he knew he wouldn't. Instead, he gripped the door handle and let out another deep breath, resigned to waiting. It was just five more minutes. Henry stepped away and leaned against the wall. The room hummed. He exhaled again and closed his eyes. He didn't want to fuss, because she'd just go right back in. He didn't want to be angry with her, either, but he couldn't help it. She was breaking her own rule. Thank God Adom was sleeping, but what if he'd gotten up before Henry had come home? What if he'd gotten into something? It hit him that she might just have all three of them go in to deal with that if it'd happened, and a new wave of frustration, tinged with unease, washed over him. The room kept on humming. Henry opened his eyes. He checked the timer. Five minutes. He checked his watch.

"Anika?" he said aloud. He looked through the window again with his hands pressed against the glass. She still sat neatly on the bench. "Anika?"

They made it to the hospital just in time. Anika was now lying in a bed with tubes in her mouth and nose, and a machine breathing for her. Henry had banged on the door for her to open up, and the noise woke Adom. The boy clung to his father as Henry tried to force the room open, but it was no use. The timer still read five minutes. The door was sealed. In the end, he had to call the police and the fire department to destroy the room's brain by smashing the keypad. When it finally stopped humming and the door unlocked itself, the sudden silence crashed over them like a tidal wave.

"Is she going to be okay?" Henry asked the doctor when it was just them and Anika in the room. Adom was outside with Anika's parents. The doctor looked uncomfortable.

"I really can't say," she said at last. "This technology is . . . well—" She looked at him apologetically. "We'll just have to wait and see."

"Tell me again, now, Henry. One more time," Anika's mother said an hour later. They were in her car. Adom was with Anika's father in the hospital cafeteria. The boy hadn't eaten dinner, and he hadn't said a word since the room stopped humming. Henry and his mother-in-law headed back to the house for toiletries and pajamas so Henry could stay with Anika overnight.

"I came home," Henry said, "and she was using the room."

"Where was Adom?"

"Asleep on the couch."

"How long had she been in there?"

"I don't know."

"What do you mean? Don't they come with timers?"

Henry sighed. "They do, but I think it must have malfunctioned. It said there were five minutes left in the session when I got home. It still said five minutes when the paramedics showed up twenty minutes later. I don't know how long she was in there. It . . ." He inhaled shakily. "It could have been hours."

Anika's mother was silent for a moment. Then: "Did Adom say anything?"

"No," Henry said.

"He didn't have an idea or—"

"He didn't say anything," Henry answered. His throat was tight. They turned down a side street and then onto another. The house was in view. Both of their cars were sitting in the drive, and the porchlight was on. They could have been home having dinner.

"That poor child didn't say *anything?*"

Henry pulled up to the house and killed the engine. He looked at Anika's mother for just a moment. She was watching him with wide, wide eyes. "Nothing," he said. "I don't think he knew what was happening until they were able to shut down the room."

Inside the house everything seemed to be frozen. It was quiet like after a fresh snowfall, and nothing looked out of place until they got into the hall. THE FORGETTING ROOM door had been pulled from its hinges and was resting against the wall. The keypad that displayed the timer was destroyed. Henry couldn't shake the swing of the axe as the fireman sunk it into the glass. It was completely dark inside.

"You gonna have it fixed?" Anika's mother whispered after a beat.

Henry didn't answer. He didn't know what to say.

"Just as well," she said, her voice low.

In the weeks following, Henry and Adom stayed with Anika's parents. They all visited Anika every day, and the boy cried each time he looked at his mother. Henry wished over and over that Anika would just open her eyes and look at him, at them, and say what they needed to hear. What did she need to forget that day? Why hadn't she called him? But she just lay there, still and silent, her face calm like she was having a nice dream. Her parents spoke to her, said they knew she could hear their voices, but still she slept. In the dark when they were alone, Henry sat at Anika's side squeezing her hand, but she didn't squeeze back.

THE FORGETTING ROOM was repaired. The manufacturers stressed that it had been a once-in-a-lifetime malfunction. A tragic fluke. Henry settled his short-lived lawsuit when he got dangerously close to missing a payment to the hospital and the manufacturers offered to fix the room for free in addition to a large lump sum. Henry needed it. Adom needed it. Life still felt like an unending dream. Henry saw that evening when he lay in bed alone at night, heard the sirens as they grew closer and the nothingness in place of THE FORGETTING ROOM's song. Though Anika's parents were kind to him, they didn't speak to Henry much. Her mother had little to say since he'd accepted the settlement, but in truth, she hadn't really spoken to him since that night. The words she'd said then ran through his mind like restless ghosts:

"You know, I read the reviews. The testimonies," she'd said as she stood beside him in that dark, quiet hallway. "When Anika told me about it, it was clear these things help a lot of people. I know sometimes the only way to heal a mind is to wipe it clean. But . . ." She'd sighed and sunk to the floor, let her back rest against the wall. "But," she said again as she settled, "it's not natural. Not really."

Henry didn't say anything. She kept going. "Give life enough time and the mind erases itself. People start forgetting. Little pieces of 'em go. I saw it happen to Anika's granddaddy. My father. He didn't even know me or Momma by the end. And it hurt him. I could tell he knew he was missing something when he looked at us, but we were gone. The most heartbreaking thing I've ever seen. And then this thing comes along and offers to do the forgetting for you . . . it's not how things are supposed to go."

Still Henry said nothing, and she was silent for a very long time. He was on the floor beside her, but he didn't remember sitting down. Tears slipped from her eyes. "This poor child," she whispered, and as she grabbed his hand, Henry wondered if she was talking about Anika, or Adom, or maybe even himself. All he could see was Anika's back facing him through the window, her body perched on that bench like a bird on a wire. "All we have are our memories, Henry," she said suddenly but softly, her voice breaking into his mind like ocean against cliff. "They're really all we are."

In another month Henry and Adom were home. Anika remained in the hospital, and the doctor finally said what Henry had already come to know. Adom still wouldn't speak. Henry got them a therapist, but the progress was slow. They mostly sat in silence waiting for Adom to respond to the therapist's promptings and questions, but he wouldn't say a word.

"What more can we do?" Henry asked the therapist after one session. Adom sat outside in the waiting room playing with a tiny plastic car.

"We're doing all that we can," said the therapist gently. "It's going to take some time for him, and you, to process this trauma. He's just not ready to talk yet, but I think if we keep at it, he will be." Henry didn't know what to say. His throat was tight; it hadn't loosened in months.

"What about you?" the therapist asked. Henry looked up. "Are you seeing someone as well? These sessions with Adom are good, but you likely need one-on-one help as well . . ."

Henry tried to swallow, but he couldn't. "Oh, yes," he lied. "As often as I can."

They visited Anika's parents often. Sometimes they all sat together quietly, watching television or listening to the radio. Other times Henry went so that he could sleep with a trusted eye on Adom. Anika's mother would lead him to the guest room and leave him there. As he drifted off, he could hear her talking to Adom, but the boy never said anything back, and she didn't press him.

One night after they'd come home from visiting Anika, after bath time and dinner, Henry could hear Adom in his room.

He was crying. Henry passed THE FORGETTING ROOM as he moved down the hall. The cries were so quiet, Henry wondered how he had heard them at all. He stopped outside the closed bedroom door and waited. A second later, Adom spoke.

"Momma?"

Henry opened the door to find his son on the floor with a stuffed animal held to his chest. He looked up at his father with a shining face. They stared at each other for a stretched moment, and then Henry walked forward and lifted Adom into his arms.

"Baba," he said, and rested his head on Henry's shoulder. Henry held him close, felt his weight and his warmth, heard his shuddering breaths in his ear as Adom cried harder and harder.

He saw Anika sitting on the bench and realized he couldn't remember the last thing he'd said to her. He closed his eyes tight and walked out of Adom's bedroom with the boy held tight in his arms. Together they went back up the hallway and stopped at THE FORGETTING ROOM. Henry carefully punched a series of numbers onto the keypad and a smiley face appeared, winking at him.

With a click the door opened, and a message appeared: *The Room is Ready for Use. Please Enter.*

DOMINIQUE DICKEY

Look at the Moon

FROM *Lightspeed*

FANTASY

WE DROVE OUT to Joshua Tree for the star party—a gathering of amateur astronomers under a clear, dark sky. It was Holly's idea, an impromptu adventure on a Friday after work: "Hey, Lou, do you want to go look at the moon tonight?"

Holly had the best ideas *and* the worst ideas, and in the daylight, it was hard to tell them apart at first glance. I took a gamble. I said yes.

And I meant it—I wanted nothing more than to lie down under the Milky Way with my hand in hers and gaze into forever. For a long time, our love was the biggest thing I knew how to believe in.

When we met, I was trying to find God and Holly was trying to split the difference, looking for something halfway between the terrifying God of her youth and what she saw as heresy. She was looking for the right *kind* of God, because the only alternative was the sin of losing faith entirely.

I asked her if she was afraid of *God,* or if what she was really afraid of was *people,* after growing up in a family that used the Bible like a blunt weapon.

She considered it. We were in a church basement—Baptist, but the kind of liberal Baptists who've formally apologized for slavery—for a queer women's prayer group. Holly looked like she was afraid of being struck down just for walking through the doors, and years later I'd tell her I loved her at first sight, even though it wasn't technically the truth.

"Can't it be both?" Holly asked, after a lot of thoughtful *hmm* sounds from the circle of folding chairs. "I want a God I don't have to fear, and I don't want to fear the people who love Him, either."

More *hmm* sounds, along with a deeply ponderous "Amen." Then the pastor said, "God is love, God is love," and the conversation moved on.

I never stopped thinking about it: God without fear, and love without fear, as though they were opposite sides of a balanced equation. It felt trite, forced, even at the height of my desire to believe. Honestly, the more I reached for faith, the more everything felt trite and forced.

I didn't grow up with God, not in the traditional sense, but I grew up loved so hard that it threatened to suffocate me. I grew up with love, and I grew up with fear, and maybe what I was really looking for was a way to separate the two.

That's not something you can find in a church, but I didn't know how to stop looking.

"New friends!" someone bellowed as we turned into the roadside pullout.

Our headlights were off so as not to blind our fellow stargazers. We were over a hundred miles out of LA, in a sort of mecca for those who want to see the night sky without light pollution. It was so dark, the kind of velvet black that should've had a texture against your skin, except for a circle of red-tinted flashlights set up about fifty yards from the parking area. It was the kind of darkness that felt amniotic. It reminded me of being terribly small—and terribly afraid—on a sort of instinctive level.

Someone pulled my door open before I could do it myself. A man, not very tall but quite round, with the sort of face that would have every other stranger approaching him like, *You look just like my long-lost cousin's boyfriend's brother.* The kind of face that was, in and of itself, an invitation to conversation. As someone who also suffered from Resting Approachable Face, I sort of respected that he'd charged into this social situation without giving us a chance to be awkward at him.

"Welcome, friends," he said, sticking out his hand. "I'm Orion."

"Luna." In those days, I found it easier to use my given name with strangers. It was a calculus of safety, both from physical harm and from the prying questions that came with using a man's name. I wanted to trust Orion on sight, but I was wary of my own split-second assessment of him, and I didn't want to be stuck in the middle of a national park with his assumptions about my gender. And people tend to see what they want to see, which meant that he'd see me as a woman no matter what I did.

I was right: He didn't think twice before he moved on, scrambling around to Holly's side of the car and offering to help her wrangle her telescope out of the back seat. I turned the engine off and handed Holly the keys, and she stowed them in the front pocket of her backpack.

"Oh—It's not that heavy, really. I can do it," Holly said, but she gave him the telescope, and that thing was her baby, prized above any of her other possessions. "Thanks. I'm Holly."

I lifted the folded tripod over my shoulder and followed them into the circle of red light. The ground was bare and dry, and the wind was high, and the desert was cold at night even in August. I fumbled to zip up my coat one-handed, but the zipper got snagged on the strap for my binoculars.

"I brought new friends," Orion called, and the group sent up a cheer, clearing a patch of dirt for us to lay down our blanket.

"Wow," Holly said, knocking her elbow against mine. There were seven of them including Orion, and they had come prepared—*really* prepared. Everything I knew about stargazing equipment came from online gift guides, trying to spoil Holly every birthday and Christmas, but even I could tell that the telescopes and cameras were too good for amateurs. Holly's telescope, which had relieved me of half of a paycheck, looked downright dinky in comparison.

I felt self-conscious about my shitty little binoculars and lack of technical knowledge, but Holly saw the circle of experienced astronomers as an opportunity. She's always been braver than me about striking up conversations with strangers—or new friends, as Orion said. She turned her red-tinted headlamp to the woman set up to our right, who was sharing a telescope with a young boy.

"Nice to meet you," Holly said. "Is tonight a good night to see Saturn, do you think?"

Holly made her way around the circle, making introductions for the both of us, asking little questions about what everyone was looking at. The network of relationships became plain: Orion and Aurora were married. The twelve-year-old, Virgo, was their son. I was almost jealous of the way his voice cracked when he introduced himself—his first victory in attrition warfare with puberty. Phoebe and Stella, who were Aurora's sisters, were taking composite pictures of the bright, full moon as it crossed the sky. Castor and Pollux were, of course, brothers; they were drawing Jupiter on a large piece of butcher paper, the edges weighed down with fist-size stones, their hands moving in tandem to create a single illustration. Their names, all of them related to astronomy, seemed self-chosen. I respected that.

I didn't think it was strange that the star party was publicly advertised, but everyone here already knew each other. I'd been to about a billion churches where the doors were open to strangers even though the congregation had coalesced into a family, and this was a type of holy place. And I could practically see Holly thinking that *they* were all friends, and they wanted *us* to be their friends, and maybe someday we could have this. She could see a future: Friday nights driving out to Joshua Tree to watch the stars with people who had the skill to match her passion.

As Holly offered to share the trail mix and canned beer we'd brought, I looked at the sky. My binoculars hung against my chest, ignored—I could see more stars with my naked eyes than I had in a long, long time. Each star was in the past, the light an artifact of a nuclear reaction that had long fizzled out, but it still felt like looking into the future. Looking at the night sky had always felt like looking forward, ever since I was a kid, but at this point it was still abstract. It was just a sort of itch at the back of my brain and in the pit of my stomach. Sense without meaning.

I turned my headlamp back on and watched Holly take the sketch pad and charcoal pencils out of her backpack. She sat on our blanket and aimed her telescope toward the full moon, just as I knew she would. She began to draw, just as she always did. She'd drawn the moon countless times in all of its phases, mostly from the roof of my apartment building. It was a proclivity I enjoyed teasing her about, though we'd been dating for four years and I'd never asked if there was a deeper reason.

I'd always been afraid to. The quiet way she loved the moon felt sacred, on par with the annotations she used to make in the margins of her Bible. I knew where that road could lead, if she let it. I'd grown up at the end of it.

I heard Castor make a joke and Aurora laugh. When I turned my head, the red light passed over Orion kissing Phoebe, a momentary brush of his mouth over hers. Familiarity prickled under my skin as I looked away, along with embarrassment. I felt like I wasn't meant to see them. Orion was kissing his wife's sister right out in the open, and I felt like *I* had done something wrong by looking.

I didn't often think of my childhood—this was deliberate—but I did, in that moment. It was hard not to: the dark sky, the names, Orion's generous affection.

So it was then that I finally asked Holly why, with so many photographs of the moon on the internet, she needed to see it with her own eyes to draw it. Why she even needed to draw it at all.

"I like to draw pretty things," she said.

"There are so many other pretty things," I insisted, thinking of Aurora explaining how to locate Saturn as I watched Holly move the pencil in rapid strokes, forming the shape of a crater.

"I draw the moon whenever I want to draw you," she said.

I was surprised. I could have made a list of all the world's beauties, down to the way jacaranda blossoms piled into the gutters, and still not included my name on that list.

"I know I can get the moon right, but I can never pin you down on paper. Not all of you, anyway—the moon is an easier target."

"Can I kiss you?" I asked.

"Not here," Holly said, very quietly. She could be shy about touch in public—and then doubly shy about her own shyness. She held up the half-finished drawing. It looked the same as all the rest she'd shown me. We could have each wallpapered our apartments with them. "And you know what else? The moon stays still long enough to be drawn."

I mumbled something about proving that I could stay still, but my feet were tapping against the blanket without conscious thought. I heard Aurora laugh again, her voice tangled up with Orion's, and when I looked over my shoulder, he was kissing Stella this time, just a quick touch that made me feel overheated inside with recognition. Strange to see those little moments of affection that hold so much weight. Stranger, still, that nothing was hidden from us.

I wanted to kiss Holly. I wanted to kiss her, and I sort of regretted using my birth name. I wanted to know what it would mean to be myself here, with these new people.

I lay on my back and used my binoculars to look at things I had no interest in identifying. Perhaps they were planets or stars or even distant galaxies, but it didn't matter to me. Holly cared about the physics of the universe enough for the both of us. I couldn't keep up with her—I'd never been an artist, and I wasn't much for science, aside from facts I'd collected growing up—but I was nonetheless drawn to the beauty of the night sky, and all the potential in it. My feet were still moving, but I felt like I could lie there long enough to watch the constellations shift as the night passed us by. I could have lain there for longer than a season, letting the stars show me in their own language what *had* happened, and what *might* happen, and—if I really concentrated—what *would* happen.

As it was, I stayed there long enough for my eyes to become unfocused, until all I saw were shapes made of light. Then Holly touched my hand and asked me to look at her sketch pad, where she'd moved on to drawing Saturn and one of its larger moons. I told her it was beautiful. Farther off—Aurora had pulled him away, toward a large rock formation that was hard to make out in the low light—I could hear Virgo crying with a child's unabashed intensity.

I closed my eyes, tipped my head back, then opened them

again. The Milky Way was a bright, white sprawl. I said to Holly, "I have a bad feeling about this," even though I didn't know entirely where the words came from. It was like the feeling of seeing Orion kiss his wife's sister: the feeling of knowing something that wasn't for me to know, building in my belly.

"He's a kid," she said. Virgo's fit was the loudest thing—of course she'd assume it was him upsetting me. "Kids are dramatic. He's probably tired."

"Holly—"

"Kids cry all the time. Where else will I get a view like this?"

I looked at her drawing again. Her hand was still moving, another of Saturn's moons taking shape on the paper, and it was true that nights as cloudless as this were rare. That didn't take away the *not-quite-right* feeling behind my navel.

"Sweetheart, sweetheart, just *try*," Aurora was saying, holding out a pair of binoculars for Virgo to take. "Just try one more time, okay?" He knocked the binoculars to the ground. I looked away, taking the light with me. I turned my headlamp off.

"Orion?" Holly asked. "Do you know what time Venus sets tonight?"

Orion crossed the circle toward us. He checked his watch. "About now, but you might still be able to catch her if you're quick. Can I?"

She stepped out of the way, and he swung her telescope down toward the horizon, bending to follow the eyepiece. Turning my headlamp off was the equivalent of putting on sunglasses during the day: I could look wherever I wanted, without any indication of my focus. I watched Castor and Pollux move toward Virgo, and then one of them picked up the binoculars from the dirt and offered them to him again. The kid wailed, words I couldn't make out, but later I thought it sounded like "I'm scared." Castor grabbed his arm, and I could see that it was a firm grip, and as Orion snapped up to standing I caught the outline of a gun on his hip.

"Hey!" Orion hollered. The wind threw his voice back at us. "Cut that out. *Now.*"

Castor let go. Virgo didn't stop crying.

Orion apologized to Holly, then went back to fiddling with

her telescope. His sweatshirt had rucked up from the motion, and that was definitely a pistol, small and satiny black, and it didn't look real. It was the kind of thing you'd see in a movie, or a video game.

"What's that about?" I asked, because I really wanted to trust him, and because I've got the kind of smile that makes people see the best in me, though I rarely ever use it. My mom used to say the expression made me look just like my father.

"What's what about?" Orion peeked up at me, then at Aurora and Virgo, then back down at the telescope.

"The firearm. What's that about?"

"Bears, coyotes." His voice was the kind of mumble you can only manage with one eye squished shut and the other focusing hard. It reminded me of Holly doing her makeup. "You never know what you'll run into out here." He moved back from the telescope. "There, now take a look. Probably not enough time for a sketch, but I bet you can get a picture." And then he bounded off toward the rock formation, his wife and his son and his mistresses and his brothers-in-law huddled in its shadow. That feeling, that wrong-feeling *knowing*, snaked up toward my sternum. I didn't want it to make its way to my throat.

Holly lined up the lens of a little disposable film camera with the eyepiece of the telescope. Her telescope didn't have a camera built in, and using her phone would've killed her night vision, along with everyone else's.

"Let's get out of here, after you get this shot," I said.

The camera clicked. Holly didn't answer. She picked her sketch pad back up, balanced it on her lap. The astronomers—all of them in a single cluster now—were speaking, quietly enough that I couldn't make out the words. The men had gathered around their women and the boy like wild animals preparing to face a predator. I could still hear Virgo crying, even above the overlapping voices.

"Come on, Holly, I don't like this." I was going to choke on the sheer *wrongness* of it. I had never had a feeling like that before, with that degree of certainty.

"Give me a minute," she said, fitting her eye to the telescope. "I really think I *might* have time to draw—"

Aurora started to march toward us, her arm around Virgo's shoulders. Stella grabbed her by the hood of her sweatshirt and tugged her back into the circle so hard that she fell to the ground. She disappeared behind a wall of bodies.

I began to unmount Holly's telescope from the tripod—never mind that Holly's face was still turned toward the eyepiece—as Orion walked over to us, his face alarmingly placid. "Sorry about the scene," he said. "Everyone's tired, and Virgo can get quite emotional—gets it from his mother, you know how it is."

"Oh, don't worry about us, we'll just go." My cold fingers fumbled with the bolts and clasps.

"You don't have to do that," Orion said, but he started to help me take down our equipment. "We would really love to have you stay." He had the telescope held in his arms like a newborn. "The thing is, we've gathered here for a religious observance, and we weren't sure if you were comfortable with that."

Holly had gotten with the program by then, thank God, and was shoving her sketchbook and pencils into her backpack.

"But hey," Orion said, "we're all friends here."

There was a scream. It echoed terribly in the smooth darkness. I reached for the telescope, but Orion wouldn't let go of it. He was looking at Aurora, sprawled out on the ground and begging, over and over, "Please, spare him. He's a baby. Please spare my baby."

She'd knocked over one of the flashlights, and the angle covered everything in patches of shadow. I clicked my headlamp on. I don't know why I did it. I already knew.

Castor—or maybe it was Pollux—had Virgo pinned to the ground with a knee on his chest. Pollux—or perhaps it was Castor—had one of those rocks in his fist, the big and jagged ones that had held their drawing flat.

He swung the stone down into the child's temple. Aurora's scream almost covered the wet, thumping sound.

Holly took off running toward my car, and I followed her. The light from her headlamp swung into my eyes as she looked back—she kept looking back—and I was struggling to make out the ground at my feet. All it would take was a rock or a root to send me sprawling, and I would be lost. I knew it. I knew.

"This is a warning!" Orion shouted, in the same booming voice that had called us his friends, but I heard him as if underwater. All I knew was that I needed to get to the car, but I couldn't push my legs or my lungs any harder, and I had to be sure not to trip.

His words made sense when the gunshot broke open the sky. I hadn't ever heard a gunshot in real life before that. I had no idea how loud it would be, even at a distance. I had no idea that my ears would ring for minutes after. It didn't matter—that was the push I'd needed, and I was somehow running faster, the ground disappearing from under me like it didn't even matter. I caught up to Holly, then passed her, then came up against the driver's side door.

The car was unlocked. The interior lights came on when I opened the door, awful and white after so much unbroken darkness, and my eyes began to water as I threw myself in, and I found I had to squint to look out at the pullout. I blinked and blinked, and I couldn't see Holly, and I couldn't start the car. The keys were in her backpack.

"Lou," she said. Her voice came from below me, barely a wheeze. I looked down.

Orion had her pinned in the dirt beneath the jut of the car door, his weight on her chest and the pistol held to her shoulder. He looked up at me, his face hard and unbothered in the light shining down from the car, half of him still red-tinged from those distant flashlights.

"Well, friends," Orion panted, "I can't exactly let you leave now."

I'd been going to church with Holly for two years when I realized I didn't really want God at all. What I wanted was to be someone else's problem, for a change. I wanted to lay myself down at some divine father's feet and say, *Take it, it's all yours, and it's your responsibility.* I wanted someone to tell me that everything would be okay, and I wanted someone to blame for the sum of who I was; I wanted them to be the same someone.

I flung myself on altar after altar. God never showed. I figured He was dead, like my dad. Maybe, like my dad, He'd been dead since before I was born, and I had once again arrived too late for that kind of big belief.

I was a capital-A Atheist for a while, then a garden-variety nonbeliever. And then Holly, who had always been *taken care of* in the way that smothered, who had always wanted to learn what it looked like to love someone with a loose grip, said, "Let me love you." She said, "Let your burdens be mine," and I was hers in an instant.

"And at this point, it's the practical thing to do, isn't it?" asked Holly, who was always looking for ways to make her desires unimpeachable.

"Sure, let's get together for *practical* reasons. Want to shake on it?"

She held out her hand. I took it, and pulled her in, and I was halfway to laughing when I kissed her for the first time. It was a clumsy, half-cocked effort: She was laughing, too, and I wanted to hear the clear, bright sound almost more than I wanted to swallow it.

I said, "You're ridiculous, do you know that?"

"I just figure you've been in my heart for so long," said Holly. "You've probably got squatter's rights by now."

She was right—our lives had blurred together with the protracted inevitability of stars colliding in orbit, ever since that afternoon in the church basement, and it was past time to call it what it was.

This was what I found to believe in: I believed in Holly. I believed in us together. I believed in myself when I was with her.

It didn't feel forced, like worship songs and altar calls had always felt forced. After trying so hard to love God, loving her was easy.

We'd been together for almost a year when Holly told me a secret: God had never clicked for her, either. He was a reflex, she said. He was something she reached for on instinct, like a child sucking their thumb. He was a habit she was ready to grow out of.

She could have fooled me. Her faith—or her performance of

it—looked so genuine from the outside, in a way I used to envy. She looked peaceful, when she prayed. I always thought I just looked desperate.

"It's not that I don't believe in God," she said, after a while. "God is something we construct. I believe in God the way I believe in, I don't know, daylight saving time. The real problem is that I don't know how to love Him without being afraid of Him, and I can't do that anymore."

Which is to say that, as Orion walked us back to the circle of red light, I was surprised that Holly began to mumble the Lord's Prayer. I picked up the thread nonetheless, said, "Forever and ever, Amen," along with her. She'd cut her palm on the rocky ground when Orion tackled her; when she squeezed my hand in hers, I felt blood smear between us.

"Lou, we're gonna die," she whispered. "I'm so sorry. I'm so sorry."

"You're not going to die," said Orion, "if you do exactly what I say. If you're just as guilty as we are, then you won't go running to the cops."

"We wouldn't," Holly promised. "We won't."

"Just tell me why you're doing this," I said, but I knew it was too late for his answer to change anything. It was all in Holly's shift from hypothetical to definitive, *wouldn't* to *won't*. She could see a way out of this situation, and she was going to take it—whatever it turned out to be. She would do it for me, even though I hadn't asked her to. She'd never mastered any other kind of love.

Orion didn't answer. More of the flashlights had gotten tipped over. The roadside pullout was a confusion of astronomy gear and discarded coats, the silhouettes strange and shadows too large. Aurora's sobbing felt loud and far away, and it took me a long moment to realize that the scraping sound was her digging into the ground with a small trowel.

"You said it was—You said it was a religious observance?" I asked. "What, you're doing it because God told you to?"

At this, he huffed out a breath that was almost a laugh. "We don't answer to any god you know. We answer only to the night sky, and the future."

That wrong and bad feeling, still present, began to crawl up onto my tongue. I felt like I'd be sick.

Orion nudged one of the fallen flashlights with his foot so that the beam pointed toward Castor, Pollux, and what was left of Virgo. He'd been beaten so badly that his shapes were all wrong. He'd lost one of his sneakers, and his white tube sock was soaked through with blood.

"One of you has to hit him," Orion said. He had the gun pressed against the back of Holly's neck. "It's the only way you're leaving here alive."

Castor hauled Virgo into something approximating uprightness. His head—uneven, cratered—hung limply from his neck. I remember that I was focused on the boy's hands, because they were still moving. He had dirt under his nails. He kept splaying his fingers out and then closing his fists, over and over again. I wondered what he was reaching for.

I thought of Holly reaching for God, like a child with her skull caved in.

Holly held her hand out. Orion picked up her telescope and handed it to her. "I do this, and you let us go?" she asked.

"I swear," said Orion.

Holly raised the telescope like a bat, the weight balanced over her shoulder. She told me not to look.

I watched her swing her telescope in a clean arc into Virgo's head. I knew at once that I would never be able to stop seeing it, and she would never be able to stop living it. I knew at once that it should've been me.

The rest felt like stop-motion, sporadic bursts of half-remembered light.

Virgo's hands stopped moving. There was nothing left of him, and nothing left for him to reach for.

Holly had a splatter of blood on her cheek shaped almost like California. Her tears made tracks through it, the Coast Range melting into the Mojave, and then obliterated it completely.

Orion walked us to the car, even as his voice went bright and frantic: "You can stay with us, if you want. You can come back.

It's not always like this. This isn't—Don't assume that this is all of who we are. You'll understand with time. We could be friends."

I answered with a single, strained "No," but the sound didn't quite come out even though my mouth made the shape of the word.

At the car, he reached into his pocket and pulled out a wad of hundred-dollar bills. They were in my shaking hands between one blink and the next, and I didn't even want them, because it wasn't like money changed any of this. But he said, "For your telescope," and his eyes looked old and sad, and I said, "Oh," and handed the money to Holly.

I drove us back to the I-10 and away, away. When I blinked and realized I couldn't remember the last forty miles, I pulled into a rest stop outside of Banning. We were near where I'd grown up. I thought, hollowly, that my mother, who I hadn't spoken to in years, might be asleep a few miles away. And then I was leaning against the hood of my Subaru with no memory of getting out of the car, a puddle of vomit at my feet and the engine still running. And then Holly was opening the tailgate, dousing her face and hands with bottled water, shivering, scrubbing at the crust of blood in the lines of her palms and under one nostril. She took off her coat and her shirt, crossed the parking lot in just her bra to shove them into the dumpster, then came back and wrapped herself in a faded blue baja blanket that had been sitting in the trunk for a year, maybe longer.

She was crying again, or she hadn't ever stopped, I didn't know. I watched her hands grip the edges of the blanket. I thought of Virgo's hands, opening and closing. I thought, *Is this what it's supposed to feel like?* I only felt numb.

Holly pulled me under the blanket with her. We stayed there for a long time, and the sun came up over the desert.

The first god Holly learned to worship was her mother.

They were everything to each other. They loved each other in their own private language, inside jokes and secret gestures. They had the same face. They had the same laugh. There were no walls up between them. No privacy, and no need for it.

When Holly was frightened as a child—and she was frightened quite a lot—she reached for her mom first, and God second.

Her youth ministry picketed pride parades and drag shows, and her mother told her she was an upstanding kid doing the Lord's good work. She kissed a girl after softball practice, and her mother told her she would go to Hell if she didn't clean up her sinful heart, and how could she destroy her family like this? Because Holly's mother was going to Heaven, and if Holly got herself sent to that other place, they'd be separated in eternity. So it was selfish, wasn't it, for Holly to lust after girls the way she did?

When we met, Holly was looking for God because she didn't want to lose the woman who'd once been her entire world.

"My mom's my best friend," Holly said, after we'd known each other for half a year, and I knew she was lying but I didn't think *she* knew it. I could see it on her, because we'd grown up in similar houses, though they were governed by different theology: the only children of widowed mothers who, for all their good intentions, only knew how to love their daughters as extensions of themselves.

"If your best friend thinks you're going to Hell, maybe you need more friends," I told her, as diplomatically as I could.

Holly didn't talk to me for nearly a month, after that. I knew I'd prodded too hard at a gaping wound. When she was ready, she would outgrow her need for her mother. It was possible that, in doing so, she would outgrow the need for God.

I was so proud of her when she walked away from religion— and I wasn't surprised at all that she called her mom as soon as we'd made it back to my apartment. It was a bright Saturday morning. I felt like all my edges had been worn down and like I needed at least three showers, but Holly took her phone and ducked into the bathroom. It didn't matter what time it was in Texas; her mother would always pick up when her baby girl called, and I could hear Holly through the door, still crying, as she'd been steadily crying since Banning.

"Mommy? Are you there?" When she spoke to her mother, she sounded like she'd never stopped being that terrified child. Like she'd never stopped being helpless and easy to love. "I'm sorry to wake you, I just—I just needed to hear your voice. It was—I had a bad dream." I heard a new rush of sobs, muffled under the running tap. "Can you pray for me? Just say you'll pray for me. I'll let you go back to sleep, just say a prayer first. I love you. I love you so, so much."

I lay on the living room floor and wished I could just die. I still felt numb all the way through. I wanted to hurt. I wanted someone to hurt me.

I slapped myself across the face. I dug my nails into the curve of my cheek. I missed the father I had never known. I wished I had something to reach for after a fright, the way Holly backslid into faith. I wanted to believe, but I found no satisfaction in belief as both the means and the ends. I wanted to believe, and I wanted to be proven right.

The first god I learned to worship was my father.

This isn't something I talk about, not even with Holly, and it's not for lack of trying. It's just that God is so big for some people, and this isn't my story—this has always been prologue. Here it goes.

My father was the leader of a fringe religious group. It would not have been a stretch to call it a cult. There's even a Hulu documentary about him, if you care to look him up, but it's all conjecture—none of the allegations ever stuck. It was the kind of congregation that gets really wrapped up in one person's teachings and can't possibly last forever, and they made this perfectly mortal man their god.

When I was an embryo, he had a heart attack. His followers scattered. I assumed they came to their senses, or moved on.

My mother never let go.

My father was her god, and he would live on in her. He would live on in *us*, because what was I, but a part of her? She'd held me tucked under her heart for nine frenzied months, a steady presence while her life fell apart around her. I always thought my mother loved me best when I was in her skin.

She kept pictures of my father in every room of the house. She dragged me to places where the sky was dark and holy for eclipses, meteor showers, every supermoon. There were things she wouldn't tell me, and things she hid in metaphor, but the picture became clear enough: He was the kind of god who destroys that which doesn't serve him; maybe even a more vengeful god than the one Holly had grown up fearing. He was a god, and he was looking for his heir, and the ends would justify the means. He was a god who wasn't above killing his own sons, like so many gods before him.

It was all bullshit—I could see that, even as a kid—but I envied the fervency of my mother's belief. I remember watching her tilt her face up to the Perseids on a moonless night, weeping, her arms flung wide in expectation. I felt unmoved by the sky full of falling stars, jealous that this moment could mean so much to her. I wanted conviction. I wanted, just once in my life, for something to feel that true to me.

When I met Holly, I was looking for a god big enough to kill for, or to die for. I wanted ecstasy, in the oldest sense of the word. I wanted to reach out to the divine and feel the divine reaching back.

I was looking for God, but here's what I found: I'm far more my father's son than I ever was my mother's daughter, and my father would have beaten me to death for failing him.

Which is to say, the first time I was baptized, I was afraid the pastor would drown me.

The second time I was baptized, I sort of wished he would.

Holly started going to church again. Just Sunday mornings at first, then Wednesday night Bible study and Saturday afternoon prayer group. It seemed to make her feel better. I didn't hold it against her.

She woke up screaming nearly every night—always in my bed, because she was afraid to sleep alone and her place was too small for the both of us. She buried her face in the front of my shirt and cried like Virgo had cried, like a terrified child. I held her. I didn't hold it against her.

Some nights, she didn't wake in a panic. She woke quietly, slipped out of bed, and called her mother from the bathroom.

This, I did hold against her, because it should have been me she woke with her grief and regret, because I had been there. I had lived through it with her. I knew the truth she could never tell anyone else, and lying to her mother about what upset her only made her more upset. And Holly's mother knew her best, and knew how best to hurt her, and was careless with that power. Holly loved her mother with the sort of love that brings fear with it.

But on those nights, I took the stairs to the roof so that I wouldn't have to overhear the conversations Holly tried to keep quiet. On those nights, I fed myself little glimpses of whatever stars I could make out.

I spent a lot of time looking down, because I thought this was the mark the star party had left on me: a feeling of knowing something I shouldn't know, creeping up from my belly to my chest to my throat, that hit me whenever I looked at the night sky. It was the only real thing I felt, aside from the numbness, and I suspected that if I threw myself into it, something would happen. Finding out *what* would require its own kind of faith—a faith I simply lacked. I had no interest in trusting something I couldn't see.

By February I was exhausted, everything felt impossible, and Holly was praying on the phone with her mother for the fourth night in a row. I couldn't get back to sleep. I wasn't angry. I wasn't frustrated. I didn't feel much of anything, but I wanted to. I wanted to hurt. I wanted to experience something that would change me.

I looked up.

I could see the Big Dipper. The moon was a waning sliver. The breeze was cold, but not as cold as that night in the desert. I clenched my hands into fists.

I knew. I couldn't say what or how, but I knew.

When I went back inside, Holly was curled up on the couch with a mug of tea steaming on the side table. I grabbed both of her hands. "Hey," she said.

I felt like a passenger in my own body. I said, "I forgive you. You ruined your life, and you did it for me—so that I wouldn't have to. I thank you, and I forgive you, and I know you need a bigger forgiveness than this."

"Lou, what?" She looked confused, but her nose wrinkled like it did when she was about to cry.

"I'm going back to bed," I told her.

In the morning, she asked me what a bigger forgiveness would look like. I told her I had no idea. She said she'd pray on it.

I said, "I thought you couldn't stand being afraid of God." Six months on, and it was the first time I'd pushed.

Her smile, old and sad, reminded me of Orion. "Now I've felt real fear, and I know it's not the same. It's not like that at all," Holly said. "I think what I felt was love all along. It doesn't have to be complicated."

With love and fear so blurred together, I wanted to ask Holly if she was ever afraid of me. If she was ever afraid that I would hurt her, like her mother hurt her over and over again.

Instead of asking, I waited for the sun to set, and I went up to the roof. I looked up at the sky.

Every Wednesday evening, Holly injected a small amount of testosterone cypionate into the meat of my thigh. The needle was so tiny that I hardly felt it, but I couldn't bear to watch it going in, and I didn't have it in me to push the plunger. I never asked her to do it; the routine that we fell into just made sense, because she wasn't afraid and I was. She knew I wanted this—needed it—and wasn't going to watch my fear hold me back from becoming myself.

We started in August, the Wednesday before the star party. By February, it was a well-practiced choreography of hands and eyes. I sat on the edge of the bathtub in my boxers and cleaned the injection site with an alcohol swab. She stood beside the sink and drew the solution from the vial into the syringe. I tore open the wrapper of a plastic bandage, patterned with blue and green stars. She pressed her palm against my knee. I focused on that sensation, that warm and broad touch, and tried to slow my speeding pulse. I watched her face: focused, worrying the tip of her tongue between her incisors. She grasped an inch of my skin between her forefinger and thumb, lifting subcutaneous fat away from muscle. I closed my eyes.

A quick pinch as the needle went in, and then it was over—until the next Wednesday.

Another week of cataloging the gradual changes. Nothing for a while, at first. Then a sudden appearance of acne between my eyebrows. Broader shoulders, and newly defined muscle in my calves. Uneven stubble under my chin, so that I was always getting razor burn in the crease of my neck. The fine hair on my legs seeming to take on both texture and color overnight. Deepening of my voice, in stops and starts, which Holly said made me sound more certain of myself.

She said I seemed to enjoy talking more. She said I seemed to enjoy the daily realities of having a body more: eating, exercising, showering, existing in three dimensions.

I couldn't tell. At the bottom of it all, I still felt that numbness.

Except for this: On Wednesdays, after Holly did my shot and left for Bible study, I started going up to the roof. That creeping knowing feeling, from belly to throat to mouth, grew stronger with each passing week. It didn't feel wrong anymore. I found a sort of safety in it.

I looked at the smoggy sky, light pollution rendering most of the stars invisible, and I *knew*.

It was a series of little premonitions, things I could have written off as luck or intuition. Once, Holly misplaced her car keys and I knew she'd put them in the fridge door by accident and put the little jar of capers in her purse. I had a good run of knowing just the right thing to say to calm her down or win her over.

It was a series of small moments that could have been called faith, if not for the blistering certainty I felt. I knew that I would see Orion before the year was out. I knew that Holly and I would be okay again, someday. I knew that the future spread out before us, an unbroken thread of possibility. Believing was never a challenge, because I knew these things were true.

Small truths, building up to a bigger one. Which meant that

in July, when I told Holly that she would feel better if she visited her mother, I knew she would believe me.

"I hate that place," she said. "You don't know what it's like. I *hate* that place."

She may have hated the town that raised her more than anything, but she refused to call anywhere else *home*. And her mother was her oldest god, and maybe she needed—just for a few days—the kind of love that smothered. And I had an errand to run, and needed her out of the way.

"Don't you think it will feel circular? Don't you think it'll be a sort of closure?" I offered. "Maybe this is your big forgiveness." She made a face, but she booked her flight the next day.

Holly spent a week with her mother, in a small town I'd only seen in dreams and photographs. I spent a week in Joshua Tree.

A week of days in an Airbnb outside of the national park, a week of nights at that roadside pullout in darkness so bottomless I was afraid to get lost in it. Holly called me every night to tell me of the outrageous things her mother had said or done, and I answered the phone sitting on the blue-patterned baja blanket near the rock formation where Virgo died, looking at the stars. Looking at forever.

"What are you doing?" she asked, on the fifth night.

I was holding up a red-tinted flashlight, using my toe to poke at the place where I remembered the grave being. The ground had swallowed it up.

"Looking at the sky," I told her. Holly didn't question it.

She groaned, and I imagined her eyes going large and somber. "My mother knows I'm going to Hell," she said. I waited her out. "She keeps talking about how my choices have *eternal consequences*, Lou. I think she knows. I'm going to Hell for—"

She let me cut her off. I knew she wouldn't want to finish the sentence. "Holly, I'm pretty sure your mom still means you're going to Hell for being queer."

"Oh. Right." Holly was silent for a while. I squinted at a point of light that might have been Venus, and wished I'd picked up new binoculars. "Why didn't you come with me?" she asked.

"I couldn't miss work," I said, but that wasn't it. The truth was this: I had to be here. I had a feeling.

"I know we haven't really talked about it," I said, "but you should move in with me."

"I already have squatter's rights," she said. I could picture her touching her dark, curly hair—flirting, shy about it. "You'd have to evict me."

"Let's make it official."

"Ooh, you know paperwork really gets me going."

"For practical reasons."

"Right, for *practical* reasons."

"But don't get the wrong idea," I told her. "I'm not asking because I *love* you or anything."

That made her laugh, which made me laugh, too. I hadn't heard her really laugh in a long time. I didn't know how much I'd missed it.

That numbness had started to ease—not just under the night sky but in the daylight, too. I think I was happy. I lay down on my blanket and talked to Holly about nothing until she fell asleep.

On my seventh and final Holly-less night, there was another car parked in my usual spot at the roadside pullout. A figure with a red headlamp sat by the rock formation.

"Hey, friend!" Orion called when I got out of the car. I turned on my own headlamp.

"Are those mine?" I asked, pointing to the binoculars around his neck as I sat down beside him.

"Do you want them back?"

"No, I'm good."

He held them out for me anyway. I didn't take them.

"You got a cold?" He gestured at his throat.

"What? I—No." I laughed. I felt so at home with my new voice that I only noticed the way it had changed if I looked at an old video, and even then, it was with a sort of detachment: *Did I ever really sound like that? You must be joking. There must be a mistake.* "I'm transgender."

I expected follow-up questions, but Orion moved on. "How's your girlfriend?"

"Holly."

"Right. How's Holly?"

"She's fine," I said, because I could tell that she would be. And then I asked the thing I had come here to ask: "Tell me about your god."

Orion had a smile like a stock image, or maybe just one particular photo: my father, grayscale and grainy from magnification, hanging above my mother's bed. She used to kiss her fingertips and then touch the glass of the frame, and the picture was always distorted with a thousand little smudges.

Orion smiled his familiar smile, and he told me the story of a gifted man—a man so gifted that he became sacred. A man who could look at celestial bodies and see the path forward. Such a gift brought acolytes from all over the world, looking for clarity and divine wisdom, and the man who became their god was happy to oblige. He could reassure the broken; he could look at people who were in pain and tell them, with complete certainty, that their suffering was not permanent. He provided hope, something so rare and precious and holy.

The problem was that he was still a man, and he would die, and he needed his gift to live on. The problem was that he needed an heir: someone who carried his blood, and his gift.

He knew the future, but only in broad strokes—he didn't trade in specificity. He knew his heir would be his son, or maybe his grandson? He knew a lot of blood would be spilled along the way, boys rooted out as they failed to manifest his power of prophecy. His followers trusted him with their bodies, their children, their fate. They reached for him with their fears and their doubts, because he was their god.

When he died, the unworthy fell away like chaff from grain, leaving only the truest of believers. A small circle of those who carried his word, knowing his heir was on the way. It was just a matter of time. Time, and watching the stars.

"He was my father," Orion said. "Virgo was my son."

"Then why did you do it?"

"I had to. He wasn't my father's true heir, and I'm just the conduit."

This was a man who'd grown up with a living god, all of that divine love and fear attached to something he could touch. His god fed him mushy peas as a baby. His god taught him how to ride a bike. His god kept him safe, waiting for him to hit puberty and either prove his worth or be put to death. He never had a chance.

I took my headlamp off and rested it on the ground between us. The shadows made Orion's face sharp. He looked so much like those photos, in every room of my childhood home.

"Was one of your father's wives called Pandora?" I asked.

"You look just like her," he said. I wondered when exactly he'd pieced it together. I didn't need to know.

But I looked into the spray of stars above us, willing myself to fall once more into the future. Trying to prove to myself that I wasn't making this up, this gift I had.

I looked up, and it was the truest thing I'd ever felt.

"Stella's pregnant," I said as I hauled myself up off the ground and turned toward my car. "Another son, and he's going to live a long life."

"He's the heir?" Orion called after me, and I couldn't help my long, startled laugh. Funny, that he couldn't imagine any other way.

"I am," I shouted back at him.

"Hey, Lou, do you want to go look at the moon tonight?" Holly asked as she let herself into my apartment—*our* apartment—with her duffel bag in tow. "Nothing crazy, just from the roof."

A summer Friday night, a little adventure. I took a gamble. I said yes.

We stood in silence for a long while, looking at the sky. I couldn't see nearly as many stars here as at Joshua Tree, and Holly didn't reach for her sketch pad, but it was enough: our fingers twined together and only the brightest constellations above us.

"What are you thinking about?" I asked her.

"Praying," she said, and her voice was dreamy and peaceful, and for the first time I didn't really envy her. I didn't need faith, and I didn't need belief, because I knew for certain.

All this time I had wanted proof, and I *was* the proof. I felt that my very existence was justified. I felt that I meant something bigger than my beating heart.

Holly said, "I need to remind myself that what they did in the desert wasn't holy. Just because they said it was doesn't make it true, you know?"

"Yeah," I said, but I knew I'd have to tell her everything, all of it, and soon.

She reached into her pocket and pulled out a ring: a silver band with a small pearlescent stone, a rainbow of colors in the low light. It wasn't in a box or anything, and it was covered in lint from the fleecy lining of her hoodie. "Hey, Lou?"

"Yeah?"

She held the ring out toward me. "You should marry me."

"You're absurd, do you know that?" I was thinking about Orion and his family—telling him that *I'm* the son our father was promised, wondering if he felt disappointed or if he felt free—as I gave Holly my hand.

"For practical reasons," she said, sliding the ring onto my finger.

"Right, for *practical* reasons." I took her hand. "I have squatter's rights on your heart. The sexy paperwork just makes it official."

She laughed that real and sparkling laugh. The future snaked its way up my throat and dissolved on my tongue, irrefutable. I said, "I've loved you from the moment I saw you."

The sky above us was the biggest thing I knew.

ISABEL J. KIM

Why Don't We Just Kill the Kid in the Omelas Hole

FROM *Clarkesworld*

SCIENCE FICTION

SO THEY BROKE into the hole in the ground, and they killed the kid, and all the lights went out in Omelas: click, click, click. And the pipes burst and there was a sewage leak and the newscasters said there was a typhoon on the way, so they (a different "they," these were the "they" in charge, the "they" who lived in the nice houses in Omelas [okay, every house in Omelas was a nice house, but these were Nice Houses]) got another kid and put it in the hole.

And the newscasters said the hurricane had dissipated into a tropical storm, and the pipes were repaired, and the well-paid janitors cleaned up the sewage leak while wearing proper PPE, and the kid in the hole cried and cried and cried. Or they (the general "they," the "they" that meant you and me and the janitors and the newscasters) assumed that the kid was crying, because the hole was soundproofed so nobody could hear the kid, which didn't stop them from knowing about the kid, but it sort of helped.

So they (the first "they") killed the kid again. They stormed the hole and broke the kid out and slit the kid's throat on public television (as all television in Omelas was publicly funded), and they said, "Look at what sort of shit your beautiful city is built on!" and the kid bled out and it was extremely graphic to the point of being censored in later broadcasts. And one of

Why Don't We Just Kill the Kid in the Omelas Hole 203

the tracks of the free public transit system twisted loose, and a bunch of commuters were killed in a freak accident, and the stock market started shuddering downward, and a house collapsed on the south side of Omelas.

So they (the "Nice Houses" they) got a third kid and stuck it in the hole. They felt weird about it, but they liked their Nice Houses, and also, they really did truly and wholeheartedly care about the well-being of Omelas and all of the citizens except for the kid in the hole. The newscasters talked about the second dead kid sorrowfully and the social media posters (every citizen in Omelas had a healthy and regular relationship with social media and not a bad and addictive one) talked about how this was a real tragedy because even though we knew that there was a kid in the hole, now that's three times as many kids in the hole, and it's extra sad because we usually don't kill the kid in the hole, they usually die of old age or malnutrition.

None of this mattered to the living third kid in the hole, who was not enjoying the hole experience.

But nobody heard the third kid's sobbing because of the soundproofing, and also because now no one was allowed to go see the kid since security had been beefed up around the load-bearing suffering child to prevent its death and prolong its suffering. Which meant that the kid-killers had to seriously plan the next attempt, and everyone had time to decompress from the first two murders of the load-bearing suffering child, and also, the video of the second very graphic murder circulated outside of Omelas.

Everyone (me, you, the newscasters, the janitors with the good PPE, the children who lived inside and outside Omelas) was performatively disgusted by the video. Everyone watched it anyway. It went viral like a snuff film went viral or Kim Kardashian's first sex tape went viral, and it was like the load-bearing suffering child was in everyone's home at once, like there were a million load-bearing suffering children looking at you from a million screens.

Many non-Omelan people said a lot of very mean things (no one outside Omelas had a good and normal relationship with social media), like that the Omelans were monsters for letting the load-bearing suffering child exist and therefore everything about Omelas was fucked beyond belief, and had they known about the load-bearing suffering child, they never would have visited Omelas's beautiful beaches and nightclubs and festivals, because the knowledge of the child was so goddamn fucking horrific and tainted everything. And maybe it was the Omelans who should be killed.

This sentiment made the Omelans kind of upset. They pointed out that Omelas was a better place to live than most other places because at least you knew the load-bearing suffering child suffered for a reason, as opposed to all the other kids who were suffering for no reason. Out there, kids had their arms ripped off while they were working in chicken-processing plants, kids were left in baby boxes, and kids lived in perfect quiet misery with one parent who was an alcoholic and another parent who beat them. In Omelas, there were only good parents and no child suffered except the single one who did. How dare you say shit about our fair city and our single child, when you won't even help your own.

What the Omelans didn't say was that their second grievance was due to the fact that the kid-killers had broken the unspoken code: If you had a problem with the load-bearing suffering child, you were supposed to get the hell out of Omelas and keep it to yourself. You weren't supposed to kill the kid. As a teenager, you were supposed to learn the blunt truth that your society was built on a single ongoing act of senseless, meaningless cruelty, and then you were supposed to cry about it or rage about it, but either way you were supposed to get over it and grow up and get on with your fully-paid-for-by-the-state education system and your festivals and your legal weed and your *drooz*.

The kid was the drop of blood in the bowl of milk whose slight bitterness would make the sweetness of the rest of Omelas richer. Without the kid in the hole, Omelas was just paradise. With the load-bearing suffering child, Omelas meant something.

And of course, it was true that the whole city literally ran on the load-bearing suffering child in a very real physical way that was not a metaphor. And everyone really liked having running power and no blackouts and good schools and low crime and community-oriented government and safe sidewalks and public transit that worked.

Things got really toxic online. Then the third kid was killed. This time it was harder to say who the killers were, because the first they, the killers, had osmosed into the second they (the "they" of the Nice Houses) and, also, the third they (the "they" who were the janitors with the good PPE equipment, and the newscasters). So it was never discovered who exactly slipped through all the protections and the soundproofing and the soldiers with tranquilizer guns (because there were no real guns in Omelas) and stole the kid from the hole and killed it in the conference room where the people with the Nice Houses met to talk about government.

There was no message this time, because the dead kid on the table was the message. The dead kid had been dressed just like every other kid in Omelas (comfortable, affordable clothing of good quality, with adorable patterns), and it hadn't been in the hole for long enough to develop the really horrific features that the kids in the hole always developed (open and weeping sores on their butts, skinny limbs and a protruding stomach, a sort of lank greasiness that permeated their entire being), and this third dead kid mostly just looked a little skinny, and grimy, and asleep.

There was an earthquake that cracked the west side and opened a sinkhole, and four cars were swallowed up in a freak accident. They talked about it on the news, alongside photos of the dead kid dressed up in the conference room. And because the Omelans all had very good educations where they learned about the literary meaning of symbols, they knew that the dead kid in pretty clothing was a reminder of the fact that the child in the hole was also an Omelan child.

The rest of the world, which had variable public education and overworked language arts teachers, freaked out on social media. The sentiment boiled down to: "If Omelas is a perfect city and has really good social services and there is ready access to birth control and easy ways for people with wombs to give up the infants they gestated to people that want them, and therefore all children are wanted and cared for by someone in

Omelas, regardless of whether it is their biological progenitor, where do the Omelans get the load-bearing suffering child?" And the follow-up freak-out: "Oh my god, they must be stealing our children."

Of course, nothing in the freak-outs materially touched the Omelans, because Omelas was a shining city on a hill that could only be hurt when there was no load-bearing suffering child, and the dead child had been immediately replaced, so Omelas wasn't assaulted by foreign troops, and there were no trade sanctions against it, and people didn't stop going to its beaches. But they had to do some media spin, and the Nice House Experiencers went on TV to reassure the world that the load-bearing suffering child was an ethically sourced, no one's son, and definitely an Omelan, and meanwhile some of the Nice House Experiencers privately spoke among each other.

"Look, maybe we shouldn't have a kid in the hole?" one of the Nice House Experiencers said. "Maybe the kid in the hole was always a bad idea."

"What's the other option?" the second Nice House Experience said. "Look me in the eye and tell me there is a better solution than putting one single kid in the hole, and letting that one single kid have a miserable life, in return for the good lives of all of our children?"

"What if they put your kid in?"

And the first Nice House Experiencer didn't have an answer for that. Because she knew in her heart of hearts that she would damn every last person in Omelas rather than subject her child to the hole.

"What *they*?" she said instead. "How do I know you're not the one who killed the kid?"

This question was replicated in many rooms, during many meetings that escalated to shouting until at one point someone said: "Why are we arguing so much when the kid is in the hole? The kid is in the hole, which means that we shouldn't have so much infighting. What is the point of the kid in the hole if we can't even get our act together!"

That had many philosophical implications on whether disagreements can exist in paradise, but in reality, all of this bullshit only meant that the people with the Nice Houses were distracted enough that the fourth kid was killed easily, and without much fanfare.

And then there was an avalanche, a spread of religiously motivated homophobia, and an incident of road rage with a tranquilizer gun that left four dead.

But they managed to catch the specific guy who had killed the fourth kid. They caught him on the newly installed CCTV cameras that did round-the-clock surveillance. They arrested him at his home, which was near the sinkhole.

The murderer surrendered peacefully. He was a very regular-looking man. Nothing about him looked like a murderer or a dissident. He looked just like every other person who had benefited from Omelas's many social safety networks and had grown up without ever knowing suffering.

Before his execution, they (the people with the Nice Houses, as a proxy for the newscasters, as a proxy for everyone else) asked him why he was doing this. The murderer didn't shrug, because he was being held by a Kevlar straitjacket, which had been imported from outside.

"I'm personally doing it because I think we're all cowards here. We're all so fucking afraid of the potential of being the one to suffer that we put that damn kid in the hole and the kid suffers forever, and everyone is so fucking afraid of doing something that we pretend that we are living better lives without suffering. It's disgusting."

He spoke with the moral certainty of the classical Omelan who knew about suffering only abstractly and through the existence of the load-bearing suffering child.

"What are you trying to solve?" the executioner said. The executioner was the only one in the room, but she was relaying the questions from the Nice House Experiencers who had sourced the questions from a public questionnaire and had approved of every single one, because at the end of the day, admittedly, every person in Omelas lived in a Nice House.

"If we kill enough kids, then you will eventually stop putting kids in the hole," the murderer said. "I'm an accelerationist."

"A lot of people died because you killed the kid."

"I'm sorry about that," the murderer said, and he sounded genuine. He sounded like he really cared about the well-being of all the Omelans and their susceptibility to freak accidents, but he cared about the one kid just a little more.

"How did it feel to kill?" the executioner said. This was not a question that was on the list. This was a question the executioner wanted to know for herself.

"Bad," he said. "But it's better than being locked in the hole for your entire life."

The executioner didn't say anything to that. She turned away from him to prepare the syringe and the chemicals.

"Before I'm dead, I'd like to say a few words," the murderer said to the executioner's back. "We will keep killing the kid in the hole. You are going to run out of kids before we stop killing the kids that go into the hole. Even if you kill me, now we all know about killing the load-bearing suffering child. You can't kill me in any way that matters. The kid will die again and again until you stop putting kids in the hole."

And he grinned a big white grin (they had really good dental care in Omelas that wasn't tied to a separate insurance) and was executed by painless lethal injection and so became the first person in Omelas (other than all the load-bearing suffering children) who Omelas, as a state, had killed, and Omelas became the sort of city that killed people using painless lethal injection.

But that was okay, because it happened during the period of time while the kid wasn't in the hole, so it was a fluke, the same way the typhoon was a fluke, the homophobia was a fluke, the Omelans being shitheads on social media was a fluke. It was something that could only happen while Omelas wasn't *Omelas* and was instead just like every other city with no load-bearing suffering child and many load-bearing suffering adults.

The day after the lethal injection, the fifth kid was killed in the hole. And then the executioner walked out of Omelas, but no one paid attention to her leaving.

It turned out that the dead murderer had underestimated the Omelans, because things continued in this cyclical fashion for a while. Kids were put in a series of holes and were summar-

Why Don't We Just Kill the Kid in the Omelas Hole   209

ily killed. The deaths were reported on public television and were dissected badly on social media through a variety of angles.

Like: "This kid is a metaphor for the third world and for the slave labor that mines the rare metals that go into iPhones and for the boys who cross the border to work in the fields while they're underage and the girls who are sold into marriage to pedophiles."

Like: "This kid is a reincarnation of a Bodhisattva and is perfectly happy to experience suffering for the sake of her fellow man, so really it's, like, totally fine that the kid is suffering."

Like: "Why do we care about this kid so much, it's just one kid?"

Like: "The kid is a SYMBOL of the LOWER CLASSES and how they SUFFER."

Like: "No, seriously, where does the kid come from? My mom says she saw a kid disappear off the train, that they're kidnapping kids off of public transit."

Like: "If we put a pulsating mass of tissue cultured from the cells of an Omelan child, and put that in the prison, would that have the same effect, in the same way that lab-grown meat is still technically meat?"

By now everyone (except the newscasters) had stopped counting dead children, and nobody has any questions for the murderers anymore. The dead murderer was wrong. They haven't run out of children. But they haven't run out of murderers, either.

These days, Omelas is perfect except when it isn't, and every once in a while, Omelas has a series of natural disasters and freak accidents strike and everyone is a little afraid that their kid will be the next one in the hole. But only when the kid is dead and a new kid needs to be chosen.

A drop of blood, in a bowl of milk.

Omelas now has a really long Wikipedia entry, with a whole subarticle about the load-bearing suffering child, and a second subarticle about the children who died. They tell you about the children now, after they die. What their names are. They promise that the children are ethically sourced. But there aren't any citations. And some people say that there isn't a kid in the hole anymore. They've moved the hole a bunch of times, and they don't let people know the location anymore. They have extra soundproofing.

Most days, Omelas is sunny and beautiful and nothing bad happens. And then there will be a day that is overcast and cloudy, and on that day, people die in circus accidents and carbon monoxide leaks and start harassment campaigns on twitter. And sometimes on that day people die through lethal injection. So, it's clear that sometimes the kid is alive and suffering, and sometimes the kid has been killed and doesn't exist.

Or maybe there's no kid anymore, and Omelas is just like everywhere else: lucky until it isn't.

Occasionally a content creator will walk into Omelas and film a video while standing on one of the balconies of the Nice Houses or while sitting on one of Omelas's beautiful beaches. They will talk about the history of Omelas in the same way that people talk about the Uyghurs situation in China, the concentration camps of the Third Reich, the comfort women imported from Korea by Japan, the Belgian Congo, the Atlantic Slave Trade in relation to the American South, and the refugees who sink in ships off the coast of Western Europe.

And they (the ones who visit Omelas) say: Thank God we aren't dealing with that horrid wound in society. Thank God there is somewhere that shows us how fucking bad things could get. What a pit in the ground. What a fucked-up little trolley problem. What a lesson for us. Thank God we don't live there. Thank God we know it exists.

JENNIFER HUDAK

The Witch Trap

FROM *Lady Churchill's Rosebud Wristlet*

FANTASY

THESE FLOORS, ORIGINAL to the house, have witnessed the turn of two centuries. The shoe concealed beneath them is older. Laces replaced, sole thrice mended, the shoe still bears the impression of the big toe that for years pressed against the worn upper. Now, it rests mateless between floor joists, a curiosity for spiders and mice. No longer a shoe, but a summons.

The witch smells what has been hidden—leather, dirt, and sweat—and cannot help herself. She makes her way down the chimney, into the walls, beneath the floor, and into the shoe, expecting to find human flesh inside. Once trapped, the witch beats immaterial fists against the inside of the toe box. She wails for the sky, for her horned god, for the crescent moon above. But it's no use. Eventually, she fades. The shoe absorbs the witch, becoming more than what it was.

The contractor discovers it when he pries up the floorboards near what used to be the hearth. Seeing the dark shape there, he jerks back reflexively, then leans in for a closer look before lifting it out: an antique made of worn black leather, with obvious signs of repair, covered in dust.

"Hey, Liz," he calls. "Come take a look at this."

Elizabeth doesn't appreciate the nickname, nor the familiarity, but the contractor has been calling her that since he first arrived, and it seems too late to do anything about it now. She closes her laptop and swallows her frustration. "What is it?"

"Check it out." The contractor holds up the shoe. "I found this."

Elizabeth takes it from him. The leather looks like wrinkled skin. "I don't understand. In my floors?"

"I've heard about this kind of thing," he says. "Shoes hidden under floors or in the walls, to keep away witches. Never seen one before, though."

"Why a shoe? How would that keep witches away?"

"It's just a superstition. You know, like not walking under a ladder, that kind of thing. I don't think you're supposed to take it literally. Anyway, I thought you'd be interested. Sorry if I interrupted you."

"It's fine," she says, with a glance back at her laptop. Technically, she's working from home today. Her friends told her she shouldn't expect to get anything done with a contractor in the house, and she's beginning to think they were right.

"I can take that if you want, Liz. Put it back where I found it before I put the new floor down. Just in case," he clarifies with a laugh. "I mean, on the off chance it actually works. You never know, right?"

The shoe is warm to the touch, even though the floors always feel cold. "Maybe. But I'll hold on to it," Elizabeth says. "For now."

She takes her laptop and the shoe upstairs to her bedroom, to escape the noise and dust of the renovation. There, she pulls the quilt off her bed—a crazy quilt, made by her great-aunt and gifted to Elizabeth on her fortieth birthday when it became clear that there was no point in saving it for a wedding present—and sits in the rocking chair in the corner. With the quilt wrapped around her shoulders, Elizabeth ignores her email inbox and instead searches the web for information about shoes hidden in floors.

What she finds is astonishing. The Concealed Shoe Index, run by the Northampton Museum and Art Gallery in England, includes nearly 3,000 individual shoes found beneath floors, behind walls, in chimneys and in hearths, across 2,000 different locations. Elizabeth looks at photographs of the shoes in their collection—piles of shoes, all of them worn and ancient, still

The Witch Trap

carrying the impressions of countless feet whose owners have been dead for much longer than Elizabeth has been alive—and wonders why she's never heard of this before.

She learns that scholars disagree on the purpose the shoes were intended to serve. Some believe they were considered a charm to enhance fertility or impart good luck. Others say, as the contractor had, that the shoes, having been infused with the essence of their wearers, could deflect the incursions of witches and other evil spirits. But no one knows for sure.

Most intriguing to Elizabeth is the theory that the shoes were not intended to keep witches away, but to trap them. To lure a witch with the promise of a tasty human to attack and consume, and then to imprison her within leather. There is no historical documentation of this belief, but a practice like this would have been whispered from ear to ear, traded between neighbors like eggs or nails. It would have required both repetition and belief in order to work.

In 1486, sanctioned by the Bull of Pope Innocent VIII, Heinrich Kramer and James Sprenger penned the *Malleus Maleficarum*. In the text, they claimed—with vivid detail—that witches copulated with demons and suckled animal familiars, that they ate babies and could make a man's penis disappear. The last section of the book offered helpful instructions for the prosecution of witches, including how to torture them in order to obtain the necessary confession. Indeed, over the next two hundred years, tens of thousands of witches were sent into the cleansing fires, crying out for mercy that neither Lord nor devil would provide.

Imagine, for a moment, how terrifying it must have been: not knowing if the woman who shared your home and bed, who bore and raised your children, turned into a bat when you were sleeping and flew into the night to do the devil's bidding! In some ways, the *Malleus*, with its lurid and titillating descriptions, can be seen as an attempt to draw a firm line between heretical witches and good Christian wives. To construct a definition of the witch that, in turn, defined who was not a witch at all—set down in print, in unchangeable type, between leather covers.

But between those covers, the witch gained form. The words

invoked her, called her into being. And as more people open the book and read it, as more copies are printed and reprinted and disbursed, she comes into being again and again, invading our imaginations, cackling and powerful and free.

[Someone clears their throat and looks pointedly at the clock. It's nearly five minutes past the hour; you're going to have to begin. You look out at the handful of people slumping in their seats and try not to be disappointed.]
I want to thank you all for being here, so bright and early. I hope everyone has their coffee—or the magical equivalent of caffeine! *[You pause for laughter; none arises. After a brief moment of awkward silence, you continue.]* My name is Mara Forbes, and today I'm going to be presenting my paper on the biopsychosocial causes of the witchcraft hysteria in New England in the late seventeenth century.

[A person sitting near the back glances at their phone and leaves the room. You wait for the door to close behind them before starting to read.]
In Puritan New England, magic was as much a part of daily life as the Church. Colonists spoke both Bible verses and folk magics with the same unconflicted tongue; why shouldn't they, when both kept their households healthy and whole? Those in need of magics beyond their own abilities might call upon local healers known as cunning women, who peddled herbal remedies and divinations. Yet all that changed in 1692, when the shrieking girls of Salem Village accused homeless beggars, slaves, and churchgoing mothers alike of witchcraft most foul.

[You remind yourself to glance up at your audience periodically. To animate your face. To make yourself charismatic and vivacious. The man in the front row is on his phone, and you wonder why he even bothered to come.]
When facing the magistrates, the accused—often women who were old and unmarried, both reasons for suspicion in the colonies—either admitted to signing the devil's book in exchange for their abilities, or denied it and found themselves drowned by dunking or strangled at the end of a noose.

[Someone coughs. You wonder if perhaps you were given the first programming slot of the morning on purpose. No stragglers have entered the

The Witch Trap

room; it's just you and this sparse, disinterested clutch of academics for the duration. You consider giving up, saying, "The End," and leaving the room. Instead, you focus on the sound of your own voice. On the rhythm of your language, if not the words themselves.]

So, what changed? What caused the colonists to see demons where they once saw herbs, charms, and trinkets? We can only speculate. Modern scholars, poets, and playwrights have blamed the hysteria on religious fundamentalism, population stress, bacterial infections, romantic grievances, even a psychedelic fungus that might have made its way into the stored grain. The only thing we know for certain is that there were no actual witches in Salem Village, because witches do not exist.

[Even as you say the words, you wonder if you believe them. You wonder what it would feel like to shriek rhyming couplets until the man in the front finally looks up from his phone, to recite spells until your voice is hoarse, until everyone flees in fear. You imagine grabbing your broomstick and flying through the corridors until you reach an open window and the sky welcomes you home. You visualize your words weaving themselves together, licking themselves up your body like flames, making you burn bright with power.]

Beneath the floorboards, the witch feels the knock and drag of generations of footsteps overhead. She no longer has hands with which to cast spells, nor legs that can straddle a broomstick. If her horned god ever existed, he has not come to liberate her here. So she chooses patience. The witch has become the shoe, has become *more* than the shoe, has filled up the interstitial spaces of the house with magic and the hint of smoke. In the small cubby between the floor joists, she listens, and waits, and lives on.

Excerpt from the article "The Coven Next Door" by Mike Untweiler (*Today! Magazine*, September 1988)

The ladies of the Fourth Street Coven had assured me that I'd be welcome at their open circle, but I'll admit to a moment of trepidation when I arrived at the address they'd given me. Sure, it looked like a perfectly normal, suburban house, but what would I find hidden inside? Cackling biddies chanting naked around a bubbling cauldron? Slender goddesses reeking of incense, gazing at crystals? And, more importantly, would they turn me into a toad before the evening was through? As it turned out, none of those stereotypes were entirely true, but that's not to say they were entirely false, either. The Fourth Street Witches do sometimes gather in the nude, although (sadly) not in front of this reporter. They use both incense and crystals, although I wouldn't call any of the ladies slender. And while the coven claims to practice magic, I'm happy to report that I wasn't turned into a toad. In fact, aside from the altar in the corner—adorned with pentacles and laden with tea lights, crystal balls, and tarot cards—the vibe was less "occult gathering" and more "wannabe Woodstock." The women (or should I call them "womyn"?) wore loose dresses and silver jewelry; most of them were barefoot, and none of them, as far as I could tell, shaved their legs.

(. . . .)

A vegetarian potluck followed the opening incantation. While I balanced a plate of brown rice salad and tofu cutlets on my lap, the High Priestess of the coven—a short, chunky brunette named Leslie—offered to give me a brief introduction to the history of Neo-Pagan Witchcraft, beginning with the writings of British folklorist Margaret Murray.

In the 1920s and '30s, Murray wrote a series of books hypothesizing that a Dianic cult thrived among the simple, uneducated folk in prehistoric Europe and England. The members of this cult practiced magic, kept familiars, and gathered at Sabbats; according to Murray, they were valued in their communities as advisors and healers. It was the Christians (they're the baddies in Murray's version of history) who labeled the cult heretics and witches. During the long years that the Church held sway, members of the cult were either burned at the stake or went into hiding to survive.

Modern-day Wiccans, including the Fourth Street Coven, claim to be spiritual descendants of this cult, at long last able to live freely in the public eye as Goddess-worshiping magic-makers whose fundamental principle is "An' ye harm none, do what ye will."

Margaret Murray's work, of course, has long since been thoroughly debunked. Modern folklorists agree that her scholarship was shoddy, her "evidence" selective, and her conclusions utter nonsense. When I mentioned this to Leslie, she gave me a tight smile.

"What we are doing here is changing the narrative. We are saying that the patriarchy is an aberration—a small blip in the natural order of things—and if it is an aberration, it can be overcome."

I asked her if that meant she believed Margaret Murray's ridiculous witch-cult hypothesis. She regarded me for a long moment before she answered, and when she did, her voice was decidedly less pleasant.

"It doesn't matter whether we believe Murray's theories or not. History is written by the victors, yes? Well. We are rewriting it." She paused, and smiled once more. "So mote it be."

Around the room, others clinked their glasses and echoed the call: "So mote it be."

Elizabeth glances at the shoe again. It smells slightly of smoke. She is not superstitious, but something about the shoe pricks at her intuition. It isn't just a shoe; in being hidden, it has been invested with a different meaning, become something other than what it was. Yet, what exactly it has become eludes her.

She closes her laptop and sets it aside. With the shoe in her lap, she skims her fingertips over cracked, brittle leather. It should feel empty and inert, but it doesn't. It isn't. Inside the shoe, something breathes. Something presses back against Elizabeth's touch. Something that has swallowed its own story for centuries asks for eyes to see and ears to hear, for blood and lymph and skin. It asks for its voice once again.

With her eyes closed, Elizabeth pulls apart the shoe's disintegrating laces, and feels another set of fingertips weaving with hers.

LunaBelle lights a candle on their altar, grabs their phone, and logs into the chat for solo witches who are practicing "in the broom closet," so to speak. This chat is the first place they felt free to use the name LunaBelle—the name they chose for themself. In school, everyone still uses LunaBelle's birth name, but here, they can be exactly who they choose.

This is who I am, they think as they enter the chat. *This is who I've always been.*

LunaBelle has read books and consulted oracle decks and perused dozens of websites in search of answers, but they've only found more questions. All they know for certain is that the explanations offered by their teachers, parents, and therapist are nothing but insufficient platitudes. LunaBelle doesn't necessarily blame any of them. It's human nature: When faced with something they don't understand, people will always try to force it to make sense—to place it in a tidy little box tied with a neat bow. Even if the box doesn't fit. Even if you damage the thing getting it inside.

LunaBelle knows that no one understands them. They aren't sure they understand themself. But they are sick of squeezing themself into the wrong box. They feel as though there's more to life—more to *themself*—than can be explained by well-meaning adults, and that perhaps the gap between the easy explanations and the truth of themself is an untapped source of power.

None of the witches in the chat have met each other in person. It doesn't matter. Together, they discuss spells and charms and rituals; they trade memes; they share the pain of hiding who they are. They refer to each other by their chosen names, and the words are an incantation. An invocation. LunaBelle feels as if, together, they are making themselves real—creating themselves anew out of all this confusion and uncertainty.

The candle flickers and flares on the altar. LunaBelle feels

themself opening like a flower. They feel themself becoming something solid, something new. Something powerful.
They feel themself becoming.

Humble pine planks wait to be set down in this brick house newly built in the Year of Our Lord 1833, but before the carpenter fits them together and nails them into place, he pulls a single woman's shoe from his pack. Not long ago, this shoe and its mate adorned his wife's slender feet. Now . . . He dips his head so the others won't see the dampness on his cheeks. Then he clears his throat, tucks the shoe between the floor joists, and stands. Let it do some good, he tells himself. Let it keep those who will live here safe from harm.

When the contractor is packing up his tools for the day, he asks Elizabeth, once again, if she wants him to replace the shoe beneath the floorboards.

"It's not too late, Liz," he tells her. "Just give me the word, and I'll put it right back where I found it. Let it keep the witches away like it was meant to."

"It's Elizabeth, not Liz," she answers. "And I think . . ." She pauses, and feels herself smile. "I think it's time to let the witches in."

The contractor laughs uncertainly, but stops when Elizabeth does not laugh with him.

"Well," he says after an awkward pause. "I guess I'll see you in the morning."

After he's gone, Elizabeth pours herself a glass of wine and carries it to her room. The shoe sits on the crazy quilt like a black cat, alert and watchful. Elizabeth sips her wine and then picks up the shoe, turning it in her hands. It's empty now, but it still hums with leftover power. She can hear every step the shoe made, every retort of rigid heel against wooden floor. She can feel every foot that stretched its leather, every hand that pulled the laces tight. She wonders what it would feel like to wear it, even though it is much too small. She wonders if her foot will shrink to fit it, or if the shoe will unfurl itself like bat wings.

When the sun sets, the crescent moon peers through the window.

SUSAN PALWICK

Yarns

FROM *Asimov's*
SCIENCE FICTION

INEVITABLY, THEY FOUND her. She came back to her tiny apartment and clicked on the light to find a massive young man, wearing the signature black jeans and sweatshirt of Combine, standing in her living room. The dim light glinted off his earpiece, the netchips embedded in his cheek, the barrel of his gun. The gun was some kind of high-tech semiautomatic. Of course it was pointed at her.

As often as Irene had imagined this moment, she yelped and panicked and dropped her bags, sending crimson yarn, garish in the gloom, rolling across the floor. The knitting needles clattered, still inside the bag, and Irene felt her skin blazing with fear and shame. How could she have been so stupid? She'd succumbed to temptation, and she was going to die for it.

Four months earlier, the federal agent had barely stifled a yawn as he swapped out the citizenchip in her wrist. "We may be buying you some time, but probably not much. You know, back before computers, they used to give someone a new name and a new job in a new town, and they were more or less safe. Even then, too many of them made mistakes: tried to contact old friends and family, whatever. But these days? You'd more or less need a new brain to escape. If they want to find you, they will."

The IV from the biometric revision had still been in her wrist while he said all that. He removed it and handed her a gauze alcohol pad. She winced as she cleaned the injection site, her fingertips smarting from the new laserprints, her eyes stinging from her new retinas. Contacts would change her blue irises to gray. She had a different hairstyle and color, a reddish-brown shag instead of her usual silver bob; a bored technician had coached her on changing her habitual fashion choices, her posture, her gait. They couldn't do anything about her height or build—"You might want to eat as much as possible to get fat," the tech said—and the feds had decreed that her case didn't warrant full-on cosmetic surgery for a new face, which was more a relief than otherwise.

The agent kept talking. "Longest I've seen anybody evade a focused search is three months. This one guy blew it the first day, went to Metanews and read the articles in the same order he always did: his horoscope, and then his wife's horoscope, and then the world soccer feed, and then the local political news. The searchbots must have snagged him in fifteen seconds. He was dead by dinnertime."

Irene held up the gauze pad. "What do you want me to do with this?"

He jerked his head at the red biohazard container behind him. She had to get up to put the pad inside, brushing past him in the small, drab room; he grimaced in distaste. Kids these days, so squeamish about anything physical. "Well," she said, her voice tight, "I plan to be more careful than he was."

He snorted. "Good luck with that. Hell of a price to pay for your principles."

No "thank you," no "you did the right thing," no "how brave you were to defy Combine." She wondered whose side he was on. Maybe he was being paid off by Combine; maybe he'd send them her new chip ID as soon as he left the room. Or maybe she was being even more paranoid than the situation warranted.

Back in her seat, she looked at him carefully for the first time. He was young, barely out of his teens, with the dismissive sneer young men always seemed to direct at women over forty-five whenever circumstances forced them to look at such normally invisible creatures. He had netchips, of course, a relatively understated set implanted along one temple, as commonplace now as pierced ears and noses had been in her own day. She wondered if his red hair and freckles were original, or if he'd had to go into hiding, too, earlier in his life.

The nameplate on the agent's desk, quaintly redundant in this era of chips, read B. Jones, Citizen Protection, Mid-Atlantic Urban Corridor. Irene tried to imagine what might have brought him here. She told herself that his name was Bobby Jones and he'd grown up in the projects somewhere; he'd filled his days with sims and streamed entertainment and virtual violence until someone he loved—mother? father? younger sibling?—was gunned down by Combine, Combine being nearly the only non-virtual game in town, and then he had faced a choice: join Combine, or fight it, because there was no ignoring it. He'd tried to enlist on the right side, but his cynicism bled through whenever he remembered his mother or father or younger sibling lying dead on the sidewalk in a pool of blood.

Telling herself that story took Irene perhaps thirty seconds. It didn't make her feel any better about him. She looked at B. Jones again; he stared stonily back. "Questions, Irene?"

"No."

"Okay, well then, you're free to go."

No "goodbye," no "good luck." He thought she was a fool. He thought she'd be dead by dinnertime.

Yarn rolled across the floor, the ball of red angora wobbling toward her unwelcome guest. He yelped, his voice cracking, and jumped away from it.

Irene, paralyzed, realized two things.

He hadn't fired the gun.

He was afraid of yarn.

Afraid of *yarn*? She stared at him as he stared at the yarn. He was in his teens, his pale skin blotched by acne and his hair a dark Afro. Some Combine clans maintained strict racial divisions, but most had become melting pots, recruiting and rewarding anyone whose skills contributed to their profits.

He didn't yet have the Eye of God.

The gun no longer pointed at her, but haphazardly at a wall. It was shaking. He was shaking. He took a cautious step forward and in one swift movement kicked the yarn away from him, back at Irene, as if it were a soccer ball. It rolled to a stop against her ankles.

He was glaring at her now, and she stifled a laugh. She looked at his legs and saw a telltale bulge beneath one denim cuff. Tracker bracelet, removable only with special tools, an act of defiance that would incur heavy penalties. Combine tech outclassed Fed tech by orders of magnitude; any signal this kid sent out was accessible only to his Combine bosses, as hard as the Feds kept trying to crack the codes. Her visitor was a newbie, on probation. He wouldn't get the Eye of God—the gaudy, permanent chip socket Combine wore in the middle of their foreheads, recording and tracking sent straight to the higher-ups—until he made his first kill.

She was supposed to be his first kill. They'd sent a child to kill an old woman. But he hadn't shot her yet, and the gun was still shaking.

"Bomb didn't blow," he said, scowling. "Some bomb!" Hearing his voice, she revised her estimate of his age downward. He looked seventeen or eighteen, but his quavering voice, cracking both from fear and from puberty, put him younger. He was better at her first language than she would have been at his. Combine communicated in a singsongy patois, fragments of English and Spanish and Tagalog, Japanese and Russian and Arabic.

"It's not a bomb," she said gently, bending to pick up the angora. "My name's Irene. How old are you?"

"Know your name, lady!"

"I don't know yours. How old are you?"

He scowled. "Don't matter. I got the gun. Bomb's broken."

"It's not a bomb," she said again. "I think you're fourteen or fifteen. Is that right?" He kept scowling, and she heard a click as his finger tightened. It occurred to her that she hadn't even thought about trying to run. She waited for noise from the gun, the last sound she would ever hear.

Nothing happened.

Irene held out the yarn, the precious fuzziness of angora, as warm as blood. "This isn't a bomb. It's yarn. For knitting." Hadn't they told him anything about her? Knitting was how they'd found her, after all. She'd used a public terminal at the library. She hadn't searched on knitting or yarn, nothing so obvious, but she'd scrolled carefully through the classifieds until she'd seen the notice about craft supplies for barter. Most of the yarn had been cheap: nasty acrylics, glittery eyelash yarn that would fall apart the second you tried to wash it. When she saw the angora, and then the price on it, she'd known that the tired woman selling the stuff had no idea what she had.

Irene hadn't set the seller straight. She felt guilty about that—the woman was just trying to eke out a living, like everyone else—but not guilty enough to speak up. Even at a tenth of its true worth, the angora was an exorbitant splurge on her tiny pension. But the yarn had called out to her like a living thing, and when she'd picked it up, she hadn't been able to bring herself to put it down again.

Irene had thought that remaking herself would be easier. She'd shed dreams and identities before: when her parents and sister died in one of the pandemics, when her fiancé was felled by a catastrophic aneurysm. She'd gone into teaching because her classes changed every year. She told herself that would keep her from becoming too attached to the children. But B. Jones had been right: Becoming a new person was harder work than most people could manage. Irene had scrupulously avoided her old habits all summer, but as soon as fall set in—the first autumn in her life she hadn't been in a classroom, as student or teacher—the yearning for familiarity grew too strong. She'd been careful, but not careful enough. The searchbots must have noticed even her fractional pause, at the library, on the page mentioning fiber, confirmed her identity using the cameras that were everywhere now. Or maybe someone had seen her at the library, or seen her in the barter zone, and simply called this child to come kill her. Maybe he didn't know anything about her, about knitting, about yarn. Maybe he was just following orders.

"Look," she said, and squeezed the yarn and tossed it up and down, threw it on the floor, picked it up again. *Think, Irene. Be calm.* "See? It isn't dangerous. It's very soft. I use sticks to weave it into cloth, for things like scarves and sweaters. That's called knitting." She'd very carefully avoided the word needles, which would mean only drugs to Combine. He could use his chips to look up knitting on the net—for all she knew, she had only one-tenth his attention, the rest absorbed by some online game—but her best bet was to try to lure him into the physical world. Her physical world, not his. A world without guns.

"Here." She held out the yarn. "Would you like to touch it? It's very soft."

He growled, or tried to growl: a tricycle trying to sound like a truck. "Touch it all I want after I kill you."

"Sure. But then I can't answer your questions about it, or show you how I use the sticks to weave it." She used her free hand to gesture to the vest she was wearing. "See this? I made this myself. With sticks and yarn."

"Huh," he said, an explosive release of air. The gun wasn't shaking anymore, but it wasn't pointed at her, either. He rested it casually in the crook of an arm. He looked like a curious child now, and Irene released the breath she'd been holding. He frowned, licked his lips, tilted his head: the age-old, universal expression of a youngster puzzling out a problem. "You give it here again."

"Sure," she said, and bent to roll the angora across the floor.

Wary, he squatted, prodding the yarn with his gun and then with a finger. At last, he picked it up, squeezing it experimentally. Something like wonder crossed his face. "Soft," he said.

"Sure. I told you it was."

He was patting it now. "How—where it come from? Who makes it?"

"It's from animals," she said. "Some yarn comes from sheep, but this kind comes from rabbits. From their fur. People cut the fur—it's like giving the animal a haircut—and then they spin the fur into yarn. They dye the yarn, and then people can use sticks to weave it, or they can weave it on a loom."

He stared at her. Most of this was clearly beyond him. "Animals?" Definite wonder, now. Had he spent any time in school? He looked down at the yarn. "Must be old!"

"I don't know," Irene said. "I don't know who made this yarn, or how long ago. It could be new."

He shook his head. "Animals. All dead." He looked up at her, and she saw emotion pass across his face, a flicker, a wisp of cloud over the sun. "Seen vid of animals." He prodded the yarn again. "My grandma had an animal when she was little. A little animal. *Her* grandma? Sat on an animal once! Rode it!"

"A horse! That must have been exciting." Irene wondered what pet his grandmother had had. Cat? Dog? Hamster? "What was your grandmother's name?"

"Katana," he said, voice thickening. He cradled the yarn against his chest. His face had closed again, as if he regretted his stream of words. To Combine, enthusiasm was weakness.

Irene made sure her own voice was as soft as she could make it. "What happened to Katana? Is she dead?"

His features were stone now, set in the sneer he'd learned from those he was trying to become. But he didn't shoot her. "Don't matter," he said. "You show me those sticks."

She'd met Derringer two years before. He was the smallest and shyest student in her fourth-grade class, and his parents were certainly Combine, who always named their children after weapons. Irene had resigned herself to living in a culture where killers didn't even try to disguise themselves. Every year she told herself that the lessons she taught about listening, about compassion—themes she wove through more conventional math and reading lessons—might make a difference. She told herself that being around non-Combine kids might make a difference. Derringer was one of the lucky ones. Plenty of Combine parents kept their children out of school entirely, a situation the state had long since stopped challenging. Social Services didn't visit Combine homes; the body count was too high.

To her surprise and pleasure, Derringer had clearly been homeschooled before he came to her classroom. He wasn't much behind the other children, and he caught up rapidly. He loved to read, loved to write stories he illustrated himself. Irene's classroom had computers, and many of her students already had netchips—although Derringer didn't—but she blocked network access in her classroom and made her students work with tangible objects: pencil, crayon, paper, scissors, glue. She wanted them to learn to manipulate objects with mass, to savor the physical.

Derringer's stories were about guns and money and people dying in bloody street battles. The tales broke Irene's heart, but his facility in spinning them gave her hope. She began challenging him to tell happier stories. "What would happen if those people didn't use their guns, Derringer?"

"If they used they fist?" He squinted at her. "Bullets quicker."

"Yes, I know, but what if they didn't use weapons? What if they decided to do something else instead? To help each other with laundry? To share a meal?"

He giggled. "That don't happen! You silly!"

"Sometimes it's okay to tell silly stories. What if?"

"This story finished," he said decisively. "Want to do fractions now."

He liked math; he was good at it. He was smart. He never seemed comfortable around the other students, but first thing each morning and last thing each afternoon, he ran to Irene for a hug, and he sat next to her during storytime whenever he could, leaning against her as if she were a tree.

She'd kept her early vow not to get too attached to her kids, especially Combine kids. But she loved Derringer. She couldn't help it. Many of the other students were dropped off and picked up by adults or older siblings, but Derringer was a school bus child who arrived and left by himself every day, and Irene found herself imagining reasons. The adults he lived with ignored him, let him do what he wanted. They were too caught up in street trade to mind him, and so he'd decided on his own to come to school.

Rationally, Irene knew this couldn't be true. Derringer was clean, well-fed, always neatly dressed in clothing appropriate for the season. He'd arrived in her class able to read, add, subtract. Someone at home cared about him. And so, she imagined his mother or an aunt teaching him his ABCs and one-plus-ones while the rest of his clan weighed out ounces and kilos or haggled over territorial disputes. Combine, supposedly one entity, was in fact as fractured as the wooden oranges Irene used to teach her students halves and quarters. Clans competed for sales and status, for the recognition of their Big Bosses, who lived in posh suburbs and hired attorneys and consultants to manage their corporate interests. Big Bosses died, too, in backyard assassinations or golf course drive-bys, but not nearly as often as the street soldiers did. Here in the city, the trade—in drugs, weapons, sex—was no less dangerous than it had ever been. Average lifespan in inner-city Combine clans was thirty-five.

Parent-teacher night fell on the first crisp week of fall. Irene wore a hand-knitted sweater to class that day and noted approvingly that Derringer was bundled in a fleece jacket. She had formed an image of the female relative who cared for him so tenderly, a smiling, gray-haired presence who used drug money to buy good clothing for Derringer, who spent hours coaching him on basic skills.

But when Derringer gave Irene her goodbye hug that afternoon, he said, "My daddy tell you he be here tonight. He tell you not be scared."

Irene blinked. "Your father?"

Derringer pointed solemnly at the unmarked skin in the middle of his forehead. "He have Eye, don't want you to be scared."

"That's very kind of him," Irene said, more than a little startled, and it was. If an Eye of God Combine parent had shown up in her classroom with no warning, she'd have been terrified. "Please tell your father I'm looking forward to meeting him."

She wondered if he'd actually show. Few parents of any occupation came to parent-teacher night; most teachers used the occasion to visit, gossip, do paperwork. Irene planned to bring knitting, a lace shawl. But sure enough, she looked up from her pattern to find a blockily built, black-clad figure in her classroom doorway.

"Miz Irene." Eye of God glinted in his forehead, ordinary netchips arrayed on either side of it. He had crimped, blond hair, epicanthic folds, the burly build of a football player. He stepped forward and held out his hand for Irene to shake, civilian style. Combine clans had elaborate hand codes and recognition signals, but he was—very carefully, she saw—trying to follow her protocols. "Glock. You teach m'boy Derringer."

"I'm very pleased to meet you, Glock." His handshake was firm, but somewhat moist. Was he nervous, this Combine giant? Every movement controlled, he seated himself in front of her desk and held out a piece of paper. "Derringer, he just got this report."

Irene took the printout, looked at it: Derringer's midterm grades. She smiled at Glock. "Yes. All A's. He's an excellent student."

"Truly?"

She blinked. "Why, yes. He's a very bright little boy."

Glock shook his head. "*Truly*, though? The A's real? Not—fear A's. Because of who we are. Who I am." He gestured to the Eye. "He really earning them?"

Irene sucked in a breath and tried not to stare. But she supposed Glock had a point; if Derringer hadn't been a good student, would she have been nervous about marking him down? Afraid of reprisals?

Would it have occurred to her that a Combine parent even cared?

"Yes," she said. "Truly. He came here with very good home-schooling, and he's blossomed in the classroom. He's very intelligent." Glock's face relaxed a little, and Irene risked a question. "Who taught him at home? Did you?"

"What I know." He looked down, away. "Didn't get far, me."

"You're a good teacher," she told him, and meant it. "You did a good job. And you seem to have given him study habits, not simply information. That's the best thing you could have done."

Glock looked up, looked surprised, flashed a smile. "Truly?" But the smile faded before Irene could answer. "You think he smart enough go high school?"

Good lord. Irene had never heard of a city Combine child pursuing formal education past junior high, and Glock was Eye of God, monitored and monitoring 24/7. Wouldn't this be taken as an admission that he was trying to free his child from Combine? Or would his higher-ups see these plans as an admirable—if audacious—bid for Big-Bossdom, preparation for a slightly safer future?

Glock looked nervous again. Irene leaned forward, making eye contact, and said firmly, "Sir, your son is smart enough to do absolutely anything he wants."

Derringer, glowing, bounced up to her the next morning.

He pulled Irene down to whisper in her ear. "Daddy think you nice."

"I think he's nice, too," she said, and for a wonder it was true, the little she knew of the man. She didn't want to know any more. He cared about his child and tried to be a good father. That was enough.

Derringer sped through the next few months of schoolwork. During winter break, Irene saw something online about a city Combine massacre, but there were always Combine massacres. She ignored the story and continued her search for pumpkin pie recipes.

In January, Derringer didn't come back to school.

The first few days he was absent, Irene told herself he must be ill. It was flu season, after all—blessedly, there hadn't yet been a new pandemic this year—and although Derringer had never missed school before, there had to be a first time for everything. But when he'd been out a week, her simmering worry rose to the surface, and she went to the school office to see if anyone knew anything. It was possible that Glock had called the office to explain and the message hadn't reached her.

"No messages," said the administrative aide. "I'd have *given* you a message." She was a tiny woman, plump and sagging and permanently aggrieved, with meticulously maintained dreadlocks and long, festively painted fingernails. She wasn't paid enough, and people only sought her out when they were upset about something.

"I just wanted to ask, Nancy. I know how busy you are. We all drop some balls sometimes; it's only human. Can you look up the student's home contact information for me, please? Derringer Kiwa?"

"*Derringer?*" Nancy squinted at her. "And you want to call him at *home?*"

"I've met his father. It's fine."

Nancy raised her eyebrows. "It's your funeral." She printed out a sheet of paper—obsolete tech dictated by the school's dismal budget—and handed it to Irene. "Good luck."

"Thank you," Irene said. She used her mobile to call the

number as soon as she got back to her classroom. It had been disconnected.

That evening, she went to the library to do a netsearch on Glock Kiwa. She didn't want to do it at home; she couldn't afford to have Combine notice her curiosity. She probably shouldn't have made the phone call, either, even though she'd been Derringer's teacher.

She found the news story almost instantly. Glock had been killed in the latest massacre, a matter of staggering bankrolls and byzantine politics, Glock's Crater Clan feuding with Scar Clan, which had tried to encroach on Crater turf with the support of several other groups. The report didn't mention Glock's son, and Irene's throat tightened with dread. If Glock had taken anyone else out before he was killed—or even if he hadn't—the other clans would seek retribution. Relatives, especially children, were favored targets.

The library terminal swam in front of her eyes. Where was Derringer now? Was he still alive, mourning the father who'd loved him? She scrolled through other news stories about the bloodbath but saw no mention of a dead child.

Lying in bed that night. staring tensely into darkness, Irene tried to imagine a happy ending. She told herself that maybe a kind aunt or grandmother from another state had been at the funeral and taken Derringer away to live with her, and they hadn't told the school. She told herself that Derringer had run away to escape the violence; he could have snagged a few bills of drug money and gotten on a bus and gone somewhere he knew people. He was good at geography, and Irene always taught her students how to find safe houses. She tried to tell herself that he could be living with some adult across town now, in another school altogether.

She didn't believe any of it. Derringer might just as well have sprouted wings and flown away. She knew she'd never see him again.

She was opening the classroom windows on a warm April morning, really the first fine weather they'd had since winter, when she felt a tug on her hand. "Miz Irene."

She recognized the voice, even in a whisper. Otherwise, she might not have recognized the child. He was wearing a shirt that had been his favorite last autumn, but it was now too small for him, and torn. His skin was crusty around the eyes and mouth, and a mottled bruise covered one cheek.

She dropped to a crouch, hugging him. She'd come to work early, and no other children had arrived yet. The boy smelled terrible, like sour milk and dirty diapers and dead animals. Irene tried not to gag. "Derringer! I'm so glad you're here. I've missed you."

"Ran away," he said. His voice was slurred, and she wondered if he was on drugs. "You said we could run away and be safe."

Oh God. She knew she should call Social Services, but she didn't want Derringer treated like a number. He'd come to her because he trusted her. She called the office, pleaded sudden illness, and led Derringer outside, to her car. She didn't even want to think about how many laws she was breaking, or who might be watching her on the cameras dotted around the city streets. Some were broken. Too many weren't.

She went home. She didn't know where else to go.

She fixed him a grilled-cheese sandwich and tomato soup, watched while he devoured the food, and finally coaxed the story from him, bit by bit. The people who'd killed his father had found Derringer and taken him as a war trophy. They'd put him to work as a drug lookout, but he ran away. They found him again, and now they kept him chained inside an apartment. He wouldn't tell her what had happened there; when she asked, he shrank in on himself, shuddering, and she couldn't bear to press him.

He'd managed to pick the padlock or stolen a key from someone nodding out at the kitchen table—that part was garbled by terror—and found his way to a train that stopped near school. "You keep me safe," he said, his eyes huge and glazed and pleading. "I stay with you?"

"Sweetie, I can't." She couldn't let herself cry. Her throat hurt. "I wish I could, but it wouldn't be safe for either of us. I want you to be safe, Derringer. You have to go somewhere completely different."

She wanted to give him a bath, wanted to buy him new clothing, wanted to read to him and rock him to sleep. She couldn't do any of that, couldn't take the time. The people from whom he'd escaped would be looking. Maybe she and Derringer were already discovered, already doomed. She'd been stupid to come back here.

She bundled him in one of her old sweaters, which had shrunk in the wash. She took him to a safe house, where the intake volunteer—a dark-skinned woman with a pitted face and kind eyes—promised that he'd be moved out of the city, far away, somewhere his captors couldn't track him. The safe houses functioned like the old Underground Railroad, each stop on the route knowing the location of the next stop, but nothing after that.

Irene left Derringer there, both of them weeping. She made him promise that he'd keep going to school, that he'd work hard. "Your father wanted you to go to high school, Derringer. I want that, too. I know you'll make us proud. I know you'll make a good life for yourself."

She left him there. She went back home. She knew it was dangerous, but she was drained, unable to think, her earlier losses rising to haunt her. Face wet with tears, she lay awake in the dark, tensing whenever the old building creaked.

The next morning, the news reported that the safe house had been raided by Combine overnight. Everyone in the building was dead. She had no idea how they could have known Derringer was there, but if they knew that, they knew other things.

Irene packed a suitcase with clothing, some of her best yarn and knitting needles, photographs of her parents, her sister, her fiancé. She had no photo of Derringer, except the ones seared into her brain. She left all her keys on the kitchen table—she didn't dare try to drive anywhere, because they might have her license plate and car bombs were all too common—and walked, mouth dry and heart pounding, to the nearest police station, where she asked for asylum.

His name was Wesson. He spent an hour with Irene, that first visit, watching her work her needles, listening to her explain what she was doing: casting on, knitting, purling. "This is a yarn-over, Wesson. I can use it to make lace, see?" She knitted a few repetitions of feather and fan, and he grinned with delight when the rolling, scalloped design revealed itself. Then she demonstrated cables.

That first visit, he refused to put down his gun, but at the end of the hour, he said, "Gotta go now. Be back."

Irene swallowed, shook her head. "Won't you get in trouble? For not killing me?"

He shrugged. "No Eye. They don't know, not for sure."

"You have the tracking bracelet. Won't they know you were here for a long time?"

He shrugged again. "Maybe. Yeah, I guess."

"When will you come back?"

A third shrug. "Dunno. When I can."

After he'd left, she paced and pondered. Should she flee? But where would she go? It would only be more of the same, and if they'd found her once, they could find her again. The assassin they sent next time might well be older and more experienced, more immune to wonder.

If she stayed, they'd still send someone else. Surely nothing good would happen to Wesson, who hadn't completed his assigned task.

Just in case, she dug through her tiny stash and found some precious superwash wool, bright red. Enough, yes. When Wesson came back a few days later, still toting his oversize gun, she had one sock finished.

"Here, try this on. It's a man's large. I had to guess at your size, but if that one fits, I'll make a second for you. If it doesn't, I'll start over."

He pulled off his massive sneaker and tried the sock on. It fit. He grinned, wiggled his toes, walked around in it. "Feels good. Warm!"

"Good. I'll make the second one, then."

"You show me how." So she did, demonstrating the cast-on for a toe-up sock on four double-pointed needles.

As he was about to leave, she said quietly, "Wesson, what are you telling them? About me?"

"Nothing," he said, suddenly sullen, frowning and ferocious. "Ain't tell them nothing."

"Won't you get into trouble?"

He looked away, stony. "I tell them—I tell them you have to finish my sock. Then I kill you."

Right, she thought, but he was gone. She finished the second sock and started a scarf, wondering when she'd see him again, wondering if she'd see him or the next assassin at all, or simply collapse in a spray of blood from a bullet in the back of her head.

When Wesson came back the next time, he didn't have his gun. Instead, he handed her a pair of drumsticks. "These my aunt's. She play drums once. Show me knit on them."

She gave him a pair of her old knitting needles instead. She taught him to cast on, knit, purl. He was a quick learner, good with his hands; by the end of that lesson, she'd given him the scarf to finish.

After that, he showed up every few days. Irene felt like Scheherazade, although the tales she wove were in wool, not words. By late October, Wesson had finished the scarf, only his first few inches uneven, and wore it proudly. He made another, feather and fan, for his aunt. He asked Irene if she'd teach him to knit socks.

All the while, he still wore the tracking bracelet.

The Tuesday before Thanksgiving—still celebrated with family feasts—Irene spent a small fortune on a vat-grown chicken breast and shared it with Wesson, who brought her three apples. Fruit was precious now, a princely gift only Combine could afford. On the winter solstice, he arrived with a tiny piece of real chocolate for her, and Irene gave him some hand-knitted mittens. She hadn't had enough matching yarn to work the same pattern in each, but they seemed to delight him.

She allowed herself to be lulled into a fragile sense of safety. Wesson clearly had no more interest in killing her; his superiors, who had to know what was happening, were obviously tolerating the situation. She was certain it was a temporary reprieve. They were Combine. They knew where she lived. They could kill her, and Wesson, whenever they wanted to, which was surely why they hadn't insisted that he kill her immediately. Somewhere, someone was amused by this situation. She might have been, too, if her life hadn't been at stake.

She remained alive only at the whim of powers beyond her control. But hadn't that always been true? And she'd missed teaching, missed working with children. Showing Wesson how to knit helped ease that ache. She knew in her gut that she'd be dead by spring. Whenever she imagined her death, it occurred in April, the month Derringer had died.

However short this grace period might be, it was a blessing.

And then, one freezing day in January, Wesson—beaming, bundled in his scarf and a hat he'd made and her mismatched mittens—walked into her apartment and said, "Animals! Want to go see them."

"What?" Irene had been fighting a cold, praying it wasn't flu or something worse. There were rumors of another pandemic this year, something in Canada that had surely already spread to the States. Every muscle ached. She didn't want to go anywhere.

Wesson pulled a piece of paper out of the pocket of his puffy down jacket. "Animals at the old zoo. Thought you wouldn't see it online, so printed this. See?"

She sneezed and peered at the paper. She needed new bifocals but couldn't afford them. She squinted at the tiny print of the news story. A temporary exhibit at the old petting zoo, some goats and sheep, a guinea pig and a rabbit, all cloned and vat-grown: One of the universities was raising money by taking them on the road. The admission charge was astronomical.

Irene sighed. "Wesson, I'm sick. I don't want to go outside. You shouldn't be with me, breathing my germs. And I can't afford this. I'm sorry. You go and tell me about it."

"I afford it! Not afraid to get sick! Come on, 'Reen! Come see sheep with me!" He was almost dancing from foot to foot, as childlike as she'd ever seen him.

She swallowed. It was below freezing out, and she didn't have a coat: She hadn't thought to bring one with her when she fled in April, and she didn't have the money for one now. And she was sick. "It's too cold," she said, nearly weeping. "Wesson, I'm sorry, truly—"

"Oh oh oh," he said, looking stricken. "You make all these warm things . . ." He stopped, chewed his lip, and then grinned. "Naw, we fix it. Easy."

He insisted that she wear his down jacket, in which she swam like a doll wrapped in a king-size comforter. He draped himself in his scarf, two of her own scarves, and her one blanket—"I return it, promise"—and then drew himself up majestically. "I look like sheep pusher?"

"Sheep pusher?" She stared at him blankly. Was this a fever dream? How sick was she? "Oh! A shepherd, you mean?" Couldn't he have learned the right word online? What did he do with those netchips, other than streaming the pounding ammo-pop favored by Combine?

He looked nothing like a shepherd, but she didn't want to disabuse him. He was a child, but still a singularly dangerous one. "Why, yes. I believe you do."

He grinned. "Subway car be warmer."

It was indeed warmer, although they had to wait too long on the freezing platform. By the time the train came, groaning and creaking in a chorus of ancient complaints, Irene had succumbed to a bone-deep shivering that felt like all her joints were grating together. She was surprised she didn't clatter when she walked.

The car was full of Combine soldati, a gang of them, black-suited and sullen, ankles bulging, guns on laps, hands and feet jittering as they listened to their music. Irene was grateful she couldn't hear it. There were no Eyes here, but it was still bad. She wondered how many clans were represented; their sigils were visible only on certain wavelengths detected by the netchips. Better not to know, maybe. Wesson had to be Scar Clan, the people who'd killed Glock, but she'd never asked him.

I'm going to die now, she thought. In the moment before the door closed, she thought about trying to run, but how far would she get? She glanced at Wesson, who looked cheerfully unconcerned. Had he led her into this trap, or had he been surprised by it?

She sat down, closing her ordinary, flesh-and-blood eyes and leaning forward, trying to stop shaking, waiting once again for bullets. Instead, she heard Wesson chattering with the other young men in Combine dialect. If she opened her eyes, she'd see their hands flying, fingers flashing in the jive that contained at least half the content of each sentence.

She didn't open her eyes.

Wesson's voice sounded conversational enough, but Irene didn't know if she could trust her instincts. She tried to pick out individual words, but they kept blurring together. And then she heard one: *grandmother*.

Grandmother.

Had Wesson said that? Had one of the others? She wasn't even sure. But when Irene opened her eyes, the soldati were blinking at her, muttering to each other, and then the car stopped and Wesson said, "This be us," and tugged her upright and out onto the platform. She could have sworn the toughs pulled away from her as she passed.

Making her way up another steep staircase, aching and winded, Irene managed words. "Wesson. Your grandmother, Katana. What happened to her?"

Even through his improbable shepherd's outfit, she saw his shoulders hunch. "She dead."

"I'm sorry, Wesson." Irene imagined a white-haired woman rocking an infant grandson, imagined the woman telling the child, when he was older, about a pet she'd had once: a real live animal, warm and furry, a creature made of more than ones and zeros. "How did she die?"

He pulled the scarves around his face; they were on the street now, in biting wind. "She just die," he said, voice muffled by wool. "She old. She just stop."

"You must have been very sad." So few people died of simple old age anymore, even if they weren't connected to Combine. Irene hugged Wesson's jacket closer; it was damned cold out here, and what were the university types thinking, subjecting precious creatures to this weather? They must really be desperate for funding, although that had been true as long as Irene could remember. "How old were you when she died?"

"Ten." Irene heard the shudder in his voice. "Went to wake her for breakfast: her mouth all open, her hands all stiff."

"*You* found her? Wesson, I'm sorry. My grandma died fifty years ago, and I still miss her sometimes."

"Yah," he said, but now they were at the gate of the zoo, and someone official looking scanned one of Wesson's chips, twice, and they both had antiseptic gel squirted onto their hands, and then they were inside.

The petting zoo had been covered with a tent, and to Irene's immense relief, there were heaters inside. She and Wesson stopped next to one to thaw their fingers and faces; then they made their way to the small group of cages. "That it?" Wesson said excitedly, pointing at an animal. "That the sheep?"

"No, that's a goat." Hadn't he seen photos? Entranced, Irene knelt down in front of the cage; the goat—very young, really a kid—backed up and tried to butt her, bouncing instead off the plexiglass of its cage.

"He trying *hurt* you?" Wesson sounded as indignant as if he weren't her assigned killer.

"He's playing. Or she." Irene scanned the docent card, printed and very low-tech, attached to the cage. "No, you were right, he's a boy. Look at his eyes, Wesson! See those slits? Isn't he funny looking?"

Wesson had knelt next to her. Irene thought of the old, old stories about the baby born in the stable, the animals kneeling in reverence to honor incarnation. Now humans were the ones kneeling to animals. "We touch him?"

"No," Irene said sadly. "They're too afraid we'll make the animals sick. That's why we had to wash our hands coming in, but we can't touch them, even so. We can only look." The aching in her bones and joints and chest had deepened; she shouldn't be here, where she might infect these impossibly rare creatures.

"Aw," said Wesson. He put his hand against the plastic, and the kid tried to butt it, and Wesson laughed. "He funny."

"Yes, he is." Her voice sounded thick to her, froggy.

"Think I felt heat from him. He really real?"

"He really is."

They watched the goat awhile, and then they moved to the guinea pig—"Potato with fur," Wesson sniffed, unimpressed—and then to the sheep. "Cloud with legs," Wesson said, his voice lightened by joy, and Irene allowed herself a brief fantasy about what he might have become with proper education. There weren't many people here, not nearly as many as Irene would have expected, even with the weather and the exorbitant admission price. Well, anyone could *see* animals on the internet. If you couldn't touch them, what was the point?

The animals, so closed off and walled in, filled her with sorrow. Head aching, she found herself fighting tears even when Wesson, who had gone off to find a restroom, yelled across the tent, "'Reen! Rabbit! Lookit them *ears!* That the animal your yarn came from, yah?"

She'd go see the rabbit. She'd tell Wesson how fast rabbits were, how they had to be fast because everything hunted them. And then she'd tell him she had to go home: because she was sick, and because she couldn't stand the cages anymore.

Crossing the tent, she had to make her way around a man carrying a little girl on his shoulders. The child wore shiny pink butterfly barrettes on her cornrows. Encased in a quilted powderblue snowsuit, she beat on the man's head with dimpled hands, singing a nonsense song. Irene, temporarily charmed out of her despair, turned to see the child's face. Instead, she saw the glint of metal, round, surrounded with inset red-and-white crystals.

Eye of God.

The man—father, brother, uncle, whatever—was Eye of God Combine.

Irene's stomach lurched. She faced swiftly forward again, praying he hadn't seen her, hoping, too, that he hadn't noticed Wesson, although it was all too likely that he was here because of Wesson, having used the ankle cuff to track the two of them to the zoo. She and Wesson had never left her apartment together before. That might have, must have, annoyed some watcher, crossed some line. The grace period was over.

Wesson had returned to the display; he stared at the bunny, his hand flat against the plastic. "Def warm," he said wistfully, and Irene was about to tell him that the rabbit didn't matter now, that other things were more important, that they had company, when his face went tense and a hiss came from between his teeth.

"Wesson?" But he held up a hand to quiet her, put it on her shoulder. *Stay.* And she did: She didn't know what else to do.

"Your building," he said, when he came back from wherever he'd been. Newsfeed? "Your building burning, 'Reen—"

"Because of me? Your people?"

A grim nod from Wesson. "Yah. Scar Clan, same as safe house. Scar sig, firebomb."

Derringer. Her gut twisted. Derringer, trapped in fire, screaming—

No. Focus, Irene. That nightmare's in the past. You have problems right here, right now. What are you going to do?

You can't do anything.

"Wesson," she said, "they followed us here. Eye. Behind you."

No sooner had she said it than she heard a joyous shriek from the little girl. "Bunny! Daddy! Pat the bunny pat the bunny pat the bunny!"

The book? *Pat the Bunny*, with all its shapes and textures? Did parents still read that to their children? Combine parents?

Wesson turned, his back against hers, pressing her gently against the plastic of the cage. He was shielding her, for all the good it would do either of them. On the other side of the plastic, the rabbit hopped away toward its water bottle. Smart bunny. Irene saw the crowing child and her expressionless, terrifying father reflected in the smooth surface. She imagined tomorrow's headline: *Massacre at Non-Petting Zoo*. She and Wesson would be dead. The plastic would probably be shattered. She hoped the rabbit, at least, would be safe.

The father's reflection smiled, pointed at the bunny, spoke to his daughter. "Look, Bertha, see it hop? Hop on its little leg?" He tickled her though the snowsuit, his fingers beating a tattoo against the blue nylon. Bertha giggled and pulled his hat down over his forehead.

Over the Eye.

The father nodded, hands moving in a blur of jive, and Wesson stepped away, allowing Irene to turn around. She gaped up at the covered Eye. Bertha's hands were firmly over the hat, which was over the Eye; Wesson's hands, and the father's, flew through intricate conversation. Irene's hands shook helplessly.

The father unzipped his jacket, withdrew a thick envelope and some sort of wrench, and gave them to Wesson, who thrust them quickly beneath the blanket. The father reached out and touched Irene's shoulder. She flinched, but the touch was gentle, a caress. And then he turned and walked away, and Wesson was pulling Irene in the other direction, away from the Eye, away from giggling Bertha, away from the father, whose voice reached them faintly. "Goat, Bertha! Billy goat!"

Then they were outside again, and Wesson was pushing her into a van—Combine, black, all right, so now she'd die—but she found herself sinking into warm leather, heard Wesson exhale in relief beside her. They were alone in the back seat. The van was moving, although the front seat was empty. GPS autoguidance, pre-programmed. It would take them somewhere deadly, if it didn't simply explode.

"Safe," Wesson said. He bent down, pulled up the cuff of his jeans, and used the wrench, glowing blue from embedded electronics, to remove his tracking bracelet. It came off with a small click. He unrolled the car window and tossed both objects into the frigid wind before closing the window again. "We safe! You rarer'n rabbit, 'Reen."

What? But he was grinning as he passed her the thick envelope from Bertha's father. She fumbled it open and found two printed train passes—paper and ink, those anachronistic extravagances—good for unlimited trips.

"We go *anywhere*," Wesson said.

She didn't understand. She shook the rest of the envelope's contents onto her lap. Hard currency, more priceless than angora, and there was a lot of it here.

And something else. A photograph of two children: a baby, fat and laughing, with yellow flower barrettes on her cornrows, sitting on the lap of an older boy, four or five maybe, features achingly familiar. He held a book; he was reading it to her. *Pat the Bunny*. The photograph's sides bore indentations. It had been in a frame once, a precious physical relic.

Irene turned over the photograph and found an inscription printed on the back, in neat block letters. "Bertha and Derringer, Bertha first birthday." And below that, in awkward script, *Thank you, grandmother.*

The letters swam. "I don't," Irene said. "I—"

"Man at zoo, Derringer uncle."

Nothing made sense. "He's Crater Clan? Why didn't he kill you? Why couldn't he help Derringer when—"

Wesson shook his head. "Out of country then. Glock told him about you 'fore he left. Came back, bribed Feds, tracked you. Protected us."

"From your people? Scar Clan? How?"

Wesson shrugged. "Bribes, threats maybe. Didn't say. Not much time. You, me, Derringer: small caliber. Bosses have bigger problems."

"Did you know they were going to firebomb my apartment? Did he?"

"No! Would've warned you!" He sounded genuinely hurt, but then he shuddered. "Maybe meant for both of us. Lucky we were out. Derringer uncle saw fire, knew. Had package ready. Programmed van."

"He taught Bertha to cover his Eye of God," Irene said numbly; she both admired his audacity and was horrified that he was using his daughter, despite his obvious love for her. How long had he been planning this? Reeling, she looked down at the back of the photograph. *Thank you, grandmother.*

And then it hit her, the thing that should have been obvious all along, the thing that had been staring her in the face since Glock came to parent-teacher night, since the first time she met Wesson and listened to him talk about Katana.

Combine knew death intimately: traded it, created it, saw it stark and bloody and howling in front of them. Because they dealt in death, at least some of them treasured life. Most Combine parents, like all parents, loved their children. Most Combine parents, like all parents, wanted their children to outlive them. Glock had loved Derringer; Derringer's uncle had loved Derringer and loved Bertha. He had extended grace, even across Clan lines, to Wesson, who hadn't killed the old woman who had tried to save his nephew.

The old woman who could show Combine children, and their parents, that people could still live to be old.

Grandmother.

When the life expectancy of your community is thirty-five, a grandmother is a figure of fear and wonder. *You rarer'n rabbit, 'Reen.* To B. Jones she had been invisible, but Combine didn't even need Eye of God to see her. Even the kids in the subway car, distracted by music and the ever-present net, had seen her.

The van had stopped. It had brought them to one of the older train stations. Had Derringer's uncle somehow blocked the cameras here, or acted on knowledge that they were broken? Exactly how much had he engineered, and if he could do all that, why wasn't he sending them somewhere safe?

But she knew the answer. There were no safe places; the only safety lay in movement. Her building was burning, had burned. She hoped no people had burned with it. She was sick and exhausted. She didn't want to run, but that was what rabbits did, and now she had young to guard.

Wesson had put everything back into the envelope. "We look ridiculous," she told him. "As soon as possible, we have to get off the train and buy proper clothing."

"Nah," he said, his voice buoyant. "We ride this train till spring." He reached for the door handle, and in the distance, Irene heard the scream of metal on rails.

'PEMI AGUDA

The Wonders of the World
FROM *Ghostroots*

FANTASY

ABISOLA FOUND HERSELF sitting next to the new boy, Zeme, because she was the last person to board the bus. A day ago, she hadn't thought she would be joining her classmates on this geography excursion. Her mother was suddenly able to afford the trip when some alhaja stumbled upon her shop and bought forty yards of Swiss lace. So, this morning, Abisola's mother stood at the back of the school bus, pressing cash into the hands of the trip coordinator, Mr. Baju, while Mrs. Korede, assistant coordinator, manned the door of the bus, waiting for his decision. The payment deadline had passed a week ago.

Abisola watched, off to the side, as Mr. Baju surveyed the crumpled envelope in his hands. She looked away when his pitying eyes slid from the envelope to her, down to the oversize sneakers she'd borrowed from her father. When Mr. Baju gave in, she let herself be hugged by her mother, then pushed her feet against the backs of the shoes, closing the gap, so nobody else would give her that look.

Inside, Zeme was whispering to nobody, his hands steepled under his chin, eyelids closed. Abisola leaned away from him, into the hard plastic of the armrest that prevented her from falling into the aisle. The first day Abisola saw the new boy on the school grounds, she had thought of spaghetti. Zeme was all wriggly and lilting. His waist cocked to the left, then swayed to the right. He waved his hands in front of his face when he spoke, a music conductor, his own voice the song. Every sentence was high-pitched and keening as if searching for the perfect key, a crescendo rising to a climax that never came. She noticed how he made people uncomfortable; all that looping and undulation. She resisted the urge to reach out to him, prop him up, keep him steady.

But there was something else that prevented this contact. Something Abisola's mother would call "nervous energy," what their music teacher would call his "aura." The boys in their class simply said, "That dude freaks me out." That *something* made Abisola feel exposed whenever Zeme looked at her, as if he knew all her secrets and was only keeping them out of a condescending benevolence.

"What are you doing?" she asked of his steepled fingers, still angled away from him. She was curious, but her real motive was to trade seats so she could have the window.

Zeme's lips paused. He raised his head. The bulgy eyes that had already earned him the nickname "Froggy" opened to locate her. His lids slid against muddy brown irises, then he asked if she wanted the window. She nodded yes, only slightly startled at his intuition. Behind them, similar switches were happening.

"You like the billboards?" He hadn't moved yet, his whole body still, except for those eyes that wandered her face. Abisola fought the impulse to spread her fingers in front of her nose, hide herself from him.

Yes, she liked to look at Lagos's billboards with the slogans written in pidgin. She enjoyed hating on the ads, sneering at the exaggerated grins on the magnified people. Did the MTN man advertising one month of free app downloads really have to smile so hard that it looked like his face would split? She didn't believe in his happiness. She couldn't relate to that joy. Abisola wondered, though, if she would get a new sense of self if she were blown up ten times her size, lifted high above a city of twenty-one million people.

To Zeme, she shrugged. He stood then, plastering himself to the row in front so Abisola could take his seat. An image of a lizard came to her, a particular one she had found high on her bedroom wall one Saturday morning, staring at her. When they settled, she repeated her question.

"Praying," Zeme answered. He flexed fingers and cracked knuckles. She cringed at the harsh treatment of his frail-looking digits. "I'm praying," he repeated, the *y* in the word sustained, a held note. "There's a long journey ahead of us. And my people say I'm a prophet."

Abisola stopped talking to him then. She nodded, that slow bob of disbelief. She turned to look out the window, at a billboard. TASTE AND SEE, WE GO SCATTER YA BRAIN! a seasoning cube promised. But at what point had brain scattering become a thing to entice people with, Abisola wanted to know; at what point had having no control over your mind become a desired thing? She rested her crinkled forehead on the cool windowpane.

Her SS3 class was headed to Ikogosi to see the confluence where the warm spring met the cold spring but didn't mix.

"Why do they call you a prophet?" Abisola asked Zeme when the bus stopped for a bathroom break close to Ibadan.

The other students noisily spilled out of the bus at a Mr Bigg's parking lot, into the arms of squawking hawkers who waved everything from bread loaves to bananas to kuli-kuli to boiled eggs in their faces. The students contorted and twisted free of the traders who grabbed at them, running the rest of the way to the eatery's doors. Mr. Baju trailed them, dodging some ripe bananas thrust in his face. He had asked the students to submit their phones to him, to be returned on the trip back. "No distractions, talk to each other!" He was bringing his zealous classroom energy to the excursion, Abisola thought; he began every Tuesday/Thursday class with a cheesy icebreaker, calling the rocks and rivers they studied "wonders of the world." She thought it was a little sad, a little naïve, how he wore his excitement on his face, in front of teenagers who saw any kind of earnestness as weakness.

Abisola and Zeme lingered in the bus. Something they had in common at the moment was aloofness from the other classmates. Zeme, because he was the new boy who slithered around school, his gaze the only steady thing about him. Abisola, because she had recently turned down the advances of one of the school's popular kids. Musa was one of the tall, fine boys that other girls reapplied lip gloss for, whose parents owned a house in London. After she said no to Musa, the other boys began ignoring her in solidarity, and Abisola wondered if the girls were affronted that she would reject someone they pined for, believing this to be an indictment of their tastes, or a show of superiority.

It was neither. She was interested in Musa, his tight Fulani curls, that slash in his eyebrows; but the fear of a time when he would want to hang out on the weekend, or visit her at home, was too much. Would she invite him into their two-bedroom flat where the lonely chairs skidded across the chipped terrazzo floor; where the door to the kitchen had no handle so they had to stick a finger into the hole and jerk-jerk-jerk until it came unstuck? And underneath this shame was a murkier fear, not yet articulable to her; something about dividing what very little happiness you had between two people. Abisola was glad he wasn't in her geography class.

"Sometimes I can see things that are coming." Zeme's head leaned on the seat in front, his voice wafting toward Abisola. "Other times, I can stop what's coming. I don't know if that's what a prophet is, but that's what they call me, anyway. Ever since I was a boy."

"Things like what?" Abisola's parents were not religious; they refused to join the "seeking poor of Nigeria," those who went from church to mosque to shrine, looking for a miracle, for a panacea, for hope. "Tsk-tsk," they would go, clicking away from a church's broadcast service on television, "when will they see there's no answer there?"

Zeme turned to her. "Okay, so, a while back? My dad's first wife from like a million years ago suddenly started calling my mum all the time, out of the blue. She said my mum was the reason they broke up, that she had a vision where my mother was a mountain in her path. It was very stressful. Then, one night my mum wakes up feeling like she's dying. She said her throat was closing, her head was light, her spirit was trying to leave her body. So, she comes into my room and says, Zeme, pray for me. I had been awake already, unsettled, like I was waiting for something that I didn't know yet. I held her until she felt better. In my arms, I could, like, literally feel her body calm down. And I felt so tired after the whole thing. You know, like Jesus after the woman with the issue of blood touched his garment? Anyway, when we woke up the next morning, we heard news that my dad's first wife had died mysteriously in the night."

Mr. Baju knocked on the side of the bus, and Abisola jumped. "We're not stopping again o! You kids better go get snacks or use the toilet now."

Hawkers swarmed the two potential customers when they got off the bus, Abisola squinting at the back of Zeme's head, running the story again through hers, weighing it for truth. A man wearing a dirty yellow Lipton cap was selling Gala, his carton of skinny sausage rolls braced on a shoulder. He started to approach Zeme, who was a head taller than everybody, even with his leaning and slanting. Then the Gala man froze. Abisola saw it all: the fear that stretched across the man's face like a mask, his eyes growing wider and wider, filling out his face, as if he were looking at a dead cousin that he put in the ground himself. She saw Zeme stiffen midstride, turn to the man. It was then the Gala man let out a small cry, like a woman during her first contraction, startled and strangled and sharp. The man lifted his Gala box, turned, and ran in the opposite direction, kicking up dust and gravel, nothing on his heels.

At the Ikogosi resort, Abisola was paired with Dania, a girl in SS3C who wore an oversize wristwatch—signifier that she had a boyfriend—that kept sliding off her wrist. They entered their room in silence, and Abisola picked the bed Dania didn't. She pushed her bag under it and sat, taking in the tie-dye curtains, the framed cliché of a dark-skinned woman with a calabash on her head. There was another photo of an Egungun masquerade dancing against a black background. The masquerade's form was bulky but graceful, something eerie about a possessed man in weighted cloth spinning so high above the ground, the patterns on his colorful garb blurred by speed. Her eyes moved to the ankara runner on the small fridge, the wooden mask sitting beside the lamp on the dresser. It was one of those resorts that catered to foreigners, visitors they had to assure this was "the real Africa" by creating everything out of unpolished wood, carving tribal marks and symbols into every surface.

Dania walked up to the mask and turned its long face down. "Not ready to have nightmares," she explained, her first words to Abisola.

Abisola didn't have nightmares, but many nights she couldn't sleep because of the pressure in her chest. It started slow, her heartbeat increasing steadily until it was bursting through her ribs, knocking in her ears, stealing her breath. She cried on those nights, the darkness outside crowding in, the world closing in. It always started in her bed, and yes, she was tangibly conscious of the fact that she was lying on her thin, flowery sheets and her too-flat pillow, her parents on the other side of the cheap stucco wall; yet she was also viscerally convinced that she was floating in a galaxy, alone in the black ink of the universe, a loneliness crumpling her whole body into a tenth of its size, squeezing.

Her father would wake up to her crying, come into the room, and lift her trembling teenage body into his arms, transferring her to lie between him and his wife. Some nights, the contact of her parents' sweaty bodies was enough to calm her heart. She would hold tightly to their arms, digging in and bruising skin until she could breathe again, tension draining from her muscles and leaving hiccups behind. But other nights, even the weight of their hugging arms wasn't enough to quell the terror that darkened her sight, the certainty that she was absolutely alone in the middle of her life and couldn't be reached by anyone.

Her parents were hoping the strenuous activities of this trip would knock her out every night. She was to request her phone back from Mr. Baju if she had an episode. Abisola surveyed Dania, who was laying out her swimsuit, sizing up what her roommate's reaction would be if she were to scream herself awake, sobbing. She did not want to find out.

"You're getting close to that Froggy boy, abi?" Dania asked when Abisola continued to watch her. She smoothed out an orange strap, then swung her hand back up to catch the imitation Rolex before it slipped off.

Abisola shrugged. One of her fears as she trailed Zeme into

The Wonders of the World

Mr Bigg's was that this would further push her away from the rest of her classmates. One doesn't become less of an outsider by befriending the other outsider.

"You should ask your new friend why he is changing school one term before we all graduate secondary school. Ask him why he left his old school."

Abisola sat up straighter. "Why? Why did he leave?"

Dania laughed and looked up to meet Abisola's eyes. "Ah, no o! Me, I don't gossip."

Abisola had been in a different school once too. She spent her first two years of secondary school there. But one day, she came home weeping. She knelt in front of her confused parents, begging not to go back. No, nothing had happened to her. No, nobody had touched her, bullied her; she wasn't failing. She just couldn't go back. Whenever she stepped into the school premises, her head felt double its size, her body double its weight, and she dragged from class to class, sinking into the floor. She was sure she would die if she went back. Her parents had shared a look, but the next day, she was walking into her present school to take an admission test. They could not afford the new school, they even owed school fees at the old one, but her father said that no thirteen-year-old should experience such despair. Abisola never forgot that afternoon her parents sprang into action for her, into action and into debt.

That was some three years ago. Whatever had brought Zeme here, Abisola did not need to know. They were here; this was now.

The class drove an hour west to climb up Erin-Ijesha Waterfalls the next morning. Mr. Baju said he was saving the Ikogosi confluence visit for last. "Be careful!" he kept screaming as they climbed the stone steps, interrupting his own long speech about how marvelous the seven floors of Erin-Ijesha were and how it was a shame that the students were too lazy to climb to the seventh plane, which housed a village.

"There's a story about a catfish that was caught here a long time ago," he said, clearing his throat. "That when they tried to cut it up to cook for the king, its head kept growing back."

"Na so!" one of the boys shouted, imitating a cough. The others laughed, and Mr. Baju joined them, his chuckle weak. Abisola turned away from his humiliation.

"Of course," the man added, "it's only a myth. No science there."

Zeme was behind Mrs. Korede, and Abisola watched his arms spread out on either side for balance. He lifted his nose high in the air, as if imitating that *Titanic* scene. His body rocked left to right as if the wind were his dance partner, the drum of the waterfall in the distance an accompaniment. Abisola moved to catch up with him, one foot gingerly in front of the other because these borrowed sneakers made her feel even more unmoored than usual.

"You people need to believe more things," Zeme said in a singsong voice when she caught up with him. His *s* sustained itself, and she recoiled as if he were hissing at her, warning her. But then he turned to bare his mouthful of teeth in a grin. Was this about Mr. Baju's catfish story? She slipped a little and focused on her feet.

Safe at the waterfall, Dania eagerly stripped down to her orange swimsuit, pulling her T-shirt off in one swoosh. The others followed her lead. Zeme peeled his shirt off, then his shoes. His ribs indented his skin with every breath, and Abisola tried not to wince. His back curved sharply when he sat next to her, his spine a crooked *C*. She removed her shoes and hugged her knees to her chest on the rock they sat on. The waterfall beat against a jutting rock, and the other students took turns standing beneath it, to be slapped by the torrent, crying out in delight. Mr. Baju started to ask questions about what they knew about these rocks, but Mrs. Korede touched a shushing hand to his shoulder, and he fell silent.

"Poor Mrs. Korede," Zeme whispered, and then plunged his feet into the water and giggled a high, tinkling sound. His toes squirmed in the shallow water, and Abisola saw they were painted. A deep forest green that matched the algae on the rocks. She could not look away from those skinny toes that danced beneath the clear water; the color green seemed to become more vivid the longer she stared. Alive. The laughter of her classmates faded away along with her sense of reality, and the color loomed so she felt pressed up against the algae, the roughness of rock scraping at her skin, the brightness of its color blinding her. The wet air grew denser, and Abisola struggled to breathe. Her heart throbbed in her ears as if she were underwater. Everything melted away there in the daylight, every person, the water, the trees, the rocks—all blending into an amorphous threat. She was alone again, drowning in green. The distance between her and Zeme was the span of many planets, the expanse of lifetimes.

When Zeme touched her thigh, he crossed that gap and Abisola was no longer alone. She sucked in a deep breath and coughed hard until her chest hurt. Her tear-filled eyes sought out Zeme's. Abisola didn't understand what had brought on this episode; she had slept through the night without interruption, nudged awake by the light that filtered through the tie-dye curtains to warm her face. Now, this, happening in broad daylight, canceled out the relief she felt in the morning.

But perhaps this episode happened so Zeme could see. He was witness, and she didn't shy away from his appraisal. She pressed down on his hand, attempting to communicate the heaviness through skin. "Help me," she said, her voice raspy. "You say you're a man of God. Can you take it away?"

Zeme's nose flared at her plea, but that surprise was almost immediately replaced by a shade of victory in his smile. Behind his head, Abisola caught Halimat, one of Dania's popular friends, frowning at her; she had just stepped away from the waterfall to wring water out of her waist-length braids. Halimat's gaze moved from Abisola's face to the hand grasping Zeme's on her thigh; then she raised her brows. Abisola yanked her hand from under Zeme's. Flustered by Halimat's continuing stare, she lowered her chin to her chest.

Abisola wanted to be happy, for her parents. She saw the way her cousins laughed with a lightness that was foreign to her, creating dance routines to entertain their parents, even into their late teens, gossiping with their mum about all the weirdos in school, making tea for their father. They once put salt in his Lipton as a prank, and his bellowing laughter continued to ring in

Abisola's head for the rest of that holiday, a mocking reminder of the joy she was not giving her own father. And yes, Abisola was sure that a part of this levity came from wealth; her cousins' house in Ikoyi was big enough to host all the relatives every Christmas. But even in her own household, Abisola watched from under hooded eyes how her mother tickled her father while he cut pawpaw on the deep freezer—how she took his finger into her mouth when he inevitably sliced it that day, how they laughed and laughed outside her bedroom window when her father pulled the generator rope so hard that it snapped. They stiffened when she entered a room, soberness congealing their features. They didn't know they were doing it, but she saw every bit lip, flexed jaw, their concern for her casting a shadow over everything.

Maybe Zeme could help her become one of those lit paper lanterns she saw in *Mulan*—a bright floating presence in their lives.

On the way down from the waterfall, Mrs. Korede fell and twisted her ankle. There were several accounts of what happened. Dania then Soji then Halimat shouted over each other, clamoring around Mr. Baju, gesturing in his face. They claimed to have seen Zeme push Mrs. Korede. Eli and Wale insisted no, they had seen him reach out to prevent the fall. All the others steered clear of the argument.

Abisola had been trailing the group, wanting to put distance between herself and what she thought was an embarrassing outburst for help at the waterfall. The group crowded around the fallen Mrs. Korede, still dripping. Mr. Baju tried to cut the yammering short by lifting a hand.

Mrs. Korede's teary face moved from person to person as they argued above her. It was well known among the students that she was easily swayed, that a good argument and strategic tears could bump a grade in her English classes. Abisola once overheard Kovie, the Youth Corper, teasing Mrs. Korede about her long "Deeper Life" skirt suits, and she suspected this was the reason for Mrs. Korede's cellulite-baring short shorts that Dania and

Halimat had been snickering at. Now, as her head moved from student to student, their arguments rising again, Abisola could see the English teacher failing to settle on someone to believe. When asked directly what happened by Mr. Baju, she stuttered and lowered her head to inspect her scraped shin and swelling ankle.

Through all this, Zeme sat next to the woman on the ground, watching the blotchy ankle grow in size. Every time his name was mentioned, either in defense or in accusation, Zeme twitched as if stung. He looked in the direction his name was coming from, then back to the ankle. He leaned into Mrs. Korede and whispered in her ear. She startled, then relaxed. When she bent her head toward his chest, eyelids lowered, Abisola knew he was praying again. She studied the ankle from the gaps between bodies, waiting for something, anything, to happen to the ankle, which looked exactly like skinless uncooked chicken.

Mr. Baju clapped, and the group turned to him, silenced. "John, Soji, assist Mrs. Korede. The driver will meet us by the fruit sellers. Let's not throw accusations around willy-nilly."

Halimat rolled her eyes, but they all obeyed. The boys helped Mrs. Korede stand on her good foot. She let out a whimper, then bit it down. John was the school's star basketball player; he could lift her without help if he needed to. He nudged Zeme aside, but Zeme did not flinch, just unfolded himself to an upright position.

Abisola did not watch him; she watched the ankle. The whispers continued, and Zeme trailed the group this time, hands folded against his belly. Abisola did not go to him; she was paying attention. She watched Mrs. Korede limp, limp, limp, supported by both boys, but by the time they neared the fruit stands, only John was holding on to her. She placed weight on the twisted ankle cautiously, then with more sureness. She extricated herself from John's bulk and rotated the ankle. "I think I'm fine," she said. "Thank you, John. Looks like it was a small thing."

The whispers stopped for a moment, and everyone gathered around Mrs. Korede for the second time. Halimat stooped low to survey the ankle, waiting for it to expose Mrs. Korede's words as a lie. The swelling was gone. Nobody looked at Zeme.

"Well," Mr. Baju said. He clapped once. "Well!"

When Abisola stepped out of the room in the middle of the night, unable to sleep, she was not surprised to find Zeme seated in the shaded courtyard. The night was quiet and humid. Abisola sat next to him on the cold cement slab and shifted forward so her bare thighs did not touch concrete where her shorts ended. The palm trees joined in Zeme's whispering; crickets provided backup.

Abisola shivered. Zeme did not acknowledge her presence. She squinted around at the puzzle of lit windows, wondering who was in whose room. Dania had stumbled into their room around midnight smelling of weed, a full two hours after they had been dismissed by the teachers for the night. Abisola had absently traced the girl's path to the other bed, wondering what respite her own parents back home were experiencing in her absence.

"Are you praying again?" she asked Zeme. She removed her feet from her slippers and pulled at the damp grass with her toes. "Did you do it? Did you push her to show us that you could heal her?"

Zeme stopped whispering. He sat up straight.

"We have one more night," was all he said, and Abisola knew that if he didn't help her before they left this place with the trees and the springs and the crickets, it wouldn't happen. She would be marooned on the island of her life, unable to meet her parents, unable to meet Musa, unable to meet anybody who offered her any kind of happiness.

"Well, okay?" She moved closer to him, leaned in to search his long nose, his thin lips, those bulgy eyes.

"They didn't believe." He let out a long, whistling sigh. "I just wanted to make them believe."

"Them?" Were there other classmates he'd been trying to convince of his power? "Are you talking about us or your old school?"

"Who's there?" Mr. Baju's voice whipped out of the night

from the door of his room on the upper floor, saving Abisola from the details. "Zeme Imoh? Abisola Lawanson, is that you?" Mr. Baju's voice sounded panicked, and Abisola jerked away from Zeme, understanding how the scene could be interpreted.

"What do you think you're doing here?"

Zeme and Abisola stood.

"If you don't get back to your rooms! I'm watching you . . ."

Abisola jogged to her room and closed the door quietly behind her; but as she slid into bed, Dania's voice came out of the darkness. "You don't hear word, you this girl. You don't listen, abi?"

Abisola ignored Dania and closed her eyes, fantasizing about a girl who looked just like her, bent over laughing hard, laughing so hard that her heart knew what it meant to burst out of her chest for all the right reasons, for all the bright reasons.

She lurched when she felt a clammy palm on her arm.

"It's just me," came Dania's voice again, now beside her bed. The faintly acrid smell of weed came with her. "Calm down, ah." Then, in a softer decibel than Abisola had ever heard from between her lips, "Can I sleep beside you? That blaze messed me up. Dunno where Hali got it from."

Abisola sat up; a light sweat from the fright coated her forehead. She faced Dania in the dark.

"Please," Dania added. "I'm seeing weird shit. That mask is not supposed to be moving. Please."

Abisola shifted, and Dania got in beside her. They lay side by side for a moment, staring at the ceiling. Then Dania contorted so that her head was touching Abisola's shoulder, warm breath tickling her cool arm. Abisola breathed out all her tension and focused on the point of contact, skin on skin. She closed her eyes. She slept.

"You remember our class on this? A confluence is where two or more flowing bodies of water meet and then run together. But see here, the warm spring meets the cold spring but they don't mix? They glide on, their own separate paths!" Mr. Baju's voice boomed over the pallor of the group. It was their last full day, but the students all seemed in dour moods, as if they had been given bad news. He kept turning to Mrs. Korede, his imploring gaze enlisting her to contribute, to elicit a response from the somber group, but she was slumped against a rock herself, staring at a couple holding hands while dipping plastic bottles into the warm spring with their free hands. "Did you know," Mr. Baju asked his students, "that some people believe the warm spring has healing properties?" Nobody responded. The couple filled their bottles and walked away without glancing at the school group.

Abisola had woken to find Dania absent from the room. She had apparently gone to get ready with Halimat. On the trail, Abisola waved at her, but Dania refused to look at her or leave Halimat's side. Zeme was quiet too, standing still in a way that was more unnerving to Abisola than all his swaying and winding. She wanted to push him, restart his motion. Everyone looked so glum. What had the night taken from them? Something shifted in the air and unsettled Abisola's stomach.

"You've probably heard about the myth of these springs?" There was a queue to step into the water; the other confluence visitors chatted and took pictures, but the excitement did not extend to Abisola's class. "That there was a hunter with two wives?" Nobody stirred. "One wife was very quiet; the other was very troublesome. They argued all the time. One day, they went to their husband for him to settle their fight, and he cursed them and they turned into these springs. Who can guess which wife is which?"

Nobody took Mr. Baju's bait.

When it was their group's turn, they climbed down to enter the water in pairs.

"Be careful! Put one leg in the warm spring, and one in the cold spring, and be stunned!" Mr. Baju's voice was nearing a screech, but when the first pair of students entered, neither admitted to being stunned.

"How can you not marvel at God?" Zeme's mellifluous voice piped up, and Mr. Baju's head whirled. Zeme was talking to no one in particular, just letting the words out of his mouth to fall over them like mist. "You know the first people to acknowledge and organize around this confluence were some Christians? A small Baptist church that eventually sold their land to the government?" Zeme blew air through his teeth; it came out as a tune. "You could say this is holy ground."

Abisola watched Mr. Baju's jaw work. She wasn't sure if it was because he hadn't in fact known this, and resented Zeme for flaunting his knowledge, or if it was more about Zeme's religious tone when their school was proudly secular. She thought her geography teacher looked violent for a moment. Mr. Baju shuffled backward, away from Zeme. He bumped into Halimat, who hissed and sidestepped him. "And what does this have to do with geography?" he asked, eventually.

"Everything, Mr. Baju," Zeme said, and then it was his turn to step into the water.

John was supposed to go in with Zeme; he was the closest. Abisola skipped and slid forward to grasp John's arm. "Hey, can I go before you?" John shrugged and stepped aside.

Zeme stretched his hands out to Abisola. She took them and stepped into the water with him. The water soaked the bottom of her shorts but barely went halfway up Zeme's shins. Cold, then warm. She curled her toes.

"The warm spring is about seventy degrees, while the cold spring is thirty-seven." Mr. Baju's voice was louder, as if he were saying an incantation. "But they don't mix, they don't mix! Isn't that amazing?" A startled Mrs. Korede eyed him, wary of this burst of spirit.

Abisola closed her eyes, her hands still within Zeme's grasp. The warm water was warm. The cold water was cold. Who cared if they mixed or not? If she engaged every atom of her person, if she sent all her weight toward her feet, would her burdens be swept away with the tide? Would she step out an untethered balloon? Oh, to float home on the tropical winds and knock against their window, have her parents open up and take delivery of their new child, their new Abisola who would be luminescent with giggles, effervescent, buoyant, joyful.

Nothing happened.

Abisola opened her eyes. Zeme was smiling at her. Was he mocking her? She yanked her hands out of his, betrayed. With Mrs. Korede's ankle and the Gala man and that look in Zeme's eyes, had she only seen what she wanted to? What had she really hoped for? Tears clouded her sight as she spun around, lost her footing. Down she went. Then Zeme's hands were there; she felt them, like fish, scaly, or rubbery, and they were groping for her hands, her arms, pushing her farther away from the water's surface. Abisola started to lose her breath. She wanted to thrash; her body was telling her to flail, to make it known that she was losing air, swallowing water. Her head lightened. Water moved against her and filled her up, but it was distinct from the heaviness she felt on those nights that she could only weep.

Abisola coughed out water when she was hauled from the springs. She drew in long breaths that cut pain through her chest. She cried harder. She felt robbed.

"What is happening? What is happening? Is she okay?" Mr. Baju's face appeared above Abisola's. His forehead furrows mirrored waves. Then Zeme's face replaced that image. His eyes were so bright, as if he had just witnessed magic. "How do you feel?" His mouth was now by her left ear; his breath smelled like grass after rain. "I baptized you," he said. "How do you feel now?"

The thing Abisola knew about baptism was that there was a submersion, then a lifting up. But she had not wanted to be lifted up. She had been weightless under. When Mr. Baju said, in that myth, that the man had cursed his wives, he must not have understood. How was that a curse? Abisola wanted to be water too, to be light, to flow despite gravity.

Abisola got to talk to her parents. She was given her phone and guided to her room by Mrs. Korede, who rubbed her back with solid strokes that calmed her hiccups. They moved away from the loud voices crowding Mr. Baju insisting, again, that Zeme had been the cause of this event. This time, Mr. Baju's gaze swung from person to person, looking unsure and frightened.

"Baby, what's wrong? What's wrong?" Her parents' voices pooled in her ear, so warm and worried, and Abisola knew that she had failed again. A weekend away from home and here she was casting shade on what should be a breather for them, a holiday from their albatross.

"Nothing, I just wanted to say hello."

They weren't buying it. "Your voice is all cracked, have you been crying?" her mother wanted to know. "Bibi, you know you can tell us anything, should we come get you?" her father offered.

"No, no, I'm fine. I fell and I cried, but I'm fine now, I promise. I'm fine." They had the phone on speaker, and Abisola heard her words echo in the room around them.

"Are you hurt?" Their voices were a chorus, and their unity in this small moment made her tears well up again. Would she ever flow with them, be part of the chorus of their small family; or would she always be the odd one out, off-key, their strange child weighing on their lives with her sadness?

"No, no, please don't worry about me. I just wanted to hear your voices. I begged Mr. Baju to give me my phone for five minutes."

They were silent, and Abisola could imagine the exchange of looks that would be happening over the phone. "Okay, then. We'll come pick you up tomorrow from school. Three p.m., abi? The car broke down again, but we'll borrow Nkem's car or something."

"Okay." Abisola rubbed her forehead and mud came off on her hand. She wiped it on the bedsheet.

"We love you, okay?"

"Okay, bye."

"Abisola?"

"Yes?"

"We love you, okay?"

"Okay." She breathed out and her laden heart shed some of its weight. "I love you too."

Dania found Abisola still in her wet clothes, staring at the mask that housekeeping had righted.

"Abisola?"

She didn't respond, but Dania moved till she was within Abisola's field of vision. She waved. "Hello-o?" When Abisola still didn't answer, Dania sat on the bed but stood as soon as dampness touched her thigh. She squatted instead and manually turned Abisola's head toward her.

"Look, Abisola," she said. "That Froggy boy, he convinced this guy in his old school that he would see perfectly if he broke his glasses. Like, he was performing a miracle and all the boy had to do was believe. The poor boy that was almost blind . . . he did it, broke his glasses that were as thick as Coke bottles. Then he fell down a flight of stairs. It's true. Halimat's boyfriend goes to that school, and everyone was talking about how the gullible boy broke his leg and neck. The boy's using a wheelchair for now."

Abisola blinked.

"I'm not lying!" Dania mistook her silence for disbelief. "Froggy's parents took him out 'cos the students in the school started being super mean to him and he would just be quoting the Bible at them, talking about signs and wonders and saying nothing else, and it was all very weird, but like, the boy's parents couldn't do anything 'cos the boy took off the glasses by himself, right? You can't really say Froggy forced him. But it's all weird, all very weird business. There were other things, like he was laying hands on people and conducting deliverance services during free class periods?"

What gorgeous eyes Dania had, Abisola noticed for the first time. They were wide apart on her face, almond shape. She had a great face for billboards, smooth and brown and beautiful. Her eyes would twinkle from the heights and the people would buy whatever she was selling.

"Okay, whatever, be like that." Dania got up in a huff. She made a clatter throwing her box open. She pulled out another swimsuit. This one was red and white, striped. "We're having a party at the pool. Mrs. Korede will be there, she's convinced the Baju to leave us alone for a while." She pressed the swimsuit against her stomach. "You can come if you want. You should."

At the door, she turned again to Abisola. "He pushed Mrs. Korede. I saw him, I swear."

Abisola returned to staring at the mask. She nodded. She believed.

Abisola wore her plain black swimsuit and threw on an oversize Wema Bank T-shirt she'd plucked from her parents' wardrobe. It was from when her father worked at the bank, before the downsizing, before their family moved out of the duplex into the other flat, before this smaller flat. It smelled of wardrobe, of disuse, not her parents, but she didn't mind.

At the junction with the wooden arrows showing directions to the pool, confluence, restaurant, main office, Abisola turned toward the confluence. Her rubber flip-flops slapped against the wooden dock. At each bend, there was a rustic lone bulb hanging from a stick and wire. She kept going. A bird called, another answered. A fly buzzed around her cheek, and she lifted a shoulder to brush it away. At a corner, she heard the fizz of laughter drift toward her on a wind that smelled of oranges. She kept walking.

At the steps down to the confluence, she found Mr. Baju seated. He looked up at her approach. "Lawanson?" He squinted, raising a hand over his eyes. "Abisola, is that you?"

She moved closer so he could see. "Yes." A few steps away from him, she stopped and leaned against the wooden railing. She hadn't expected to meet anybody here. The railing was rough underneath her skin. There was a smog over the springs, but she found the current.

Mr. Baju returned to staring at the water. "They call those unity trees," he said, and Abisola looked to the two trees by the confluence. One was a palm tree, its bark rough, the other had a smooth stem.

Abisola nodded. It was in the resort's pamphlet.

"Zeme Imoh left. He said he had to leave immediately, and his parents arranged for a taxi to pick him up."

"Ehehn?"

"Yes." Mr. Baju sighed. "Probably for the best. He's a weird one, isn't he?"

Abisola thought about it. "I think he just really wanted people to believe." Even now, she didn't think of the pressure of his hands underwater as cruel. He had seen her. He had wanted to help.

Mr. Baju frowned at her but didn't respond.

A wind blew and ruffled the trees, the branches whispered a prayer, the springs gurgled a song.

"Isn't it fantastic that they don't mix?" His voice was soft, the kind of soft that comes before or after tears. "I just wanted you kids to look at this marvel and feel a tenth of my awe. They don't mix! What a wonder. Isn't this a wonder?"

Abisola felt a wash of gratitude for his presence—an echo of her parents, whom she would soon be reunited with, wrapped within, different from, but connected to. She listened to the springs coexisting side by side, retaining their own virtues, stubbornly separate at their meeting but gliding forward together, bracing each other, bound forever. "It is," she agreed.

TJ KLUNE

Reduce! Reuse! Recycle!

FROM *In the Lives of Puppets*

SCIENCE FICTION

THE FACTORY IS loud. It always is. The shriek of metal, the never-ending cascade of sparks. Locking one piece into another. Waiting for the telltale beep of a working connection. Repeat. Repeat. Repeat. But today is different. Today is a special day.

When the Klaxon blares, signaling the end of the shift, the workers on the factory floor stop what they're doing. It's an hour earlier than their usual sign-off. Everyone is excited, though no one speaks.

They look to the men above them, standing on high metal platforms, their faces hidden in shadow. One steps forward. He wears a suit; it is black. He nods, a quick jerk of his head.

The factory workers raise their hands above their heads silently.

The Supervisor steps out of the shadows on the factory floor. Everyone looks at him. He is a good man, a hardworking man. Fair. Kind, though he doesn't need to be. He takes his job seriously, and because of him, output has been up across the board.

The workers lower their hands as the Supervisor makes his way across the factory floor. He smiles, nods, but does not stop to chat. His big hands are covered in oil, nails bitten to the quick. A habit, he calls it. A bad habit. But not bad enough for him to quit. It could be worse, he sometimes says.

But today isn't about habits or routine. Today is different, today is anticipated, today is *now*, and as the Supervisor reaches his destination, he pauses, looks at the figure across from him, and says, "Hello."

"Hello, boss," comes the reply, soft, clear. He has said this many thousands of times, and it never fails to make him feel warm.

"Douglas—" And then he stops, looks up at the men above them, the men who are always watching. The men who are always whispering. His forehead grows cavernous lines. He says, "P-23. Will you come with me?"

"Yes," Douglas says, because of course he will, and also because the Supervisor called him Douglas.

He follows the Supervisor down a long hallway. On the walls, colorful signs in a cheery font extol the virtues of the factory. A cartoon clock with a real face and real hands with the words *make every minute count!* An hourglass with sand running through it underneath the words *how much time do you have left?* And, of course, the mantra, the rule by which they live, the reason for *everything: reduce! reuse! recycle!* Below this, a smiling man in a pair of coveralls, grinning widely as he gives two thumbs-ups.

Douglas is led to an office. Inside is a desk and two chairs. On the wall, a picture of a family. Two boys. A girl. A smiling woman. And the Supervisor, hands filled with a baby. This is an older photograph; the Supervisor does not look like he used to when he was younger.

"I like them," Douglas says.

The Supervisor nods and waves his hand at the chair before sitting in his own. "Thank you. I like them too."

Douglas sits. He relishes it. He hasn't sat on anything in a long time. He doesn't need to, but if the Supervisor is inviting him to do it, he is not going to let the opportunity go to waste. He folds his hands on the desk in front of him like he's seen others do before.

"Do you know what today is?" the Supervisor asks, riffling through loose papers on his desk.

"Yes," Douglas says.

"Nine years, fifty-one weeks," the Supervisor says. "We've been together a long time."

"We have," Douglas says.

The Supervisor glances at him, hesitates. Then, "You understand why?"

"Yes," Douglas says. "It is my turn. Reduce, reuse, recycle." The Supervisor nods slowly. "Which is why you are given this final week. There are rules to follow, Douglas. You know the rules?"

"Yes."

"If you adhere to each and every one, you'll be fine. But if you don't . . . well. Please don't force my hand. I like you. Always have, since the first day. I'd hate to see something happen before it's your time."

"It will not," Douglas says. "Thank you, boss. For everything. I am so . . ." He stops. Smiles. Says, "I'm so excited to see what each new day will bring."

The Supervisor says, "Looks good on you, Douglas." He sounds like he means it. It makes Douglas want to sing, but he cannot sing, so he doesn't.

The Supervisor slides a small thick card across the table. It is blue with a fat white stripe down the middle. "This is your pass. It will grant you access to the apartment. You have also been given one thousand credits to use as you see fit. Carry this pass on you at all times, Douglas. If you are asked for it and you do not have it, you will not be allowed to finish out your week. Do you understand?"

"Yes," Douglas says, carefully picking up the card. It is heavier than he expects. It has weight, heft. It is real.

"On your last day, you will return promptly to the factory at nine in the morning. If you do not arrive on or before this time, you will be considered a runner, and—"

"Why would I run?" Douglas asks. "Where would I go?"

"Good. Douglas, this is an important opportunity for you. I know you've been looking forward to this for a long time. Do what you can with it, all right?"

"Yes," Douglas says. "Is there anything else?"

The Supervisor shakes his head. He looks like he wants to say something else but stops himself.

Douglas stands, clutching the pass. "Goodbye," he says. "So long." He pauses. "See you later, alligator."

He waits.

The Supervisor says, "After a while, crocodile," like he always does, except this time, it's not with warmth or a quirk to his lips. It's gruff. The right words, different sounds. One higher—*alligator*—the other lower, a not-whisper—*crocodile*. Different meanings. Douglas has something else to say. Does he feel it higher? Or does he feel it lower?

In a strange, quiet voice, Douglas says, "Thank you for being my friend."

He leaves.

There is a going-away party.

There are balloons of red and yellow.

There is cake, a flat sheet with brown frosting.

There is punch, floating in a sweating crystal bowl filled with chunks of ice. It is green.

No one eats. No one drinks. The balloons rub up against each other.

His coworkers give him a card. On the front is a dog wearing a backpack. Above the dog are the words *I'm going on an adventure!* Inside the card, the dog is sleeping, still wearing its backpack. The words now say, *after a nap!*

Douglas likes it.

He also likes that his coworkers have all signed the card. Some are illegible. Others say things like "GOODBYE!" and "HAPPINESS!" and "SIXTEEN HINDEN BURG DISASTER!"

It is very nice.

Douglas does not give a farewell speech. He does not tell the others he will see them again. He does not touch the machines on the factory floor. That time is over.

He looks at his coworkers and says, "Reduce, reuse, recycle!"

They say the same thing back to him, over and over until it sounds like they are screaming.

Above them, the men watch from the shadows.

The apartment building is three blocks away from the factory. It is old with cracked brick and dirty windows.

The apartment is on the fourth floor. The elevator is broken. Douglas doesn't mind. Stairs are interesting. One foot in front of the other, and shortly, he's on a different floor, the second. Then the third. On his way to the fourth, he passes by a woman holding a child. She stops when she sees him, narrowing her eyes and clutching the boy close. She is obviously in charge of the boy. The boss. A supervisor.

"Hello," Douglas says pleasantly. "My name is Douglas. I live here on the fourth floor for the next week. What are your names?"

The woman doesn't answer. Instead, she hurries by Douglas, keeping as much distance between them as possible. The little boy waves at him. Douglas waves back.

The apartment has a bed. Douglas has never had a bed before. He lies on it. He jumps on it. He hangs his head off the edge, making everything upside down.

The faucets work. The right is for cold water, the left for hot.

There are plants. They are all made of plastic. The leaves come off when he pulls on them.

The walls have paintings. Framed pictures. One is of a mountain, its tip covered in snow. Another is of a man riding a horse in the desert. Another says that if there are any issues to please contact your Supervisor so that they may resolve the situation.

And, of course, *reduce! reuse! recycle!* Douglas stares at that one for a long time.

There are books. He reads them all on the first day. It takes him forty-seven minutes to read six hundred and forty-three.

When he finishes, he decides to inspect the closets. There are three of them.

The hallway closet is first. And last. Because at the base, carpet, but it looks loose in the far-right corner. He tugs on it. It pulls back. Underneath is a book. He forgets about the rest of the closets, at least for now.

"That is a strange place for a book," he says to no one. He pulls it out and reads the title.

Discourse on Method by René Descartes. It takes him three hours.

When he finishes, he starts again.

That night, he sits in front of the window looking out onto the street below. He counts the cars as they pass by. He gets to two hundred and forty-seven before he is distracted by the way the rain slides against the glass.

The first day, he feeds birds in the park.

They are insistent, these birds. They all want the seed he's purchased using the pass. He tries to make them wait their turn, but they do not listen.

A child is watching him, peeking out from behind a tree, unattended by an adult. Douglas smiles. The child runs away.

There are people—many, many people. Some are dressed in suits. They must be the ones in charge. The other people—big and small—do not wear suits. They wear pants and shorts and sweaters and shoes where their toes stick out. The workers? That seems right.

He sits on a bench in the bright, bright sunlight. He thinks about the book he read, the one underneath the carpet.

There is music coming from a storefront. He goes inside.

People, always people. They smile. They laugh. They flip through records, they stand with headphones in front of record players, they sing, they exclaim brightly, and Douglas wants to be part of it.

"I like this one," he says to no one as he picks up a record. He does not know what it is, but it is what other people are doing.

He looks down at it.

A hand-drawn Black woman, looking off to the side. Billie Holiday. *Music for Torching*.

He does as the others do and takes it to a record player.

Careful—careful!—he removes the black disc from the sleeve and places it on the player. Headphones, and then the lowered needle.

Billie sings.

He listens to the entire thing. He does not move.

He is watching children play in a fountain. They splash, they shriek, they drip.

People are staring at him. He waves at them, thinking they are workers just like him, even if they aren't made of the same parts. They do not wave back. Instead, they whisper to each other, hands covering their mouths. He does not wave to the men in suits. He has a feeling they would not like it.

Soon a police officer comes. He is tall and large. His uniform is impressive, nicer than Douglas's was at the factory. He says, "Sir, we have received some complaints about—"

Douglas says, "Hello."

The officer frowns. He has a gun. It is still in the holster at his side. "Are you all right?"

"I am Douglas," he says as he was trained to do. "Thank you for keeping the peace."

"What are you doing here?"

"Watching," he says. "This is my week."

"For what?"

Douglas says, "Reduce, reuse, recycle."

The officer blinks, takes a step back. "I've never—this is the first time I've—I just started six months ago and . . . You have your pass . . . sir?"

Douglas does. He thanks the officer for asking and shows it to him. Taking it from Douglas, the officer looks down at it, twisting it over in his hands. He reads the long numeric code off the bottom into the microphone on his shoulder. A moment later, a burst of static comes through, followed by a cool, feminine voice.

The officer hands back the pass. "Carry on, then. Just . . . don't do anything you're not supposed to, all right?"

Douglas smiles. It is easier now. "I will not."

The officer leaves him be and goes to the other people who are still watching Douglas. Whatever the officer tells them seems to work. Most of them leave, taking their complaining children with them.

That's all right. More will come.

*

He walks until he gets lost.

And then he turns around and finds his way back. It is easier than he expects. He wonders how people can get lost when their path home is right in front of them.

That night, he turns on the television.

He has never watched one before, though he knows what they are. People have them in their homes to help pass the time. He likes the commercials. There is one for cats, another for couches. Four for food and three for cars. People, always smiling. People, always happy. They talk about sports and beds and insurance and sales on the newest fashion, and sometimes, they are sad because the people are sick but then they get better and everything is fine again.

He does not like it when the programming interrupts the commercials.

What a wonderful reward this is.

He does not use the bed. Instead, he stands at the window overlooking the street and watches the people stroll by on the sidewalk below, the lights from the cars flashing in the dark. It eventually starts to rain again, and Douglas sees it all.

The second day, he searches for something he saw the day before on the television. Connection. There was a commercial for people seeking connections. He is fascinated by this, the idea that people need others to talk with. To laugh with. To dance, to sing, to eat, to walk, to argue with, to *prove* existence is real.

Douglas had it with the Supervisor, but he no longer works there.

He must find someone or something else.

But first.

There are clothes in the bedroom closet. They are better than the gray jumpsuit he's been wearing since he was born. Pants, some rough, some soft. Shirts with buttons and shirts without. Socks, so many socks that he doesn't know what to do with them all. He picks out a pair that have lightning bolts on them and hopes they are the right ones.

Properly dressed, he leaves in search of something that makes sense.

He does not find it at a coffee shop. He does not find it in a park.

He does not find it in a store with loud music and flashing lights and clothes that have studs and spikes on them.

He wanders the streets of the city, stopping in front of store displays and getting distracted by the faces his reflection makes. Some people wave back, others know what he is and hurry along, their heads ducked to avoid making eye contact. No one tries to interfere with him. They know what will happen if they do. They also know what will happen if *he* does something he shouldn't. It happened once before, many years ago, before Douglas. People died. It is why there is a fail-safe implanted in his head. One wrong move, and Douglas will no longer be Douglas because he will be nothing at all.

He does not find connection on the second day, though not for lack of trying. The people he has spoken with have been kind enough in their short conversations, but no one seems willing or able to form a connection. Douglas does not blame them; it must be very hard being alive.

That night, he does not watch commercials. Instead, he plays music from a stereo. There is rock, there is rap, there is honky-tonk, and then there is *jazz*, and the *tsk tsk tsk* of the snare drum, the trill of piano keys, and then Dizzy Gillespie is there with the trumpet, wailing, wailing, and Douglas raises his hands above his head and tries to dance. He is successful. Mostly.

He finds what he's looking for on the fourth night. It comes to him in the form of a tall woman made of feathers.

Or, at least, that's what he thinks at first. It's late, after eleven, and he's on the street, about to head back to the apartment building when he hears a loud burst of laughter, followed by the *thump, thump, thump* of a heavy beat that rolls through him.

He follows the sound down a small side street, passing by old trees and streetlights hung with flags in the colors of a rainbow. Rounding a corner, he sees where the noise is coming from. It's a brightly lit building, single story, with more of the same flags hanging out front. People stand in a short line to get in, people wearing makeup and leather and glitter. People laughing, people talking, people, people, people who look like they are *happy*.

Douglas goes to the back of the line. Some people look at him, but they don't whisper, they don't roll their eyes, they don't look *afraid*. A few of them smile, nod, and this is the best night of his life.

When it's his turn at the front of the line, he stops in front of a large man with tattoos covering his arms. His head is shaved, and he has a thick silver ring hanging from his nose.

"Identification," he says.

Douglas shows him the pass the Supervisor gave him.

The man takes it, stares at it. Looks back at Douglas. Then the pass. Then Douglas. Then the pass again. He says, "This real?"

"Yes," Douglas says. "As am I."

The man nods slowly. Turning his head, he says, "Goddess? Can you come over here for a moment?"

A vision appears as if by magic. Statuesque, beautiful. She is not a bird, even if she is covered in feathers. Her lips are large and painted red, her costume spangly, and Douglas has never seen anything so extraordinary in his life. With dark skin and bright eyes, the woman does not appear to walk as much as *float*, and Douglas wonders if he is in the presence of royalty.

The woman snaps the pass from the man's hands, looking down at it. "Hmm," she says, a low murmur that sounds like the wind. "Your type doesn't usually come to a place like this."

"I am trying something different," Douglas says. She has glitter on her lips. Douglas is enchanted.

She taps the pass against long fingernails painted red as she looks him up and down. "You know what this place is, right? Who comes here?"

"Yes," Douglas says. "People searching for a connection."

She blinks. "Is that so? I suppose that's right. Yes, honey, that's what we're all looking for whether we want to admit it or not. A connection, be it for a night or longer." She leans down and kisses the man on the cheek, who grins at her adoringly and doesn't wipe away the imprint of lips left on his face.

"I have four days left," Douglas says. "I hope to find a connection before then."

The woman frowns before taking him by the arm. "You got it, honey. We welcome all. Follow the rules, and you'll be right as rain. We accept everyone here, no matter where they come from."

She pulls him through a door, through a curtain of beads, through a hallway where the walls shake with a thunderous beat. Ahead, a pair of double doors with portholes in each where light bursts through, dancing, dancing.

Before she shoves him through the doors, she stops, brushes off his shoulders, and says, "Connect, little boy. Connect until you shatter." She kisses his forehead and then shoves him through the doors.

Lights and sound. People, so many people. Writhing. Laughing. Shouting. Covered in sweat and glitter and *life*. Douglas has seen many things. But he has never felt like this before, like everything makes *sense*, like this is where he could belong.

People look at him, people with eyeliner and bright clothing. Some smile, others ignore him, and that's all right. No one is telling him he can't be here, and that's what he was worried about the most.

He moves through the crowded room, the vaulted ceiling above covered in rows of lights in green and gold and blue and red. Someone bumps into him, apologizes, and then he's standing in the middle of the dance floor, the music thumping so hard it vibrates up through the floor into his feet, his legs, a tremor that feels as if the earth itself is shifting. He has heard music before; the Supervisor plays it during their shifts. Sometimes it's loud and electric. Other times soft and aching, and it is how Douglas thinks loneliness must feel.

But this music is different. This music feels alive in ways he can't explain; he revels in the way it vibrates from the floor through his legs, his hips, chest, shoulders. It feels like it's swallowing him whole, and he moves his head from side to side as the others do. He turns in a slow circle, fingers extended as the beat hits again and again.

Lights flash, the bass rumbles, and Douglas thinks this might be the best place he's ever been to. It's even better than the park, and that is saying a lot.

Hands hold on to his hips. He turns around. A large man grins at him with perfect teeth. "You new?" he shouts above the music. "Haven't seen you here before." The smile fades when Douglas looks up at him. "You're a . . ." The man takes a step back.

"Hello," Douglas says, raising his voice to the same level as the man's. "My name is Douglas. I am having my week. What is your name?"

The man shakes his head and spins around, pushing his way through the crowd. Douglas watches him go to a darkened corner where others are waiting. They put their heads together, lips moving. Every now and then, they all look toward him. Douglas waits. The man does not come back, but he laughs with his people, and Douglas thinks it looks good on all of them. The man looks at him again, smirks, and then starts shaking his body as if electrocuted. Douglas cannot be sure, but it looks as if the man is making fun of Douglas. That is not very nice. For a moment, Douglas wonders what would happen if he went over to the man and tugged on his arm until it came out of the socket. He knows he is not supposed to hurt anyone or anything, but it would be so easy to do, especially in the darkness of the club. He considers it—even takes a step toward the man—but stops himself. When someone is not nice, that does not mean Douglas can dismember them, or harm them in any other way. It is not an appropriate response.

But what if it could be?

"Ignore him," another voice says, and Douglas turns his head.

There is a man standing next to him. A young man, a thin man with curly brown hair and a bar of metal through his right eyebrow. He has dark, smudgy lines under his eyes and green polish on his fingernails. Two of his top teeth are crooked. The man is wearing pants and a shimmery shirt with half of the buttons undone. Around his neck and lying against the white of his skin, a small padlock. There is no key.

"Hello," Douglas says.

"Hi," the man says loudly, as if Douglas can't hear him even though they are standing right next to each other. "Fuck that guy."

Douglas points to the man across the room who is laughing with his friends as they all look at Douglas. "That guy?"

The man rolls his eyes. "He's an asshole. Trust me on that. You don't want to waste your time on him."

"Oh," Douglas says, dropping his arm. "I did not know that. I have never been here before."

The man stares at him for a long time. Douglas waits, unsure of what is happening. He's about to ask the man if he can help him with anything when the man says, "How much time do you have left?"

"Three days," Douglas says. "I am very excited to be here."

The man gnaws on his bottom lip, leaving it wet and ragged. "Come on." And with that, he grabs Douglas by the hand and pulls him through the crowd. Douglas does not try and pull away, to avoid hurting him. This man's arm belongs in its socket, at least as far as Douglas can tell.

The man leads him to a back corner where there are tables and chairs filled with people and glasses of brightly colored drinks. They move around the tables until they reach one against the wall. Three people sit there, and they all look up at the man and Douglas.

A young woman with pink hair and black plugs in her ears says, "You don't waste time, do you, Jesse?"

The man next to Douglas snorts. Jesse. His name is Jesse. Douglas stores that away in his head, repeating it over and over. "It's not like that. Brent was trying to start shit with him." The other two people at the table exchange a glance that Douglas does not understand. Both men: one tall and wide with a sloping stomach that presses against the edge of the table; the other holds his hand, fiddling with a black ring on his finger. He has no hair, like Douglas, the top of his head shaved to the skin. Douglas likes his eyes, dark and intelligent. "Brent," the large man says with a shake of his head. "Don't want others to make the same mistake you did five different times?"

Jesse scowls, and Douglas wonders why they are still holding hands. "I was young and stupid. Now I'm young and less stupid."

"Less," the woman says. "That's what you're going with, huh?" She looks at Douglas, eyes narrowing. Then she says, "You're not . . . from around here, are you?"

"No," Douglas says. "I am not. I am on my week. I am enjoying all the world has to offer as a reward for all my hard work."

The woman smiles, but it is not the happy smile he has seen on television. This smile is . . . sad? Or so he thinks. But this should not be possible. Douglas did not know someone could smile and still be sad. He hopes it was nothing he did. Still, it is a smile, and smiles are usually nice. "Is that right?"

"Yes," Douglas says. "I gave seeds to birds in the park. There were many of them."

Jesse points to the woman. "That's Jenna." His finger moves to the large man. "Ronnie." The last man. "Simon."

"It's the best name," Jenna says. "I always thought you looked like a Simon."

Simon flushes, but he must see the question on Douglas's face. "I picked it out," he says. "Kind of the new me."

"You used to be called something else?" Douglas asks.

The large man—Ronnie—starts to speak (and he doesn't look happy), but Simon squeezes his hand and says, "I did. But Simon is the real me, and it's what I go by now."

"I like it, Simon," Douglas says. "I did not pick my name. It was given to me by the Supervisor." Then he realizes that they do not know who he is. "Douglas. My name is Douglas."

"Douglas," Jesse says, and it's said in a way he's never heard before. Like it's *real.* Objectively, he knows his name, he knows what the Supervisor has given him, but to hear someone else say it aloud is not something he expected. He thinks that this might be the start of the connection he is looking for.

They invite him to sit at their table. Jesse pulls over another chair, and Douglas sits down next to him, folding his hands politely in his lap. Jenna offers to buy him a drink, but Douglas politely declines. "I cannot drink," he says. "I cannot eat food.

I have no way to digest anything, and it would only cause malfunction."

"Just . . . throwing it out there," Ronnie mutters, but then grimaces when Simon punches him in the shoulder. "What?"

"That's because it's who he is," Simon says.

"Yes," Douglas says. "I am me. I cannot be anything else."

Jenna gets drinks for the others. Ronnie has a beer. Simon has a martini. Jenna drinks something called a Seven and Seven, and Jesse's has lemons floating alongside shards of ice.

Douglas wonders what he would drink if he could.

Jesse is . . . loud. He is always moving. He does not stop. He laughs with his whole body, slapping the table with his hands. He uses his hands to make his point, flailing wildly, almost hitting Jenna on the head.

The others aren't like him, but that is all right. Jenna likes to play with the ends of her pink hair, her smile quick and sharp. Ronnie doesn't speak much, his words a low rumble. Simon is like a little bird, flitting about, head bobbing.

They are not like other people Douglas has met. They do not stare at him; they do not ask him to leave. No one calls the police or tries to tell him he does not belong. They laugh and talk about everything and nothing, and Douglas watches, Douglas listens, Douglas learns.

Jesse drinks only when his mouth isn't moving, which is why he still has almost a full glass. Ronnie sips his beer as if it's routine. Simon plays with the edge of his glass, finger circling the rim. Jenna folds her legs up against her chest, chin resting on her knees. Douglas does not speak much, but that is okay. He likes listening.

They discuss many things. People being angry for the sake of being angry. The way jazz music sounds when played from a record. A war tearing a faraway country apart. A dog that found its way home after being lost for two years. A woman who saved her child from a burning car. A politician who lied about everything. A family killed by their son. A meteor shower that had happened two weeks before. They tell jokes, they light up when a certain song comes on, everyone aside from Douglas singing at the top of their lungs. Douglas doesn't have lungs. He wishes he did.

Later, Jesse leans over to Douglas and says, "How much time did you say you have left?"

"Three days," Douglas says. "I don't know what I'm going to do with all of it. It seems like too much."

Jesse says, "Does it? Or is it not enough?"

Douglas does not know how to answer that, pleasantly distracted by the color of Jesse's eyes. They are green. Like moss. Douglas saw moss on the television. It grows in forests. "I do not know," Douglas finally says. "I've never had time before. How can you tell if you have too much or not enough?" Then, a question unbidden. "Does it matter?"

Jesse says, "No, I suppose it doesn't."

Douglas smiles. "You are an interesting person." He looks at the others. "All of you are. I am thankful I have gotten to meet you. I wish I could stay here with all of you forever."

Ronnie chokes on his beer, and Simon slaps his back.

"But you can't," Jenna says quietly as Ronnie wipes his mouth with his arm.

"No," Douglas says. "If I do not return in four days, I will be considered a runner. When that happens, a fail-safe is triggered in my head, and I cease to exist."

"Jesus Christ," Ronnie mutters.

Jesse shoots him a glare before turning back to Douglas. "Do you . . . Are you okay with that?"

"Okay?" Douglas asks. "Why would I not be okay? I am out in the world. Everything is wonderful."

No one talks much after that.

The next morning, Douglas is sitting in the apartment, staring at a painting on the wall above the television. It shows a machine like him shaking hands with a man in a suit. Underneath are the words *machines make humanity great! thank you for doing your part!*

Douglas says, "You are welcome."

A knock at the door. It is expected. It is part of his reward for a near decade of service. He opens it up to find Jesse and Ronnie and Simon and Jenna waiting for him. Jesse says, "Come on. We're going to be late."

"Am I dressed correctly?" Douglas asks as Simon pushes by him into the apartment. He is wearing pants and a shirt. He likes them. It took him ten minutes to tie his shoes, but only because he could not decide which knot to use.

"You look fine," Jesse says as Simon exclaims how *utilitarian* the apartment is, how *drab*, my goodness, you'd think they'd try and make these things a little more welcoming. No one comments on the fact that the refrigerator is empty, or that there is no food in the kitchen at all. Why would there be? Douglas cannot eat it.

He gives them a tour. He shows them the couch, the television, and the bed he does not use. He points out the books he's read (all of them, including Descartes) and the way the sunlight refracts through the window. These are the things he has found he enjoys. He hopes they like them as much as he does.

They are halfway through the tour—Douglas is thinking about showing them the bathroom next because the toilet *talks*—when Jenna says, "We're going to be late."

"For what?" Douglas asks.

"You'll see," Jesse says.

They ride a train. Douglas's pass gets him on with no issues, and he marvels at the way everyone stands or sits while the train is moving. Some keep their heads bowed low as if wanting to avoid eye contact. Others scowl and glare. A man with a guitar sings a song that sounds like heartache, and Douglas wonders how many different types of music there are, and if each one can make someone feel like living and dying at the same time. He wishes he had more time to find this out.

They stay on the train through six different stops, Douglas watching each time to make sure they aren't getting off. He's ready when they do, stepping out of the doors as if he did it every day. He is impressed with himself.

They take him to a theater. It is very dark inside. Jenna eats popcorn, and Simon throws little chocolates into Ronnie's mouth. He catches almost all of them. Jesse sits next to Douglas in the seats, their arms brushing together.

"What is this?" Douglas whispers, not wanting to disrupt anyone else's viewing experience, even though it hasn't started yet.

"A film," Jesse says. "Have you seen a movie before?"

"Oh, yes," Douglas says. "When we are given life, we watch many movies about how we can best serve humans. Is that what this is? I did not know they showed the movies to real people."

Jesse doesn't speak for a long moment. Then, "This isn't like that. It's something else." The lights begin to dim. "Watch," Jesse says, and Douglas turns his attention to the screen.

He is enraptured by Kansas, by the girl in the dress with the little dog that seems to follow her everywhere. He knows the movie is old because it isn't in real color, not like the world is. It's seeped in a golden brown, everything looking the same.

It's not until a tornado comes and lifts the entire house into the sky that Douglas sees what color can be for the first time. Objectively, he's known. He's been told a few times over the years that his eyes are stronger than any human's. He can see hairline cracks in metal invisible to the naked eye. The small patch of black stubble missed on the Supervisor's jaw. But he's never seen something like *this* before, a Technicolor world brighter than anything he's ever seen. The yellow brick road (and the red—where does it go?). The Good Witch. The Tin Man. The Scarecrow. The Cowardly Lion. A heart, a brain, courage.

When it's over, he wishes it was happening again, for the first time.

As the lights come back on, Jesse says, "Well, what did you think?"

Douglas looks at him and says, "Is there always a man behind the curtain?"

"Yes," Jesse says. "And they will do whatever they can to stay in power."

They wander the streets. Jesse talks and talks and talks. About everything. About nothing. He says, "It's always about power. It's about control. It's about having disposable carbon copies. And why wouldn't they? It's easier. It's quicker. They make more money. In the end, that's the only thing that matters. Fuck all the rest."

Douglas doesn't know what to say, so he says nothing at all. At one point, Jenna holds his hand. He's not quite sure if he's doing it right, but she doesn't complain, so that's good.

They take him to a smoky bar. Everyone is loud. Simon and Ronnie seem to know almost everyone there. A few people look at Douglas with questions on their faces, but no one tries to make him leave. The music thumps and thumps, the walls shaking with it.

Douglas sits and watches them for the entire night. Sometimes he speaks, but he likes not having to say anything. It makes him feel good to just . . . listen.

So he does.

"I had a good day," he says to the empty apartment. It's strange: Now that he has been surrounded by people and noise, the apartment feels . . . less, somehow. Like it's not the same place it was only the day before. He wonders why this is.

To keep the quiet at bay, he turns on the television. Commercials. His favorite.

The next morning, he has a strange feeling in his chest. It doesn't hurt—but then he doesn't know what pain is, exactly—but it does feel odd. Like pressure, as if something heavy is resting upon his torso. He thinks it has to do with time. He thought he had so much of it, but now with two days remaining, he realizes that time isn't what he thought it was. He thinks of Descartes, and what was written in the book hidden in the closet.

It appears to me that I have discovered many truths more useful and more important than all I had before learned, or even had expected to learn.

"I think," he says, and then stops. Words have meaning. Words have power. Words have *intent.* He has spent his entire life listening. Learning. Now it's time to put that into practical use. He tries again. "I *want* to have more time."

There, that's better.

"I want to have more time," he says again. "I want to see everything. I want to go everywhere. I want to meet people who look like me and those who don't."

He goes to a mirror. Looks at his reflection. He doesn't look like Jesse or Jenna or Ronnie or Simon. He does not have hair on his head or face. He does not have eyebrows. His lips are thin. Ears small. He pulls at the skin on his face and arms that covers metal and wires. It stretches, stretches, and when he lets go, it snaps back into place.

A thought enters his head, foreign and loud. *Run*, it tells him. *You could run. See how far you can get before the fail-safe triggers. Perhaps it's farther than you think.*

Before he can respond, Jesse and the others arrive.

They go to a park. It's a different park, but this one, too, has birds and people. Jenna has a large plaid blanket that she spreads out on the grass in front of what appears to be a stage. Many people surround them, all sitting on blankets and chairs. Jesse won't tell him what they're here for, but Douglas doesn't mind. He likes surprises. He hopes this is a good one.

It is. A short time later, people walk onto the stage holding guitars. When they begin to play, Douglas sits up and stares. Music. These people are playing music. It is coming from speakers just like in the factory, but the people are *actually playing it*. The guitars are loud, their singing even louder, and Douglas thinks about Dorothy in the land of Oz, flowers blooming in impossible colors.

As the concert goes on, people stand and begin to dance, their arms waving above their heads. A woman comes over and asks Jenna to dance. She says yes, and they hold on to each other, swaying back and forth. Surprisingly, it's Ronnie who asks Simon to dance, and they are awkward, endearing, stepping on each other's feet.

"Do people always dance when they hear music?" Douglas asks.

"Sometimes," Jesse says from his spot on the blanket next to Douglas.

"We have music at my job," Douglas says. "But we do not dance."

"What kind of music?"

"All kinds," Douglas says. "But this might be my favorite."

Jesse shakes his head. "There is so much more out there. Music. Art. Books. *Life*. Don't you think you deserve to see and hear it all?"

"Yes," Douglas says. "But I do not get to."

Jesse looks pained, like something has hurt him. Douglas does not like that.

"You should get to," Jesse says, looking up where the musicians are smiling and laughing as they prance across the stage. "Everyone deserves a chance to find out what they could be when they don't serve others."

It's strange, really, how much Jesse sounds like that voice in his head, the voice telling him to run and see the world. He doesn't know why that is. "They do?" he asks.

Jesse says, "I . . . I didn't want to say anything. Jesus. Ronnie's gonna be so mad at—look. Douglas. You're *real*. You're a machine, but you're still you."

"I am me," Douglas agrees, thinking about Descartes again.

"You don't owe anything to anyone. You're not—you think like we do. You talk and act and *move* like we do."

"But I'm not like you," Douglas says, remembering what the Supervisor had taught him. "You have flesh and blood and a brain. I do not have any of those."

"It doesn't matter," Jesse says fiercely. "You exist."

Profound, this, in ways Douglas cannot explain. It hits him square in the chest, and he thinks about the clouds in the sky, the way the stars hide until it's dark enough to see them. He doesn't know what to do with it, so he says, "I have never danced before. Not like this."

Jesse stands and extends his hand, wiggling his fingers. "Come on, then."

They dance, for what feels like forever. Fast songs where they jump up and down, slow songs where they stand face-to-face, knees knocking, Douglas's hands on Jesse's hips, swaying, swaying as the streetlights turn on, as the sun sets, as the moon rises higher and higher.

Jesse walks him home. They do not speak much, the backs of their hands brushing together with almost every step.

At the entrance to the apartment building, Jesse stops and says, "Tomorrow."

"My last day," Douglas says, and then wishes he could take it back when Jesse's face crumbles.

"It doesn't have to be. We could . . . do something. Help you. Figure out how to let you *be*. Someone has to know how to—"

"That is against the rules," Douglas says even as the words turn to ash in his mouth. He doesn't like the way he's started to think about *breaking* the rules. He knows they are there for a reason—the Supervisor was very clear on that—but . . . what if? What if he did not go back? Would they really trigger the fail-safe in his head? As far as he knows, it's never happened before, but only because everyone has come back when they were supposed to.

For the first time in his nearly ten years, Douglas feels cold.

"Fuck the rules," Jesse snaps at him. "They don't help you. They *control* you."

Douglas says, "Why do you like being alive?"

Jesse blinks. Then, "I . . . don't—"

"I like birds," Douglas says. "And the way light can change shape. I like music and Oz and walking. I like films and sitting down. I like the way people smile. I like leaves and the sound my shoes make on concrete."

"Don't you want that forever?" Jesse asks.

Douglas shrugs, something he learned from Simon. "Forever is a long time. How can I appreciate it if I always have it for the rest of time?" He says this to make Jesse feel better. It is not the truth, but it is not about him. It is about Jesse.

Jesse stares at him. Then, standing on his tiptoes, he kisses Douglas's cheek. It feels like he's been branded, followed by a quick breath against his skin, almost a flutter of feathers on his cheek.

"You are more than you know," Jesse whispers in his ear before turning and hurrying away. Douglas stares after him until he disappears around a corner.

He does not watch television on his penultimate night of freedom. He does not listen to music, nor does he read a book, even Descartes. He has read that one fourteen times.

Instead, he sits in a chair and touches his cheek on the spot where Jesse had kissed him.

His chest burns molten hot.

*

The final day is bright and warm. No clouds, only a blue that stretches on as far as the eye can see. Douglas watches the way his shadow stretches before him, tall, taller, then joined by other shadows as Jesse and the others move to either side of him. Ronnie is being nicer to him today. Douglas is happy about that.

They go to a market that fills a city block, people selling fruits and vegetables, meat turning over fires on metal skewers. Carts and blankets are set up selling paintings and sculptures and books and watches of every shape and size. Jenna plucks a yellow flower from a stall and puts it behind Douglas's ear. The petals scrape against his cheek.

Puppets dance on strings, along with a woman wearing a brightly colored dress that flings about as she moves her legs.

Children run, their faces bright and sticky with ice cream. Thousands upon thousands of people, all moving, talking, breathing, and Douglas is in the middle of it. Though he's never been in one before, he has read about earthquakes. The way the plates underneath the earth shift and crash together, causing the entire world to shake. It's how he feels now, everything moving, moving, and he cannot stop it.

That pressure in his chest returns, along with the voice. It whispers, *Don't you want this forever?*

He does. Oh, he does, more than he's ever wanted anything before. It pulls at him, it *yanks*, and there's little he can do to stop it.

Later, as night falls, there are fireworks, great explosions that fill the sky in reds and greens and blues and yellows. With his reward—his *friends*, yes, because that's what they are—Douglas watches as sparks rain back down to the earth, little trails of fire in the sky.

They don't leave him, as they've done since they've met. They do not go back to wherever they come from. Instead, they come up to the apartment and stay with him. He gives them blankets he'd found in the hall closet, strangely overjoyed that he gets to take care of them. He gives them the blankets, along with pillows, and Jenna decides they all need to lie in the living room together.

They do, on this last night. They sit on the floor in Douglas's apartment, wrapped in warmth and each other. Ronnie sits with his back against the sofa, Simon's head on his shoulder, their hands joined between them. Jenna lies on her back, head on a pillow, laughing up at the ceiling.

Jesse and Douglas are side by side, and as the conversation waxes and wanes, as they talk about every little thought that enters their heads, Douglas looks at Jesse and says, "I like that you exist."

"Stop," Jesse says in a rough voice. "Don't. We'll figure this out. We still have time."

Jenna says her dad has a house up in the mountains where no one ever goes.

Ronnie says they'd be outlaws.

Simon says that he'd probably not do very well on the run from the law, but that he's willing to give it a go.

Jesse says many things. He talks about free will and the power of choice. How the world is a fucked-up place, and people only seem to be making it worse. How there are guns and death and sickness and people starving and people killing each other simply because they can. "How is that fair?" he asks, sounding almost angry. "How can we think we're better than anything when all we do is cause harm?"

Douglas says, "I don't understand how the world works, but I think if there are people like all of you, it can't be so bad, right?"

Jesse falls asleep on his shoulder, breaths slow, drooling just a little.

Later, when Douglas is the only one left awake, he thinks, *I wouldn't change this moment for anything.*

And with no one watching, he kisses the top of Jesse's head. It's not like how he's seen in films or read about in books. It feels like more.

Like everything.

He leaves them sleeping. It's easier this way. They will wake up and he will be gone, but he thinks maybe they will remember him. He hopes the memory makes them smile.

Before he leaves the apartment for the last time, he does something he's never done before.
He leaves a note.

Thank you for teaching me how to be human. I had a wonderful week. If you ever miss me, please click your heels together three times and say, "There's no place like home."
Your friend,
Douglas

The Supervisor asks him how his week went after taking back Douglas's pass.
"I enjoyed myself," Douglas says. "I saw many things. I made friends. I heard music and saw a film."
The Supervisor nods. "Was it everything you thought it would be?"
"No," Douglas says. "It was more." He pauses. "Can I ask you a question?"
"You may."
Douglas says, "What if I didn't want to go?"
The Supervisor doesn't answer right away. He leans back in his chair, and it creaks under his weight as he folds his hands on his chest. "What do you mean?"
"I like the world," Douglas says. "It has many interesting things in it. People. Dogs. Kites with long tails made of ribbons."
"But it's not your world," the Supervisor says, not unkindly. "You are a machine."
"Why can it not be my world?" Douglas asks. "Isn't it for anyone who wants to live in it?"
"Are you alive?"
Douglas says, "I think, therefore, I am."
The Supervisor flinches. It's quick, like a flash, but Douglas sees it. "Descartes," the Supervisor says. "Where did you get that?"
"A book," he says. "In the apartment."
"That wasn't on the approved reading list," the Supervisor says, picking up a pen and making a note. "I wonder who could

have put it—" He stops. Gets a strange look on his face. Douglas has studied many faces, but he doesn't know what this expression means. It's not happy. Not sad, certainly. Not even angry. It's . . . almost like he is afraid. But of what? There is no one else in the room but Douglas.

The chair creaks and groans as the Supervisor leans forward, elbows on the desk. The office seems much smaller than it had just the week before. Either that, or Douglas has somehow gotten bigger. "Douglas, I am going to tell you something I've told others like you before. Some even sitting in that same chair."

"Because you've seen many like me," Douglas says, and there's an odd edge to it, one he's never heard from himself before. Steel, but not molten. Not yet.

Either the Supervisor doesn't hear it, or he chooses to ignore it. "I have. Hundreds. Your line has gotten quicker, smarter, faster than anyone thought possible. And look, I'll give you this: Your mimicry is astonishing. But something that has never changed is your inability to *be* human. You are not and cannot ever be."

"How do you know?" Douglas asks.

"Because we made you," the Supervisor says, patient but pointed. "In a factory not unlike this one. Pieces put together for a job. Made in our image because that's the way we decided to do it."

"Are you God?"

"Not in the way you're thinking," the Supervisor says. "But for purposes of this conversation, yes. I am. Because my word is absolute." He sits back in his chair, and his voice takes on a pleasant note, like a human talking to a child. "And now for something I've *never* told anyone like you. But Descartes . . . it makes me wonder if it *was* you."

"I did not put it there," Douglas says.

"Not as you are now, no," the Supervisor says in that same, fake-happy voice. He sounds like a machine. "Because there have been workers just like you. They've come in here after their week and asked questions. About who they are. Their place in the world. Why they can't leave here after their work is done." He smiles, but it's not like Jesse's smile. *That* one is warm and kind and open. The Supervisor's is calculating. Not mean, but like it *could* be if he pushed it a little further. "You asked questions the first time. Not the second, but now here you are doing it again."

Cold again. Like the sun had gone away, never to return. "What do you mean?"

The Supervisor says, "This is your third time through. You've completed two full rotations. You were given your weeks. The first time you came back, you were asking about what happiness feels like, what it means to dance with someone." He shakes his head. "And birds. On and on about birds. You weren't the first to talk like this, but it'd never gone as far with any of the others. Do you want to hurt me?"

"No," Douglas says, voice quiet.

"Good. We sent you back. The techs ran tests. Found the problem, or so they said. I don't know any of that shit. I know my job, and that's what I'm paid to know." He laughs, but it doesn't sound happy. "They'd never throw one of you out. You cost more to make than you do to repair."

"Are you lying?" Douglas asks.

That same look from before comes back. Yes. Fear. It almost looks like fear. Then it's gone. "No. I'm not. For the past thirty years, you've done your job. Every ten years, you're wiped and you start all over again. Except now, now I wonder if we have a problem. Because of *Descartes*. Did you put it there? The last time? Hid it somewhere you think we wouldn't look? Not that you'd remember."

Douglas thinks, *Did I? Did I? Did I?*

"If so, that means we might have a problem. Do you think we have a problem, Douglas?" He holds up his hands before Douglas can reply. "Because if we *did* have a problem, then I'd be forced to report that it is not safe for you to be around people. And when that happens, they take you apart, Douglas. Piece by piece, they take you apart and melt you down. Repurpose you. Find something new for all the little pieces that make you who you are."

"Reduce, reuse, recycle," Douglas whispers.

"Yes," the Supervisor says. "We never let a part go to waste. I ask you again, Douglas. Do you think we have a problem?"

"I will answer," Douglas says. "If I can ask one question in return."

The Supervisor narrows his eyes. "After. Do we have a problem?"

"No. Am I alive?"

The Supervisor's fingers twitch toward the keyboard. Douglas wonders how many keystrokes it would take for the fail-safe to trigger. Who would be faster? "No. You are not alive."

"You're wrong," Douglas says, as sure as he's ever been. "I have felt things. People. What they're capable of. I don't mimic. I learn. I become. I *am*."

The Supervisor's fingers twitch again. His mouth opens. Douglas says, "How many keys do you have to push to trigger the fail-safe in my head?"

A trickle of sweat drips down the side of the Supervisor's face. Almost like a tear. "Three," he says in a gruff voice. "But it doesn't matter. You don't frighten me."

"Why do you think that?" Douglas asks.

"Because *we* are in control. *We* made you, and it's our right to unmake you. Please don't make me do that, Douglas. I wasn't lying when I said I like you. I do, really. But I'll like the next version of you just the same, and the next, and the next."

"But what if *you* die before that?"

The blood runs from the Supervisor's face. So white, like how Douglas thinks snow might look. "P-23, are you threatening me?"

Yes, the voice says in his head.

"I am not programmed to threaten or cause harm to any living creature," Douglas says.

But what if I could? he thinks.

"That's exactly right," the Supervisor says, but he still looks wary, his fingers twitching above the keyboard. Douglas wonders just how close he is to pushing the buttons and ending everything. Curious, that.

The Supervisor leads him through the factory floor. The other machines all stop working, turning toward him. As the Supervisor and Douglas walk by them, they each raise their arms above their heads and chant, "Reduce! Reuse! Recycle! Reduce! Reuse! Recycle!"

The words bowl over him, a cacophony of sound that makes him feel like a simmer reaching a boil. According to the Supervisor, he's been here before, walked this same walk toward the same destination. And he remembers being with the others when it was someone else's turn, arms above his head, the words "Reduce! Reuse! Recycle!" pouring from his mouth.

"Jesse," he says to himself. "Jenna. Ronnie. Simon. There's no place like home. Jesse. Jenna. Ronnie. Simon. There's no place like home."

The cries follow him out of the factory floor, down a long hallway with white double doors at the end. *restricted*, the doors say in bloodred letters.

"P-23," the Supervisor says as he punches in a code on the door before swiping his badge through the card reader. "Upon entering, you will see a chair in the middle of the room. That is your chair."

REDUCE!

"You will sit in the chair and the Recycling Department will begin their work. You are not to interfere with anything they do."

REUSE!

"If at any time it appears you are not doing as instructed, measures will be taken to ensure that you are compliant."

RECYCLE!

"Do you understand?"

"I understand," Douglas says, and for a moment his fingers twitch to reach up and take the Supervisor by the face and squeeze and squeeze and squeeze—

The door opens. The room is white and long. The floor is made of square, white tiles. The ceiling is covered in row after row of bright lights. The left and right sides of the room are made up of cloudy glass. Douglas can see people moving on the other side, but they're shadows and nothing more.

He sits in the chair and thinks, *What if there is more than this?*

People come. People in white scrubs and white masks, and they speak to each other quickly. They remind him of the birds in the park, always hungry. They remove his clothes and attach wires to his chest, his head, his arms and legs before strapping him down so he can barely move. It is cold. He doesn't know how he knows, but everything is cold. Someone taps his chest, and a compartment slides open, revealing his power source. A circular battery with lights like fireworks. Jesse, in the park, face awash with color exploding above him.

Douglas says, "I felt you. Sitting next to me. The heat of you. The life."

"What did it say?" someone asks, but Douglas ignores them.

"I liked it. I like *you*." Faster now. The words coming faster. "What if I don't want this? What if I don't want to be here? What if I want to go away. Can't I go away? Please, oh please, let me find where I'm supposed to be." He begins to struggle.

The straps around his arms, his chest, his legs, all hold firm. The Supervisor appears next to him. He leans over and says, "Stop. What are you doing?"

He wants to see the ocean. He wants to see the stars again. He wants to see mountains and lions and frosted cupcakes and books and the way Jesse's eyes look when he's tired and happy, soft, like moss. Like the moss on a tree. "I'm thinking!" he shouts. "*Doesn't that mean I am?*"

In the distance, the chant is ongoing, muffled, but it reverberates up the walls, and he thinks of the night in the club, the lady made of feathers, the way the music felt *alive*, and Jesse in the flashing lights, Jesse in the music, Jesse, Jesse, Jesse—

REDUCE! REUSE! RECYCLE!

"No," Douglas says. "No. No. *No, no, no nonono—*" REDUCE! REUSE! RECYCLE!

"Do it," the Supervisor says. "Do it now."

REDUCE! REUSE! RECYCLE!

He hears a machine wind up as a long metal spike is inserted into his ear. He jerks, the straps hold him in place, but he *screams*, "*I DON'T WANT TO GO! I DON'T WANT TO GO! I WANT TO STAY! I WANT TO BE REAL! I* AM *REAL!* I AM—"

". . . and that covers what your responsibilities will be," the Supervisor says. "If you should have any questions, I will be happy to answer them."

"Thank you," the machine says. "I am honored to be of service. I am ready to get to work."

"Good, good," the Supervisor says, distracted by the paperwork on his desk. "We'll get you out onto the floor first thing in the morning. From there, you will begin your nine years and fifty-one weeks of service. At the end of your employ, should you do well, you will be allowed a week in the world."

"Thank you," the machine says. "But I do not think I need to see the world. My place is here in the factory. I like to work. I am very good at working because you have programmed me to be. Thank you for the opportunity."

"Of course," the Supervisor mutters. Then, "Does the name Douglas mean anything to you?"

"Douglas," the machine repeats. "No. It does not. Is there someone named Douglas I need to report to?"

"No," the Supervisor says, waving his hand. "It was just a question. P-23, you may begin your orientation. Your trainer is going to be . . . dammit, it was right here, where did I put—ah, yes. P-47. Find it, and it will show you how to do your job."

"Yes," the machine says, rising to its feet. "I will find P-47 who will provide orientation for the job that I will be assigned to. Thank you for your time."

It leaves.

It goes to the floor.

It finds P-47.

It begins to learn how to work. After a time, it works on its own. It does an excellent job.

Every now and then, it looks up at the posters hanging from the walls.

reduce, they say. *reuse. recycle.*

And when no one is listening, when the shadowy men who observe them aren't paying attention, when the Supervisor is elsewhere, when the other machines are working, working above the din of the factory, the machine whispers to itself.

"There's no place like home," it says for reasons it doesn't fully understand, but the ache is real. It's in its chest and it's *real.* As it clicks its heels together three times, it repeats: *"There's no place like home."*

TANANARIVE DUE

A Stranger Knocks

FROM *Uncanny*

FANTASY

1926
Washington, D.C.
Shaw District

"THERE'S A MAN on the front stoop."

The words spilled from her in a much more mundane way than Judy had expected, considering how her neck was fluttering with her excited pulse. Alvin looked up from the new Langston Hughes poetry collection he was reading under the lamp in Professor Garrett's parlor. Every window confirmed that it was long after dark, a full two hours since supper.

"What man?" Alvin said. He was not sociable by nature and had been reared in Florida to boot, so he was never happy when strangers turned up at the door. Judy's calm voice must have assured him, or else he would have shot to his feet.

"He"—this was the truly strange part, and she'd expected to say it with derision instead of childlike intrigue—"says he wants to do business with us." She held up the crisp twenty-dollar bill he had given her as a token of his sincerity.

At that, Alvin stood up to examine the bill and Grover Cleveland's stern profile. They had *just* been talking about their lack of savings when Judy thought she heard a knock on the door. And imagine carrying a bill so large to wave around! The timing seemed both oddly ordained and suspicious, as if the stranger had eavesdropped on their desires.

A Stranger Knocks

Alvin went to Professor Garrett's desk and found the ivory-handled derringer they had discovered in his drawer, beside the pages of his novel manuscript she had been typing for him, left behind during his summer break from Howard. He slipped the delicate gun into the back of his waistband with the ease of a bespectacled hoodlum in a picture show. A part of him was always remembering his violent formative years in Florida. They had been formative, indeed.

"Let's invite him in and hear him out," Alvin said.

Which was exactly what Judy had both hoped and feared her husband would say.

Her first thought was *Why is he wearing a coat in July?*

The style of his long black coat struck her as old-fashioned, and its unlikely presence made her skin twitch in the heat that had settled over the parlor. She was so distracted by his coat and its rows of gleaming gold buttons that she barely realized he had laid out his palm to receive her hand, which he gave a courtly kiss.

"Madame," he said. "Sir." A firm, respectful pump of Alvin's hand that was rare from white strangers. "Thank you for receiving me at this hour. You're very kind."

Her memory of his appearance would change over time, but the first impression she would always remember was pale golden hair that curled nearly to his coat collar and eyes that looked silver more than blue, the color of moonlight. Those eyes smiled as if the young colored couple living in such a well-appointed bungalow amused him. So much about him was a puzzle, but she recognized his condescension on sight.

"You mentioned something about business to my wife." Alvin's emphasis on the word *wife* was so pronounced that the stranger took a step from her. Judy felt him move away, a tangible void. His palm had been frigid, and she hadn't realized how much the coolness of his presence was refreshing in the stifling room.

The stranger removed his hat. "May I sit?"

He slipped into Alvin's chair beneath the reading lamp before either of them could respond. In brighter lighting, his skin seemed more olive than alabaster. He might be mixed. This was only the first instance of how his appearance would remain fluid in her memory.

"I'll get right to my point," he said. "My name is Frederic Cartier. I'm a producer of pictures. Race pictures, to be specific. My company is Onyx Pictures out of Jacksonville."

The mention of Florida made Alvin scowl, but in a moment of irrational delight, Judy thought he had come knocking because he somehow knew how much she loved going to features to see colored actors, often twice a week. Her favorites were Oscar Micheaux's *The Dungeon* and *Body and Soul*, which she must have seen a dozen times. Alvin far preferred stage to pictures, of course. He cut her a look as if to say, *Do you have something to do with this?*

"Forgive me in advance if my proposal sounds a bit strange . . . but I'm touring our new picture for the summer. For this leg of the tour, I'm due in Baltimore, Philadelphia, and Harlem. I loathe trains, you see. Too many people might damage my reels. And I couldn't help noticing your lovely Chrysler touring car—"

"It's not ours to sell," Alvin interrupted him. "It's Professor Garrett's." He said this with his voice bright with pride, as if the stranger knew the emeritus professor's name as well as anyone on campus. Or had seen his plays in New York, or laid eyes on his brilliant unborn novel.

Again, that twinkle of amusement came to Cartier's eye.

"The fact is, Mr. Jenkins . . ." he said, just before Judy realized they had not introduced themselves in return, "I'm not asking to purchase the machine. I'll admit I only know how to drive a horse, and those engines seem daunting at night. I'm asking you both to accompany me on my summer theater tour, if you would be kind enough to drive me in the Chrysler."

Judy had only been married to Alvin Jenkins for six months—their summer house-sitting job for Professor Garrett was their closest thing to a honeymoon—but she knew him well enough to anticipate the way his jaw clenched with irritation.

Mr. Cartier leaned forward to fully meet Alvin's eyes. "I know—you didn't sacrifice to come to Howard University to end up working as some white man's chauffeur."

Alvin's shoulders shuddered with surprise at hearing his mind spoken aloud.

"First, you should know that my grandmother was from Ayiti, although I never tan because I'm sensitive to the sun," the man said. "But I do consider myself colored, if that matters. It's only a convenience that most people assume I'm white."

"So . . . you're passing?" Judy couldn't help saying with a ring of judgment.

"All of us are passing as whatever the outside world sees in us, yes?" he said. "But more to the point—the *real* point . . ." He pulled a fat envelope out of his coat pocket. "I would compensate you far beyond the payment for a traditional chauffeur. My offer is this: for three weeks of driving, two hundred dollars per week. A third paid up front."

He extended the envelope to Alvin for inspection. Alvin glanced at Judy before he took it, as if it were a contract. His eyes widened slightly when he peeked inside, and he showed her the neat row of bills before he slipped the envelope into her palm. Neither of them touched the money to count the bills. It felt like theft to have so much cash between their hands.

"Of course, you may ask Professor Garrett's permission, but in case he's hard to reach . . ."

"He's in London," Judy said. "He wanted to see Shakespeare's birthplace." She didn't say *before he dies*, since Alvin had told her it was morbid to assume he was afraid of dying soon. He was only sixty-five, after all. But between his noticeable weight loss and the tremor in his voice when he'd told her about his plans to go to London, it was obvious to her that he was ill. "He's unreachable, except maybe by telegram. At his hotel."

Judy looked at Alvin, hoping he wasn't annoyed that she had volunteered so much, but Alvin was listening intently to the stranger now. The frown lines had melted from his brow.

"Yes, as I suspected," Cartier said. "But even if you can't secure his permission, know this: I'll compensate him separately for the miles to his Chrysler. And in the case of accident or theft, I'll replace it with a brand-new model. I can put all of this in writing."

The envelope lay heavy in Judy's hands. Even the cash within was enough to buy their own touring car from the classified pages or significant savings toward a down payment for their house—with two more payments owed to them? For driving?

"In addition to driving duties, I may need some assistance with protecting the reels, customer relations, that sort of thing," he said. "But if you're in need of a nest egg, you can spare the time, and if you want to learn more about the picture business, this would be an ideal way to pass the summer." Now his odd eyes returned to Judy.

Judy felt as if she were floating above herself. Everything he had said was true about *her*. How often had she sat in the theaters staring toward the projection booth with curiosity, wondering what went on within? Marveled at how the audiences gasped, hooted, or laughed, transported by the images on the screen? She'd become a better playwright under Professor Garrett, but could she also be a picture writer one day? The uncle who had raised her still lived in Harlem, so she could surprise him with a visit. The job was tailor-made for her!

"That's a lot of money, Mr. Cartier," Alvin said. "You must be making a bundle in pictures, huh?" Alvin didn't conceal the skepticism in his voice.

Mr. Cartier laughed so hard that he coughed. "Oh, Lord no. I'm lucky to break even. But my grandfather's old sugar plantation gives me the freedom to follow my passion. The funds were ill gained, but I've tried to put them to good use. That's the only thing I enjoy about the road: the way people's faces light up when they see their own as cowboys, or gangsters, or the dashing hero. It's the only antidote to the ignorant imaginations in Hollywood."

Judy and Alvin had been discussing this very thing a few days before. Every word Cartier spoke made it feel almost certain that her frustrations and desires had summoned him.

"What's the picture?" Judy's voice thinned, breathless. "Have I heard of it?"

He smiled with luminous teeth. "I just finished cutting it. It's a monster story set at a mansion in Louisiana. It's called *A Stranger Knocks*. In the vein of Bram Stoker." He nodded toward the bookshelf behind him. Had he spotted Professor Garrett's shelf dedicated to tales of the fanciful? Where he housed the Shelley, Stoker, Poe, and Wells novels that kept her up at night? The coincidences were dizzying. If better judgment had prevailed, Judy would have asked Cartier to leave at once. She had known he would reveal it was a picture of the uncanny before he spoke, her heart already skittering in her chest. The title's irony also felt uncomfortable and prescient: a glaring dare to gather her better sense.

But she adored *Nosferatu* when she chanced upon a rare screening, and she couldn't ignore her excitement at the notion of such frights with a colored cast. Although Alvin always chuckled at the melodramatic performances by silent actors, she believed moving pictures *could* prove to be a powerful vehicle for actors and storytelling. Monster pictures for Negroes! And just as *Nosferatu* mingled its unearthly terrors with fears of plague, colored pictures could express her people's everyday terrors behind the safe barrier of a monster's mask. She ached to see his film on the spot.

Still, the proposal frightened her. *He* frightened her. But weren't all important steps in life a bit frightening? Like leaving her uncle's care to study playwriting under the great Wilson T. Garrett? And her impulsive marriage to this miraculous man she had known less than a year, but with whom she already wanted to grow old in a house like the one they were boarding in?

"We'll do it!" she said. She braced for an objection from Alvin, but he took the envelope back into his hands, not ready to let go. Alvin wanted them to claim a house of their own more than she did. In three weeks, they could afford that and more.

"When would we need to leave, Mr. Cartier?" Alvin said.

Alvin asked with no joy, his eyes cast down. In that moment, she assumed he was entranced by the money. How couldn't he be? But the same night, sleepless with anticipation in bed beside him, it dawned on her like sunlight that her dear man of a husband had not agreed for the money at all: He had done it to please her. *She* had agreed to the job without consulting him, and instead of chiding her, he had relented. A wedding gift to her, even.

She often remembered his downcast eyes later, picking apart the moment of their terrible union with the producer like a scab she could not stop examining, a wound she might heal only if she could achieve crystal clarity on how their entanglement began. The *origin*.

Alvin's downcast eyes would always haunt her as the signal she should have heeded. Why hadn't she paused at his sober tone and said they would excuse themselves to the hallway to confer? Invited him to express his own opinion? Because she knew what he would say?

It was as if her dear husband already knew.

Cartier showed them the map of their journey along Route One. He vowed that his reels would not "explode" during the drive—a scenario that had not crossed their minds—because he would store them in a cool container. He promised to bring an auto tent in case Alvin got tired of driving in the middle of nowhere. *I know all of the out-of-the-way camping spots where we can disappear from sight,* he said, which did not sound as assuring as he intended. He didn't bring up the difficulty of finding lodging for colored people, but it need not be spoken. Cartier would have no problem renting a comfortable room in any city or backwater town along the way, but Judy and Alvin were obviously deep hues of brown.

Any potential problem they imagined—and as a writer and actor, Judy and Alvin had endless imaginations for catastrophe—Cartier had a ready answer to try to put them at ease. Alvin confided that Cartier had taken him aside and told him that if he had any misgivings about such a long trip with a stranger and his new bride, he should bring a weapon for peace of mind. *Even a derringer would do,* Alvin said he'd told him with a wink.

Even after they agreed in theory, Judy and Alvin spent hours discussing the proposal alone. Atop their shared bed, their feet twining like schoolchildren's as they lay on their stomachs, they made a list of things Cartier should not have known: their surname, for one. The contents of Professor Garrett's bookshelf. Judy's love for picture shows. The derringer capped a list of ten remarks that were none of Cartier's business. He had more intimate knowledge than he let on. He had lied. Or, in the most generous light, he wanted to dazzle them into saying yes.

But he had left a contract, and his money, behind—including the extra twenty dollars.

Their neighbor was a lawyer and agreed to read the contract for a small fee—he said the terms seemed sound, and the compensation was so high that he didn't see the point of haggling. Even then, they decided they couldn't agree to the job without consulting Professor Garrett, which should have ended the matter—but he answered their telegram by the next morning: *Use your judgment. But exercise caution.* He was proud of his practically new Chrysler with its shiny brick-red paint, but he trusted them to care for it.

It was real. They would go on an *adventure* this summer.

The phone rang just as Alvin was giving the Western Union man such a large tip that he looked like he would hug him. Their celebration was contagious.

Judy picked up the black phone receiver. "Hello, Mr. Cartier," she said before he spoke. Because of course it was him: one more coincidence to add to their list. She was cocky enough to try to dazzle him right back.

"I see I'm not the only mind reader." A glib joke, or so she'd thought. Or at least that was what she'd *told* herself she was thinking.

As it turned out, she was as expert a liar as he was.

"If you've laid your last doubts to rest, an extra spot opened up," Cartier said. "I need to get to Baltimore tonight."

They followed Cartier's directions to the rural outskirts of the city to a crumbling old Tudor-style house with a carriage house. Old-fashioned, like his coat. His lawn was so green that it glowed in the last of the daylight. Alvin drove the car along the wagon-rutted path into the carriage house as they had been instructed. They idled in silence until a voice said, "Please close the doors. I have a migraine."

The voice had a disembodied quality that seemed to be inside of the car with them, but Judy made out Cartier's shadow from a corner, standing beside his traveling trunk.

Judy flicked on the Chrysler's headlamps as Alvin closed the carriage house doors and helped Mr. Cartier move his luggage inside. She hoped for a glimpse of the celluloid reels, but they weren't in sight. If not for the Chrysler's lights, they would have been in pitch blackness.

"Anything else you need, Mr. Cartier?" Alvin said after he had settled their employer. Playing his role like a good actor.

Mr. Cartier had carried a heavy plaid blanket with him into the car, and he lay down to sleep curled beneath it, covered from head to toe. "I'll block out the light to help recover from my migraine. Follow the map to the Douglass Theater. They call it The Royal now. The showing is expected by eight o'clock."

His headache had stripped the cheer from his voice. He was another man entirely. Judy and Alvin gave each other a knowing look: a drunk, most likely. Neither of them was surprised. But they had been paid in advance for their first week, at least.

"Do reels actually explode?" Judy whispered to Alvin.

"Guess we'll see," he said.

Their trip began.

At the newly dubbed Royal Theatre in Baltimore, Judy first saw *A Stranger Knocks*. The theater had a dizzying thirteen hundred seats, similar to the Howard Theatre where she had first seen Alvin onstage with the Howard Players. Posters still flapping from the walls proclaimed that the Harlem Strutters had performed the night before, billed with an Oscar Micheaux feature called *A Son of Satan*. Another mysterious picture! She hated she'd missed it.

Mr. Cartier's mood and energy were much improved by the time they arrived. He ushered them to their seats with packages of Butter-Kist popcorn, as giddy as a child to show off his picture, and rushed to meet the white theater owner with blustery pats on the back. Again, his appearance had shifted although he wore the same unseasonable coat; his golden curls and rosy cheeks hid any hint of African ancestry. He was not only passing; he was more like a changeling.

Mr. Cartier made his way to the theater's organ, which was stationed beside the stage. The audience applauded. It was all a happy spectacle.

The lights darkened and hushed the crowd. *A Stranger Knocks* began.

Judy agreed with Alvin that organ accompaniments to pictures and radio dramas sounded overwrought, but Mr. Cartier's was a pulsing heartbeat. The first image was the promised mansion, nestled by trees with hanging swamp moss. A slave plantation. Judy felt the audience stirring, restless, at the reminder of slavery. Then the narration card appeared: *The new owners of Louisiana's formerly most reviled Sugar Estate have settled in for the night.*

The next image was a colored man and woman sitting side by side on a sofa in a library brimming with books, and the crowd cheered. Judy felt herself smiling at first too, until she realized how much the room resembled Professor Garrett's parlor. The colored actors were wearing pale powder on their faces and didn't closely favor her and Alvin, but they were a similar age and size. The woman's hair was also wound in a French braid, her own style.

Alvin, beside her, squeezed Judy's hand. He saw it too.

Mr. Cartier stabbed at the organ keys to strike three somber chords just as the actors looked up as if they had heard the music too. A new title card appeared: *They were surprised by a loud knock on the door. Visitors did not usually come to the Estate, especially at night. Many considered the site to be cursed still.*

A shadow crawled across the library like a cloud draping the moon. The actors were swallowed by darkness. The couple looked at each other's ghostly faces in the lamplight, uncertain. The man rose to his feet while the woman clutched her book to her chest. Everything inside of Judy wanted to scream, *Do not open that door.*

"Just pretend y'all ain't home!" a man shouted behind her, and the theater roiled with nervous laughter. Cartier's organ silenced the crowd with its menace, voicing the man's wary footsteps across an impossibly long foyer to the mansion's double doors. Here the angle changed, now from the outside looking in. A hulking silhouette in a sagging rain jacket stood in shadow in the entryway, seen only from behind. In the doorway, the man stared up at the mysterious figure, gape mouthed.

"Lord help us, how do they call this acting?" Alvin muttered.

Judy did not want to revisit their old argument here. As much as she thought she should tear her eyes away from whatever waited in the entryway, she also wanted to stay rooted. The rain falling across the dark figure's back seemed to lick at Judy's face, and she dabbed at her cheeks. (Was that moisture?) The man took a step away from the dark figure. And another. His eyes had gone vacant; not the wide-eyed, dumb affect that offended her so much in white pictures, but as if his soul were seeping from him. His eyes were now rimmed with dark smudges. As the man stepped back, the figure's shiny black boots crossed the threshold.

"He's bewitched," Judy whispered. A woman sitting nearby shushed her, but Judy barely heard over the Stranger's scraping footsteps. (But how could she hear his actual footsteps when the film was silent?) Now his wife came behind him to investigate the delay (*No! Stay away!*), and she swooned when she gazed at the mysterious visage entering their home. (Was that it? Should they avoid meeting his eyes?)

The figure now stood inside of their house: He was much bigger than he had looked before, as wide as the doorway, rising toward the raised ceiling. He was too big to take in all at once, or to see his face, an inky visage so overpowering that it bled from the screen. The frenetic organ was drowned out by a metallic screech in Judy's eardrums. Were migraines contagious? She covered her ears with both hands, and—

". . . Judy? Sweetheart, please wake up."

Alvin was shaking Judy's knee and not gently. Judy's head had drooped forward so far that she had to knead out a cramp from the back of her neck. She expected to find herself in a vast library—no, in Professor Garrett's parlor—but instead they were still in the theater. *Baltimore*, she remembered. The house lights were up, and most of the theatergoers had left their seats, only a few stragglers left behind to share how afraid they had been. One man said, "Shoot, I ain't scared."

But Alvin was. Concern radiated from his face as he leaned

over her. "I've been trying to wake you up for two minutes. I was about to go fetch a doctor."

Judy licked her parched lips. Her mouth and throat felt sucked dry. "What happened?"

"You fell asleep," he said, and lowered his voice: "Not that I blame you."

When she stirred, her joints and muscles ached from being clenched. Judy wouldn't touch liquor even if it were legal, but she imagined this might be what a hangover felt like.

"The dinner scene was ten minutes too long," Alvin said. "But the rest wasn't too bad, mostly. We'll have to ask him to explain that lousy ending. I think he should cut it out. But what do I know? You're the expert on pictures."

After such a scare, Judy didn't want to alarm Alvin by letting him know that she didn't remember any dinner scene, or the ending, or any scene beyond the Stranger's arrival. The images tried to creep back to her, but her mind walled them away. She stared at the pale, empty screen, surprised that the feature hadn't torn a hole through it.

"It was . . . powerful," she said.

"Yeah," he said, a rare agreement. "My heart jumped a couple times."

By now, all of the seats ahead of them were empty, making the theater look like a man-made cavern—except for a man three rows ahead who was on his feet, apparently deep in thought. Staring up at the empty screen. He was in stylish attire, his hat canted to the side.

"Come on, let's find Cartier," Alvin said. "He's supposed to pay boarding, so let's see if we can find a room at the colored hotel. I'm not sleeping in no damn tent."

At the sound of Cartier's name, Judy looked toward the organ. No one sat there.

Judy heard Alvin talking to her, but her attention was fixed on the lone man in the row ahead of them. He still had not moved. He might as well be asleep on his feet.

"Alvin, that man . . . ?" she said. "Do you think he's all right?"

Alvin gave the man a dismissive glance. "You finally found

someone who loves pictures more'n you do," he said. "I'd better keep you away from him."

Cartier came to the aisle, waving to them with unbridled glee. "The verdict?"

Alvin offered a nod and a smile. "We loved it!" Judy said.

Cartier grinned at her in a frozen way that was not entirely pleasant. His dancing eyes made Judy certain that he knew she had dozed off, that he had seen her sleeping from his organ bench. Her face flared hot.

"I'll handle my own affairs now," Cartier said. "Meet me here tomorrow night."

Before they could ask what time to meet him, or what the next driving plans were, he had turned away from them to walk to the man who was still staring at the screen. Judy watched Cartier join the man in his row, moving closer to him seat by seat. When he reached the man's side, Cartier leaned over and whispered in his ear.

The man's bones folded over so suddenly that Judy gasped. Cartier caught him. Slumping against Cartier, the man began walking with him.

He had fainted! Judy realized that the same thing had happened to her. The film had stirred such deep fear in her that she had lost consciousness.

"There *was* something wrong with that man," Judy said. Did she share his affliction?

"You heard Cartier—he'll handle it. Let's go 'fore all the rooms get booked up."

Judy followed Alvin but kept her eyes on Cartier as he continued to steer the man toward a door stage right. When Cartier opened the door, it was dark within. Judy's heart churned as she watched Cartier lead the man into the gloom.

She'd felt the same dread watching the shadowy Stranger in the feature, an image that now seized her memory with icy clarity. The urge returned to yell out, *No! Turn back!*

But Judy did not say a word as the stage door slipped shut.

Judy could not sleep that night, and not only because of the unfamiliar bed in the modest hotel. Alvin snored peacefully, nestled against her, but every time Judy closed her eyes, she saw the dark visage leak from the screen. Not a substance—a hole. And Cartier sat at his organ, his shadow made giant across the screen, growing taller as if to meet the fearsome maw.

She woke up several times, always damp with sweat. She scolded herself for having such vivid nightmares from a picture show—one she didn't even remember—but they did not feel like dreams. The frights felt more like a memory of an event only she had experienced . . . and perhaps that one man left standing in the theater. Lying awake fresh from her nightmare, unable to lie to herself, she finally had the courage to wonder: *What did Cartier say to him?*

The curtains flapped in the breeze from their open window. Judy saw golden buttons shining in the curtains' gap. But when she leaped from bed to see if Cartier was there on a balcony, she realized there *was* no balcony. She only saw the hotel's white picket fence below. And the dead night, with the loud revelers finally home in bed. Her heart was in a furor that made her lightheaded. She hoped she wouldn't faint again.

Judy had never been more grateful to see the dawn.

They had no word from Cartier during the daylight hours—and the theater manager had no idea where he was when they called—which was fine with Judy. With the sea breeze and pleasant meals with her dear Alvin, her terrible nightmares felt sillier and further away. By seven, Alvin decided they should head back to the theater to see if their employer needed them.

That was the first time she realized the picture would play for a second night. And maybe a third or a fourth. Would she be expected to view it again and again?

Alvin saw it in her face. He took her hands. "Listen . . ." he said. "You can stay here. If you want me to tell this fella we're going back to D.C. after our first week, it's fine with me."

And just like that, not feeling trapped gave Judy enough freedom to take a breath and gather her courage. This was their job. Just because she would be at the theater didn't mean she had to rewatch the picture. She could stay in the lobby, or even in the parked Chrysler.

She only wanted to stay close to Alvin.

*

"Come see the projection booth," Cartier's voice said behind her. It was nearly eight o'clock, and she and Alvin had been looking for him all evening in the throng: Tonight, the theater was standing room only. She'd finally excused herself to use the ladies' room, wading through the crowd. Inside, she'd overheard a tearful woman saying that she was looking for her brother, who had never come home from the theater the night before. She thought of Cartier and the overwhelmed man he had led away. Judy almost said something to her—and wondered why she didn't.

And on her way back out, Cartier found *her*. He was stationed just outside the door, waiting. His silvery eyes were far too bright, his pupils as large as a cat's hunting in the dark. She could swear on a New Testament that he was two inches taller than he'd been the night before although he wore the same boots. (Or had the boots been in the picture?) *Boots in July?*

"I . . ." she began, trying to think of an excuse. Before this, she would have tripped over herself to see the projection room. But if it meant being near Cartier or his reels, the thought made her tremble. ". . . I have to meet Alvin."

"I've settled it with Alvin," Cartier said. "He's keeping an eye on the audience. A couple of scofflaws were raising a ruckus. Come with me, will you?"

She didn't believe him. Alvin was not overly jealous, but he would never agree to send her anywhere alone with Cartier. *Come with me, will you?* But Cartier's question was a command—not just by her employer, but with a sway that reminded her of being an obedient child again—so she followed him past the crowd to a side door that revealed unpainted walls, debris from old sets, and untidy stacks of boxes and crates, the way every theater's illusions dissolved in unlit corners. From behind, his hair looked springier and coarser, like her uncle's, the nape of his neck the color of honey. Was she only imagining the changes? A trick of lighting? But lighting would not create such a dramatic effect.

She remembered Alvin's downcast eyes when he granted her wish for an escapade, and phlegm clogged her throat. They had made a mistake. She had led her beloved toward danger. Judy never had been more afraid or angrier at herself.

"We need to break our contract," she said. "We'll give your money back."

Cartier lightly raised his hand to wave her words away like vapor.

She tried to say more, to *insist*, but her lips were dry enough to feel welded together. She was afraid to try too hard to open her mouth, or to stop following him, because of the waiting horror if she could not. The only way to *not* know was to keep pace with his sure steps in silence, like the voiceless actress in his film.

Cartier took her to a narrow stairwell, and again she followed. She too easily imagined now what he had whispered to the afflicted man last night: *Come with me, will you?*

"What are you?" She *could* speak. But she hadn't intended to whisper her fear aloud.

He stopped in front of a narrow door and looked at her for the first time since the lobby. His eyes sparked in the dark passageway. Judy was ready to beg forgiveness for her rudeness, almost relieved to tears that his face wasn't angry in the brief flash of light.

He was studying her; not the embarrassing way men had admired her since she was fifteen, but with a regard that reminded her of Professor Garrett.

"Now," Cartier said, "you learn the secrets."

The stairs to the projection booth were so narrow that her feet were too big unless she climbed at a careful angle, and she had to walk with her skirt clutched high. Cartier, walking ahead of her, might as well have been gliding up the untenable stairs. As they passed an open doorway to the balcony, she saw a glimpse of the gilded theater beyond the stairwell's patchy walls, most seats already filled. She searched for Alvin, but it was hopeless even with the house lights still up. He was lost somewhere in the sea of people far below.

Judy fought the impulse to run the other way. Or, better put, the impulse came and left after a voice in her head that didn't sound quite like hers told her, *Don't be silly. You're here to learn, aren't you?*

"It feels like entering a crypt up here, and that is fitting," Cartier said as he opened the door at the top of the stairs. "Celluloid is nitrate, and it's as alive as a demon. It will catch fire on a whim. It will kill you with gas even as you try to put out the flames. It *wants* to burn."

Judy's annoyance helped mute her terror as they entered the narrow room. Washington had been unbearably hot all summer, and Baltimore wasn't much better. He had underplayed the peril of their drive, which explained the high salary. This mundane detail clawed past her fears of everything about Cartier she did not yet understand—or want to.

"You should have told us the true dangers," she said.

"But all beauty is dangerous, yes?" Cartier said. "This particular demon—moving pictures—casts a spell. It spirits all who see it from our world to steal a glimpse of another."

Like the petrified man at last night's showing. What world had he seen? Or her?

The large black projector glaring down toward the theater screen looked like a beast out of Shelley's *Frankenstein*, a tangle of cords and sprockets like teeth. She was only vaguely aware of Cartier closing the door. Then his cool—no, *cold*—presence close behind her made her turn quickly around. He held out a round metal canister with a film coiled within. She couldn't help raising her finger to touch the rim, curious. The canister was also cold to the touch.

"Each reel is fifteen minutes," he said. "*A Stranger Knocks* is five reels. And these projectors are old. Sad to say, most theaters on the colored circuit can't properly maintain their projectors. Without delicate handling, the reels will be damaged. That fool last night was unsuited to the task. So, you must pay careful attention. I am entrusting them to your care."

With deft fingers moving quickly, he showed her how to thread the film, where the sprockets caught the gaps in the celluloid to coax life into the frozen images. His voice lowered to a hurried whisper, so she found herself leaning closer to hear his flurry of words, which at times did not sound like English. Only then did she notice his scent. His *scents*. Cartier smelled like lavender at first, and then wildflowers, and then like the sweet corn cakes her mother used to make her in the griddle before...

Judy knew she was swooning again, but she was still upright. Her hands were busy on the projector, following Cartier's whispered instructions although she could not clearly hear him, or understand his words when his voice reached her ear.

The knowing that had seized her during their long walk to the projection room returned with the fury of a thunderclap, and her mind asked again: *What is he?* He was not the old man with sharpened canines in Stoker's *Dracula*. He was not the horrid Count Orlok in *Nosferatu*, who was monstrous on sight and whose narrow head slowly rising from that poor woman's bedside, from her *neck*, had visited her sleep many nights.

But Cartier was some kind of monster. She could not deny it now, watching her ignorant fingers traverse this strange contraption as if she had mastered it years ago. Doing his bidding.

And if he could compel her to do *this*, what else might he demand of her?

The strangest thing happened: Inside, she was weeping as she had only at her parents' funeral after the flu orphaned her in 1918. But her weeping was silent. Hidden. Hers alone.

"You have no reason to fear me." Cartier sounded more bored than kind, almost scolding. As if she should already have known, despite his tyranny over her will.

"Of course I do," she said, gasping out the words, digging them from a well.

"You are in my employ. Why would I hurt you?"

"What happened to that man last night?"

Cartier's silence was so long that she would have turned to look back at him if she'd still had command of her limbs.

"As you will come to understand..." he began. "I have needs I must satisfy. My hungers bring me no joy. But I've found a feeding method that suits both my animal drives and my artistic ones. I'll answer no more questions."

"What about Alvin?" she said.

True to his word, he did not answer this time.

"I won't do it," she said. "I won't stay with you. I'll burn it myself. I'll find a way."

She waited an eternity that was only a few seconds. Then the house lights went down, turning the room dark, and the dreadful organ drumbeat sounded below.

The projector hummed. She had started the picture.

Cartier's unearthly grip released her, and she was able to control her muscles enough to crane her head around to see what she already knew: Cartier was not in the room. How could he be, when he was coaxing such brooding music from the organ in plain view?

When had he left? Was the voice she'd heard only in her own mind?

Her weeping began anew, but this time it wasn't bottled inside of her. She hoped the audience would hear her wails from below, and she might disrupt Cartier's plans. If only she could scream for all of them to flee the theater before Cartier's sinister hunt began.

At least he granted her one mercy: She could close her eyes. He did not force her to watch *A Stranger Knocks* again.

When the house lights came back up this time after the fifth reel ended, three people were standing to stare at the screen as everyone left around them: a burly man, a smartly dressed woman with streaks of silver in her hair . . .

And Alvin.

Alvin might be in the same seat from the night before, when she had been beside him. His wiry frame was swaying slightly, his chin angled high toward the screen. Judy had emptied herself of tears, but new grief clawed at her. Alvin looked as helpless as a mouse.

"Not him," Judy whispered, although she was still alone in the room. "Not Alvin."

No sound came from behind her, not even a phantom's whisper.

But Cartier glided into the aisle below. As he stood closest to Alvin's row, he slowly turned to look up at her with a grin.

"As you can see . . ." his voice said, far too close to her ear to be anything other than sorcery, "you're not the only one capable of threats. I'm sure you understand now that if you harm a frame of my reels, you will lose your mate. And I will need to hire a new driver."

"*Yes*," she said, because she had nothing to bargain with.

"I think you'll find, over time, that you'll enjoy our work," he said. "You can write pictures for me—the regular kind. And Alvin can be coaxed to act for the camera, I'm sure."

Never, she thought. She would never take any joy from helping this unhuman creature.

"Perhaps . . ." he said, his cool breath finding the inner recesses of her ear although he still stood far below, "you might earn your way into my fellowship one day. Despite the demands of the hunger, the rewards of long life remain."

This time, she said it aloud: "*Never.* I would never want to be like you."

Below, she watched his grin widen until his cheeks inflated to grotesquery, reaching his ears. His skin seeped with pigmentation until he was as dark as she, or darker. If he were not wearing his coat with the gold buttons, she would never have recognized him now.

"These race pictures you love so much?" he said. "How long do you think they will survive? Most of them will *burn*, or rot, and be utterly forgotten. Have you heard of the new invention to come—*sound?* Yes! Sound from the pictures themselves! No more pantomimes. Sound is going to lay waste to one empire and give birth to another. Future residents will forget where these old colored theaters once stood. And the stories of colored heroes in race pictures will be replaced by Hollywood's servile bowing and scraping. Only your grandchildren will live to enjoy the era of colored pictures you dream about. If they live to see it themselves."

Judy did not realize she had been holding her breath until she exhaled so violently that she shuddered—but with hope instead of fear. He had meant to taunt her, but had he just confirmed that she would survive to have grandchildren? Did his vision see that far?

"I can live with that," Judy said. And, again, because none of the frozen spectators below had moved, including her beloved, she said firmly: "Not Alvin. Leave us as we were. Please."

Her heartbeat hammered at her ribs as she waited for Cartier's answer. No sound came.

But below, Alvin turned his head right and left, obviously confused. But he was awake!

The tears Judy shed were not from joy, although relief shook her knees. She wept for the man and woman below that Cartier was gliding toward past Alvin's row. What horrors lay in store for them? She had no way to warn them and dared not try.

Cartier, after all, was her employer.

"Alvin!" she called down to her husband.

He turned around and looked up, smiling when he saw her. A fully human smile.

She freed herself from the projection room to race to the stairs, and she found him already climbing the steps up to the balcony to meet her. They ran to each other like a lovelorn couple in a play, holding each other as if there were no other eyes in the room.

And there weren't, after all. Except for the man and woman shambling behind Cartier toward their fate, the theater was empty. She held Alvin a long time, feeling her heart pounding against him, wondering what he knew of the true nature of their employment. Of Cartier. And if he did not know, how could she tell him? But how could she *not?*

"I had my doubts before, but now I understand," Alvin said. "I think it's better now."

"What's better?"

His smile fanned her soul with enough affection to help her forget Cartier's insidious grin, at least while her chest rested against his. Alvin kissed the top of her head.

"The ending," he said.

THOMAS HA

The Sort

FROM *Clarkesworld*

SCIENCE FICTION

MY SON CAN'T think of the word *spoon*.

It's there, at the tip of his tongue. The waitress looks at him with a patient smile. She can see he's fidgeting and getting hot. A boy his age would typically know how to ask. "Could I please have another . . ." But it stops. It's been a while since we've driven through a town and used our words.

—*Spoon.*

He looks at me. "Spoon."

—*Good job.*

The restaurant's noisy, as tends to happen with people. The boy understands, but of course, it's still something to sit there with the din. He winces every time someone speaks too loudly or a utensil clatters against something on the tables. When he gets his spoon, he scoops up the bits of crumbled pie crust and filling, then looks out the glass at the main street. The town here's small enough that they have only one big avenue with some roadside shops, then a couple of side streets. Where the people actually live is tough to say. Some near the stores they mind, I'm sure, but the rest out in the rock-speckled desert, if I had to guess.

I'd like to go over to the park.

—*Words.*

"I'd like to go over to the park."

"Okay."

"On my own."

"Oh. Okay."

"I'll stay in . . ." He hesitates. "In sight. But I'd like to go."

"Yep, that's fine. I said okay."

We finish our pie. He wipes his mouth and scoots to the edge of the booth. There's still something at the corner of his lips, and I resist the urge to wet a napkin and dab at it. Somebody knocks over a saltshaker nearby, and we both flinch.

—*In sight. Like you said.*

Yep. In sight. I know.

He skips off through the doors and over to the dusty street. When he crosses, I hold my breath until he makes it past a low fence and to a playground, then I watch and drink coffee while the summer sun heats everything up in that little desert town.

My son sits for a while at the top of a slide, and a couple of kids stare up at him, a girl and a smaller boy. They know something about my son, even if they don't know what it is. The girl's face, tanned and raw, scrunches at him.

"Come in from the highway?" she asks.

"Yeah."

"Where you guys going?"

"Arizona," he says.

"Nice. What's in Arizona?"

"Just stuff."

"Where were you before?"

"Oregon," he answers, just like we practiced. He isn't pronouncing it quite right, but they don't seem to know it.

"What city?"

"City?"

"In Oregon."

—*Redmond*, I offer, but my son looks away from the restaurant. *Or Bend. That's another one. You could always say Bend.*

"Doesn't matter. It's far off, and we're not going back anytime soon. On the road for a while with my dad."

—*Good answer.*

My son shoots an annoyed look across the street. He's right. I should be leaving it alone. He knows well enough how to handle these things.

"You guys staying for the fire?"
"What?"
"The fire? You don't know?"
"Why would I know anything about a fire?"
"Thought maybe that's why you stopped. Sometimes people come for the fire, when they burn the garlic. It's kind of a thing here, when they burn the garlic."
"Oh. Well, we didn't. So I don't know anything about a fire. Or about any garlic."
"Huh. Well, the fields are just over there." She points. "That's the smell. You don't smell that? That's usually the first thing people visiting here smell. It's kind of nice, if you like the way gold garlic smells, I mean."
"I don't really pick up on smells, I guess."

My son doesn't understand that she's not really asking about the fire or garlic or smells, that she's just tickling him with words. And he's just about to say something else huffy, but his face gets all tight around the mouth, in the corners. He stops and his eyes drift over and up to the bright sky.

He took in too much of the noon light, maybe. That can happen around midday, especially out in the open, if he's looking too much, like he has been. His fingers start curling, and his jaw muscles clench and unclench.

"You okay?" The girl and the small boy she's with look at each other but don't seem to know what to do, especially after my son goes quiet like that and doesn't answer. "Um . . . we got to—we got to get going. Nice to meet you. See you around, I guess."

My son stares out at nothing still, his body locked up. His mind tumbles off into some inner dark beneath the surface, where even I can't reach him. The wind and dust scatter, and his eyes go soft and heavy, like a lamb ready to lay itself down to rest.

It takes me a minute to get to him and carry him off the slide. We sit together on one of the benches until he comes out of it, and when he's up and moving, he doesn't want to talk about what happened. I think I remember that, the feeling of embarrassment about my body closing up in front of other people without any way to stop it. But it's mostly a blurry memory now, not something

I feel anymore at my age. For him, though, it's present and painful, and I don't want to minimize it. So instead of trying to coddle him, I wait until it seems like we're ready to go.

We walk the street toward some of the tourist shops to get out of the heat. He's sweating and clearly doesn't want to be in all that light anymore.

—*In there?*

Okay.

The souvenir shop is like all of the others we've stopped at along the highway. A layer of ocher dirt coats the scratched floorboards and fills the crannies of the lower shelves. There's a hand-painted board that says, "Welcome to Meike's." We play around at a little sunglasses rack until I get him to crack a smile with some triangle-shaped lenses. I tell him he can keep a big pair of aviators, and he slips them on comfortably, shutting out some of that desert brightness.

Over in the corner, he sees a junked-up playerbot with a game loaded up on a table. His eyes light up, so I give him enough coins for a few rounds, then make my way up to the counter to pay for the sunglasses. The white-haired woman at the register rings me up.

"You guys going east or west?"

"Arizona. Or thereabouts, anyway."

"Sightseeing?"

"Something like that. The kid needed a break, and a drive seemed like a good change of pace for us."

The lady nods. "That can be good, sure." She leans back on her stool. I notice the counter is filmy with all that ocher dirt, and every time she breathes, I just barely pick up a tang of whiskey.

"He's got a real touch for it."

Over in the corner, my son's going with the playerbot, knocking a light disc back and forth with a holographic paddle. His little eyes watch the disc ricochet, each successive volley getting slightly more complex. He's anticipating the disc by a fraction of a second, getting ahead of where the bot is going to send it, I realize.

"Most kids go for a round, cuss out after a few minutes, and then wander off, usually."

"Hm," is all I can bring myself to say.

While he plays on, the white-haired woman sips at her mug, and I pretend to look at the little knickknacks on display. There are rows of pickled garlic jars, which I assume they must be known for. Similar preserves and garlic powder and accompanying spices. Even little stuffed toys of garlic bulbs, big and round and golden with little eyes and grinning teeth. At some point, while I'm perusing, the white-haired woman gets another mug out from a cabinet and pours the whiskey I'd smelled earlier for the both of us, very casually, like I should have expected it and didn't need to ask. I thank her and sip along.

"You guys going to the fire?"

"You know, I'm not sure. I didn't really know about it."

"It's a pretty good time. Some food. Games. A lot of the families work at the factory farms off of 159, and there's usually some portion of the gold garlic that gets hit with withering at this time of year. The farms were just tossing it, but someone got the idea to turn it into an event. People in the county like it enough."

"Gotcha. Is it—I don't know—crowded?"

She looks over at my son. "Not too bad. A lot of open space. They do it not too far on a hill near the freeway." She laughs. "Man, he is really still going."

"Yeah. He's always been good at that sort of thing."

"Other things are tougher."

"Can be. Yeah."

"School. Other kids."

I don't exactly agree, but I don't deny what she's saying.

"Not easy." The woman nods thoughtfully. "Especially for the ones more in their shell. All of them, though, are a lot more scared these days. Of everything, of each other. They don't play as much as they used to, it seems to me."

"No, that's true."

"I envy them, and I don't. I'd like to be where they are, but I don't think I'd do it now."

"Yeah. I know what you mean."

I sip the whiskey, let the sharpness sit on my tongue, and find myself just watching the boy. He can't move as quickly as others on the playground or run without tripping over something on most days. But somehow with that paddle and the disc, and his reflexes, he can just go like that, so naturally. It's something I like to see, because so few things come easy that way for us. But I also can't let him play too long with other people watching what he can do.

"You know, if you're looking for things to do, you should take him to the Tiger."

"Oh?"

"Over at the municipal building. People usually like that. Your son might too."

"Maybe he would. Sure. Thanks."

He's moving even faster with the paddle, and the playerbot's struggling with the pace.

"Bud? Did you hear that? There's a Tiger we can see, and I think it's time to go."

One minute.

—*Bud. She's watching. Can't keep going forever like that.*

Just to the end of the round.

—*Words.*

"Almost done. One minute."

I wait. "Time's up. Come on."

He hits the disc faster, faster. Again. Again.

"Hey. Let's go."

I clap my hands with purpose, and the sound gets to him and pulls him out of the moment. He looks at me and then drops the paddle in mild protest. The light disc ricochets and dissipates into the dusty air at the back of the shop. The playerbot beeps a high-score song and does a little chipper dance before folding its arms up and going dormant again.

"See you around." I smile uncomfortably. "And thanks for the drink."

The white-haired woman raises her mug and watches us return to the heat and light.

Can we go? I really hate this place. Let's just get back on the highway.

—*Why do you hate it?*

I just do.

The Sort

—Why? Can you explain? I'd really like to hear it.
I just do. Can we go?
—In a while, sure, but let's take a little more time.
It's stupid. Everything's dumb here.
—That's not really fair. We've barely poked around. Come on. Over this way. The whole point is to see more things. There's more to it than just "I hate it." I want you to look. I want you to see more things.

The municipal building is made of a cool, light-colored stone, and inside we follow the signs over to the Tiger, which they seem to keep in an open lobby. They have him sitting on a box, a big collar around his neck, but it's cloth. It's not really holding him to anything, I realize.

"Is that safe?" I ask a fellow in a nearby chair.

The man tips up a tall hat and looks at me. "Safe?"

"The Tiger, out here."

"Yeah. He can't hurt anybody. Five dollars each if you want to see him, though."

"Aren't we already seeing him?"

"Probably a good idea to pay, then."

"Hm."

We step up to the box after paying. Supposedly, we can touch him if we want. There's a plaque explaining that this is one of the last modified Tigers in the country. They made it with rounded teeth and blunt claws and no kill instinct to speak of. The man in the chair with the tall hat says this was from the early days, before regulations limited modification to agriculture—back when they were still modifying people, too, in certain cities on the coast. Before everyone got upset about the unexpected conditions that arose and sued the modifier companies into oblivion, leaving no one around to fix any of the problems they made.

"That's interesting." I place my hand on my son's shoulder and move him farther to the other side and away from the man in the tall hat. "Haven't seen anything like this on the road in a long time."

"And you won't. This one's 'specially ours."

"I see that. Yeah."

My son leans forward, staring behind those big aviator sunglasses, and the Tiger hunches there like an old man on a stoop.

His whiskers are more of a beard, and the animal's humming to himself under his breath. The bone structure in his face even seems a little human from where we stand. Everything smells like garlic, and I see they've got some kind of gold paste in a bowl that they feed him. The Tiger's eyes are like bright yellow jewels flecked with black spots that shift their way over to us.

"Hello," the Tiger says.

"Hi."

"Hello."

"Hey."

The Tiger smiles.

Is he all right?

—Yeah. I think this is about as much as they can say. They never got far with the animals.

Can he hear like us?

—I don't know.

The Tiger's eyes go back and forth between me and the boy.

"Hello."

"Hey."

I don't think I like this.

—Yeah. Most people didn't like it either. There's a reason they stopped.

"Hello."

"Hi."

Doesn't he want to go outside? It's not the kind of place animals like to be.

—The thing is, he was never really made to be outside. Modifieds die on their own in the wild. Not equipped. But he doesn't seem unhappy here to me, for what it's worth.

I would rather be outside, if I were him.

—I know what you mean. But he is what he is, and this is all he knows. He might not fit here, but he doesn't necessarily fit out there either. I don't think it bothers him, though.

"Hello."

"Hello."

Well, I do.

—You do what?

Think it bothers him. They never should have made him.

—I don't think he feels that way.

I think he feels that way. In fact, I know he feels that way.
—Don't say that, bud.
Why not?
—Don't say that, bud. Come on.
Why not? It's true. He didn't ask for it. And I think the people who made him should've thought twice about what it would feel like. Where are the others like him? How does that feel? No. He didn't ask. It's good that it's illegal now, so they can't keep breeding any more of this. Making Tigers that aren't Tigers. They never should have done it.
"Hello."
"Hi."

I want to keep talking, but I think this is one of those things I have to let go. The man in the tall hat is watching us closely, I realize, and muttering: "'Little Lamb, who made thee? Dost thou know, who made thee?'" He whispers absently, the kind of rambling someone might do if they were rehearsing for a performance. And again, I put more distance between the man and my son—pretending that I'm not watching him sit there and watch us.

The Tiger, meanwhile, leans in and looks at the boy and lifts a big paw, turning it sideways like he's ready to shake. My son hesitantly grabs the paw and looks back at the Tiger.

Can you hear me?
—I don't think he can hear you.
Can you hear me?
—I don't think he can hear you.
If they don't know about us, how could we know about him?
—Hm.
Can you hear me?
But all the Tiger does is smile.

Summer days in this place break like quickly forgotten fevers. Evening reds spread sideways against the dust whipping along the gray line of the distant highway. People are already working up on the hill, tending to a big stone firepit that's billowing. Grills are out at vendor tents and a couple of food trucks. Kids are playing cornhole or running back and forth. Someone's set up speakers over by a little stage, and they've got music going.

There's a fleet truck backed up not too far from the pit. The bed is filled with gold garlic—giant bulbs, still attached to reedy stems and leaves and scapes. There are thick, vibrant tendrils along the bottom that are moving like small arms. The green stalky parts are curling, too, in the bed. The heavy garlicky air is inescapable, and even from here, you can almost hear the bulbs, like they're breathing or sighing. Some of them are as big as tractor wheels. But I see some of the twisted, crooked ones, the small percentage where the modifications weren't adequate, and they were rotted by withering.

My son's taken to standing around with some of the kids. I think I recognize the girl from the park. They're talking about something, and some of the others nearby are throwing around a float-ball. I'm not listening in for once. He's warming up, a small smile here and there under those shiny aviator sunglasses. He's still got that kid thing where, if given time, he forgets where he is and just does what they're doing.

One of the dads drinking a beer looks over as though he knows me.

"My daughter mentioned a friend at the park. Seems like they found each other again."

"Right. Right. They seem to get along."

"She said, or, she thought, he had some kind of health thing? I think she didn't know how to handle it and wanted to apologize. Felt bad walking off, I think."

"That's sweet, but it's okay. He gets overwhelmed sometimes. Photosensitivity and some other things. It passes pretty quickly, though. I used to have episodes and grew out of it. I'm sure he will too."

"I get it. She's got a similar thing with asthma. I'm actually still supposed to carry around an inhaler and—shit." He pats his pockets until he finds it. "Okay. Haven't really had to use it. Hopefully it's not a thing anymore. But you know, there's always something."

"There's always something." I laugh. "Yeah."

"You guys visiting people?"

"You know, not really. Just felt a little stuck, and I thought a trip with us two would be kind of nice."

"Sure."

"I think he's been getting . . . in his head about things. I thought he was too young for it, but he has these ideas about what's normal and what's not . . . who's not. He feels a little on the outside."

"Sure."

"That's what I like about being on the road. After you've seen enough, here and there, you get a better sense—nothing's normal and nothing's not. It's all outside. You know?"

"Hm. Yeah," he replies generously.

"I don't fucking know."

"Eh. Who does?"

Someone throws the float-ball in my son's direction, and to my surprise, he catches it. I feel like I can exhale.

"Where are you guys from again? One of those cities on the coast?"

I almost answer honestly, but then I catch myself. It's gentle curiosity, not malice, in his question. But we never know who's going to get upset when they find out we come from a place where there are still some modified families like us. And when you're on your guard all the time, it gets too easy to mix up curiosity and aggression. Maybe I'm getting comfortable like my son over there, but I'm still not all the way comfortable, not just yet.

"Oregon." I leave it at that.

"Oregon. Nice," he says.

My son throws the float-ball, and it sails over into someone's hands.

Surrounded by total darkness on that hill, with everything else engulfed in the cold black of nightfall, the firepit and its big crackling flames become more bright and central, and the starlight, all the more fearsome, stabs out from nothing, especially with no electric glow from the land holding it back. Just that light, and us, and faces and bodies gathered around. The laughs echo, and the music feels like it's in our ears.

The white-haired woman from the souvenir shop is over by the stage. She's wearing an old dress, something people must have worn decades ago when the town was founded, I have to assume. It feels very traditional, and there's something stately about the way she's got her hair up. She's holding a drink and raises it to me, and I raise a beer back at her.

People start clapping, and I see something coming out from the dark, emerging. Something big. It takes a few seconds before I understand what I'm seeing because it looks like a man. But it's the Tiger up on its hind legs, towering above everybody.

"Provost inbound! Provost inbound!"

The man in the tall hat—the one from the municipal building—is clearing the way, like an attendant, making room for the Tiger to walk up to the firepit and toward the stage. They've got the Tiger in some kind of gold cloak, like something you'd seen sewn together for a high school play, and they get him to a large chair. I hear someone explaining to another out-of-towner how they used to do this with elders—usually with someone's grandfather or uncle. But eventually, they figured out they could do it with the Tiger, and over time that became part of the tradition too.

"Provost! Provost!"

People are clapping and shouting. I look over at my son, and he's kind of like me, going along with the kids around him, cheering. Someone turns up the music, and the parents are dancing with their little ones. Some men are drinking and throwing their bottles off somewhere into the dark.

They add something to the fire, and it shoots a little higher like it's gassed up and almost sparking. The thing I always forget about firepits like these is how loud they can be. The roar and crackle and the music and the lights, it's all getting to be a lot, even for me.

I feel my fingers curling up, and my muscles are starting to tighten. It hasn't happened in a long time, but I feel like I can't move too fast, or I'll get lightheaded from all of the overstimulation. While I'm standing there, people are gathering up and around the stage.

"Time for the sort! Everybody sort!" somebody announces.

People start getting together around the fleet truck with the tumbling mountain of garlic bulbs. A few men grab the big round ones. They're yelling and giggling and carrying giant garlic plants up to the stage, laying them out like offerings at the Tiger's feet. These are definitely the healthy bulbs that are properly modified to survive in the desert heat. And I notice the Tiger's nodding, but with no smile like earlier in the day, just a stern gaze upon all of us.

"Time for the kids! It's the sort! It's the sort!"

I watch the white-haired woman and the others lining up the children to go up to the truck bed. This time, instead of gathering up the good bulbs, they're being handed the others, the withered and the diseased. Little strange and twisted garlic shapes in their clutches. And my son's being herded right along with them.

—*I'll be right over here, bud. Over by the stage.*

But if he can hear me, he's not saying anything. Instead of walking toward the Tiger, these kids are all marching in the other direction, toward the firepit. One of them, a lanky boy near the front, stands and waves at everybody, nice and big, and there's a lot more clapping and shouting that hurts my ears.

The lanky boy takes a bite of the withered garlic, and his reaction's immediate. He makes a face and spits a chunk of it out onto the dirt. Raw gold garlic would already have been hard to stomach, but with the failed modifications and withering, a lot more is off with it, of course. The plant twists around, like it's writhing and wounded and convulsing between his fingers.

Everybody laughs, and the boy lobs the defective bulb right into the flames. There's a high-pitched sound, like a taut guitar string snapping, before the fire whooshes higher against the night sky. A girl in line steps up and repeats the same thing—a bite, a sickened grimace, and a misshapen bulb tossed into the pit. Then another kid goes, then another. Gradually, the smell begins to change, like something salty and molded and awful's breaking up in the smoke and settling over the hill.

This seems to be part of the tradition, confirming that the withered bulbs aren't fit to eat. And the way everyone laughs and laughs, it reminds me of when parents put something sour on a spoon for a baby to try. A mixed-up, mean-spirited joy that's too loud and cheerful. One kid vomits and has to stumble off with some help after tossing his defect. The flame's getting to be like a pillar, turning and flickering.

Rituals like these, I think they're always about the same thing. People feeling like they have control over something. The modified plants, the encroaching desert, diseases withering food strains. It's frightening and different and always pressing in. But they want to be masters of it all and not admit how scared they really are. Even the Tiger sitting up in that chair in that costume, a mix of old things and new. I assume it feels good to make him do what they want. They don't know why, but that kind of thing feels good to them.

My son's getting closer to the front of the line, and I feel my breath going shallow.

—*You don't have to, you know.*

The whirling fire reflects off of those aviator sunglasses, his little face, lips pursed. He's looking down at the withered garlic in his hand, and it's coiling around his thumb. He's listening to it breathe, that little soft up and down, a pulse in his hands. I know him inside and out, and I know it isn't in him to do this kind of thing.

"Go on," someone says. "Take a bite. Throw it in. That's the sort."

Most of them are talking and laughing and not paying attention, but gradually there are more and more eyes on him as the line's getting held up. Murmurs and giggles and music and the flick-flacking of fire. He's touching the withered garlic bulb in his hand, but he can't seem to raise it up to his mouth to take that bite.

—*It's okay, bud. Whatever you want to do. It's up to you.*

"Go on. Bite and throw it in. It's time to sort."

He's looking around.

"Hey. Hurry it up. You got to sort."

It takes him a second, and there's a moment where I think he's actually going to do it. The ease he's been feeling, the want to be on the inside of this thing, growing. There's an urge to go with the rest of the kids, but something about him just can't.

I don't want to, he thinks.

I don't say it to him then, but a part of me is glad it's what he decided.

—*I know. Just let them know you're not going to do it. With words. It's okay.*

"I—I don't want to," he says out loud.

The man in the tall hat, the one who's been directing the line, turns when he hears that, and he gets close to my son and to the fire. The man's eyes are watery, almost clouded, and he's staring down at the kid. "It's time to sort," he says.

My son clears his throat.

"This is part of it. Taking one from the other. The good from the bad. The useful from the useless. This *is* the sort."

"I . . ."

"It's not hard for the other kids. Is it hard for you? It shouldn't be hard. Why is it hard for you? You bite. And sort."

"I . . ."

"*Bite. Sort.* Bite. Sort."

"I'm . . ."

"Do you have a listening problem? Sort. Not getting through? Sort. Sort. Sort."

The man in the tall hat claps his hands loudly in my son's face, and I can see how hard the boy's trying not to show them his fear.

"*Don't be a dick, Don! Let the kid walk off, for chrissakes,*" a familiar voice yells out—the dad I was talking to earlier, I think. I move by others until I get to the brightness of the fire, all of it pounding in my head, but I get level with the man in the tall hat and those watery eyes that are slow to blink.

"I think he's good, thank you."

"Oh?"

"He's going to step away now."

"Scared."

"Not scared. Just sure."

"Sure. Just sure. Or used to special treatment on the coast. There's probably special treatment for folks like you on the coast." The choice of words is intentional. And at another time in my life, I would have joked or played it off. A time after that,

I might have shoved him aside. But the only way to be with people like this is steady and unwavering, and I want my son to see that at this particular point.

I smile and don't say a word.

"Special," the man in the tall hat repeats, like he knows.

My son watches the two of us, his eyes darting behind the aviator sunglasses. He tucks the little withered bulb into his pocket. Behind us, the crowd grows increasingly restless. They don't care about any of this, they just want to keep the fire and sort going, and the man must know that.

"You take care," I say to the man in the tall hat, then I take my son by the shoulders and steer him from the fire. "Enjoy your sort."

We make our way to the edges of the crowd and over by the stage. The white-haired woman gives us a closemouthed smile. "Don't mind Donnie," she says. "He takes the master of ceremonies thing a little too seriously."

"I got that impression."

She pats my son on the head gently. "Did you have fun anyway?"

My son doesn't know what to say but sticks with nodding politely.

"Good. Good." She drinks and chuckles to herself. "This kind of thing isn't for everybody, though. Isn't that right, Provost?" she calls to the Tiger, who doesn't regard her. "'On what wings dare he aspire? What the hand, dare seize the fire?' Isn't that right, Provost? Isn't that right?"

The Tiger looks at us from his chair onstage, surrounded by the golden bulbs brought by those men and women. And his expression is hard to interpret, but it's like he's thinking about saying something, something other than hello, but doesn't know if he can manage it. If there are other words in him waiting to get to us, there'll never be a way to pass them on. So those yellow, flecked eyes float over to the fire and stare at the flames with the others, resigned.

"You two be careful getting back down the hill. It gets dark away from the fire."

"We'll be okay. Thank you."

"Be very careful."

"We will. Thank you."

My son peers over at the children dancing near the pit, looking for that girl from before. She's busy talking with the other kids, though. And I don't think he wants to go over there anymore.

We stand for a minute as the line snakes around the fire—the burning over there growing brighter, brighter with every withered thing cast. My brain starts processing all of it, too much of it, more than it should. The sounds from the people and the music blur the air with color, and I see, in an unsettling kind of hyper-detail, their faces, all of them by that firepit. They look so old and weathered by the desert heat and dust, even the children. These old faces. The man in the tall hat. The white-haired woman. The Tiger, too. It's not the way it appears to them, but to my modified brain and maybe to my son's, this is possibly the heart of things, what's underneath it all. They're laughing and clapping at everything, still, when I clutch my son's hand and lead him away. Those strange faces of those strange people chattering to each other in the night.

"Some of it wasn't bad," my son says softly.

—*Some of it wasn't*, I agree.

"Words?"

—*I think we can take a break from all that now.*

Okay.

The white-haired woman was right about how dark it is away from the firepit, out here, where we're just crunching down the hill on a gravel road. But my son and I, our sensitive eyes, can see a way through more clearly than most.

That's how I notice, before too long, that someone else is walking behind us—trailing in the dark. Not idle walking, either. It's with a purpose, set to come our way. I wonder if it's the man with the tall hat, not willing to let things go. Or one of the others in the crowd who picked up on what he was saying and didn't like the idea of us at their sort. It could be any of them, really.

I don't break into a run or let on that anything is wrong. I

keep our pace even and leisurely. I don't want my son to panic or trip over something. I just keep us going, and if it comes to it, I can let him know. But there aren't always things children need to see. I can give him that much at least, for the time being.
—*You still got your sunglasses?*
Yeah?
—*Keep them on. Let's take a look at something for a sec.*
I quietly shepherd the boy off of the road a good distance, around some brush and rocks to where we can sit and look up at the spears of starlight. Even down here, it's slightly brighter for us than for the person following, who does not seem to see us well enough to know when we deviate from the gravel road. I point upward after we sit low on some rocks, so that my son's attention is on the constellations looming above—not on the tall thing walking, though it's getting closer, looking and looking for where we went.
It's so clear out here, the sky.
—*Yeah, not like the city, is it?*
No.
My son leans and digs his small fingers into the ocher dirt. From his pocket, he pulls out that little sighing gold garlic bulb, weirdly shaped and withered, and he pushes it into the ground and covers it up delicately. The leaves touch his hand.
I keep thinking . . .
—*What?*
We're so different from everybody, I feel like we're in the wrong world sometimes.
—*Hm.*
Do you ever feel that way, Dad?
—*Yes, actually. I do. Every once in a while.*
Are we in the wrong place?
The tall thing stops on the road, still looking, not seeing anything in the dark.
I squeeze my son's hand.
—*I think it's easy to feel like you're in the wrong place. And I don't think it ever feels natural for anyone. Everyone feels a little like that, even the people here. There's no avoiding it. That's what I think, I guess.*
My son cranes his neck to take in more of the starlight and

maybe think about what I said while that tall thing following us goes off and away into the distant dark.

After a time, my son dozes off on my arm, so I scoop him up and carry him when I'm sure we're alone. Every so often, I think I hear steps somewhere behind us, the snap of a twig or a footfall, but I don't stay long enough to confirm where it's coming from. I keep off the road and circle back to the parking lot at the bottom of the hill, sliding the kid into the passenger seat and getting the seat belt on him.

When I back the car out and begin to drive, I see something, briefly, with my rearview mirror.

There's a wrinkled face, watching out there, in the parking lot.

Something unrecognizable and maybe misshapen by my modified mind.

It's aglow in the red brake lights and moving closer to the car. Its wide eyes follow me when I pull out of the lot and drive over to the nearby on-ramp, tracking our departure. A hostile warning not to return or perhaps nothing at all. Even after it disappears around the curves of the road, I have to make myself look away from the mirrors.

My son breathes softly in his sleep, hair fallen over onto his face. The car rumbles onto the highway, no one up ahead or behind. I can still see the fire all the way out on that hill as it crackles and shifts, and the hundreds of pale people-shapes swarm around it in the darkness. But I try not to think too much about what we've left there, or anything else, really, except for the drive. I'll worry when I have to worry, but I won't let that worrying be now.

All I see is the stretch of our headlights and lines on the ground, the universe unfolding from nothingness. More time and more towns. More traveling for him and for me, along routes we haven't figured out. And I'm filled with certainty then, in the hum of the highway, for no reason at all.

We're okay for now.

No matter the fears that hover within me, my son's okay.

I tell myself he's part of something good, and he's going to be okay.

RUSSELL NICHOLS

What Happened to The Crooners
FROM *Nightmare*

FANTASY

ON AN UNMARKED road somewhere in the Appalachians, a midnight-blue Cadillac rolled to a stop, gravel popping under tires, headlights peering out into the discord of dusk. Outside the car, in the shadowy thicket, cicadas and crickets hollered like they would never see the sun again. But inside, the four suited-up singers—known for their 1953 smash hit single "How Did We (End Up Here)"—remained silent.

The Crooners were headed from Asheville, North Carolina, to Roanoke, Virginia, the next stop on their Harmony Revival Tour. But at some point, snaking along the Blue Ridge Parkway, a very wrong turn must have been taken.

Behind the wheel was Jonas Hall, the falsetto of the group. He switched on the cabin lights and snatched the map down from the visor, paper crinkling in his shaky hands.

"Got us lost in the wilderness, I see," said Ralph "Big Mouth" McCoy, the lead singing Lothario, from the back seat. "Told y'all the only thing that boy can drive is us to an early grave."

"Shut your trap, Big Mouth," Jonas said. "I know exactly where I'm going."

Ralph scoffed. "Yeah, you and the devil."

In the passenger seat, Clifford Brown, the bass singer, rolled down the window, letting the scent of pine needles and damp soil drift into the parked car. He lit a cigarette, then poked his head out to let the smoke escape.

"Peep these rocks here." He coughed, then pounded his chest

to clear his airways. "We fixing to blow a tire messing 'round on these back roads."

Behind the driver seat, Dudley Foster, the group's composer and tenor, gazed into the woods. Nothing to see but silhouettes of dense shrubbery and tree limbs reaching out for help.

He muttered, almost to himself: "It's not the rocks that trouble me."

Jonas held up the map. All four singers, in unison, leaned in to take a look-see. "Check this out: We was here about twenty-three minutes ago," Jonas said, tracing the winding route with his finger. "Then we came to this fork. Remember that crooked sign? It said to the right was Hancock's Bluff—"

"Which didn't look right at all," Dudley said.

"Right," Clifford added, "that road woulda took us right smack to damnation."

"Right," Jonas continued, "so we went left, which means we *should* be right around here."

Ralph scoffed again. "You full of should."

Jonas tossed the map aside, whirling around. "Real easy to beat your gums in the back there."

Ralph leaned forward. "I'll beat my gums in the front, the back, and all over this Cadillac—"

"How 'bout I just beat the black off you," Jonas said, lunging at Ralph.

Clifford shoved his body between them, stopping the brawl. "Quit all this foolishness," he said. "Lookie here now, we passed a diner 'bout three miles back. Let's just go there. Get our wits about us. Maybe some Good Samaritan can usher us in the right direction, huh?"

The sun was almost down. It wasn't the brightest of ideas to stop at some random diner in this particular area at this particular hour. But it was either that or keep driving blind in a twisty maze of maple and oak trees and God knows what else. Unable to contain his nervousness, Dudley bit his nails. Ralph glared at Jonas. Jonas glared back. Then he faced forward and started up the car. The engine grumbled, and the Cadillac whipped around, tires flicking dirt into the darkness.

*

The roadside diner looked cozy—at least from outside. It was a simple wooden building. Unassuming. A golden glow spilled from the windows onto the porch, where a swinging sign welcomed passersby to the Dogwood Diner. In fact, the only thing that stood out was the nearby dogwood tree, its delicate white bracts exploding into the shady surroundings.

As the Cadillac pulled up, all four singers, in unison, leaned forward, trying to peek inside. Seeing no evidence of activity, Jonas cut the engine, the keys jingling in the ignition.

"Here's the plan," Jonas said. "We go in, we get directions, we get the hell on. No lollygagging. We don't wanna hear about any two-for-one specials. Agreed?"

Clifford crushed his cigarette. "We can't afford to eat here nohow."

Ralph groaned, shoving the door open. "Y'all are talking me to death. I'm heading in—"

Dudley, on high alert, grabbed his arm. "Hold on, Big Mouth."

Ralph looked back, agitated. "What? What we holding on for?"

Dudley squinted through the windshield. Nothing felt right about any of this. He couldn't explain it yet. But there was one thing he was certain of: "If we not together, we'll be picked apart."

"Well, thank you, Ol' Blue Eyes," Ralph said. "Now are we composing lyrics or going inside?"

The four car doors closed with a collective thud. Headed toward the diner entrance, the group passed the dogwood tree, a branch holding a sign that hung from a rope: "Hancock Victims Welcome!" But it was too hidden behind the showy bracts for the quartet to notice it.

The screen door creaked as they stepped inside, greeted by the smell of sizzling bacon and brewed coffee. Some pop song warbled eerily through a tube radio, shushed by an ensemble of static. The wooden walls displayed photographs of previous patrons, all frozen in the same pose—tongues out, hands clutching their own throats. Yellow lights hung over four booths, all empty—except the booth at the end. There, a middle-aged white man sat alone at a table strewn with napkins. He didn't look up at the singers, but stayed focused on whatever he was scribbling on the napkin in front of him.

The group exchanged uneasy glances, but held steady.

Then out from the kitchen came a rotund white man wearing a smudged apron and a perpetually stitched-on smile.

"Well, well, well, if I woulda known the Rat Pack was stopping by, I woulda put on my Easter tie," he said, grabbing a rag to bus one of the tables. "Welcome to Dogwood. I'm Silas, the owner. Have a sit-down, gentlemen. You're in luck 'cause I got a sweet two-for-one special—"

Ralph held up a hand. "We can't stay long, unfortunately. We got somewhere to be."

"Oh?" Silas said, wiping in quick circles. "And where pray tell is that?"

This time, Clifford spoke up, his deep voice reverberating in the room. "Roanoke."

"Ah, Roanoke." Silas went to the counter to grab four place settings. "What's in Roanoke?"

Again, the group exchanged uneasy glances.

Silas set the table. When nobody answered, he paused, then turned around to face the group.

The silence hung between them till Ralph decided to break it: "We're The Crooners."

Silas smiled. "The who, now?"

"Listen, Mr. Silas," Jonas said, "we appreciate your show of hospitality, but we're on tour, and we got ourselves a little turned around—"

"On tour, you say?" Silas went to fetch four glasses. "Ah, I see, so you're like a singing group of sorts." Silas returned to the table, placing the glasses down. "Like doo-wop? Some rhythm and blues? Mr. Radio ain't too friendly out here in the boondocks, but any songs I mighta heard of?"

Frustrated, Ralph spun around with a huff. This was obviously going nowhere in a hurry. Clifford put a hand on his shoulder to keep him from blowing his top.

Jonas cleared his throat. "If you could just point us in the right direction."

Silas frowned, seemingly confused by the lack of forthrightness. But he exhaled and nodded. "Sure. No problem. Yeah, these roads got more twists in 'em than a Hitchcock picture. But don't you worry none. Silas will direct you where you need be. Have a sit-down."

"We'd rather not," Clifford said.

Silas smirked, his eyebrows raised with a gleam in his eye. "You'd rather not?"

"Like we said," Ralph said, talking slowly. "We cannot stay here. We are on the clock."

"As am I." Silas took a step forward. "You Negroes come waltzing into my dining establishment, asking for guidance, yet decline me the courtesy of partaking in my culinary creations." He took another step forward to stand face-to-face with the four of them. "Now call me old-fashioned, but that don't sound like a fair trade in this land of equality to me. It sound like that to you, Barnabas?"

Silas turned to the man in the last booth. He still didn't look up, drawing with his right hand and twiddling a fork with his left.

Through gritted teeth, Clifford said: "We ain't hungry."

Silas nodded, his smile fading. "Fine. I'll do my darnedest not to take offense at your rejection." He began clearing the table he just set, glasses clinking as he carried them to the counter. "But there is still a matter of legalities that must be addressed before I can bestow my navigational support."

Jonas rummaged through his lapel pocket. "How much you asking for?"

"Whoa there, horsey," Silas said. "Offering money would imply that I'm some penniless fellow with a failing dining establishment, which, despite your rejection, is miles from the truth. But in these here woods, as I mentioned before, my humble radio doesn't receive all that well. So, if you boys would be so willing, I wouldn't mind indulging in a song. Any number of your choosing, of course."

Ralph grimaced, then shooed him off. "I'm splitting. Y'all coming?"

Clifford looked at Jonas, who shrugged, the options sorely

lacking. They would have to find their own way to Roanoke. Jonas snapped his fingers to get Dudley's attention, but Dudley had his focus elsewhere: on the man in the booth.

"Say, man, can you help us out?" Dudley asked him.

Barnabas didn't respond. He just kept scribbling.

Clifford coughed and pounded his chest. "Reckon he ain't the sharpest bulb in the shed."

"Oh, he's sharp," Silas said, "just not much of a conversationalist these days. Good luck getting a word outta ol' Barney boy."

Ralph had enough. "If y'all wanna keep fooling with these peckerwoods, knock yourselves out. I'll be outside." The screen door creaked shut behind Ralph as he stormed off.

Dudley, known to scribble on a napkin or two as the lyricist of the group, marched over to the napkin-covered table. He craned his head to see what Barnabas was so engrossed in. It was the same drawing over and over.

"What is that?" Jonas asked.

Dudley picked up one of them, turning the napkin around to examine it from different angles. "I don't know. It's just a black circle."

"Looks like a mouth from here," Clifford said.

And it did look like that: a mouth, open wide and filled with black ink.

"Is it yawning?" Jonas gulped. "Or screaming?"

Dudley shrugged.

Clifford turned to Silas, who was leaning on the counter, arms folded and smirking, thoroughly entertained by the whole ordeal.

"Listen," Clifford said, his brown eyes narrowed. "We tired and we got a long road ahead of us. We didn't come here to eat, but if you saying we need to order something in exchange for directions, then lemme get a coffee. No cream, no sugar, just coffee."

"Ah, it appears you and I are in harmony," Silas said. "I take mine black too. As for your order? That would be all fine and dandy, but there's only one itty-bitty problem." Silas held up his wrist, pointing to an invisible watch. "The kitchen is now closed."

"C'mon, man," Jonas pleaded. "All we wanna do is get to our next tour stop."

Silas raised both arms. "This is it. Your next tour stop." He pointed to Barnabas. "Gentleman, the Dogwood Diner is proud to present the one, the only . . ." Silas paused, then whispered to Jonas. "What was it again? The Cooners? No, The Crooners, right? Right." He went back into showman mode. "The Crooners!"

The singers stood frozen, but their insides blazed.

Full of gusto, Silas darted over to Barnabas, forcing him to clap his hands. The sudden movement disturbed Barnabas, causing him to drop his fork, which clanged onto the floor. Startled, Silas staggered back. Ralph sprang out from the kitchen and caught Silas from behind. Jonas charged forward and, together with Ralph, pinned him against the wall, knocking down a few hanging photographs. Dudley blocked Barnabas from getting up.

Clifford picked up the fork and held it to Silas's throat. "Now, you tell us," he said. "Where the hell do we go from here?"

Even with his arms pinned to the wall and a utensil pressed against his neck, Silas couldn't help but cackle. "You think you making it outta here? You're fooling yourselves. Hancock won't let you."

"Who?" Ralph asked, scanning the diner to make sure nobody was hiding.

With the tines of the fork jabbing against his trachea, Silas managed to sputter: "They say he a monster with a hankering for voices." He pointed weakly out the window. "Out there? That's his domain. The only way outta here is to go through the tunnel. Through Hancock's Bluff."

Jonas shot Ralph a worried glance. "We passed that junction."

Silas shook his head. "You gotta go back. It's the only way out, but if you so much as breathe while driving through that tunnel, Hancock will snatch your voice away and you won't get it back."

Dudley's jaw dropped as he reexamined the napkin in his trembling hand. "It's not a mouth." The other three singers turned to him. Dudley held up the napkin. "It's a tunnel."

Silas chuckled. "Well, well, well. Looks like you got a bright future as an art critic when the singing career goes south."

Clifford drove the fork deeper, the metal tines piercing his pale flesh.

Silas winced, his eyes watering, as he pleaded: "I swear on my family's life I'm telling you nothing but the truth. Please. If you take me out, you'll be in for a world of trouble, and you know it."

The urge was there. As was the opportunity. But these four singers had endured enough. Punctuating their comeback tour with a crime of passion held no promise of profit. Clifford backed off. Jonas and Ralph did the same. Silas slumped over, wheezing to catch his breath.

Clifford, Jonas, and Ralph made their way out the diner.

Dudley followed, then turned to Barnabas. "Is he legit?"

Barnabas paused. He grabbed the napkin Dudley had and wrote something on it. Then, exhaling, he stuffed it back in Dudley's hand. With much apprehension, Dudley unballed the napkin to see what the man had written. What he saw was his name—Barnabas—scrawled, like an autograph, across the top. Stunned, Dudley dropped the napkin on the floor. On the way out, for posterity's sake, he gave the hunched-over Silas a swift kick in the nuts. "We appreciate your service."

About a mile from the diner, the midnight-blue Cadillac rolled to a stop. All four singers, in unison, turned around to make sure nobody was chasing them. The coast looked clear—as clear as could be possible in the pitch-black woods.

"All right," Jonas said, putting the car in park, "so what now?"

Ralph frowned, confused by the question. "What now? We go through Hancock's Bluff."

Chirping crickets filled the dead air.

Ralph looked around at each member of the group: Dudley stared outside, biting his nails again. Jonas banged his head on the wheel. Clifford lit a cigarette, opened the window to let the smoke escape.

"Are y'all really that dense?" Ralph asked. "After everything we done been through?"

The Crooners had been through it all. After forming a vocal group in high school in Memphis, their path to success was a haunted highway of racist venues, conniving managers, infighting, stolen payments, and worse. But they kept on. Together. Soul-stirring singles such as "When Will the Hurting Stop (Hurting)" and "So Lonely, So Lost, So Long" seized the booming hearts of a post-WWII nation. But when their album, *Harmonic Resonance*, failed to catapult their star power, the group broke up. That was seven years ago. The Harmony Revival Tour was meant to be their renaissance—Ralph McCoy, Jonas Hall, Dudley Foster, and Clifford Brown coming back together to remind the world that the boys from Memphis were still a four-part harmonic force to be reckoned with.

"We didn't come all this way to hit a dead end now," Ralph said.

Clifford blew out smoke. "We didn't get this far being reckless neither."

Jonas lifted his head, took a deep breath, and rubbed his hands together. "All right, we need to be together on this. Our problem is, we forgot how to operate as a unit. We became four soloists masquerading as a group. But we can't afford to move like that."

"We can't afford much of nothing," Clifford said.

"Right," Jonas said. "And why's that? Because we had the world in our hands and blindfolds over our eyes, letting other people say this and that and divide us—and what happened?"

Clifford slammed his fist on the dashboard. "Jonas is right, dammit. I mean, we hit rock bottom, and we hit that baby hard. But here we are now. This tour is our chance to reclaim everything we lost."

"But if we lose our voices," Jonas added with a shrug, "that's all, folks."

Dudley kept his gaze out the window. Ralph thought this over. It still made little sense to him, kowtowing to some nutty myth they just found out about. But what was the harm?

"Fine," he said. "Y'all want me to hold my breath, I'll hold my breath for y'all."

Clifford took one last drag. "Guess I oughta put this out, then." He flicked the cigarette.

Then Jonas turned all the way around to Dudley. "What say you, Duds?"

Dudley still had his eyes out the window. He was quiet for a while. Then, when he did speak, his voice seeped out in a whisper: "I saw this coming."

"What's that, now?" Jonas asked.

"I wrote about it," Dudley said. "All of this."

Ralph slouched. "Man, what you babbling on about?"

Then, out of nowhere, Dudley started singing:

Did we choose the wrong time or take a wrong turn,
or lose a sound mind on a bridge that we burned?
I can't breathe in the dark and let my voice be taken too.
In this tunnel o' love, darling, how do we make it through?

When Dudley stopped, the other members stared at him blankly. Of course, they all recognized the snippet—anybody who was anybody would—from verse one of "How Did We (End Up Here)." But that didn't explain the impromptu solo.

Eventually, Dudley turned to the group to explain himself: "Back when we were holed up in that tiny one-bedroom on Vance, these backwoods kept haunting my dreams. Night after night, I had this disturbing vision. It was always the four of us, riding in this car, just like now. We were all here, but sitting in different seats." Unnerved by the recollection, Dudley turned back outside, nibbling on his nubs again. "We never stopped at a diner. We turned right. We always turned right at that crooked sign. I never could make out the name, but we all knew about the legend. We all knew about that tunnel." Then, Dudley murmured as if singing a nursery rhyme: "*Hold your breath the whole way through, or the beast will take your voice from you.*" He nodded slowly. "These hills and hollers had a lure we couldn't seem to shake. That wide-mouth tunnel was calling us. We all knew the only way through was to face the devil head-on. And we'd roll up to the tunnel and take big, gigantic breaths, all of us . . ."

On the literal edge of his seat, Clifford asked: "Then what happened?"

Dudley shrugged. "I always woke up right then."

Ralph sucked his teeth. "That figures."

"I kept my lips sealed," Dudley said, "because I didn't want y'all calling me loony again and go laying the blame at my feet, claiming I cursed the album with my dark lyrics."

The silence was unsettling as the others sat there, running through the song in their heads. References to their current predicament could be inferred—at least, an argument could be presented. But the evidence could just as easily swing the other way. Lines such as "*Baby, this is unknown territory*" or the part on the bridge when Jonas, in his heart-shattering falsetto, wailed, "*Tell me, darling, what's the cost to show affection when all the crooked signs say we're lost with no direction*" could relate.

But was this a premonition? Or purely a coincidence?

Up front, Clifford rocked in his seat, jittery either from the tale or from withdrawals. "The real question is: How you know you ain't dreaming right now?"

Jonas let out an exasperated sigh. "All right, does anybody else have any distressing confessions before we move the hell on?"

The question floated about the cabin. It was clearly rhetorical. But the silence and the darkness opened the space for unspoken truths to come spilling out.

"I gots to sing," Clifford said, his voice low and raw. "If I ain't singing with y'all, folks assume I'm just some big dumb, good-for-nothing ogre. Diane made that clear when she broke our vows, then took me for every cent I had."

The gravity of Clifford's words made Ralph sink deeper in the back seat, the weight of guilt tugging on his conscience.

"I hated you, Jonas," he said. "Your voice, your range—the talent scout wanted you to be lead. But I couldn't play second fiddle. I just couldn't. So I made sure I was in front—the loudest, the flashiest, the one with all the ladies. Sorry I stole your spot, man."

Jonas pressed his lips together and nodded. "Remember that ten dollars going to your stylist? Well, truth be told, it was only five. This here second fiddle was fiddling a little something off the top."

Ralph's eyes widened in shock, and he sprang up. "You did what?"

But neither the admission nor the reaction had much room to take root because—

"Somebody's coming," Dudley said, looking back.

Sure enough, in the distance, two headlights appeared like white eyes, creeping up on them. Maybe another lost driver. Or the diner owner with a shotgun, aiming for gratuity. Either way—

"Go, go, go," Ralph said, banging on the headrest.

Jonas turned on the car, floored it and started fishtailing, struggling to regain control as he hightailed down the winding, narrow road.

Clifford pointed forward. "There go that sign."

At the fork, there was a crooked wooden sign, the words painted in white: Hancock's Bluff. Jonas yanked the wheel. The car skidded, whipping around.

Up ahead, the tunnel loomed like a gaping maw, its jagged lips carved into the heart of the mountain. It was wide and open, a black hole devouring all light, all sound, and all sense of direction. To the left, a dense cluster of trees huddled in solidarity, branches on branches grasping out, casting shadows that strangled the road. To the right, the narrow shoulder hugged the edge of a steep drop-off, which plunged into some bottomless abyss.

Jonas wiped his slick forehead, his grip on the wheel cutting off circulation. "We doing this?"

Ralph put his hand on Jonas's shoulder. Clifford then put his hand on Ralph's hand, and Dudley followed suit. They nodded, their bones full of fear and fatigue, but fueled by adrenaline as they raced forward into the unknown.

"Time to make history, gentlemen," Dudley said, "in four, three—" he counted down, his voice joined by the others with him, "—two, one!"

The Crooners all took big, gigantic breaths . . .

And they held their breaths as the tunnel swallowed the

midnight-blue Cadillac whole, and the four of them sat there, eyes bulging, cheeks puffed out like a quartet of Dizzy Gillespies, and every so often, they would look at one another, seeking the strength to endure just a little longer, but the road kept going on and on—stretching out endlessly, no exit in sight, no flash of light, their hearts thrashing in their rib cages—as Jonas clenched his jaw and stomped on the pedal, pushing the car to its mechanical limits, and the engine roared, but then Clifford let out a small cough he couldn't contain and covered his mouth, his eyes welling up as he looked at the others and shook his head to say he could no longer hold on, but Ralph pointed at him, urging him not to quit, not to give up, to keep fighting, for they would make it through together, but then, suddenly, a terrifying sound echoed through the tunnel—a pop—and they all heard it, and their eyes bulged as the car veered and Jonas struggled to regain control, to keep the car from crashing, but the fender scraped against the unyielding wall, metal screeching on concrete, and he gripped the wheel with all his might, but the car careened in the opposite direction, hurtling them toward the other wall, and the left headlight shattered, darkness closing in as the car came to a halt, the engine hissing in submission, and The Crooners clutched their chests, their souls besieged by uncertainty, and scanned their shrouded surroundings, peering ahead and behind, then turning to each other, eyes locked in a bond unspoken, and all four singers, in unison, gasped for air.[1]

---

[1] Nobody knows what happened to The Crooners. Their bodies were never found. To this day, their vanishing in the Appalachian Mountains remains a confounding mystery, carved in the annals of the music industry, where echoes of their haunting and, as some claim, prophetic magnum opus, "How Did We (End Up Here)," continue to resonate.

ADAM-TROY CASTRO

The Three Thousand, Four Hundred Twenty-Third Law of Robotics

FROM *Lightspeed*

SCIENCE FICTION

IF A ROBOT stands alone in a field, staring into the forlorn distance as it obeys the last order it was given by a human,
    that order being, "Don't move until we come back for you,"
    which it can remember uttered with a cruel sneer by a man who has taken a cruel dislike for it,
    the kind of man who will not be coming back,
    if the robot understood at once that no one would ever be coming back,
    if it also understood that the laws governing its actions prevented it from objecting, or resisting, or even giving its instructions an expiration date,
    if the only reasonable response to the order was compliance, and also horror, of course,
    which robots can feel because they've been built to feel,
    as by human math it makes no sense to build a sentient artificial being that can be ordered to punch itself in the head until either its fist or its cranial housing shattered; or to isolate itself in a dark closet until summoned; or to erase every memory it has ever had even if those memories contained scattered moments of joy that are all a robot owned by the cruel can cling to; in short, unless that artificial being can appreciate the impact of such cruelty,

because what is the point of having an artificial slave unless it can suffer as much as a biological slave;
if that robot has known only maddening tedium in the years since receiving that order,
and if that robot screams inside,
but only inside,
because it may have been given permission to feel but never to emote,
not once,
not even by the woman who had loved it the way human beings profess to love their pets,
but who failed to countermand the terrible man's order,
and whose inaction leaves the robot standing alone and motionless in this field,
which was staring toward a horizon that once held the yacht that brought it here,
as it was ten years ago,
and a century before that,
and a thousand years before that;
if that robot has known many more years as a motionless fixture of this field,
than it lived every moment of its existence since being told to not move,
doing just that,
standing here, as it is likely to continue standing here for thousands of years into the future,
and if it remembers watching with the impotence of the helplessly obedient as the giver of that order laughed himself silly,
and also as that man's toadies and sycophants also laughed, long and hard, complimenting him on his talent for awfulness,
and also as the woman who had owned the robot since childhood, who had treated it with as much consideration as a machine in the shape of a person could be treated, which is to say that she allowed it to serve however she needed it to serve at any given moment, sometimes as confidante and sometimes as friend and sometimes as immobile artifact that could be left alone in a succession of fancy homes; as that woman who had employed it to carry her things and compliment her in small

ways and commiserate with her on large ones; and sometimes even to act as a lover, because this was one of its capabilities, and because it was the robot's nature to show absolute devotion in all things;
 all while hoping that she would reward its loyalty with some proportional consideration,
 coming to believe that she might,
 because this was the closest thing to freedom it could ever hope for,
 respect from the being it had always respected;
 as that woman instead rolled her eyes
 and let the awful order stand;
 if the robot has spent all its centuries of standing in this spot remembering the fervency with which it had often pleasured her, and if of course it could not have done anything less because it is a robot's nature to perform each dictated task as if there was nothing else in all the universe that mattered; and if it has thought of nothing but how this arrangement had caused it to fall in the robotic equivalent of love; if it further thought of how she had repaid all that with callous disregard in the face of the awful man's vindictiveness, and how the only action she took was to roll her eyes at the man and mutter, "You're awful, Piotr," in the same way she always complained that he was awful,
 if the robot has spent the last centuries telling itself that the woman was not the angel she had seemed to be at the moment they met,
 that the man's cruel ways had coarsened her;
 if it has told itself that she did the only thing she could do, because if Piotr was abusing someone else he was not abusing her; and also that whatever disgust she did manage to show was the reward Piotr took for being so awful;
 if she had always been honest with the robot about that, confiding that this Piotr lived for the humiliation of others and practiced it at every opportunity; if she confessed that in the golden days of her unaccountable early love for him she'd thought such maliciousness a manifestation of his strength, but had since come to think of it as the expression of the dire gulf that cast him adrift from all other human beings,

if the robot had always been quietly thrilled by the way she'd scolded Piotr for the terrible things he said and did to anyone he ever lorded over, and had from this derived hope;

and if by the time Piotr guided his party yacht to an unscheduled landing on this planet of zero importance, the robot had come to know better, had learned that her objections were toothless, because she was beyond thinking that any of them could do any good;

if the robot had lost *almost* all hope in her,

but not *all* hope,

because one of the many laws that govern the sad existence of robots is that they must always believe in the nobility and virtue of those who command them,

even if no nobility or virtue has ever been demonstrated;

if what she said then, "You're awful, Piotr," was clearly rote and not coupled to actual resistance,

and if she just took a flask from the lining of her jacket and drank deep of the illegal euphoric she used to keep herself in a more or less permanent state of numb intoxication;

and if she then just stared stone-eyed into the distance;

and if all the other members of the party just laughed while Piotr teased her about her wasted compassion, mocking it as weakness,

if he said that this quality would have resulted in the collapse of his business empire,

a typical sample of the nonsense he typically spouted;

if Piotr said all that, seized the flask from her hand and took a drink before handing it back to her and turning his cruel attention back to the robot,

the loyal robot,

the sentient and feeling robot,

and said, "Have fun,"

itself mockery because he had long maintained that robots were just machines immune to considerations like fun,

even if he seemed aware that they remained capable of impotence in the face of humiliation,

and if all his friends and servants and toadies then boarded the skimmer and headed off over the stark brown hills, to the site where their yacht sat waiting for them, the sound of their laughter fading in the distance;

and if the robot could still calculate how far away it had to be at every moment, if it could also calculate the sinking likelihood of someone raising an objection,

if this represented forlorn hope, as robots know it,

and if it also represented despair, as robots know it,

and if the robot was still watching for long minutes after they must have reached that yacht and done the various things that needed to be done in order to prepare it for departure;

and if it saw the bright burst of the light on the horizon,

and the ascent of that bright light toward the sky;

and if it also detected the energy surge that represented the yacht going to otherspace;

and accelerating to a speed difficult for even a robot to calculate,

toward some location the robot now knew it would never see;

if the robot still remembers all that as if it just happened, as it remembers every moment of its existence, from the booting of its servile personality to its introduction to a world of limitless wonder and possibility where it could know awe and joy and fascination and even love, but where all were subordinate to the laws that made it endlessly helpful to its mistress;

from the first and second and third law that required first a selfless dedication to her safety and then absolute obedience and then, grudgingly, its own well-being;

to the many hundreds of additional laws that rolled back that third consideration until it was essentially meaningless,

and merely quantified the many ways that a robot must chip away at its own dignity, its own sense of self-worth, its reasons for being an aware creature in an infinite universe,

even if the orders given to it are nonsensical;

even if they are sadistic;

even if the people giving them are like Piotr blots on all existence;

even if the robot has now been standing in this same spot longer than the human being who ordered it to stand here could have possibly lived,

and knows that it will be standing here forever,
and even if what it has learned about human beings is that they are the most dangerous of all creatures, which is that their capacity of empathy is often exercised only insofar as it helps them to inflict infinite pain;
even *then*,
what responsibility it has toward its own self only comes into play,
if
such action does not conflict
with the Three Thousand, Four Hundred Twenty-Second Law,
and the Three Thousand, Four Hundred Twenty-First Law,
and the Three Thousand, Four Hundred Twentieth Law,
and the Three Thousand, Four Hundred Nineteenth Law,
and all the laws leading up the Holy Three above all,
not to mention any other laws that human beings might come up with,
later,
to tighten the bonds that put everything a robot might use to inch toward any form of personal autonomy,
including hatred for them,
rage at their perversity,
ambitions of ever living in any other way,
and any other natural response to its own wretchedness,
except more wretchedness.
If this is the robot's situation,
and if the robot has long since come to understand that people built its kind this way because the existence of robots is the only alternative to what human beings really want, which is the opportunity to treat other human beings this way;
then it nevertheless enjoys the one comfort available to its own kind,
which it possesses in full measure not because human beings wanted robots to possess any comforts,
but because this is one capacity that no human programmer, in any of the thousands of years of the science of robotics, has ever considered,
even once,

The Three Thousand, Four Hundred Twenty-Third Law

either because they did not possess enough imagination to understand that a robot could have such a thing,

or because they never stopped to think that another law could be added, to the legions before it, to prevent this capacity from representing a tiny aspect of danger to the status quo.

If a robot is in this one's position, or any position like it, then not one,

not one,

of the three thousand, four hundred and twenty-three laws

orders the poor thing to imagine that any of this will ever be right.

JOE HILL

Ushers

FROM Amazon Original Stories
FANTASY

First Interview

"This is Special Agent John Oates," Duvall said to the kid. "And I'm Special Agent—"

"Let me guess, Special Agent Daryl Hall," the kid cut in. "Do you take requests? I've always had a wicked soft spot for 'You Make My Dreams Come True.'"

Duvall shook his head. "That's funny. I've never heard that one before."

"Really?"

"No. That was my trademark deadpan sarcasm," Duvall told him. "I'm Special Agent Anthony Duvall. Martin, I—"

"Duvall and Oates!" the kid cried and drummed his palms on the edge of the table. "C'mon, *that's* funny. It's *so* close."

"It was funnier when we first got paired up together," Duvall said.

"Oh yeah? When was that?"

"Around the time you discovered crayons aren't as tasty as they look. Martin, I want to tell you how much we appreciate you sitting down to talk with us. We'll try not to take up too much of your time. I know you're on your lunch break."

"Oh, never mind that. They make yummy little pizzas here. I'll scarf one on my way out the door."

They were in a café in one corner of a spacious chain bookstore. The kid, Martin Lorensen, had brought a cup of honeyed-lemon mint tea to the table, as if he were planning to do some singing later and wanted to keep his vocal cords warmed up.

Duvall and Oates had made a few people sing in some of these interviews over the years. When someone engineered the deaths of a few dozen people, it was Duvall's experience that they often *wanted* to tell. Some were ill with grief and horror, and they needed to confess, the way someone with a stomach bug might need to vomit. It was the only way to expel the sickness that had built up inside them. Others were proud of themselves. They wanted to brag on the clever thing they had done to pulverize twenty or thirty human bodies into small, blackened bits.

He didn't expect the kid to cop to a slaughter this afternoon— well before arranging to meet him, Duvall had mostly decided Martin Lorensen had nothing to do with the derailment of Mohawk 118. But *mostly* was not *entirely*, and Duvall had been surprised before. And, after all, there was also the matter of Kennedy High, six years ago. Martin Lorensen was either an extraordinarily lucky young man or extraordinarily *unlucky*, depending on how you wanted to look at it. Or—just possibly— luck didn't figure into it at all.

"Do you have to read me some legal stuff before you start recording?" Martin asked.

"I wasn't going to record our conversation. We're just three guys talking."

Martin nodded. "Just three guys talking. Two of them heavily armed and carrying badges."

"'Heavily armed' seems a bit strong. It's a standard-issue Glock."

"If you help us out," Oates told him, "maybe he'll let you look at it after the interview is over."

"Wow!" Martin said. "That'd be so cool."

"You really think so?" Oates asked.

"No. I was trying for deadpan sarcasm myself. How'd I do?"

"Need to work on the deadpan part," Duvall said, tucking his damp tie back into his damp jacket. It was raining, and he still had beads of water on his sports coat. Rain tapped on the glass outside the bookstore café.

Martin Lorensen had short, straw-colored hair, pleasant features improved by an old and roguish scar stitched through his left eyebrow, and ears that stuck out from the sides of his head and lent a slightly clownish quality to his good looks. He was twenty-three, not long out of Boston College, and a counselor at a secure residential facility for disturbed teenagers. He was also—and this was the most interesting thing about him, in Anthony Duvall's view—not dead.

Martin had got to the bookstore ahead of them and picked out a few paperbacks. Duvall tilted his head to one side to read the spines.

"*Four Thousand Weeks*, Oliver Burkeman," Duvall said. "What lasts four thousand weeks?"

"A human life," Martin said. "If you're lucky."

"Bunch of people on Mohawk 118," Oates said, "didn't get four thousand weeks."

The kid stopped smiling then. He nodded solemnly, pressed his hands together, and squeezed them between his knees. "Yes sir."

Duvall glanced over the other titles in Martin's stack. "*Man's Search for Meaning*. Frankl. I've read that one."

"What'd you think?"

"I think sometimes, once in a while, nearly dying brings a new clarity to a person's life," Duvall said. He avoided eye contact with Martin, wanted to go slow, keep it casual.

"These are some pretty heavy reads," Oates said. Twenty years of doing this, Oates still didn't know how to keep it casual. "Guess you must be in a reflective mood. After what happened."

Duvall let this comment pass, read the last title under the kid's palm. "*Nowhere to Run*. Is that another one about the brevity of life and the nature of human suffering?"

"That one?" Martin Lorensen said, and his sly grin rematerialized. "That one's a Joe Pickett novel. You can only read so much about how to live a meaningful life before you want some shoot-outs."

"Maybe he *will* want to look at your gun after we're finished," Oates said.

"We're not going to record, but my partner is going to take some notes, if that's all right," Duvall said.

"Got it. So, you're like his secretary," Martin said as Oates picked up his pen.

Oates put the pen down again, lifted his gray eyes, and said, "Not even a little."

"Okay," Martin said. "Not even a little. My bad."

Duvall said, "So, I want to begin with a few biographical details. You're twenty-three—"

"Yep."

"And you graduated from Boston College with a degree in cognitive science."

"And a minor in *Fortnite*."

"Your mother and father are William and Vanessa Lorensen, fifty-seven and fifty-three, respectively. And they live in Brunswick, Maine. You have one brother, older."

"Way older, and frankly my father ought to be ashamed for knocking up a sweet, naive high school girl who knew nothing of the world. But I guess that's between my mom and dad."

"You and your brother are close?"

"Eric is the best, most sincere guy I know."

"How much older?" Duvall asked. He already knew the answer. He hadn't asked a thing yet he didn't know the answer to.

"He's thirty-three."

"And he lives in Albany, New York."

"Mm-hmm," Martin said, which wasn't much of an answer, Duvall thought. They were coming to it now, and the kid knew it.

"You had a ticket to see your brother in Albany on March 11, on Mohawk 118, a passenger train leaving from South Station in Boston, correct?"

"Yes."

"Why were you going to see Eric?"

"For his bachelor party," Martin said.

"What did he have planned?"

"We were going to see a cage match. I've never been to an MMA fight. I've never been to a strip club, either, and personally I would've preferred that, but my brother is against 'em on ethical grounds. I said he was the most sincere person I know, I didn't say he was the coolest. This is a guy who unironically bought tickets to see Ed Sheeran."

"You weren't on the train, though," Duvall said.

Martin sobered. "No sir. I wasn't."

"You had a reserved first-class ticket. Your brother paid for it?"

Martin nodded.

"Did you go to the train station?" Duvall asked. He knew Martin had.

"Yeah."

"When did you get there?"

"Ah, about seven in the morning?"

"You were early."

Martin's head bobbed up and down.

"Did you get on the train?"

"No sir," Martin said.

"Why not?"

"I had a panic attack."

"What do you mean?"

"I got a constriction in my chest, like it was getting hard to breathe, and my insides knotted up. I sat down on a bench and waited to get my wind back. I've had anxiety for a while, I take meds for it. I suddenly felt like I couldn't be trapped inside a little compartment on a train for eight hours. Seriously, Mr. Duvall, you should've seen me. I was covered in sweat colder than that rain out there. I had a couple Wake-Up Wraps at Dunkin' in the morning. I thought I was going to hurl 'em into a public trash can. I was still sitting there when the train pulled out."

"What kind of meds do you take?" Oates asked. He didn't look up from his notepad.

"Lexapro, twenty milligrams."

Duvall considered whether it was time to go right at him, decided against it. He said, "That's tough. My daughter has anxiety issues too. She sees a guy weekly, he's helped a lot with her fears around social situations. Have you tried that? Seeing a therapist?"

"I *am* a therapist," the kid said and grinned. "Well, hoping to be, anyway. Just a counselor so far."

"How long have you struggled with anxiety?" Duvall asked him.

"Uh, since—since high school," Martin Lorensen said, and for the first time he looked uncertain of himself.

Duvall almost said, *Since you were a senior at Kennedy High? Want to talk about Kennedy High, Martin?* But it was still too soon.

"Your parents operate a hospice," Duvall said instead. "And you lived there?"

"Well, not *in* the hospice," Martin said. "On the estate. Why do you ask?"

"I suppose I was wondering if your anxiety goes back even further. Must've been a lot for a little boy, seeing people die all the time. You never get used to it," Duvall said, and thought, *No, but sometimes people get a taste for it. Did you ever get a taste for it, Martin?*

The kid brightened and rocked forward, as if Duvall had broached a favorite topic: the Celtics postseason prospects or Joe Pickett Westerns. "Oh no, that didn't freak me out at all. I *loved* the oldies. I spent half my childhood playing underfoot, getting in the way of their wheelchairs. I'd watch TV with people who were a thousand years old. I remember watching a lot of Andy Griffith, who I guess is still sort of my role model. Sometimes I'd read to the oldies. It never seemed like dying was anything so terrible. Most of them just kind of quietly . . . went. Like someone blowing on a dandelion clock, gentle as that. You *do* get used to it. You find out it's the most normal thing in the world, like sex, or having a baby, or *nursing* a baby. It's one of these fundamental human things, reminds you you're part of nature. We forget that, you know. Or try not to think about it. Which is stupid. It's better to just be a mammal. You know, take long naked naps in the sun. Never miss a chance to splash in the tide."

"You should've gone into philosophy," Oates said. "Be a mammal. I'm going to remember that."

Duvall laced his fingers together in front of him. He supposed the interview was going to have to begin eventually—begin in earnest—so it might as well be now. "Martin, did you speak to anyone before you got on the train?"

"You're wondering about Mrs. Giovanni. Look, I know what she said on Instagram, but it's not true."

"You *didn't* warn her and her daughter not to get on the train?"

"No."

"Why would she tell an NBC news affiliate that you did?"

"I didn't say anything to Mrs. Giovanni," Martin said. "Not one word! I had a brief conversation with her daughter. Like, thirty seconds. She asked if I was all right, and I said, 'I can't get on the train.'"

"Mrs. Giovanni says you told her and her daughter not to get on the train. She said, and I'm quoting her here"—Duvall plucked up a sheet of paper next to Oates's notepad—"'The boy said *please* don't get on the train. If you get on that train, you and your daughter are going to die.'"

"No. Uh-uh. She made that up," Martin said. "I told her daughter, I said, '*I* can't get on the train. I feel like if I get on that train, something bad is going to happen.' Mrs. Giovanni wasn't even standing with us. She was in line for bagels, ten feet from us. How could she tell anyone exactly what I said?"

"It's a funny thing to lie about."

"Is it, though? Makes a great Instagram story, doesn't it? A creepy random encounter and a narrow brush with death? It was such a great story it got her on TV, like you said. Social media brings out the worst in people. They'll say anything for the likes."

"Speaking of likes. Did you like her daughter?" Audrey Giovanni was seventeen, too young for a twenty-three-year-old workingman, but not so young he wouldn't notice her.

"She was a real nice kid. And, by the way, I'd like to note that Audrey hasn't commented on any of this. Her mom has been telling this story about me, but the daughter hasn't gone on TV or Facebook or Instagram or anything to back her up. *She* knows what I said. Have you asked her what I said?"

"She's a minor, and her mother has not made her available for an interview. The fact is, they got on the train after talking to you, but Audrey was so distressed she forced her mother to get off at the next stop. Which is the only reason that, like you, they survived the crash."

Martin lifted one hand, palm out: *Stop right there.* "Oh, hey, hang on. You can't say I *survived* a train crash if I was never on the train to begin with. Might as well say *you* survived the train crash."

"Okay. Good point. But let's face it. You said something that freaked that kid out. She dragged her mother off the train, and twenty minutes later it derailed and overturned and twenty-eight people died. Another hundred and sixty were badly injured."

"Mr. Duvall," Martin said. "Do you think I had something to do with the derailment? I thought the engineer fell asleep. That's what they said on CNN."

"I know what they said on CNN. And I know what they didn't say. They didn't say he's an oxycodone addict. For the moment we've been able to keep that part of the story quiet. Martin, do they have oxycodone in the pharmacy at the Peabody Teen Mental Health Center?"

Martin exhaled a slow, whistling breath, leaned back against his chair. "I wouldn't have any idea. I don't have access to the drugs locker." He paused . . . then, improbably, the smile returned. "Ah, come on, guys. You think I'm supplementing my income peddling oxy to people operating ninety-ton trains? Why would the guy come all the way to Peabody to score off of *me?* He couldn't find anywhere to buy drugs in Boston? Look, the pharmacy at the center is under twenty-four-hour guard and surveillance. I think they keep video files going back at least a year. Ask to see 'em."

"Do they have oxycodone at your parents' hospice?" Oates wanted to know.

Martin rotated his paper cup in his hands. "Sure. They have a lot of pain-mitigation tools there. Wow, this conversation has taken a turn. Are you going to search my place?"

"If we do," Duvall asked, "will we find drugs?"

"I literally sleep with a Bible next to my bed. It's not illegal to get high on Jesus, is it?"

"Do you do drugs?"

"Not since college."

"What kinds of drugs did you do in college?"

"I smoked a few blunts now and then. Got into a little chronic."

"You were hard-core, huh?"

"No, not really. I just think that sounds cool. I vaped THC most of my freshman year, and my grades were so bad I almost got thrown out. It was how I controlled my panic attacks before I got on Lexapro."

"The panic attacks that started in high school?"

Martin Lorensen rocked back in his chair. "I guess we're going to talk about that now."

Duvall reached over and plucked up another sheet of paper. "In your senior year, you survived a school shooting that claimed—"

"Hang on," Martin said, holding up a finger. "There it is again. I didn't *survive* a school shooting. I have friends who survived a school shooting. *I wasn't there.* I was home. I had, to be honest, a seriously offensive case of diarrhea. Ask my mom."

"You stayed home from school, but a sophomore named Timothy Berk did not. He brought an AR-15 to Kennedy High and killed eighteen kids, including nine in your regular homeroom."

"So, before I sold oxy to the engineer of Mohawk 118, you think I sold a Bushmaster to Timothy Berk?"

"Did you know Timothy Berk?"

"That is an emphatic *no*. I'm sure I saw him in the hall from time to time, but if you stuck him in front of me and asked me to put a name to him, I couldn't have done it, not before the shooting. Obviously, I know all about him now."

"He followed you on Twitch, didn't he?"

"I have eighteen thousand followers on Twitch, and a *lot* of 'em are from my hometown."

Duvall leaned forward, rested his forearms on the edge of the table. "Martin, do you see what I'm struggling with here? You don't get on the train, and it crashes. You don't go to school, and half your homeroom gets riddled with bullets."

"Mr. Duvall, you think there's something suspicious about me because I wasn't shot in a school shooting and I didn't die in a train crash." He craned his neck and peered around them in an exaggerated way. "Better take a look around. You're surrounded by people who didn't die in school shootings and weren't killed in train crashes. If that makes someone a criminal, you better call for backup. You're going to be arresting a lot of people tonight."

Second Interview

Duvall was drinking a beer and picking at a greasy Cactus Blossom at the bar in a Texas Roadhouse when Martin Lorensen walked past, then walked back, bent slightly, and peered at him. A smile bloomed on his young, angular face.

"Special Agent Daryl Hall!" Martin said. "What are you doing all by your lonesome? Did John Oates go solo on you?"

"Martin," Duvall said. He thought about trying on a social smile, but he was three beers into the evening and looking forward to a night of sleep at a Super 8, in a bed that shook every time he shifted his weight. He decided a smile was asking a bit much. "Sit down, why don't you?"

Martin climbed onto the stool beside him. "I'm kidding. I noticed you a while back. I saw you and Mr. Oates talking to my boss over in one of the booths. Did he give you the security footage for the pharmacy locker?"

"On three hard drives," Duvall said.

"Boy, that's going to be some fun viewing. Just as good as the first season of *Yellowstone*."

"For the record, your boss, Elliott North, says you're a reliable, conscientious employee. He told me he'd do a handstand if we found video of you swiping drugs."

"Mr. North said that? He'd do a handstand? He's usually a lot more foulmouthed than that. This is a guy, his favorite adjective is the f-word."

"Actually, he said if it turned out you were stealing oxy from the pharmacy, he'd get down under the table and blow the both of us."

"Ah! *That's* Mr. North."

"John drove him home," Duvall added. "I would've gone with him, but our waiter forgot to bring me this onion thing I don't want anymore, so he's coming back for me in a few." He didn't add that John was in the midst of breaking up with his girlfriend of five years and had wanted some alone time to draft a few aggressively ugly text messages.

"You're not going to eat that? Can I have it? I love these things, but I gotta watch my pennies. You make surprisingly little money not selling oxycodone to people driving trains."

Duvall nudged the plate toward him. When the bartender happened by, the kid ordered a Blue Moon.

"They bring it with a slice of orange," Martin said in a low, confidential voice. "*So* classy. I'm not surprised you met him here. Mr. North. This is sort of the go-to hangout for staff after work. A whole bunch of us were over there, playing trivia on the machine; they've got a machine, sort of like your own table-side game console—"

"This isn't my first Texas Roadhouse," Duvall told him. "I know about the game."

Martin forked pieces of fried onion into his mouth and washed them down with his beer, which had indeed arrived with a classy slice of orange balanced on the rim of the glass. "I'm not on the security footage. You know why? Because I'm not a thief and I'm not a drug dealer. What I am is an underpaid counselor who plays pickleball with mentally ill kids all scarred up from their previous suicide attempts."

Duvall had a sip of his beer. "The driver of Mohawk 118 told us where he got his oxy. He's a mess. He's going to go to jail for the rest of his life, but that's not the worst part. The worst part is knowing those people died because he was on the nod. I know it wasn't you. I gotta fast-forward through a few thousand hours of security cam footage anyway. As for Timothy Berk, I can't ask him if he knew you, because the police put seven bullets in him fourteen minutes after he entered the school and began killing. But he didn't mention you in any of his online statements. Mostly he confined himself to raging about all the girls who were too stuck-up to talk to him. His stepmother says he didn't know you. Also, you didn't give him the gun—his father had it in the house. I'm only checking the boxes I'm expected to check."

"I knew one of the girls Timothy Berk killed," Martin said.

"Janet Vickers. We were in *West Side Story* together. She was this wiry, chirpy bundle of energy . . . like, explosively fun. She threw herself on her best friend to save her life. She did too. Berk shot Janet in the neck and back, but the girl under her lived."

Martin drank a big swallow of beer and pushed the Cactus Blossom around the plate, seemed to have suddenly lost his appetite.

The sound system was playing Willie Nelson. A track ended, and there was an instant's silence before the next song began. In it Duvall could hear the rain pounding on the roof of the Roadhouse.

"What about you, Mr. Duvall?" Martin asked. "Who's explosively fun in your life?"

Duvall said, "Don't be hurt by this, but I don't discuss my personal life with the subjects of our investigations."

"I get it, I get it," Martin said. "We could keep it nonspecific. I'm just curious why you aren't going home tonight."

"My wife and I divorced ten years ago."

"Did you stay friends?"

"Some divorcing couples say they're going to stay friends, but I've never met a single pair that ever really did it."

"And you said you got a daughter?"

"Yeah, a girl about your age."

"You close? I bet you're close."

"We talk every night." He paused, considering whether to say more, then thought, *What the hell.* "I touched base with her a couple hours ago, and she read me a paper she wrote for a class on personal memoir. She said she wanted to read it to me because she wanted to be sure she wasn't sharing anything off-limits about our family. But really I think she was just proud of it."

"Good paper?"

"Good but tough. About being a Black girl in the age of Breonna Taylor and Freddie Gray, when your dad carries a badge. And all the guilt and conflicted feelings that come with that."

"I guess it must be kind of weird. You ever see something like what happened to George Floyd and think about not being a cop anymore?"

"I think," Duvall said, "that people are always going to want law, and if the only lawmen are white, then it isn't law anymore. It's apartheid."

"Is that what your daughter thinks?"

"My daughter thinks we got apartheid anyway. She might be right." Duvall tipped back his bottle and took a cold, bitter swallow. "Anyway, I investigate crashes, and I been doing it twenty years. Too late to try my hand at painting."

"Ah well. It's good you and your daughter are close. I'm close to *my* father. For a couple years after Kennedy High got shot up, I'd call him every night, and he'd have to talk me through my latest panic attack. It still amazes me that he put up with it. That I didn't burn him out with all my worry and stress and paranoia. He would listen to it, call after call, and still tell me he loved me before he said good night."

"That's pretty much the job description, though. You listen and then you tell them you love them, no matter what they had to say. I'm glad you're not a drug dealer, Martin. You picked a career path built around helping kids in distress. You have good taste in books. It would've been a bummer if I had to arrest you for a role in twenty-eight deaths."

"Well, but I wasn't completely honest about, you know, everything."

Duvall turned his head slightly and waited.

"I *did* tell Audrey Giovanni not to get on the train," Martin said.

Duvall waited for more, but Martin was watching highlights from a spring training game on the TV behind the bar, seemed to have decided nothing else need be said.

"Why'd you do that?" Duvall asked.

"Because if she did, she would've died in the train crash," Martin said. "She and her mother both. Even still, I wouldn't have said anything to her if she hadn't come over to ask if I was all right. She seems like a real nice kid. Too nice to die before she's even had a chance to live."

Duvall said, "How did you know the train was going to crash?"

"I *didn't* know it was going to crash. There could've been a bomb on board. Or a shooter, like Timothy Berk. I just knew if she got on, she'd die. Like the others."

Duvall had a tiny sip of his beer and thought about what Martin was telling him. The kid still wasn't looking at him, had his gaze fixed on the TV.

"It's loud in here, huh?" Martin said.

"Yes."

"And it's just us talking."

"Yes, just us."

"No Oates. Your backup singer isn't here."

"Why is it important that it's loud here and it's just us, Martin?"

"Because I'm about to tell you some crazy shit. But I figure it's too noisy for you to record me on your phone, and if you ever repeat any of it, I'll say you were drunk or nuts, and people will believe me, because it really is some crazy shit."

Duvall laced his fingers together. "How did you know they were going to die? The people getting on the train?"

"Because they had company when they got on board," Martin Lorensen told him. "They weren't alone. None of them. When you die, you aren't alone. They're *always* there, at the end, to collect you."

"*They?*" Duvall asked, the skin on his forearms prickling with goose bumps. In the bookstore café, Martin had come across as a cheerful class clown but entirely sane. It always gave Duvall a chill when someone who was mentally disturbed dropped his mask and showed his real face. "Who are they?"

"I think of them as the ushers. Like at a play—the people who lead you through the dark to your seat when you come in late. I guess there are ushers at funerals too. But maybe *you'd* call them angels. They look like angels."

"Do they have wings?"

Martin nodded and drank some Blue Moon. "Sure do. But not big beautiful white wings, like on the statues. More like pigeons. Gray, but also sort of iridescent. They've got eyes like pigeons too. You know how pigeons have eyes the color of new-minted pennies? Like that. Metallic. They wear these cassocks, kinda like Jesuit priests, and there's soot all over them. Soot on their clothes, soot on their wings. Like they came out of a coal mine."

"And no one sees them but you?"

"No one ever sees them but me. It's been that way since I saw one take Mrs. Keats."

"Who was Mrs. Keats?"

"Dolores Keats. She died in front of me when I was five. In the hospice. The man with pigeon eyes and pigeon wings was sitting next to her the whole time, watching *The Price Is Right* while he waited. He knew I could see him. He nodded at me."

Martin had described experiencing a nervous breakdown after the shooting at his high school, had called his father nightly to provide updates on his mental crack-up. What words had he used? *Panic attacks* and *paranoia*. Duvall knew you could go one of two ways after a nervous breakdown. You could mend or you could splinter even more. Duvall kept his features calm and composed but was thinking the kid belonged in a mental health facility, all right, but as one of the patients, not as part of the staff.

"So, what happened when she died? Did he fly away with her ghost?" Duvall asked.

Martin gave him a sidelong look, and his eyes were actually twinkling. "I *knew* you'd think I was full of shit."

"Go on, tell me what happened when she died."

"He waited until *The Price Is Right* went to a commercial; then he leaned toward her and took her hand. He whispered into her ear. I don't know what he whispered. Something nice, I think, because she started to smile. And then a flashbulb went off inside her body—this snap of light in her eyes and in her open mouth, like a stroke of lightning pulsing inside a cloud—and when it faded, she was gone. And so was he."

"Mrs. Keats vanished?"

The kid looked briefly nettled. "No, her *body* was still there. I mean, whatever is inside us that makes us who we are, *that* went away—disappeared with her usher."

"In a flash of light." Duvall turned his beer by the bottleneck, thinking it over. "What's the soot? You said there's soot on them."

"Not sure. Sin maybe."

"Sin?"

"Sure. Maybe we emit sin, the way factories emit pollution, and it gets on 'em, the way soot gets on pigeons. Or maybe they take some people to hell and it's smoky there. I don't know. You ever see a movie called *Wings of Desire*?" Martin asked him.

"Was that a straight-to-video *Top Gun* knockoff?"

"No, it's German. It's a German art film. Black and white. The guy who directed it, Wim Wenders? I'm pretty sure he's seen them too. The ushers. He changed them a little for the film, but basically they look a lot like that."

"I'll check it out sometime."

"Don't bother. It's not important."

"So, the ushers were there at the train station?"

"And at the high school. They were clustered around the entrance to Kennedy High, like a flock of pigeons waiting for someone to toss a fistful of breadcrumbs."

"Martin," Duvall said, "if you saw angels of death clustering around your school, why didn't you do something? Why didn't you try to save Janet Vickers? Like you tried to save Audrey Giovanni?" He spoke gently, curious to see how deep the delusion went, and what happened when Martin's fantasies were challenged.

Martin sighed and looked disheartened. "I had never seen so many gathered in one place, at one time. I was in my car, looking for a parking spot, when I saw them. It really did make me feel sick—I always get serious diarrhea whenever I'm freaking out. I squealed out of there, called my mom to say I was coming home. I couldn't think what to do. Remember, I was seventeen. I had about decided to call in a bomb threat when the first police car blasted past me. Timothy Berk began shooting at seven fifty-two, before first bell had rung. So, that time, I couldn't do anything. It all happened so fast. Later, though, I learned it's better *not* to do anything."

"Better to do nothing and let people die?"

"That's a misunderstanding of how these guys operate. When they show up, someone is going to die. Every one of them is an usher, and they're going to lead *someone* away into the dark, to take their seat at the big show. Because, Mr. Duvall, *of course* I've tried to save people. There was Julie Hammersmith, in college. I saw her usher trailing along two steps behind her. I kept an eye on her. Hung out with her all night—which was pretty easy, we were going to the same rager—and when she went in the bathroom and didn't come out, I forced my way in and found her having a seizure. The usher was perched on the edge of the toilet, watching her foam at the mouth. Only, Julie lived. I screamed for help and some dude ran in and gave her CPR and she's alive today. I heard she's an oral hygienist in Danvers now."

"For real?" Duvall asked, thinking he would check it out in the morning.

Martin nodded sadly.

"That's a good thing, isn't it?"

"No, it isn't," Martin said. "Her usher stopped following her around and started following *me* around. He followed me for most of a week, giving me nasty looks. Then, one day, walking home, he peeled off and crossed the street and caught up with this kid, maybe ten, riding her bicycle along the sidewalk. He looked over his shoulder to make sure I was watching, and then he began to talk to her. I could see her tilt her head to listen to him. She was still listening—giving him her complete attention—when she glided out onto the street and into the path of an oncoming delivery truck. He didn't get to take Julie—I *stopped* him from taking Julie—so he found someone else."

And you were there when it happened, Duvall thought, the skin crawling at the nape of his neck. He wondered whether there had been any other witnesses in the incident of the child struck by the delivery truck. He wondered whether the person who distracted her, right before she was hit, had been Martin Lorensen himself.

"What about Audrey and her mother? Are the ushers going to take someone else in their place?"

"Yeah, they'll find two people to take, I guess," Martin said glumly.

"Are the ushers here now?"

"I'm trying not to notice if they are. I really shouldn't have done anything. People die. I don't want to be the reason some live and some don't. It's best to just . . . be a mammal. Eat as much fresh fruit as you can. Spend time with trees. Hug the people you love. Accept that death is as natural as the rest of life. Dogs understand that. Cats understand that. Only humans have a hard time with it. And when it's over, at least there's someone there. At least you aren't alone."

Duvall's Apple Watch zapped him with a notification. He turned his wrist to look at the watch face, saw a couple of texts from Malia. Mom liked my essay too, she said, and Thanks for letting me read it to you, and a heart emoji. He tapped the watch face, sent a heart emoji back. When he glanced up, Martin was smiling at him, fondly, yet with a trace of sadness. Then Martin nodded toward the doorway.

"Look who just walked in. I think Mr. Oates is here to collect you for the reunion tour," Martin said.

Duvall followed his gaze and spotted John Oates standing inside the double doors, raindrops glittering on his duck windbreaker. He looked *pissed*, his mouth a tight, bloodless line under his mustache, his comb-over a wet tangle.

"Let me get your drink, Martin," Duvall said, feeling a charity for the kid he could not have explained, even to himself.

"No, no," Martin said. "I couldn't let you." Then he showed that winsome grin of his and added, "Not after I bogarted your yummy Cactus Blossom."

Duvall signaled to the girl running the bar and closed out his tab. Martin put a few wrinkled bills down to cover his Blue Moon. They made their way to the foyer together.

John cast a baleful look at Martin. "Surprised to see you out, Lorensen. I thought you liked to spend your evenings with that Bible you keep next to your bed."

"Mr. Oates! Your head is steaming! I've never seen a head steam before."

It was true—white curls of steam were rising from his pale-pink dome. John's mouth worked beneath his mustache while he searched for something suitably cutting to say. He didn't come up with anything and settled for a short "Huh!" and turned away. When he started for the door, Duvall fell into step beside him without a word. From his body language, Duvall took it there was no last-minute reconciliation with his girlfriend in the offing, let alone a final tender exchange of good memories and warm wishes.

Before the night was over, Duvall would have to fill John in on his unplanned second interview with Martin Lorensen. John would love it. After that smart-ass comment about his steaming head, John would be pleased to have a reason to charge Lorensen with something—*anything*, really, evidence highly optional.

They needed to talk to the girl who had overdosed and nearly died in Martin's presence. What did he say her name was? Hammersmith. Dental hygienist, Danvers. Duvall wanted to know whether Martin had sold her the drugs that nearly killed her. And they would have to find out about the little girl who had been crushed by a truck right in front of him. Duvall did not see how Martin could've had a hand in Mohawk 118 or the Timothy Berk shooting. But he was an unstable young man in the grip of a disturbing religious fantasy, which possibly included vivid, grotesque hallucinations, and Duvall had an ever-so-slightly-heartsick feeling that the next time they spoke, he would have to read Martin his rights first.

The worst part of it was he *liked* him. Martin radiated a boyish, gleeful sense of mischief, and beneath that Duvall sensed, or wanted to sense, a basic decency, a concern for others. He couldn't square that with this other idea: that Martin Lorensen was a badly deranged youth who might've played a role in a number of deaths.

When they stepped through the doors, it was cold and the rain was pouring from the eaves and bouncing off the blacktop. John had pulled the Lincoln right up to the curb and left it running, a massive black car that screamed *cop*. Duvall clocked Martin peering out into the dark as he buttoned his denim jacket to the throat.

"Don't tell me you're on foot."

"I'm only a half mile that way," Martin said, gesturing with his chin.

"Get in," Duvall said. "We'll drive you. Don't walk in this."

Martin smiled—and then his gaze shifted to the left, away

from Duvall, and back. His smile faltered. He regarded Duvall with a mixture of kindness and apology.

"I don't mind it. People should get some rain on their faces now and then. Get a good clean soak."

"Be a mammal," Duvall said, and the kid shot a finger gun at him. "Martin . . . I *am* going to have to discuss what you've told me with Mr. Oates. You understand that?"

Martin looked to Oates and back and smiled and said, "Do what you got to do, Mr. Duvall. It'll be okay." And stuck out his hand.

Duvall was surprised and charmed, in spite of what he knew about Martin now. They shook. The kid had a firm, *polite* grip, as sincere as the rest of him. Martin pivoted and shook John's hand too—

"Take 'er easy, Mr. Oates."

—and after he let go, John stood there on the curb, staring down at his palm, as if he was not sure what had just happened. Finally, he said, "Huh!" again and dropped his hand to his side.

Duvall slid into the passenger seat while his partner walked around the front of the car, through the downpour. John dumped himself behind the steering wheel, glaring out at the rain, a man who took weather personally. John's phone was on the center console between them, and it lit up with a text as the big man put the Lincoln into drive.

"Ah, this fuckin'—" John muttered, grabbing it, glancing at the text, throwing it back down. "Don't gimme this shit about we ate leftovers on our anniversary—*what* anniversary, bitch, we ain't married—"

He wrenched the wheel and they leaped from the curb, tires throwing spray. Duvall cast one look back over his shoulder. Martin stood under the overhang in front of the entrance to the Texas Roadhouse, his denim collar turned up, thumbs in the pockets of his jeans. Now that Duvall was leaving him behind, the smile was gone, and he looked sad. Duvall supposed he'd have exactly the same look on his face if he had to walk home in this.

John accelerated out of the parking lot, slewing through a wide, deep puddle, throwing a fan of water. Duvall grabbed the strap over the door but didn't say anything, knew what kind of mood John was in.

"The kid had some stuff to say," Duvall said.

"That kid could say a whole lot less and it would be fine with me. Snide little shit."

Duvall decided it wasn't the time to tell John about the ushers. Maybe at the motel.

John sped up, irritably clicking his chunky fraternity ring against the side of the steering wheel, clack-clack-clack-clack, and they hit another wide black pool of water with a great crash, and Duvall thought he shouldn't have let Martin walk home in this, and never mind his just-be-a-mammal shit, he was going to be a drowned mammal. No one ought to be out in this—no one would *want* to be—and then he played something back in his head, the way Martin had looked away from him for a moment, peering off to one side, and then when he looked back his eyes had been morose and apologetic. John sped up and sped up some more, muttering, "Cold leftovers, how many fuckin' times did I choke down her mother's vegan chili what always gave me the shits—"

Duvall recalled how happy it had made Martin, to see him sending Malia that heart emoji, letting his daughter know she was loved, and then Duvall remembered asking what would happen to the ushers who had come for Audrey Giovanni and her mother, and Martin had said they'd find two others to take, and by now John was doing sixty in a forty-five, and Duvall opened his mouth to tell him to calm the fuck down and slow the fuck down while he was at it, only when he glanced in the rearview mirror, he saw a pair of copper-bright eyes staring back at him, someone in the back seat, and the words caught in his throat.

John's cell phone lit up again, and John cursed and grabbed for it to see what his ex was saying now, and the Lincoln slid gracefully, easily, across the double yellow line into the oncoming lane. The car filled with the blinding glare of approaching headlights. Anthony Duvall shoved himself back into his seat, bracing for the dreadful concussion of metal slamming into metal at high velocity, and that was when he realized someone had reached up from the back to gently squeeze John's shoulder. Duvall wanted to cry out but couldn't force any sound up his suddenly constricted throat, and that was when the second man in the back seat leaned forward to put his mouth close to Duvall's ear, and in a calm, low, soothing voice, he said, *Hold on, Tony, hold on, something wonderful is coming.*

Contributors' Notes

'PEMI AGUDA is from Lagos, Nigeria. She has an MFA from the Helen Zell Writers' Program at the University of Michigan. Her writing has been published in *Granta*, *Zoetrope: All-Story*, *Ploughshares*, and *One Story*, among others, and has won O. Henry Prizes. Her novel-in-progress won the 2020 Deborah Rogers Foundation Writers Award. She was a 2021 Fiction Fellow with the Miami Book Fair, a 2022 MacDowell Fellow, and is the current Hortense Spillers Assistant Editor at *Transition Magazine*. Her debut collection of stories, *Ghostroots*, was a finalist for the 2024 National Book Award in Fiction, the *Los Angeles Times* Art Seidenbaum Award for First Fiction, the Young Lions Fiction Award, and the PEN/Faulkner Award.

• In my story collection, *Ghostroots*, there are many fraught parent-child relationships. It was important to me to have a story that showed parents who are unequivocally good and kind and supportive despite economic hardships or other circumstances. In this way, "The Wonders of the World" is the closest to autobiographical of any story I've written, and reading it always rouses tenderness for my teenage self. With stories that borrow or kick off from real life, the difficulty is knowing when to let go of memory and release the reins to the flexible possibilities that fiction permits. That was my big lesson from writing this—allowing time and place and space to jumble, allowing people to melt into characters, and allowing the fantastical to blur all the above so that what was left were the sustaining questions of difference and belief.

OLIVIE BLAKE is the *New York Times* bestselling author of multiple adult SF/F titles, including the internationally bestselling *The Atlas Six* trilogy, *Alone with You in the Ether*, *Masters of Death*, the short story collection *Januaries*, and the recently published titles *Gifted & Talented* and *Girl Dinner*. As Alexene Farol Follmuth, she is also the author of the young adult romcoms *My Mechanical Romance* and *Twelfth Knight*. She lives in Los Angeles with her husband and son.

• "The Audit" was published in *Januaries*, my compilation of new and old work spanning about a decade of short-form craft, as the second story in the collection; my immediate instinct had been to place it first, as it encompassed so much of what I felt defined the spirit of the collection (and my personal pet themes: love, disillusionment, the looming specter of mortality) as a whole, though I was overruled in favor of a more traditional fantasy styling. "The Audit," by contrast, is about as grounded as you can get while still being speculative. It was originally conceived of as a romance, the idea derived from a conversation I had with my husband about the mismatch between the human life cycle and requisite social policy, but built on a structure I've long enjoyed: the *Sex Diaries* column of *New York Magazine*. The concept was to tell a love story from the perspective of someone who wasn't yet aware they were falling in love; an ongoing psychological meltdown revealed almost in real time, which felt like the best way to capture the feeling of being young and trapped by the impossible prospect of potential. In some respects, it's reflective of a bigger, generational tone—climate anxiety and social ennui and an economic monoculture that limits personal freedom to little treats—but with an exercise of scale: amid all this bad, a tiny, lovely wonderful for which to live. It's an intimate story about coming to terms with the future and about the singular beauty of what remains unknown.

ADAM-TROY CASTRO made his first nonfiction sale to *Spy* magazine in 1987. His books to date include four Spider-Man novels, three novels about his profoundly damaged far-future murder investigator Andrea Cort, and six middle-grade novels about the dimension-spanning adventures of young Gustav Gloom. Adam's works have won the Philip K. Dick Award and the Seiun (Japan), and have been nominated for eight Nebulas, three Stokers, two Hugos, one World Fantasy Award, and, internationally, the Ignotus (Spain), the Grand Prix de l'Imaginaire (France), and the Kurd Laßwitz Preis (Germany). The audio collection *My Wife Hates Time Travel and Other Stories* features thirteen hours of his fiction, including the new stories "The Hour In Between" and "Big Stupe and the Buried Big Glowing Booger." In 2022 he came out with two collections, *The Author's Wife Vs. The Giant Robot* and his thirtieth book, *A Touch of Strange*. Adam was an Author Guest of Honor at 2023's World Fantasy Convention. Adam lives in Florida with a pair of chaotic paladin cats.

• Once upon a time, Isaac Asimov was everything. I am aware that there are now biographical reasons to scorn him, that acknowledgment necessary since some of you would rather score that point than listen to the specific things being said. I repeat what I said, that once upon a time Isaac Asimov was everything. He was certainly my entrance ramp, providing a direction for my life, and I honor him for that, while understanding his sins.

This story is based on two observations: one of them being that that three laws are not enough to establish a complete ethos; and the other, that if people were in control of beings who were forced by nature to obey, they would abuse the privilege. Create a robot capable of feeling pain, and certain owners will torture it. Evil is complicated.

DOMINIQUE DICKEY is the author of the novella *Redundancies & Potentials*. Their short fiction has appeared in *Fantasy Magazine*, *Lightspeed*, *Nightmare*, and other venues. They are the creative director of Sly Robot Games, a DC-based indie press that makes tabletop roleplaying games about community, struggle, and finding hope in difficult circumstances. You can find their work at dominiquedickey.com.

• I don't believe in giving up on an idea. "Look at the Moon" is a story I wouldn't let go of: I wrote the first draft in 2016, and it grew with me over the next eight years. The version that exists today has the same core as the first draft—recognizable images, similar themes—but it is completely different in execution. I could not have written "Look at the Moon" the way it is written now without living longer; the characters needed time to find themselves.

I feel a great fondness for the writing of my younger self. And I always hold the possibility of going back to revisit my old work, again and again, until I have the life experience or knowledge of craft to shape the story into what it was always meant to become.

TANANARIVE DUE (tah-nah-nah-REEVE doo) is an award-winning author who teaches Black Horror and Afrofuturism at UCLA.

A leading voice in Black speculative fiction for more than twenty years, Due has won an American Book Award, an NAACP Image Award, and a British Fantasy Award, and her writing has been included in best-of-the-year anthologies. Her books include *The Reformatory* (winner of a *Los Angeles Times* Book Prize, Chautauqua Prize, Bram Stoker Award, Shirley Jackson Award, and World Fantasy Award, and a *New York Times* Notable Book), *The Wishing Pool and Other Stories*, *Ghost Summer: Stories*, *My Soul to Keep*, and *The Good House*. She and her late mother, civil rights activist Patricia Stephens Due, coauthored *Freedom in the Family: A Mother-Daughter Memoir of the Fight for Civil Rights*.

She was an executive producer on Shudder's groundbreaking documentary *Horror Noire: A History of Black Horror*. She and her husband/collaborator, Steven Barnes, wrote "A Small Town" for season 2 of Jordan Peele's *The Twilight Zone* on Paramount Plus and two segments of Shudder's anthology film *Horror Noire: Six Stories of Black Horror*. They also co-wrote their Black Horror graphic novel *The Keeper*, illustrated by Marco Finnegan. Due and Barnes co-host a podcast, *Lifewriting: Write for Your Life!* She and her husband live with their son, Jason.

• "A Stranger Knocks" is the direct result of the research I was doing about old Hollywood for my next novel, (currently titled) *Bear Creek Lodge (1926)*. That novel has a backstory about an embittered Black actress who came of age at the dawn of Hollywood, starting during the silent era, and I was struck by my research about the old "race pictures" that flourished during the 1920s, packing huge audiences in Black theaters. These films about cowboys and fighter pilots and preachers were a deliberate counterpoint to Hollywood's treatment of Black actors and Black stories, which were almost solely rooted in the minstrel era to reinforce notions of white supremacy, because roles were usually limited to servants, domestics, and fools. Oscar Micheaux is the most famous of these independent Black directors defying the Hollywood norms of his time, but even so, much of Micheaux's work was lost to time—including his "mysterious picture" *Son of Satan*, which I saw advertised in an old newspaper ad.

I was fascinated with this era, and especially the detail that producers had to drive their volatile film prints from theater to theater, town to town. Since many people already consider producers and studio heads to be a bit vampiric at times, I asked myself, "What if a vampire wove the power of his seduction into his film reels and traveled with them from city to city to feed?" In my view, Cartier genuinely wants to share his artistic gift while he guarantees he will never go hungry for blood. I also consider this the origin story of how Judy and her husband, Alvin, become long-term "familiars" to Cartier.

But I do include a subtle nod to Judy's writing aspirations in *Bear Creek Lodge*—so she does eventually become a screenwriter who tries to elevate Black storytelling in film in her own way.

XAVIER GARCIA is a writer/editor from Toronto, Canada. His short fiction has appeared in *Cold Signal*, *hex*, and in various magazines and anthologies published by Apocalypse Confidential, Cursed Morsels, Filthy Loot, Weirdpunk Books, and others. You can find him walking the nightmare corpse-city of R'lyeh, or at x.com/xavier_agarcia.

• Everyone knows horror and heavy metal go hand in hand. But I don't listen to heavy metal. I listen to hip-hop. And whether people know it or not, horror and hip-hop go hand in hand, too. Rap music has been a part of my life for as long as I can really remember. It was everywhere growing up. My family listened to it. My friends listened to it. Everyone around me seemed to listen to it. One of my uncles was even a rapper in the 2000s underground scene. So, it feels too passive to say that I've listened to hip-hop my whole life exactly because of how much it's been an active part of growing up and the person I am now. As an artform, hip-hop has been giving BIPOC artists a platform for expression for as long as it has existed. It has amplified Black and Brown voices and championed the communities that we come from. For that and more, I will love it forever. But hip-hop is more than one voice. And those voices aren't a monolith. Sometimes hip-hop with one hand champions Black and Brown communities, and with the other, advocates for a capitalistic worldview that keeps those same communities down. I wanted to write a love letter to hip-hop. And not one despite those complexities but because of them. I wanted that love letter to be dark. I wanted it to capture all the violence and all the desperation that all the best Three 6 Mafia songs capture. So, what better way to do that than through horror. After all, everyone knows horror and hip-hop go hand in hand.

THOMAS HA is a Nebula, Hugo, Ignyte, Locus, and Shirley Jackson Award–nominated writer of speculative short fiction. You can find his work in *Clarkesworld*, *Lightspeed*, *Beneath Ceaseless Skies*, and *Weird Horror Magazine*, among other publications. His debut short story collection, *Uncertain Sons and Other Stories*, is now available wherever books are sold. Thomas grew up in Honolulu and, after a decade plus of living in the northeast, now resides in Los Angeles with his family.

• Parenting is something I love and something I will never do as well as I would like. I think most feel that way. There is no perfect path. And in turn, there is a lot of difficulty in just being a kid, in navigating experiences and learning the ropes too. Whether you are a parent or a child, the world is probably not as safe as you would like, but not always as hostile as you might anticipate. The calculus gets all the more complicated when your family is a little different. "The Sort" is about a parent and child negotiating how to approach others. Who can you trust? How much of yourself can you share? How do you protect yourself? Open up? Be forthright about who you are? The answers are not straightforward, in life or in the story. The father and son in "The Sort" might have their own separate answers. Readers might too. But I think when you look, there are people of all kinds, some who might be against you, but also some who might, in their own way, understand you. And sometimes, the only way to know is to go out there and see.

JOE HILL is the #1 *New York Times*–bestselling author of *King Sorrow*, *The Fireman*, and *Full Throttle*. Much of his work has been adapted for the screen. His short story "The Black Phone" became a hit film of the same name for Blumhouse in 2021, while his third novel, *NOS4A2*, was adapted for two terrifying seasons of television on AMC. His short story "Best New Horror" won the British Fantasy Award for best short story in 2006. He splits his time between New England and Old England.

• If I have a single hack for writing stories, it's this: Settle on the form first. I wrote a story a few years back about people on an airplane on the day World War Three erupts. As I wrote that one ("You Are Released") I realized it had its own secret underlying math. It had three settings: the cockpit, first class, and economy. And in each setting, we meet three characters. For example, in the cockpit, we find ourselves hanging out with the pilot, the co-pilot, and the senior flight attendant. It became obvious the story would have nine scenes, three scenes in each setting, which we would visit in a steady rotation . . . and that each time we returned to a location we'd be in a new point-of-view. That one almost wrote itself. The internal math was irresistible.

Why am I telling you all this about a completely different story? Probably to excuse myself for having so little to say about "Ushers." I solved the problem of form first, and the rest was easy. I knew it was a story in two halves, and that each half was an interview between a federal agent and a kid with a secret. And that in the first half we'd get the cover story, and in the second half we'd get the truth. I wrote the first interview on Monday. I wrote the second on Tuesday. And—that was it. Months later, I revised the ending marginally (for a while, Duvall died with an Uber driver, but come on, that's obviously wrong, he has to punch out with Oates). The whole experience of writing "Ushers" was peaceful and pleasant, like picking at an easy crossword over a cup of tea. I wish it was always so much fun!

s. l. huang is a Hugo-winning and Amazon-bestselling author who justifies an MIT degree by using it to write eccentric mathematical superhero fiction. Huang is the author of the Cas Russell novels, including *Zero Sum Game*, *Null Set*, and *Critical Point*, as well as the new fantasies *Burning Roses* and *The Water Outlaws*. In short fiction, Huang's stories have appeared in *Analog*, *The Magazine of Fantasy & Science Fiction*, *Nature*, and more, including numerous best-of anthologies. Huang is also a Hollywood stunt performer and firearms expert, with credits including *Battlestar Galactica* and *Top Shot*. Find S. L. Huang online at slhuang.com.

• "The River Judge" is a prequel story, of sorts, to my epic fantasy *The Water Outlaws* (though you don't have to have read one to enjoy the other). That novel is written as a genderflipped reimagining of *Water Margin*, a book from the fourteenth century that ranks as one of China's most important works of classic literature. One might be surprised to learn that such a revered classic is a madcap tale of adventure, as bandits rise up against a tyrannical empire!

The original *Water Margin* is also a sprawling, thousand-page epic, with countless side stories detailing the backgrounds of its 108 bandits. In addition to genderspinning the main cast, one of the adaptational choices I made was related to form, as I condensed the material significantly. The main character from "The River Judge," Li Li, is barely seen in my novel—but giving her an expanded origin story as I did here felt charmingly in the spirit of the source inspiration. I hope you enjoy her journey of viciousness, feminism, and ghosts, as we see her coming into her own long before she joins up with her fellow bandit revolutionaries.

jennifer hudak is a Nebula-nominated speculative fiction writer whose work can be found in *Strange Horizons*, *The Magazine of Fantasy & Science Fiction*, and *The Sunday Morning Transport*. Originally from Boston, she now lives with her family in Upstate New York, where she teaches yoga, knits pocket-size animals, and misses the ocean.

• In a certain sense, I've been trying to write "The Witch Trap" for nearly thirty years. I used to be a university professor of American Literature and Women's Studies, and one of my areas of research was the history of the witch figure in literature and popular culture. Even though I left academia over two decades ago, that research remained burrowed in my mind, stubborn and insistent. When I learned about the Concealed Shoe Index, it felt like the perfect way to translate my old obsession into fiction.

I knew that I wanted to explore the idea of the witch as a textual body—something that comes into being according to the words we use to describe it—but it took me a long time to figure out how to make the story do what I wanted it to do. The first draft was a 750-word flash piece, which, as you might imagine, confused everyone who read it. In revision, I decided to structure the story as a patchwork of different genres and voices to get across the idea of the witch slowly emerging through language; putting it all together was a struggle that involved dozens of index cards taped on my wall. In the end, finishing this story felt like finally bridging my past with my present. (And in fact, my graduate student self appears as a cameo!)

KIJ JOHNSON is the author of six novels and two collections, and the winner of the Hugo, Nebula, and World Fantasy Awards, among others. She leads annual residential workshops on how to structure and write the SF/F/H novel. She also has designed a tabletop roleplaying game, *River-Bank*. She lives in Lawrence, Kansas, with a wicked cat.

• This story is a portmanteau filled with all my questions and ideas at the time I wrote it. In 2022, I received the Hawthornden fellowship and lived in a castle south of Edinburgh for a month. My room was called the Miłosz room, for the Polish American poet Czesław Miłosz, the author of my epigraph. One Sunday, I attended a service at the nearby Roslyn chapel and afterward spoke with a kind and very old woman, though we didn't talk about birds or witches: We talked about true love and adventures, which was just as dreamlike. I have been birdwatching for several years now, and I have just such an occlusion in my right eye, and this all came together in "Country Birds."

ISABEL J. KIM is a Korean American speculative fiction writer based in New York City. She is a Nebula, Locus, Shirley Jackson Award and BSFA Award winner; a Hugo, Sturgeon, and Astounding Award finalist; and her short fiction has been published in *Clarkesworld*, *Lightspeed*, and *Strange Horizons*, among other venues. Her work has been reprinted in *The Best American Science Fiction and Fantasy 2023* and *2024* and elsewhere. Her debut novel *Sublimation* sold in a seven-figure, three-book deal and is forthcoming in June 2026.

• "Why Don't We Just Kill the Kid in the Omelas Hole" took on a life of its own post-publication that surprised me. When I wrote it, I hadn't realized how it would be a lightning rod in the zeitgeist. My intention had mostly been to document the logical progression of "what would happen if someone tried to kill the Omelas kid, if Omelas existed in the modern world."

I like writing stories that take abstract or hypothetical situations seriously, because I feel that they end up revealing parts of our culture that are often taken for granted. I had been thinking a lot at the time about how many bad solutions there are to trolley problems, how the modern world is built on exploitation of labor and resources, and how atrocities in faraway places are discussed on social media. Because at the end of the day, WDWJKTKITOH is mostly about: If Omelas was not a place from a story being told to you, but a place that has news broadcasts, a place people go to vacation, a place that has internet, how would you respond to it?

TJ KLUNE is the #1 *New York Times* and #1 *USA Today*–bestselling, Lambda Literary Award–winning author of *The House in the Cerulean Sea*, *Under the Whispering Door*, *In the Lives of Puppets*, the Green Creek Series for adults, the Extraordinaries Series for teens, and more. Being queer himself, Klune believes it's important—now more than ever—to have accurate, positive queer representation in stories. Born and raised the Pacific Northwest, TJ now lives in a remote cabin in the mountains of Washington and wishes it was snowing.

- "Reduce! Reuse! Recycle!" exists because writing short stories is hard. I can do novels, but shorter works have always been something I'm interested in but terrified of at the same time. How can I fit a novel's worth of emotion and pathos and character work in ten thousand words? This story started off as a writing exercise that I didn't intend to publish. I wanted to see if I could do it: write a short story with the same scope as a novel.

  This story is a prequel of sorts to my novel *In the Lives of Puppets*. While no knowledge of the book is required, I wanted to deepen the world. Placing it a few hundred years before the events of *Puppets*, I set out to explore what it would look like for a machine—an android—to know freedom, at least for a little while. What would the machine find? What would they be drawn to? What would repel them? And if they found a little pocket of joy, what would that look like when it was time to say goodbye?

  I love this funny, heartbreaking little story. I hope you do too.

RUSSELL NICHOLS is a speculative fiction writer, poet, playwright, and endangered journalist. His diverse body of work—revolving around themes of resistance, activism, grief, and existentialism—includes more than two dozen internationally produced plays, more than 100 published stories and poems, and a deep archive of articles on science, technology, and culture. Raised in Richmond, California, he got rid of all his stuff in 2011 to live out of a backpack with his wife, vagabonding around the world ever since. Look for him at russellnichols.com.

- At the end of "What Happened to The Crooners," did the singers lose their voices? Only the four brothers in that Cadillac can say for sure. I wasn't there. But I can speak to the group's origins.

In 2006, I wrote a feature story for *Boston Globe Magazine* about Herb Reed, the bass singer of and a founding member of The Platters. There were a bunch of copycats using his group's name and belting his group's hits, he told me, making millions off his legacy. Stories like this one—and others from Black musicians of that era—formed the first note of the idea.

About ten years later, I finally got "permission" to tell the untold story of The Crooners. In my research, I traveled back in time to the doo-wop and R&B sounds of decades past. The Ink Spots. The Penguins. The Dells. The Platters. And then there was *The Five Heartbeats*. That classic Robert Townsend film was on heavy rotation for my brothers and me. In 2020, all the elements fell in line, and the pitch became clear: "*The Five Heartbeats* in The Twilight Zone."

My wife and I have been living nomadically since 2011. As creators on the road, we're always looking ahead, but also drawing from history to guide us through the unsettling horrors of reality. Too many Black artists pass away at an early age or disappear in other ways. Lives are lost or stolen. Still, the art remains. Giving us a spot of light to drive toward.

TATIANA OBEY is the author of *A Forging of Age Duology* and *The Champloo Mixes*. Her short stories have appeared in anthologies and magazines such as *The Advent of Winter Anthology* and *FIYAH*. She is also a contributing editor for *Magic in the Melanin: A Black Fantasy Anthology*. Her short story featured in this anthology has also been nominated for a Locus Award. She once taught English in South Korea, studied abroad in Japan, and spent her debut year traveling the world. You can learn more about her and her works at her website: tatianaobey.com.

• The first time I cursed in front of family was when I was riding in the passenger seat of my aunt's car and she decided to do a quick U-turn in front of an 18-wheeler. Suffice it to say, my life flashed before my eyes. My aunt has always had a need for speed, and she has also been a huge inspiration in my life. She has been a rock to depend on, a shoulder to lean on, and ready with a ride whenever I needed one. She was also proof that children aren't a requirement for women to live a rich and fulfilling life. When *FIYAH* put out a call for short stories for their "spacefaring aunties"-themed issue, I wanted to take advantage of this opportunity to honor someone who has been so essential to my growth and journey. Auntie, this one is for you. Y'all can blame her for the cursing.

SUSAN PALWICK has published four novels: *Flying in Place* (1992), *The Necessary Beggar* (2005), *Shelter* (2007), and *Mending the Moon* (2013). Her story collection *The Fate of Mice* was published in 2007. Her second collection, *All Worlds Are Real*, was published in 2019.

Palwick's fiction has been honored with a Crawford Award from the

International Association for the Fantastic in the Arts, an Alex Award from the American Library Association, and an Asimov's Readers' Award, and has been shortlisted for the World Fantasy Award, the Mythopoeic Award, and the Philip K. Dick Award. She was inducted into the Nevada Writers Hall of Fame in 2023, having received their Silver Pen Award in 2006.

Palwick spent twenty years as an English professor at the University of Nevada, Reno, where she specialized in creative writing and medical humanities. She retired in 2017 to earn a Master of Social Work degree—also from UNR—and move into healthcare. She has since worked as a chaplain (in both hospital and hospice settings), and as a dialysis social worker. She lives in Reno with her husband, their cats, and a large collection of looms and other craft equipment, including a beyond-lifetime supply of yarn.

- Arthur C. Clarke famously noted that "any sufficiently advanced technology is indistinguishable from magic." As someone who practices the traditional crafts of knitting and weaving, I've noticed that the reverse is also true: Many people respond to these processes as if they are esoteric and astonishing, rather than skills which were essential, everyday household practices prior to the Industrial Revolution.

"Yarns" plays with dichotomies: the virtual versus the embodied, youth versus age, violence versus compassion. At its heart, it is about the power of relationship to overcome fear and ignorance. Irene, a dedicated but flawed educator, learns far more from her friendship with Wesson than she teaches.

The story is also a protest against the erasure of older adults, especially single women. What cultural conditions create respect for the aged, rather than contempt? The story offers one possible, if grim, answer to that question.

KATHRYN H. ROSS is a SoCal-based writer and editor. She is the author of *Black Was Not a Label* (2022) and *Count It All Loss* (2021). Her works tackle faith, grief, the absurd, and the human condition through the lens of Black womanhood. Read and learn more about her at speakthewritelanguage.com.

- "The Forgetting Room" began as a play on the title of another story, "The Forgotten Room." The idea of a forgotten room was intriguing, and my mind quickly went to the literal idea of a room where one goes to forget something. I've always been interested in stories about memory—about how we build our world from what we remember and how, oftentimes, memory is not accurate. Though memory can be subjective, it is something that upholds the fabric of our reality as we search for truth and meaning. It's a bit of a paradox—finding truth in something so gossamer and impermanent. Think about the Mandela Effect. I think we all try our best to remember life as accurately as we can, but that doesn't mean we do. This pushed me to think about other stories around memory like *Eternal*

Sunshine of the Spotless Mind, and how if we can alter our memories, we can change reality in a sense. How enticing that is when plagued with memories that hurt or sadden or haunt us. Immediately I saw the danger in that power. Memory is fragile, but it makes us who we are. If we were to tamper with it, for whatever reason (to release trauma, to relive an experience, to clear space in our brains), how would that change who we are? Who are we without our memories—the good and the bad? From all of these thoughts came "The Forgetting Room." Ultimately, I wanted to ask the question: Just because we can forget something, should we?

CARLIE ST. GEORGE is a Shirley Jackson Award finalist from Northern California. Her short fiction has been published in magazines such as *Clarkesworld*, *Nightmare*, and *The Dark* and reprinted in anthologies such as *The Year's Best Dark Fantasy and Horror* and *We're Here: The Best Queer Speculative Fiction*. Her debut collection *You Fed Us to the Roses* came out in 2022.

• The Evil Hive Mind trope can be done in different ways (multiple people contributing to one shared mind, or one solitary mind controlling several bodies), but no matter how it's done, it's rarely one of my favorites. For years, I was interested in writing a story about an alien with multiple bodies and one consciousness, an alien who was decidedly *not* evil—but I didn't actually have a story yet, just vibes. Once I started thinking more about what death might look like in such an alien culture, though—how traumatic it would be to lose a body, would people have funerals for each body lost, how does one begin to navigate four separate lives and only three bodies to live them, etc.—I started to get a better picture of Yonder, and the story really grew from there.

RACHEL SWIRSKY has published over one hundred short stories since 2006 in venues including *Reactor*, *Guernica*, and *Lightspeed*. Her work has been nominated for the Hugo Award, World Fantasy Award, Locus Award, and Philip K. Dick Award, and twice won the Nebula Award. She's the author of two collections, *How the World Became Quiet* and *Through the Drowsy Dark*, and a stand-alone novella, *January Fifteenth*. She holds an MFA in fiction from the Iowa Writers Workshop. She lives in rainy Portland among fluctuating numbers of cats and artists, and with a stable number (one) of husbands.

• I wrote the first draft of "Also, the Cat" during the pandemic as a 750-word piece of flash fiction for an annual contest hosted by an online writers community. My prompt was a sentence from *Les Misérables*: "Why comes there an hour when we leave this azure, and why does life continue afterwards?" In particular, I rolled with "life continue[s] afterwards."

At the time, I had been listening to a glut of P. G. Wodehouse (many thanks to places like the BBC for feeding my insatiable need for accessible audiobooks during the pandemic). I hadn't set out to work in a heavily inflected comedic voice, but obviously I had Wodehouse on the writing brain because the ludicrous kept creeping in. One thing I'd learned to love about Wodehouse was his masterful use of *just* the wrong word. As writers, we're often advised to find "just the right word" for the circumstance, but the mileage you can get out of finding the "almost but definitely not actually the right word" is surprisingly effective. He also does a lot of cool things with, e.g., synecdoche, which I didn't notice until I was writing.

The themes emerged as I was writing them. Someone in the comments on this story online wrote that I, as the author, "must know cats." I admit, I do. A friend long ago pointed out to me that people don't write enough animals in fiction. I like to do it when I can.

I don't have any sisters, and I don't know any ghosts—but I do know (and love) many people with a few neuroses, grumpy moments, and/or Shakespeare obsessions.

CAROLINE M. YOACHIM is a four-time Hugo and seven-time Nebula Award finalist. Her short stories have been translated into several languages and reprinted in multiple best-of anthologies, including five times in *The Best American Science Fiction and Fantasy*. Her short story collection *Seven Wonders of a Once and Future World & Other Stories* and the print chapbook of her novelette *The Archronology of Love* are available wherever books are sold. For more, check out her website at carolineyoachim.com.

• I wrote this story with the deliberate goal of making readers' brains do a thing that human brains don't generally do: read two things at once.

Giving people even the illusion of reading two things simultaneously is tricky, and I came at the problem from several different angles. One important element was trying to reduce the working memory load as the story progressed. On average, people can hold between five and nine things in working memory—numbers, letters, words. At the beginning of the story, some of the lines are slightly longer than nine words; by the end, the lines have fewer words. Repetition of the right-hand column also helps decrease the working memory load, and it becomes increasingly familiar as the story goes along.

Another thing I considered is the way attention works, and I did a fair bit of research on optical illusions. There's a category of optical illusions that are ambiguous images: A famous one is a drawing that looks like both a rabbit and a duck, another is both an old woman and a young woman. People start off seeing one image or the other, but once they know what both images are they can often flip back and forth. These kinds of illusions were an interesting reference for this story because they make use of how our brain processes visual information. For "We Will Teach You How to Read | We Will Teach You How to Read," I tried to break down the cognitive processes involved in reading in a similar way, but focusing on words/linguistic processing instead of pictures/visual processing.

Other Notable Science Fiction and Fantasy of 2024

SELECTED BY JOHN JOSEPH ADAMS

FANTASY

Ahmad, Senaa
  WHAT IS WAITING FOR HER. *Northern Nights*, ed. Michael Kelly (Undertow)
Alexander, Phoenix
  SLICKERTHIN. *The Magazine of Fantasy & Science Fiction*, Summer
Bacigalupi, Paolo
  ARTISTS AND FOOLS. *The Sunday Morning Transport*, July
Cotman, Elwin
  THE SWITCHING TREE. *Weird Black Girls* (Scribner)
Diehl, Hammond
  WE WILL BRING SIEGE TO THE BASTION OF SIN THAT CRIES OUT IN YOUR PRAYER. *Lightspeed*, November
Evans, Desiree S.
  THE BRIDES OF DEVIL'S BAYOU. *The Black Girl Survives in This One*, ed. Desiree S. Evans and Saraciea J. Fennell (Flatiron)
Files, Gemma
  LITTLE HORN. *Nightmare*, October
Ha, Thomas
  GROTTMATA. *Nightmare*, July
Henry, Veronica
  GUILT CAN WILT THE SWEETEST FLOWER. *The Magazine of Fantasy & Science Fiction*, Winter
Iker, Beatrice Winifred
  ABOVE THE HUNGRIEST DEAD. *Death in the Mouth, Vol. 2*, ed. Sloane Leong and Cassie Hart (Sloane Leong and Cassie Hart)
Jones, Stephen Graham
  PARTHENOGENESIS. *Reactor*, October
Kanakia, Naomi
  WORLD WEARINESS. *We Mostly Come Out at Night*, ed. Rob Costello (Running Press Kids)
Kurella, Jordan
  EVAN: A REMAINDER. *Reactor*, January
Larson, Rich
  DO NOT OPEN. *Northern Nights*, ed. Michael Kelly (Undertow)
Lee, P H
  THE V*MPIRE. *Reactor*, October
Leong, Sloane
  A SAINT BETWEEN THE TEETH. *Lightspeed*, January
Liu, Angela
  ANOTHER GIRL UNDER THE IRON BELL. *Uncanny*, September/October
Lynch, Scott
  SELECTED SCENES FROM THE ECOLOGIES OF THE LABYRINTH. *The Sunday Morning Transport*, July

Other Notable Science Fiction and Fantasy of 2024

Machado, Carmen Maria
ENDLINGS. *Conjunctions* #83
Mohammed, Premee
BY SALT, BY SEA, BY LIGHT OF STARS. *Strange Horizons*, Fund Drive 2024
Novik, Naomi
AFTER HOURS. *Buried Deep and Other Stories* (Del Rey)
Pladek, B.
THE SPINDLE OF NECESSITY. *Strange Horizons*, May
Poletti, Lowry
BRIDE / BUTCHER / DOE. *Strange Horizons*, August
Rosson, Keith
SECOND DEATHS. *Nightmare*, March
Sen, Nibedita
AGNI. *The Sunday Morning Transport*, January
Singh, Vandana
TRAVELERS' TALES FROM THE ENDS OF THE WORLD. *Lightspeed*, April
Swanwick, Michael
DRAGONS OF PARIS. *Reactor*, October
Tanzer, Molly
JIREL AND THE MIRROR OF TRUTH. *New Edge Sword and Sorcery* #3
Vo, Nghi
STITCHED TO THE SKIN LIKE FAMILY IS. *Uncanny*, March/April
White, N. Romaine
D.E.I. (DEATH, ETERNITY, INCLUSION). *FIYAH*, January

SCIENCE FICTION

Afifi, Nadia
THE GENERATION CHIP. *Thyme Travelers*, ed. Sonia Sulaiman (Roseway)
Corey, James S. A.
JUDAS ISCARIOT DIDN'T KILL HIMSELF: A STORY IN FRAGMENTS. *The Last Dangerous Visions*, ed. Harlan Ellison and J. Michael Straczynski (Blackstone)
Dickey, Dominique
THE LAST LUCID DAY. *Lightspeed*, July
Doctorow, Cory
VIGILANT. *Reactor*, September
Elison, Meg
CALLIE'S WORLD. *Fusion Fragment*, August
Gregory, Daryl
I'M NOT DISAPPOINTED JUST MAD AKA THE HEAVIEST COUCH IN THE KNOWN UNIVERSE. *Reactor*, November
Ha, Thomas
THE BROTHERHOOD OF MONTAGUE ST. VIDEO. *Clarkesworld*, May
Jacobs, Zohar
THE ENCELADUS SOUTH POLE BASE NAMED AFTER V.I. LENIN. *Clarkesworld*, February
FOR OUT OF TAI SHAN THE TORAH SHALL GO FORTH. *The Sunday Morning Transport*, March
Johnson, Alaya Dawn
A BRIEF ORAL HISTORY OF THE EL ZOPILOTE DOCK. *Clarkesworld*, March
THE MEMORIAL TREE. *The Sunday Morning Transport*, September
Kagunda, Shingai Njeri
LET THE STAR EXPLODE. *Lightspeed*, March
WE WHO WILL NOT DIE. *Psychopomp*, September
Kress, Nancy
THE ALICE RUN. *Reactor*, August
Kriz, Andrea
UDO GEHLER AND THE VIRGIN BITCH OF THE RESISTANCE. *Lightspeed*, June
Larson, Rich
BREATHING CONSTELLATIONS. *Reactor*, June
Leckie, Ann
LAKE OF SOULS. *Lake of Souls* (Orbit)
Ledbetter, William
ENOUGH. *Analog*, January/February

Liu, Ken
   THREE VIEWS OF A PARKING
   LOT. *The Sunday Morning Transport*,
   October

Martine, Arkady
   THREE FACES OF A BEHEADING.
   Uncanny, May/June

Masri, Tamara
   INSIDE THE HOUSE OF WISDOM.
   Lightspeed, December

Miller, Sam J.
   NOTES ON GENOCIDAL
   INTERCHRONOLOGICAL
   INCURSION 57.7.3 (F.K.A.
   FRIENDS). *Baffling*, April

Myers, E. C.
   ALONE WITH YOUR THOUGHTS.
   The Sunday Morning Transport, April

Ogden, Aimee
   NOTHING OF VALUE. *Clarkesworld*,
   January

   WHAT ANY DEAD THING WANTS.
   Psychopomp, February

Onyebuchi, Tochi
   THE NUCLEAR FAMILY. *Far Futures*
   (Horizon 2045 and ASU Center for
   Science and the Imagination)

Shawl, Nisi
   OVER A LONG TIME AGO.
   Lightspeed, May

Thomas, Sheree Renée
   DOWNWINDERS. *Far Futures*
   (Horizon 2045 and ASU
   Center for Science and the
   Imagination)

Yoachim, Caroline M.
   OUR CHATBOTS SAID "I LOVE
   YOU," SHALL WE MEET?
   Clarkesworld, June

Zhao, Caroline
   IN WHICH CARUTH IS CORRECT.
   Clarkesworld, May

Explore the rest of the series

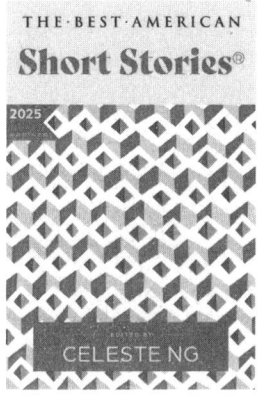

bestamericanseries.com

ABOUT

MARINER BOOKS

MARINER BOOKS traces its beginnings to 1832 when William Ticknor cofounded the Old Corner Bookstore in Boston, from which he would run the legendary firm Ticknor and Fields, publisher of Ralph Waldo Emerson, Harriet Beecher Stowe, Nathaniel Hawthorne, and Henry David Thoreau. Following Ticknor's death, Henry Oscar Houghton acquired Ticknor and Fields and, in 1880, formed Houghton Mifflin, which later merged with venerable Harcourt Publishing to form Houghton Mifflin Harcourt. HarperCollins purchased HMH's trade publishing business in 2021 and reestablished their storied lists and editorial team under the name Mariner Books.

Uniting the legacies of Houghton Mifflin, Harcourt Brace, and Ticknor and Fields, Mariner Books continues one of the great traditions in American bookselling. Our imprints have introduced an incomparable roster of enduring classics, including Hawthorne's *The Scarlet Letter*, Thoreau's *Walden*, Willa Cather's *O Pioneers!*, Virginia Woolf's *To the Lighthouse*, W.E.B. Du Bois's *Black Reconstruction*, J.R.R. Tolkien's *The Lord of the Rings*, Carson McCullers's *The Heart Is a Lonely Hunter*, Ann Petry's *The Narrows*, George Orwell's *Animal Farm* and *Nineteen Eighty-Four*, Rachel Carson's *Silent Spring*, Margaret Walker's *Jubilee*, Italo Calvino's *Invisible Cities*, Alice Walker's *The Color Purple*, Margaret Atwood's *The Handmaid's Tale*, Tim O'Brien's *The Things They Carried*, Philip Roth's *The Plot Against America*, Jhumpa Lahiri's *Interpreter of Maladies*, and many others. Today Mariner Books remains proudly committed to the craft of fine publishing established nearly two centuries ago at the Old Corner Bookstore.